Lincoln Street

A Novel

Coming of Age in Fly-Over Country

Don Burgess

Merit Associates

Fort Worth

LINCOLN STREET
Copyright © 2014 by Don Burgess

ISBN-13 978-0986156311

ISBN-10 0986156310

FIRST PRINTED EDITION: December 2014
FIRST AMAZON KINDLE EDITION: February 2015
SECOND PRINTED EDITION: August 2015

Dedication

To Lyn,

with great thanks

and soooo much more!

Table of Contents

Part III

1957-1963

Part IV

1962 – 1988

Preface

All my adult life I have been a speaker and writer. My wife Lyn and I have been blessed to have a daughter and son who, with their respective spouses, are also speakers and writers.

Thus, a few years ago, our daughter Kirsten Wilson asked if I was aware of *NaNoWriMo,* the shorthand name for *National Novel Writing Month.* I'd never heard of it.

Subsequently, I learned that *NaNoWriMo* exists to encourage authors and challenge them each year to write at least 50,000 words of a novel during the month of November.

The exhortation is to grind out at least 1,667 words per day for thirty days to hit the target of 50K. Those who do this, as verified by filing the digital text with *NaNoWriMo* for counting purposes only, receive a *Certificate of Completion* which may be printed and posted on the author's refrigerator. With such an incentive, I joined Kirsten and thousands of other writers to sit down, shut up, and *WRITE!* I am happy to say both Kirsten and I earned our certificates! Thank you, Kirsten, for the prompting!

Fairly quickly I landed on the idea of writing a *fictional* coming-of-age memoir about author *"Billy Howard's old gang of mine"* during his teenage years. I also wanted to provide *Billy* the opportunity to comment on the events of his teenage years from an adult perspective.

But when the *NaNoWriMo November* was over, I remained 68,000 words short of completing the manuscript which is now *Lincoln Street.* In the fullness of time, God gave me the words!

"Delight yourself in the LORD,
and He will give you the desires of your heart."
Psalm 37:4   (ESV)

Don Burgess
Fort Worth, Texas
December 2014

Part I

Chapter 1

Elm Trees, Chainsaws, and Body Bags

The 700 block of Lincoln Street had been barricaded by the police, forcing people parked on cross streets to walk to the site. With plenty of daylight remaining, law enforcement personnel went about their grim duties.

Two blocks away, the whine of the chainsaw carnage rose and fell in counterpoint to the melancholy chorus of the cicadas. Through the elm leaves, the afternoon sunlight flickered and danced across the porch and front yard as the gurney went back and forth from the house to the coroner's van. It seemed as if everyone on Lincoln Street had gathered to watch the procession of body bags and ultimately the departure of the killer who sat handcuffed in a rocking chair at the far end of the front porch.

The victims and their killer would be taken away in opposite directions. The deceased would head for the Montgomery County Morgue in Independence. The felon would be dispatched to the Coffeyville jail.

Horrified onlookers keeping vigil at the house were mostly silent. If they spoke, they whispered tersely to one another.

The Kansas Bureau of Investigation crime scene specialists had arrived to work with the local and county officers. The various law enforcement personnel were scouring the house for evidence and taking statements from neighbors. All the bodies had been found in the living room.

Around 6:00 p.m., the first of the flowers arrived. The trunk of the elm tree with the swings was outside the yellow-tape cordon. That's where the flowers were placed. Lindy and I stood beside the flowers. Her hand was on my shoulder as I wrote in my reporter's notebook.

It was June 21, 1962, the longest day of the year.

Chapter 2

"A Sickness Suffered by Dogs"

1958

I didn't see it. I didn't see it coming. It hit me like a rocket, on my right shin just above my ankle. I fell to the ground with a thud. Too sharply pained to cry out, I grabbed my leg and writhed on the ground. My sweaty arms were like magnets for the fresh cuttings of the lawn.

I rolled to my knees, trying to keep pressure off my right leg. I inched forward until I could get my hands on an elm tree. I slowly pulled myself up the bark. When I was upright, I turned around to lean my back against the elm so I could bend to massage my ankle, I pulled up my jeans pant leg and saw that a huge welt was forming. The skin had been only slightly broken so there was little blood. I slowly put pressure on my leg. My foot seemed numb but pain shot up my leg all the way to my gritted teeth.

I suppose it took only a minute more of my panting before I brushed off my arms and hands, ran my forearm over my forehead, and limped back to my lawnmower which was still idling where I had fallen. Damn rocks! Some genius should figure out a way to put some sort of guard on the mowers to keep rocks from being flung by the blade like missiles to smash whatever they hit. I had even heard stories of people losing eyes or breaking bones or even dying from a mower-launched rock or shard of glass.

I limped my way through the rest of old biddy Trotter's backyard. She had left my one dollar payment in an envelope clothes-pinned to her mailbox. That buck would not cover the cost of amputation!

On my way home, I knew my parents would want to know why I was limping. They wouldn't be fazed by the injury; life's tough. Man up! But my mother would be quick to demand I take a shower so that she could then apply hydrogen peroxide to the wound. As the solution bubbled in the welt, I would again grit my teeth and "man up." "Man up?" Hell, I was still a half-year from being a teenager!

War is hell and so is mowing lawns!

Two days later, the swollen welt sported a Band-Aid where the skin had been broken. The bandage was encircled by a kaleidoscopic black and blue bruise. My limp was barely noticeable but it was still generating pain, especially if the shin somehow got bumped. Yet, there were lawns to be mowed.

Thus, in the scorching mid-afternoon heat, I was pushing our hefty lawn mower down the sidewalk on Lincoln Street toward our house after having cut Mrs. Hathcock's yard. She was a retired nurse, a widow. She had picket fencing in the front yard which, along with the heat, slowed down the mowing. It had to be well into the 90s. I had a now empty plastic jug of water strapped over the mower handle. My lawn care efforts and the humidity teamed up so that I was drenched. When I got home, I would most definitely take a shower voluntarily (to my mother's astonishment)!

Fortunately, almost all of Lincoln Street was in the shade of the elm trees and I was grateful for the respite from the direct sunlight. A block from our house, I noticed Captain Jack in front of his home trimming his spirea bushes. He had his cane draped over his left forearm so he could work the trimming shears with both hands. It appeared he was manicuring the last of the four spirea bushes that fronted his porch. He always kept them from getting too tall because he didn't want his view blocked when he and friends sat on his front porch, smoking and sipping their drinks.

"Hi, Captain Jack," I said as I halted the mower and wiped my forearm across my forehead. "Another hot day!"

"Hello, Billy," the captain said as he turned to face me, holding the shears in one hand and planting his cane with the other. "Been making money, I see. How many lawns are you mowing this summer?"

"Only six," I said. "Unless they're unhappy, most people stick with the kid who's been mowing for them the past few years. This is only my second summer that Dad has let me use our mower. But every year, some of the older kids find work other than mowing and those of us who are newer pick up their accounts. But I'd surely like to do something to earn money other than pushing a lawn mower. I have to do our lawn for free."

"I see," the captain chuckled in reply. "Of course, there is the little matter of your folks providing you with three slops and a flop every day. Good luck in finding another means of employment. I don't like pushing my mower either, but I know I need the exercise. Otherwise this gimpy leg gets too stiff."

"Captain Jack, I actually sent a letter to the *Journal* to see if I could work for them."

"What? As a paperboy? That'd be a good way to put some miles on your bicycle. Good workout, too."

"No, Captain Jack," I said. "I wrote the Editor—Mr. Wilson J. Woolcott—that I'd like to be a copy boy and work my way into being a real reporter. I told him I'd even work for free for a couple of months and sweep up if they needed it. And the *Journal* building is air conditioned!"

"Hah! Air conditioned, you say! Now that's using your noggin, Billy," the captain replied. "Willie Woolcott and I used to play semi-pro baseball together. I played shortstop and he played second base. Boy, could we do a slick double play, Willie and me and ol' Orville Hargrove on first. Orville died on Corregidor. He was a Marine. Willie was in the Army and went through the Pacific without a scratch, save for picking up some malaria. He still gets the sweats and shakes."

"I actually don't know if the *Journal* has copy boys these days," I said. "I've seen them in movies. It's been a week now since I wrote Mr. Woolcott and I haven't gotten any reply. Maybe he just tossed my letter. But still, I remembered that you always say, 'Nothing ventured, nothing gained.'"

"Ben Franklin said that long before I did, Billy," the captain said. "I'm glad to know you were paying attention to my words. These days, not many do," he again chuckled to himself.

"Hello, Billy! How are you on this fine day?"

The voice belonged to Mrs. Patterson—Mrs. Eugenia Patterson—who was Captain Jack's housekeeper and occasional cook. She came by twice a week, on Tuesdays and Fridays. She was a colored lady, as we said in those days, and was always nice to me. She had a pretty smile with very white teeth.

"Hi, Mrs. Patterson," I said with a wave. "I'm doing fine. Have you had a nice day?"

"Nice day? Well, I suppose I have, now that you mention it. Captain Jack didn't mess up his house too much since Tuesday. And, with the windows open, it's cooler inside than out, except for in the kitchen where I've been baking pies. And those pies are why I've come out here, to see if Captain Jack would like a nice piece of pie on the porch or inside."

"Inside, Mrs. Patterson. I've done enough damage out here. Which of your mighty fine pies have you baked today?" the captain asked as he grabbed the rail and stepped up onto the porch.

"Your favorites, Captain Jack," Mrs. Patterson said. "Coconut meringue and pecan."

"Outstanding! I can't wait to sink my teeth into your pecan pie," the captain said with a smile. Turning back to me, the captain said, "Come on in, Billy. Let's go wash our hands and you can have a piece of Mrs. Patterson's prize-winning pie, too."

"Wow! Thanks, Captain Jack," I exclaimed, pushing my mower in front of the spirea bushes. "I'd surely like some of your coconut pie, Mrs. Patterson."

As I was finishing my slice of coconut pie, I said to the captain, "I saw you and the other soldiers at the fireworks Sunday night."

"Soldiers, sailors, Air Force, Marines, and Coast Guard. Yep. Can't say our marching formation would have passed muster back in the day. But I'm glad they still call the vets together on Independence Day. That's about the only time in the year that I see most of those fellows. I still haven't met the three WACs.

"The mayor said some nice words, I thought," the captain continued. Before the National Anthem Mayor Bowman had made a few remarks to salute the veterans and acknowledge military sacrifices. "The best thing about Mr. Bowman's speech is that it was short and sweet."

Captain Jack snapped his fingers. "Speaking of 'short and sweet,' that reminds me, Billy, that I've got something for you." With that said, he grabbed his cane and walked toward the back of the house.

Mrs. Patterson cleared the dishes. "Thank you, again, Mrs. Patterson. That was real good."

"You're welcome, Billy. I'd give you a second piece but I know your mama wouldn't be happy about that. Guess you'll just have to come back another day for a second helping."

The captain returned from the room he used as an office. He was carrying a book, a couple of sheets of typing paper, and a file folder. He sat back down and placed the empty manila folder in front of me.

"Billy, the price you're going to pay for eating my coconut pie is to listen to some advice I'm gonna give ya. How old are you now?"

"Twelve," I replied. "Thirteen in December."

"And you're not shaving yet, are you," the captain chuckled and winked at Mrs. Patterson who was looking on as she dried dishes in the kitchen.

"No, sir," I smiled. "Not shaving yet."

"Well, good, son. You got all of life ahead of you. But you need to pay attention to what's going on around you and keep a few notes as you go." The captain reached over and opened the file folder.

"Billy, when you leave here today, you can decide whether my advice is worth a bucket of warm spit or not, but I'm going to suggest that you start a file folder or a set of file folders or a box in which you can keep what I call 'Life Jottings.' If you do some such, you can call your file 'Life Jottings,' 'Jack Benny,' or 'Fried Pickles.' It's not what you write on the outside of the file that matters but rather the stuff—the 'jottings' as I say—that you put inside the folder. Follow?"

"Yes, sir," I replied, not knowing exactly where the captain was headed.

"So, now I'm going to give you your first two jottings to put into this here folder." The captain leaned toward me.

"Got a question for you, Billy," the captain began again. "Sunday night, out at Walter Johnson Park, why were the veterans invited to march across the field and come to a parade rest before the folks in the grandstand? Why?"

"Well, it was July 4," I began. "I guess people think of fireworks like 'bombs bursting in air,' like the Anthem says. So the soldiers—I mean not just the Army, but all of the branches—were represented. I think it was sort of a thank you, thanks to all the vets." I stopped,

17

uncertain that I was tracking with the captain. Mrs. Patterson hung up her dishtowel and began putting away plates and cups.

"I think you've got it right, Billy. But just one more question," the captain said. "What was the crowd there assembled thanking the veterans for?

"Well, for the war—I mean the big wars and Korea, too—service in war," I said. "Not all of Coffeyville's fighters came back. Some came back hurt. My folks say it's always a good thing to say, 'thank you!'"

"Say that again, Billy," the captain said, leaning forward.

"Uh,..you mean, 'It's a good thing to say, "thank you?"'"

"Yep." The captain picked up one of the sheets of typing paper and tore it into two pieces. He took a ballpoint pen from his pocket and wrote on one of the half-sheets: "It's a good thing to say, 'thank you!'" Underneath the sentence, he wrote in capital letters: RIGHT! Then he picked up the piece of paper and placed it into the file folder.

"There, Billy," the captain said. "Your first deposit. But let me give you a couple more."

"Yes, sir. Sure," I said, curious as to what would come next.

"Billy, I reckon you were born just as the war was coming to an end. But you're probably old enough to know who I'm speaking about if I use the name, 'Uncle Joe.'"

"Sure, Captain," I replied. "'Uncle Joe' was Stalin—Joseph Stalin, the Russian dictator. Right?"

"That's right, Billy. Uncle Joe went after the Nazis on the Eastern Front. We met up with the Soviet troops at the River Elbe. That linkage cut Germany in two and the war was over within a month.

During the war, Roosevelt, Churchill, and Uncle Joe were all good buddies. But when the war ended, things changed. Stalin's blockade of Berlin created a tinderbox that could have exploded into new super-power fighting. But Truman and the U.S. "Berlin Airlift" outlasted Stalin and broke the post-war blockade. Now, Stalin is dead and on display like a mackerel in the Kremlin with his buddy Lenin."

Mrs. Patterson refilled the captain's cup. He sipped the black coffee.

"So, Billy, I've been spending a lot of time on my front porch reading about the war. I was there, of course—four long years. But one soldier only sees a speck of the whole shooting match. So, I read and in this little volume I came across a quotation by Uncle Joe that just stuck in my craw."

"What was it, Captain Jack?" I asked.

"Well, here's the set up. A British diplomat named Carrington was dispatched by Churchill to carry a message to Uncle Joe. When Carrington arrived in Moscow, the Brit was sick with the flu. But he met with Stalin and gave him Churchill's message. Then Carrington walked out of Stalin's office and collapsed in the secretary's office. Stalin heard about it and had his personal physician tend to Carrington for twenty-four hours until others in the British legation removed Carrington to their chancery where he was recovered within a week.

While he was still weak but able to travel, Carrington was instructed to return to London. Carrington called on Stalin to pick up a return message to deliver to Churchill. Stalin was seated at his desk reading. An aide to Stalin picked up an envelope and gave it to Carrington to be transported by diplomatic pouch to the British Prime Minister. While Stalin was still reading, Carrington thanked the Premier for the medical assistance. Then he asked if he might personally visit Stalin's physician to thank him and his staff for tending to him. Without looking up, Stalin said, *"Nyet."*

Then one of Stalin's aides approached Carrington to escort him out of the Kremlin. As Carrington turned to leave, Stalin said 'Остановка,' the Russian word for *"Halt."* Carrington and his escort turned back to Stalin who had picked up his pipe and puffed on it. He leaned back in his leather chair and said a sentence in Russian and then waved his pipe in dismissal.

As Carrington left, he asked the English-speaking aide what the Premier said. The aide replied with a stony face, *"Gratitude is a sickness suffered by dogs."*

"Wow," I exclaimed. "My parents wouldn't like that."

"That's right, Billy," the captain said. He had taken the other half-sheet of typing paper and written *"Gratitude is a sickness suffered by dogs."* In capital letters beneath Uncle Joe's comment, Captain Jack printed, *"WRONG!"* He placed that half-sheet into the manila folder.

"Billy," Captain Jack began again, "I flew twenty-five B-17 bomber missions over Europe. I was shot out of the sky three times. Twice I crashed in East Anglia near our home base in England. Once I crashed in France and had to be rescued by the French resistance and smuggled across the English Channel. Eight of my crew had serious injuries. Two died. All of us knew we were at war and we had our duty to do even if that meant we'd all be blown out of the sky. But my crew—all of those men, including the two that died—knew I loved them like brothers and would forever be grateful to them for sharing in saving our collective asses—pardon my French. Saying "thank you" ain't much but it can mean a hell of lot when flak is exploding all around you."

The captain paused and glanced at Mrs. Patterson who was watching the two of us. Captain Jack sipped his coffee and cleared his throat. "Billy," the captain said, "sometimes I get a little excited about one thing or another. If war don't excite you, nothing will. But I need to finish up here with your brand new file folder."

Captain Jack picked up the remaining sheet of typing paper on which he had already written. Looking at the sheet, the captain said, "Billy, I don't know why Uncle Joe's comments riled me like they did. But Sunday night, our little town said 'thank you' to a company of veterans. That was the right thing to do. Gratitude is not *a sickness suffered by dogs.*' When thanks is rightly earned, it is wrong not to declare that thanks, whether we're talking about giving thanks to God or man. Does that make sense to you, Billy?"

"Yes, Captain Jack," I said. "I think so. Saying 'thank you' is important."

"So, Billy, on this sheet of paper, in my very own handwriting, are ten quotations about gratitude I tracked down in my own collection of books and in some books I found at the library. Now, in front of Mrs. Patterson, I am going to autograph and date this list of quotes and put it in your file. As you get older and begin to shave, peruse this file every now and again."

Captain Jack closed the folder and handed it over to me. "Billy, all my rambling boils down to me encouraging you not to go to your grave without having given due thanks to those folks who have crossed your path, have walked along side, or have waved a 'hello' as they came from the opposite direction. If you can learn this as a skinny lad who mows lawns, you'll be way ahead in the game of life when you hit eighteen and start drinking beer. And that, Billy Howard, is all the advice I can dole out for one day."

The three of us sat for a moment in silence. Then I stood, picked up the file, went to the screen door, turned back and said, *"Thank you,* Mrs. Patterson. *Thank you*, Captain Jack."

When I got home, not finding a box that was the right size for a file folder, I placed my new LIFE STUFF file in my bottom dresser drawer in my bedroom. That catch-all drawer had my baseball card collection, my plastic Hopalong Cassidy bank, slingshot, and three throw tops. Now it also had my LIFE STUFF file. Out of sight, but not out of mind.

Chapter 3

D.C. and Fort Worth Nightcaps

1987

Dr. Scott Brentano, Dean of the Humanities Department at American University in northwest Washington, D.C. had brought me back to the Willard Hotel. We were nursing nightcaps in the Round Robin and Scotch Bar that looked out upon Pershing Park. Tourists were ambling west toward the White House.

"It really was a fine night, Billy. Everyone enjoyed the lecture and the panel. It's been a while since I've seen our jaded graduate students and skeptical faculty as positively animated as they were tonight."

"Whatever!" I mocked.

Scott merely chuckled and took another handful of barroom nibbles. "Do you know when you'll be back this way again?" he asked.

I leaned back in the leather chair, sipped the scotch, and replied. "May. I'm speaking a couple of times at the Washington and Lee University writers' conference in Lexington. I'll fly into Dulles. Maybe we can all get together then. I'd love to see Claudia and the girls. Your feminist daughters must be old enough now to hear what their father thought of women as a teenager."

"The hell you say, Billy Howard!" Scott nodded to the waiter to bring another round. "The relationship between my teenage perspective of women and my present *sitz im leben* with five women in my house is clear evidence that God has a sense of humor. I can testify that the Ancient of Days extracts penance from those such as I who had a misguided youthful perspective of females."

Changing the subject, I said, "I wonder how far we walked."

"What?"

"I wonder how far we walked back and forth to school and around the neighborhood or downtown. I wonder how far we rode our bicycles. We were quick to go cruising in a car as soon as we had a license and gas money. But till then, we walked or biked. Too bad we didn't have pedometers. Today, kids get driven everywhere."

"Sure. But around here, they get driven everywhere so they don't get shot, gangbanged, or kidnapped. Back in the day, Coffeyville didn't have many of those problems."

"You're right," I said. The waiter swapped out our peanuts and pretzels bowls.

"You know Claudia grew up in Emporia," Scott said. "We tell our girls that we both had something they haven't had: A childhood. I don't know that I could ever gear down enough to reside again in Coffeyville, but I'm still glad we grew up there."

"So, what did your girls say to all that?" I asked.

"Kirsten Leigh—she's 15 now—Kirsten said, 'You had childhoods. We have VCRs. We're good, Pops. Don't worry 'bout it!'"

We looked up as three couples walked in, apparently having just come from the National Theatre, a block east on Pennsylvania Avenue. The maitre'd seated the party at the opposite end of the lounge.

"When were you last in Coffeyville?" Scott asked.

"Last June. I sent the kids' oldest sister and loving mother to Hawaii. Then I gave Frederick and Dawn a guided tour of the great state of Kansas. In Coffeyville, I took them to the Dalton Defenders' Museum and the Brown Mansion."

"That must have been a hit!" Scott said reaching for his scotch.

"They put up with it. Actually, in light of them being prepubescent world travelers, they were astonished that I had actually been happy growing up there. Frederick concluded, 'Different strokes for different folks!'"

"I read the *New Yorker* article," Scott said. "I thought it was pretty well done. Did you like it?"

"I skimmed it as I do any such pieces," I said. "I should mention that is because of my loving wife's insistence. Whatever gets written about me, she doesn't want me to wax giddy with delight or morose with despair."

"The *New Yorker* article only gave two short paragraphs to Coffeyville and Kansas, if I remember correctly," Scott said.

"You're right. Jason Goldman who wrote the piece grew up in Brooklyn. He said he'd travelled quite a bit east of the Alleghenies but only saw *"flyover-country"* from 30,000 feet enroute to California. I doubt that he has much of an understanding of or appreciation for small town America."

"On the subject of "small town America," here's a trivia question for you. Your Kansas University Jayhawk Alumni Card will be taken away from you if you don't know the answer," Scott said as the bartender put down new tumblers of scotch.

"Shoot!" I replied.

"Who was the *'Sage of Emporia?'*" Scott asked.

"You must be kidding me, Brentano," I said. "Fifth-graders in Kansas are taught the answer: William Allen White, editor of the *Emporia Gazette* and friend of presidents. What about him?"

"Okay, so you know Claudia grew up in Emporia," Scott said. "Turns out her grandparents and parents were friends of the Whites and their two kids.

"Two or three years ago, Claudia gave me a set of the *'Collected Works* of *William Allen White.'* I had read a couple of books by White and many articles, but I launched into reading the whole collection for a summer lecture series I was going to do as a guest at K-State in Manhattan."

"Did you discover any lost codes?" I smirked.

"No, Billy, I didn't find any lost codes. Just snort your scotch and listen. White was awarded ten honorary degrees. He received all sorts of journalism prizes and awards, including two Pulitzers, just like you. Almost every time he was conferred with some honor, people would ask him how was it that his writing could so well capture Midwestern life and perspectives. White said, 'I write my life.'"

Scott downed the rest of his scotch and grabbed his daytimer from the table. "Look, Claudia bought me this scheduler at Riggs Stationers in Emporia. Had them engrave my initials here in gold leaf. That same day, in that same store, she bought this post card that has a portrait of White in all his journalistic glory. But on the backside are some quotes. The first one listed is by Edna Ferber— *Edna Ferber!* She wrote *Showboat, Stage Door,* and *Giant.* She also won a Pulitzer. Listen to what she said:

> *'There is no ocean trip, no month in the country, no known drug equal to the reviving quality of twenty-four hours spent on the front porch or in the sitting room of the Whites' house in Emporia. . . .'*

"Scotty," I said looking at my wristwatch, "you have the beginning of a marvelous post card collection. But you probably need to bring your discourse in for a landing so the staff here can clean up and get some rest."

"Yeah, yeah," Scott said as he loosened his collar and tie. "Here's the big finish. These are the quotes about White they put on the back of the post card. Listen:

> *'An article in the New York Sun on October 20, 1910, hailed White as being "as much a part of Kansas as her cornstalks and sunflowers," and observed that "He thinks Kansas is the real United States, and had rather be the mouthpiece of Kansas' thought . . . than to be the richest man in the State or an United States Senator." By remaining in the small town, when his generation were flocking to the city, he eventually became not only the spokesman for Kansas but for much of the Middlewest. He always maintained that the reason he stayed in Emporia was that people were more sociable and friendly. Emporia was a personal world where neighbors' joys and sorrows were shared with others."'*

"Are you saying we should have grown up in Emporia. But then I might have met and married Claudia. Then you'd be homeless and hungry."

"Billy, you said the *New Yorker* essay author probably never set foot in small town America. He doesn't know what he's missing. William Allen White was a product of Emporia. Harper Lee was a product of small town Alabama. Larry McMurtry grew up in a town of thirteen-hundred in Nowhere, Texas.

"Bill Inge grew up in the confines of Coffeyville's arch-rival Independence, at the time a much smaller town than Coffeyville. All of a sudden, Inge is a big hit on Broadway with *Picnic, The Dark at the Top of the Stairs,* and *Come Back, Little Sheba.* Everything that Inge wrote was full of life in *"fly-over country."* The two of you grew up twenty-six miles apart and each of you garnered Pulitzers."

"Drum roll, please," I said. "I sense you've finally come to your point." The waiter cleared our glasses and nibbles.

"Billy, I've read virtually everything you've written. God, you are good, man, so good! And the whole country agrees. I've also read most of the articles and essays they've written about you. Whether it be your books or these articles, there's never much included about Coffeyville. Don't get me wrong. You're the author and you can include or exclude anything you want.

"But what White and my Claudia and her folks have said about Emporia, we can say about Coffeyville. And we do, when we get together. Maybe none of us wants to live there today, but we're all glad to call the place our hometown.

"So now I'm talking like one of the hometown folks or maybe even the Chamber of Commerce," Scott continued. "You and I know that our lives as adults have been influenced big time by where we grew up. I am amazed at how often I think of Coffeyville. As you said, it seems that we were always outdoors. There was school. The teachers. The homework. The *Kindley Kavalkade* musical. The Rousters, Lindy, the *Journal* where you were copyboy. That ex-ballplayer who lived next to you, the murders down the street. Billy, there's gotta be some stories in all that."

"Okay, Scott, I hear you loud and clear," I said. "Writing something with Coffeyville as the backdrop is not a new thought to me. But let me tell you what I have always thought to be a huge problem in writing such a great American novel."

"I'm listening," Scott said.

"For all the good times we had growing up, for all the influence our families, friends, teachers, and that little town had upon us, we were, nevertheless,....."

"What?" Scott said. "Don't leave me dangling. We were what?"

"Provincial. Naïve. Ignorant. Clueless. Unaware of the ways of the world," I said, uncertain as to how Scott would respond.

"And that was all bad?" Scott asked.

"No, Dr. Brentano, it was not all bad," I said. "And today, neither of us is provincial, naïve, ignorant, clueless, or unaware of the ways of the world. We are both on record as being glad about those halcyon days under the majestic elm trees. The challenge is to describe that time and place to people who have never set foot in fly-over country. I've already noted that it was a stretch for my own kids to grasp the implications of growing up in a place like the 'Ville.'"

Scott said, "Are you going to serve cheese with this whine? Suck it up, for heaven's sake! You're the writer, Billy. It's your job to transport readers to far-away places with strange sounding names.

"Listen to me, Billy-boy: You've probably got your next six books already outlined, but I'm telling you here and now, you need to do a Coffeyville book. I promise I'll buy at least ten copies if you mention my name."

Doubtless it was the scotch that caused me to dream that night about *Coffeyville: The Musical!*

The next night, I was home in Fort Worth. When she walked into the den, I realized that she had visited *Victoria's Secret* while I was in D.C. Leaning against the doorframe, she said, "Come to bed, Billy."

"My dear, in that lovely outfit, you will not have to ask me twice," I said. I leaned forward in the wing-backed chair, placed the file folder, yellow pad, and pencil on the side table. I drank the last bit of Chardonnay, put down the wine glass, and headed toward the door.

"What were you doing?" she asked as she hugged me and pressed her cheek against my chest.

"I was looking through an old file that Captain Jack gave me. I may need to catch up on some thank you notes. But I can elaborate on that at tomorrow. Now, I'd much rather have you show me the ins and outs of your new attire. You may need to take it off so I can examine it and you more closely."

She smiled, took my hand, and led me to where the phrase, *"Home, sweet home!"* undoubtedly originated.

Chapter 4

Added Prodding to Write the Memoir

"So, like a forgotten fire,
a childhood can always flare up again within us."

Gaston Bachelard
Philosopher

"Every author owes it to the reading public to explain himself."

John Stott
Theologian

"Not until I was about to turn forty did I awaken to the fact that
I had enjoyed an actual childhood,
something that too many children born later never experienced."

Dr. Scott Brentano
Grew Up in Coffeyville

"In normal life we hardly realize how much more we receive than
we give,
and life cannot be rich without such gratitude.
It is so easy to overestimate the importance of our own achievements
compared with what we owe to the help of others."

Dietrich Bonhoeffer
Martyr

PART II

1957-1963

Chapter 5

The Black Thunderbird

Coffeyville's two secondary schools sat side-by-side, eleven blocks west of downtown. The campus included large grassy commons in front of the school buildings. Behind them sat Ise Athletic field and an intramural field. Roosevelt Junior High School—named for Theodore, not Franklin—was on the east side of the block serving seventh through ninth grades. Field Kindley Memorial High School—named for a WWI flying ace from Coffeyville—sat on the west side of the campus for grades ten through twelve.

I had just departed a special Saturday debate team practice. The Southeast Kansas District Forensics Tournament was the following Friday and Saturday in Fredonia. Rather than heading for Lincoln Street, which came to a dead end at the junior high school, I was walking along Eighth Street, the main drag through Coffeyville at that time. Eighth Street was also U.S.166 that entered Kansas from Missouri about sixty miles east of Coffeyville. Thus, Eighth Street usually had a steady flow of traffic.

I wanted to have a burger at the A&W Root Beer which was on the other side of Eighth Street. I crossed Cherokee Street on the eastern side of the campus to await a break in the traffic to cross

Eighth Street. As I was doing so, Paulie Pyle rolled out of the A&W parking lot and pulled to the curb in front of me.

"Hi, Billy," he said. Want to go for a ride?"

"You bet, Paulie. Will you take me home?" Having an A&W burger was not as delicious as riding in a souped-up '57 black Ford Thunderbird!

"Sure, sure! I'll take you home but first I have to take some quilting patches out to my grandma's. Get in!"

I stuck my briefcase with my debate cards and yellow legal tablets behind the right front seat, sat down, and slammed the door on that beautiful machine. Paulie looked around to assure himself that the fuzz were not near and then peeled out and accelerated to the middle of the school block. But then he eased off the pedal and cruised at a steady thirty m.p.h., the speed limit on Eighth Street. He was past his final parental warning about getting another speeding ticket, parking ticket, or turning infraction ticket. Should he be pulled over by the local police again, whatever the officer might say, Paulie's parents were on record that they would pull his license and ground him for a month or more.

The Thunderbird had its ragtop up on that brisk January day. In light of the temperature in the low forties, I was glad not to have the chilly wind whistling through my hair. I did not want a cold to put a damper on my voice which I would very much need the next weekend at the district debate tournament.

Paulie glided the car past the high school and the old inter-urban train barn, past Delk's Market, the little service station with an all rock exterior, Jack's Newsstand, the florist, the VFW, the furniture store, Ted's Grill, the skating rink, into what was called "West Coffeyville," and finally up and down the overpass that marked Coffeyville's western city limit.

As soon as we came down the overpass, Paulie gunned the engine and off we went.

"Where does your Grandma live?" I asked.

"Tyro," he said. "Just off the highway, a couple blocks north, near the park. Tyro was eleven miles west of Coffeyville on 166. It hadn't occurred to me that we'd be leaving town. But my parents didn't know what time the debate practice was supposed to end, so unless I was spotted on the open road, by them or one of their friends, I should be okay.

The Thunderbird was going faster and faster. In those days, there were no shoulder seat belts and only a few new cars had lap belts. The Thunderbird had no seat belts at all. But I dared not show any hint of fear or I'd never get to ride in the black beauty again.

"Well, we just hit 100," Paulie said. "Let's see how long we can hold it."

Paulie held it at 100 for more than a mile. I kept wondering if we were being tracked by a Highway Patrol radar gun. Fortunately, we weren't and Paulie began to ease up on the gas pedal.

He told me his grandparents had been farmers with a thousand acres between Tyro and Caney. "Wheat, corn, and hay," Paulie said. "I worked on the farm every summer from when I was seven. They actually paid me. My dad thought I should donate my labor as a loving grandson which I probably would have done if Grandpop hadn't insisted to pay me. He didn't pay me a full wage till I reached thirteen. I thought I was rich, but, man, was the work hard."

"Don't they farm anymore?" I asked.

"Grandpop died two years ago, he said. He had his lunch and was sitting in his easy chair listening to Paul Harvey on KGGF. Grandma thought he'd just dozed off as he often did. But he was gone. They were married for fifty years and six months. Man, that's a long time to spend with just one woman."

"Did your grandma sell the farm?"

"No. She leased it. Then she moved into Tyro, the big city. Hah! One of their long-time hired hands leased the farm from her. Daddy worked out the deal for her. Neither Daddy nor my Uncle Alger wanted to farm. Their parents worked the land to pay for the boys to go to college which they did. Uncle Alger is a lawyer up in Olathe and Daddy's a C.P.A."

"What's a C.P.A.?" I asked. "Doesn't it have to do with bookkeeping?"

"Yeah, but, well, it's at a higher level. He checks the books—the bookkeeping at stores like Carter's Clothing Store, Oakley Plumbing, and even the school district. He does taxes for individuals, couples, and companies. He really puts in the hours when it's tax time, you know, January through April."

"Well, whatever a C.P.A. does," I thought to myself, "he must make some good dough to supply his son with a hot-rod Thunderbird."

"Are you going to be an accountant?" I asked.

"No way, my boy," Paulie said emphatically. "You know dang well I've been the number one player on the golf team. I've already heard from KU, K-State, and even the University of Arizona that they're watching my scores. I want a full ride and then I want to go pro when I graduate. Ain't nobody goin' to stop me from being the next Ben Hogan or—better yet—Arnold Palmer. I'm gonna be rich as hell. Chicks to the right of me and chicks to the left of me. Wanna be my caddy, Billy?"

"Nope. But I look forward to seeing you on TV. I'm going to be a writer."

As Paulie said, his grandma lived across from the Tyro City Park. Tyro was not then nor is now a city. In the early 1960s, it had only a few hundred residents.

Mrs. Pyle, Paulie's grandma, was delighted to see Paulie and meet me. Paulie handed over the quilting patches that Paulie's mother had sent to Mrs. Pyle to take to the Tyro Christian Church's Ladies Quilting Bee which met every Thursday morning.

"Billy, are you and Paul in the same grade?" Mrs. Pyle asked.

"No, ma'am. Paulie—I mean Paul is one year ahead of me. I guess we met when we played on the same Little League team. *'Machine Tool'* was our team. Machine Tool Company was our sponsor. Paul played centerfield. I was at first base."

"And I was great, Grandma," Paulie declared. "You oughta know that. You saw some of our games. I suppose you probably saw Billy, too. Like he said, he played first base but he wasn't any good at it and he couldn't hit a volleyball if you pitched it to him," Paulie mocked. I kept my mouth shut.

Happily, Mrs. Pyle came to my defense. "Paul, don't be! I'm sure Billy was a very fine ballplayer, including being a good hitter. Land's sake!"

On the way back to the 'Ville, Paulie kept to the fifty m.p.h. speed limit. We were talking about golf as the pro season was about to begin. I had only played miniature golf. Paulie was doing most of the talking, comparing Arnold Palmer to Jack Nicklaus, and why a wood made out of metal was an abomination compared to a wood wood. He was just about to tell me the differences between *Titleist* and *Wilson* golf balls when he suddenly leaned forward and squinted into the rear-view mirror.

"No shit!" Paulie exclaimed. "Now ain't this a cowinkydink!"

I had no side mirror. My stomach dropped as I could only envision a Kansas Highway Patrol Officer about to turn on his siren and pull us over. But Paulie showed no sign of slowing down or pulling over. He was looking down the road, into the rear-view mirror, and over to the side mirror which was affixed to his side of the car.

I did a 180-turn in my shotgun seat to find out what was happening. I saw no flashing lights, just another car that was closing fast on our tail.

"That fool is gonna blow his engine!" said Paulie.

"You know who it is?" I shouted as I saw that whoever was driving behind us seemingly wanted to ram us.

Apparently thinking along the same lines, Paulie said, "That stupid fart hasn't got the balls to ram us. Besides he won't want to bang up his hearse."

"Hearse?" I said. "You mean that's *Brillo*?"

"Of course it is, doofus! Who else drives a hearse?"

On that Saturday afternoon on U.S. 166, Brillo was coming on fast. Paulie kept steady at fifty. At the last possible moment, to avoid drop-kicking us all the way to the overpass, Brillo pulled into the oncoming lane and passed us like the *Santa Fe Zephyr* passing a freight train.

"Holy hottie rocket!" I shouted as I turned back to the front to see Brillo's 1953 Ford station wagon disappear into the distance. "What was that all about, Paulie?" I asked.

Paulie was laughing. "Hell, Billy! Brillo is pissed that I won't race him. One day, I'll race him but I gotta get Mom and Dad off my back first. I am not going to risk losing my wheels when there are too many babes wanting to take a spin with me."

Then Paulie pointed down the road to the right. Just ahead was a country road that Brillo had turned right onto, turned around on, and was now idling perpendicular to U.S. 166.

"Looks like our buddy, Brillo, wants to have a summit conference," Paulie said. "He's as fat as Khrushchev and that burr haircut makes him look bald like Comrade Nikita. He's your pal, too, Billy, so you can be the official eye-witness reporter. Just remember to spell my name right," Paulie concluded as he pulled off the highway and idled driver's window to driver's window with Brillo.

Both drivers rolled down their windows.

"What's up, Brillo Pad?" Paulie asked.

"Doin' fine, mighty fine, gentlemen. Just been blowin' some dust out of my pipes. Sadly, I was slowed to a crawl by a tortoise-like two-seater. How you doin', Billy? You trying to give this cowardly lion some courage?"

"Hi, Brillo. I'm just taking advantage of a free ride." There was no way I wanted to get into the middle of this summit meeting.

"By the way, Paulie," Brillo said, "when are the two of us going to settle things before the town folks? Lotta people want to know if your little toy Ford could get off the starting line against this here fine family vehicle."

"Brillo Stubblefield, you never cease to amaze me by wanting to get into waters that are way too deep for you," Paulie responded. "Maybe, just maybe, one day before I leave the Sunflower State for good, I might amuse myself by letting you and your hearse eat my dust. But, for the moment, I've got some other minnows to fry."

"Whatever you say, Paulie. I'll be sitting by my phone day and night. By the way, since I want you to have no excuse for why you lost to me in the drag race of the century, might I suggest you spend some of your pappy's hard earned cash on new tires. They're beginning to look a little threadbare."

"You don't know beans, Brillo. These Michelins are original equipment on this Thunderbird. They're good for 50,000 miles and this baby only has 44,000. Balding simply makes them like the Indy cars. Nevertheless, I'll keep your concerns in mind, Brillo. Now, stay alert and don't get hurt."

With that, Paulie drove a quarter mile down the country road till he could turn around and head back to town. Brillo peeled out on the gravel and sped toward Coffeyville. It seemed like he was doing more than fifty.

Paulie turned onto 166 and railed with laughter as to why Brillo Stubblefield was a loser when it came to fast cars or anything else. Keeping my mouth shut, I thought that Brillo, from my own interaction with him, was a pretty good guy who had always been straight with me, a mere plebe. As to how good either Brillo or Paulie were with their respective souped-up vehicles, I and the rest of the town would have to wait for *"the drag race of the century."*

Suddenly, I leaned forward to scope out the flashing lights ahead. "Uh-oh, Paulie! Look at that."

Just as we came down the overpass across the city limits, we saw a Coffeyville police car and Brillo's Ford. I guessed that he had entered the 'Ville too fast. Who should be waiting for his arrival but none other than Officer Shug Webb and Detective Bear Knightly. Apparently having nothing better to do on a Saturday afternoon, they parked their patrol car with side-mounted radar at the overpass entry to the city. Due to their diligence, they had caught hot-rodder Brillo Stubblefield in his 1953 Ford station wagon exceeding the posted speed limit by fourteen M.P.H., as I found out later.

As we drove by the police stop, Brillo was pleading with Bear to let him off the hook. While Brillo was intent in his conversation with Bear, he did not fail to notice our smirks as we drove by. It was an especially good laugh for Paulie and a $32.50 fine for Brillo.

It was almost 3:00 p.m. when Paulie dropped me off two blocks from my house on Lincoln Street. My folks were not keen on me riding with other teens, so, I made certain to walk the final distance to my Lincoln Street home. Paulie well understood. Like every other generation of teens—early teens or late teens—I was learning how to outfox parents. Or so I thought.

"Thanks, Paulie. That was a great ride."

"Keep your dobber dry, Billy!" The beautiful black Thunderbird drove away.

"Wow!" I thought to myself. "I had a real-deal joy ride in a black T-Bird! I have been one lucky space cadet today. *Tom Corbett* would be proud!"

Chapter 6

Getting the Light Right

None of my classmates used backpacks. Most days, we didn't have to lug all our textbooks home. More often than not, we could leave some books in our lockers if we had no homework for that night or if we chose to ignore our homework for that night. However, most students could be seen walking to and from school with a notebook and textbooks riding on a hip. We would regularly shift hips to give one arm or the other a rest.

A block away from my house, I veered into the middle of Lincoln Street to approach Captain Jack. The World War II combat veteran had his hands on either side of his prized *Leica* M3 35mm camera. His cane was dangling from the crook of his left elbow.

"Hi, Captain Jack! Whatcha doin'?"

"The light's right, Billy" the captain replied. The elm trees are in full leaf for the first time this spring. I want to get some shots of the sun filtering through the canopy of branches. Beautiful sight to these war-worn eyes."

The captain was facing east. I looked down Lincoln Street and the view was as the captain had said. The elm tree branches were loaded with full leaves that swayed in the slight breeze, permitting shafts of sunlight to pierce the canopy and dot the street. The windshield of the Bixby's old Hudson caught one of the shafts of light and reflected it like an exploding star. The elms lined either side of Lincoln Street and their stately branches touched over the center of the street.

"Billy, when I look up and down Lincoln Street, this canopy of branches reminds me of some of the naval air hangers I've walked around," the captain said as he advanced the film. "At Navy Air Station Oakland, they tethered blimps and dirigibles in arenas like this and did the same over at Treasure Island in the San Francisco Bay. But those gray hangers never warmed my heart like these elms do! I'm going to finish my roll of film and take it down to Maddon's for developing. When the prints come back next week, I may be able to sell a couple to *Kansas Highways*. Two years ago, they bought some of my shots of the Verdigris along U.S. 169. Do you know that magazine, Billy?"

"Yes, sir," I replied. "I've looked through some at the doctor's office. What speed are you shooting, Captain Jack?" I asked, as if I actually knew how to set shutter speed. Our family camera was an *Argus Argoflex*. "Point-and-click," as they say these days.

"There's no rush for shots like this. The film is ISO 100 so I'm shooting f/16 at 125. I expect that will work out just fine."

"Right," I said knowingly.

"When school's out, buy a roll of *Kodachrome* and I'll teach you how to use this *Leica*."

"That would be great, Captain! Thanks!"

The captain retrieved his cane and leaned on it as we moved to the curb to let a car pass. Captain Jack kept walking, up onto his porch. He sipped his lemonade and then pulled a slip of paper from a book he was reading. He traced his steps to rejoin me on the parking, the strip of grass between the sidewalk and the street where the city had planted many of the elm trees.

"Our talk about these here elms reminded me of this," Captain Jack said as he looked at the one column wide paper. I've used it for years as a bookmark, so I pretty well have the paragraphs memorized. I believe I tore it out of the *Kansas City Star* but I can't be certain. Read it when you get home. Maybe it will qualify for your jottings file."

"Thanks, Captain Jack," I said as I folded the bookmark and tucked it into my pocket.

Captain Jack returned to the center of Lincoln Street, again checking the sunlight and shade.

"Hi, Captain Jack!" Carolyn Rousters said as she walked off the sidewalk onto the parking, clutching her books to her chest. She ignored me.

"Hi, Carolyn. How are you today?" the Captain asked.

"I'm fine," she said. "Captain, you know how to work a sextant, don't you?"

"I can work a sextant in my sleep, Carolyn. I have my own sextant that I bought at a surplus store right after the war. Why?" the captain asked.

"Miss Dickenson, my English teacher, and Mr. Linville, the geometry teacher, are having us do a joint final paper. In English, we're reading *Billy Budd* by Herman Melville. We have to do a term paper that reports on the book and intertwines how something nautical or scientific is used to help tell the story. That's why I thought of a sextant."

"I understand, Carolyn. What may I do to help you?"

"Captain Jack, I've read about how a sextant works and I think I understand. But any chance you could show me how you work yours? It would help my paper a lot and I might even get extra points for actually holding a sextant or working it."

"Sure thing, Carolyn. If you want, you can haul it off to school for a show-and-tell if you think that would get you some extra credit. Come by some afternoon. It would probably be best to walk down to the junior high school to get a clear shot at the sky. If your parents will allow it, we can even check the stars in an evening."

"That's great, Captain. I'm sure this will be fine with my folks," Carolyn said.

"What about me? I want to come," I said.

"Fine, Billy. Come!" she said with the condescension of a ninth-grader to a mere eighth-grader. "I'll get back to you, Captain Jack. For me, the sooner the better."

"That's fine, Carolyn. Now, I have a question for you, young lady," Captain Jack said.

"Sure, Captain. Ask away," Carolyn replied, shifting her books from her left breast to her right breast.

"What do you think of Lincoln Street?" the captain asked.

"Beg pardon, sir? I don't understand," Carolyn replied.

"I told Billy that I've been out here taking pictures of the elm trees. I don't suppose you've read the *Iliad*—that's a book in Greek by Homer. There is a Latin poem called *The Aeneid* written by a man named *Virgil*. In both of those ancient books, elm trees are mentioned. Shakespeare wrote about elm trees."

Captain Jack's cane was on his forearm as he placed a hand on my shoulder to stabilize himself as he moved in a circle. In his other hand, he held his camera, using it as a pointer toward the trees.

Captain Jack said, "Elm trees grow all over the world. They were here to greet the Pilgrims when they showed up at Plymouth

Rock. They were all across North America when Lewis and Clark went exploring. They can live more than two hundred years. These here elms along Lincoln Street have doubtless been growing for at least sixty or seventy years. Look at 'em. Holding hands from one side of the street to the other. Must be sweethearts!"

"Look west toward the schools and then east to the other end of Lincoln. Every tree is in full bloom. We've got our own private *Lincoln Street Canopy of Elms.* Not every town can say that. Coffeyville's got many other streets with plenty of elms, but I believe Lincoln Street has the best formed. Really magnificent trees! The Bible even mentions elms. There are other trees that are bigger but I don't believe any tree is as neighborly as *Ulmus americana*, the American Elm. I never saw anything like this during the war."

"No, I don't suppose so, sir," Carolyn replied with a smile, framed by her neatly bobbed haircut. She should smile more often, I thought to myself.

"You probably see my folks taking an after-dinner walk up and down Lincoln Street in the summer," Carolyn said. "They always remark about the trees. I suppose I sorta take them for granted. They've always been here. I suppose I think this is the way a street is supposed to look. And you can climb them, or put a swing on them..."

"Or carve your initials in them," I piped up.

"That's right, Billy. I've done my share of initial carving over the years. Now, if you students will excuse me, I don't want to lose my light." With that the captain walked back to the center of the street and began taking more photographs.

Carolyn and I walked onto our block. She lived on the corner. I was a couple more houses down.

"You'll let me know when you want to go to Captain Jack's, right?"

"Yes, Billy. I'll let you know. I'd like to do it after the sun goes down. But I've got to run it by Mom and Dad. You sure you'll be able to go?"

"Probably," I said. "As long as my Mom thinks I'm done with my homework. Well, see ya!"

Carolyn walked onto her front porch with not a word of farewell. Ninth-graders!

When I got to my house, I went to my room. I put my books on my desk and sat down on my bed. I pulled out the short article Captain Jack had given me. After reading it, I added it to my growing LIFE STUFF file:

Regarding American Elm Trees

"During their usual strolls along the main streets of their hometowns, our parents and grandparents gazed at the scenery around them and took for granted a spectacular picture that seldom is observed nowadays and that few of us can hope to see during our lifetimes: The interweaving limbs of the stately trees that lined the streets ascended into a towering canopy with a graceful, arching beauty unmatched by any tree that is commonly seen today, spreading horizontally at heights of exceeding 100 feet (in rare cases attaining 140 feet with even greater spreads and 11 foot truck diameters), and drooping long, slender branches in abundance high above the street, blocking all view of the sky. Along countless streets for many miles in cities and towns throughout the tree's extensive native range...this scene abounded, the effect of the only species capable of giving us such majestic splendor."

Bruce Carly
"Saving the American Elm"

Chapter 7

Kick the Can

One summer night, approximately a dozen of the Lincoln Street kids were rotating among two or three clusters of conversation in the open back yard of the Rousters. It was a mellow night but lightning could be seen to the southwest. The humidity was high. Everyone worked up a sweat just by sitting on the grass watching the lightning bugs. Earle Ludlum, the KOAM TV weatherman, said a rain squall would be moving through southeast Kansas later that night.

The weather forecast was of particular concern to Carolyn Rousters' younger brother. Of all the kids in the Lincoln Street neighborhood, the most avid advocate for playing *Kick the Can* was Henry James Rousters, Jr., whose name was compressed by everyone to call the lad *Henryjuner*. The alleyway behind the Rousters' garage was the usual home base for the coffee can or bucket or whatever we could find to kick. Most of the kids enjoyed playing *Kick the Can* on a regular basis, but not every night of the summer. On this particular night, despite Henryjuner's repeated pleas, no one was interested in hiding in bushes, crawling under a porch, or making a dash to kick an already heavily-dented can.

But Henryjuner would not take no for an answer. We were all getting annoyed and no one more than Big Sis Carolyn Rousters. Finally, she exclaimed, "Knock it off, Henryjuner! Go stand over by the garage. The rest of us are going to have a huddle and make an absolutely final decision on whether we kick the can or kick your butt."

Henryjuner started to say something but Carolyn cut him off. "Shut it, Henryjuner, or I'll kick the front of your butt. Now go stand by the garage." Henryjuner obeyed and the rest of us huddled by the Rousters' back steps. After brief discussion, the conferees blossomed back into the yard. Carolyn said for all to hear, "Henryjuner, we've decided to play. But you're IT. You've got to count to 100 out-loud with your eyes shut and absolutely no peeking. Understand, little brother?"

Henryjuner said he understood and was elated that the group had accepted his petition. "Wait a minute. I'll set up the can." Henry dashed inside the Rousters' garage and quickly came out carrying an often-punted Folger's can. He turned into the alleyway, placed the can on the alley's center ridge and, without further notice, began to count aloud, "1, 2, 3, 4,.."

Back on the yard side of the garage, everyone began to scatter. "..18, 19, 20…"

In the huddle, Carolyn Rousters had proposed that we all call it a night. Let Henryjuner search the area high and low. Maybe this would teach him a lesson not to be a dweeb. We all agreed to Carolyn's plan, not so much because we couldn't enjoy the group's company for awhile longer, but rather because we supported Carolyn's brilliant perversity. Pesky siblings needed to be put in their place several times a day! Of course, I spoke from no personal experience as I was an only child.

Anyway, by the time Henryjuner reached "..99, 100. Here I come, ready or not!" everyone else was long gone, safely inside their homes. At that point in his life, Henryjuner was a few sandwiches short of a picnic in his ability to process what was or was not happening around him. Twice he shouted that Warren Nelson was lying beside the Casswell's goldfish pond. But no one rose up to race Henryjuner to the can.

Fortunately for Henryjuner, the squall arrived twenty minutes after those not IT had disappeared. The summer rain was a torrent and Henryjuner, with raindrops and perplexity upon his face, retired to the indoors of his house. There, he found sister Carolyn in robe and fuzzy slippers reading *TEEN* Magazine and chomping malted milk balls.

Final Score: Big Sister: 1. Dweeb Brother: 0.

Chapter 8

Flipping for Flowers

I was nearly twelve when I became the new kid on Lincoln Street. Within two blocks of our house, there were twenty-five to thirty kids, ages seven to seventeen. Summer, fall, winter or spring, there was steady kid traffic in the environs of Lincoln Street.

Parents were quick to exhort their kids to *"Stay in the house, get your homework done, and clean up your room!"* But parents would also pressure their kids to *"Turn off that television set and go outside to play!"* No doubt that TV was a big draw, but to be out of the house and out of visual range of our parents' eyesight was also a big incentive.

In those days, kids were very familiar with the nooks and crannies of their neighborhood. We traveled the sidewalks and rarely walked in the streets, the domain of bicycles, motorcycles, cars, and trucks. We darted between houses and across backyards. If the backyards had fences, we could drop back to the alley which virtually every block had. Alleys were not sinister places in that time and place.

As long as we didn't trample flowers or peep through house windows or steal anything, the neighborhoods had an open border policy. But most kids had figured out that there were usually some adult eyes watching.

Whoever may have been watching us, it didn't take me long to meet the cast of characters that populated Lincoln Street and its environs. The one exception to this were the children of the Madigan household.

From various kid sources, I had pieced together an interesting story about the family. Hugh and Fiona Madigan were Irish Catholics who moved to Coffeyville from Omaha because of Hugh's job as a District Manager for *National Tractor and Plow*, a farm implement company. Fiona was a homemaker and apparently the glue of the family. She accomplished the usual household chores and saw to it that everyone was on time to Sunday Mass at Holy Name Catholic Church. The Madigan children included daughter

49

Molly (Madeleine), the oldest (a year older than I), and twin brothers, Hugh III, and Cormac, two years younger than Molly. Upon arrival in Coffeyville, the kids were enrolled at Holy Name Catholic School which had classes through the eighth grade.

About eighteen months before my family moved onto Lincoln Street, Fiona Madigan was diagnosed with pancreatic cancer. She understood from the day of her diagnosis that she had only a short time to live. In fact, she died less than three months later. She spent most of those final months at Coffeyville Memorial Hospital. But in those days there really was no treatment for the disease, other than to make the patient as comfortable as possible. Mrs. Madigan requested to be sent home to die. Her wish was not contested. Three months following her terminal diagnosis, Fiona Madigan succumbed at age forty-four. Hugh was then forty-six. Mrs. Madigan died around noon on July 22, the saint day for Mary Magdalene after whom Molly had been named.

During Fiona's illness, Hugh's mother had arrived from St. Louis to provide care for the children. After Fiona died, Hugh's mother returned to Missouri where her other son, Ennis, was going to help her pack so that she could take up residence with the Hugh II's family in Coffeyville. Unfortunately, she attempted to pull down a suitcase from a closet shelf while standing upon a step-stool. She died from her fall—two "Mrs. Madigans" dead within three weeks. Only sorrow was found in these summer partings.

Hugh and his children received some welcomed encouragement from Captain Jack who was three years older than Hugh II. They had much in common. Both were Army veterans who served in the European Theatre. Both were single in their forties. Both liked to drink, Hugh more than Captain Jack. Captain Jack could hold his liquor; Hugh couldn't. Hugh and Captain Jack were members of the Coffeyville Hunt Club that held its meetings in the back room of the Newcastle Café. For years, they had tramped through cow pastures and woods stalking duck, pheasant, quail, rabbit, and squirrel.

Twice, Captain Jack had taken Molly, Hugh III, and Mac to target shoot at the hunt club firing range, northwest of Coffeyville. Captain Jack provided ammunition and three weapons. The first weapon was an old Remington 512 Tube Fed Bolt Action Rifle that had belonged to Hugh Madigan himself. Mr. Madigan had once owned several firearms but, following Fiona's death, he sold all of them except for the .22 rifle. He didn't figure he'd have much time for hunting or target practice as a single parent. The second firearm was Captain Jack's Savage 16-gauge break-barrel shotgun which he had also purchased from Hugh Madigan II. The third weapon was a .38 caliber police special hand gun which was the first weapon Captain Jack had purchased for himself many years previous.

As to the target shooting, Hugh III and Mac were very wide of center, especially Mac. Hugh III laughed at Mac, declaring that his "four-eyed brother couldn't hit the broadside of a barn." In truth, Hugh III was not all that much better. Further, Hugh III tested Captain Jack's patience when he begged to place the .38 police special into his right front jeans pocket and quick-draw to fire at the target. Captain Jack was concerned the kid would shoot off his toes or nuts and therefore declared the boys' target time completed.

Molly didn't like the weight of the police special. She bruised her shoulder and nearly fell over when she fired the shotgun. But the .22 caliber rifle seemed just right. She triangulated the center ring of the target. Captain Jack set up a couple of tin cans for her at twenty-five and fifty yards. To her delight and her brothers' dismay, Molly put a hole through both cans. Captain Jack loved telling the story of Molly's prowess with the rifle. The senior Hugh Madigan was happy to hear about Molly's skill but seemed annoyed at the reports of how poorly the boys had shot.

Fiona Madigan had admired and enjoyed Captain Jack. Originally, it was Hugh who invited Captain Jack to supper at the Madigan household. He became a Tuesday night fixture. He was like an uncle to the kids who relished his presence. After dinner, Fiona and Molly would each play a piano piece. Then, the boys went to bed. Fiona and Molly went to the kitchen. Hugh II and Captain Jack went to the porch or living room to sip scotch and smoke.

When I arrived in the neighborhood, Molly had been shipped out to St. Theresa's Catholic School for Girls in Wichita. She boarded there through high school and only came home every third or fourth weekend and summers. I had met the twins, Hugh III and Mac, as we passed one another riding bicycles. The brothers weren't impressed by me being two years older. In fact, when I met them, however angelic they may have been prior to their mother's passing, my early opinion was that they were fast becoming hellions.

And a couple of others things about the brothers: They were twins but they were fraternal twins. Hugh III outweighed his slim brother Cormac by thirty pounds. His obesity caused Hugh III to be called "Baby Huey"—after the humongous baby duck of comic book fame—by many of his peers. Hugh III would pound some fool kid—always a smaller kid—who dared to refer to Hugh III as "Baby Huey."

Whereas Hugh III was bellicose, Cormac was a kid of few words. He wore horn-rimmed glasses and always sported a shirt Pocket pen holder. He was almost always called "Mac, never *Cormac.*" That didn't faze Mac at all. What did bother him was that his acne was far more acute than the blemishes and break-outs that struck Hugh III or Molly. Mac always had an ample amount of *Clearasil* smoothed over his face. Alas, Hugh III would taunt Mac by regularly calling Mac *"Zit-Face."* As I got to know the brothers, they didn't seem to care all that much for their dad, Molly, or anyone else, including each other.

I had just ridden my bike back to our house from Pony League baseball practice. I was on the *Pepsi Cola* bottling team. As I was parking my bicycle in the carport, Henryjuner walked up.

"Hi, Billy. How 'bout some catch?" he asked.

"Okay, Henryjuner," I replied. "But only for a little while. I've got some stuff I gotta do before my mom gets home."

"Sure, sure! Maybe after supper we can get up a game across the alley with Mike and Julia."

Henryjuner, who was the same age as the Madigan twins, loved it when any older kid would do something with him. Henryjuner was as avid a baseball fan as I was. We took our positions at opposite ends of my front yard. We had only tossed a couple of throws when the florist's delivery van pulled to the curb on the other side of Lincoln Street.

Kenny the Florist offered a bouquet of cut flowers every week for a year for only one dollar per week including delivery. Customers had to pay twenty-six dollars to launch the contract and the final twenty-six bucks six months later. As my dad traveled a great deal, he thought the flowers would cheer my mother. In our case, bouquet deliveries were every Thursday afternoon.

Clydene Kime was Kenny's driver. Clydene was a natural blonde and the butt of many jokes about her being a dumb blonde. Clydene was too addlepated to recognize people were laughing at her. She generally presented a smiling countenance. Looking into her bright blue eyes, one would note eventually that the lights were on but no one was at home. On this occasion, Clydene waved at me and then turned to reach into the back of the van to grab our bouquet as she also unlatched the driver's side door which began a slow and squeaky opening arc.

Then, three things happened at once: First, coming from behind the van in the center of Lincoln Street, Hugh Madigan III zipped by on his bicycle toward the schools at the west end of Lincoln Street. Second, Clydene's driver-side door completed its lateral arc and was fully open. Third, Cormac Madigan, who had been riding behind and to the right of his brother, slammed full bore into the delivery van's open door.

Clydene screamed as Mac flew off his bike and over the door. Mac did a somersault, landing feet first. But then he fell backwards to bang his head on the front of the van's door before sliding flat onto his back where he again bonked his head on the asphalt.

Amazingly, *I knew what to do next!* "Henryjuner, go find Molly!" I shouted. I raced to the van.

Clydene was hysterical! *"I didn't see him! I didn't see him,"* she wailed! *"Kenny's gonna kill me! I didn't see him! Really, I didn't see him! Waaaaahhh!"*

"Calm down, Clydene!" I shouted. "Get out of the van and sit on the curb. Stop screaming and calm down." I shut the driver's door behind Clydene as she headed for the curb where she continued to wail.

I knelt beside Mac. He appeared unconscious but was slowly moving his head and moaning. I stuck my baseball mitt under his head. As I did so, blood oozed onto my hand and onto my fielder's glove. I looked down his body and saw that his elbows were scraped and bloody. His right jeans leg was ripped. There was a gash on his calf that was also bleeding.

I popped buttons as I pulled off my shirt. Mom was not going to be happy! I quickly folded the shirt into a makeshift pad and placed it under Mac's head. I pushed the glove aside and applied light pressure to the head wound which was pumping out a slow but steady stream of blood. As I was doing this with my right arm, I pulled my handkerchief out of my back pocket and pressed it upon Mac's ripped calf. I hoped my snot would not infect him.

Just then, Molly Madigan, Carolyn Rousters, and Henryjuner Rousters all arrived. Molly knelt on the other side of Mac and shouted, "Cormac, are you alright? Answer me, Mac!" Carolyn took one look at Mac, saw the blood, and said, "I'll go get Lindy." Lindy was a nursing student who lived across from the Madigans on my side of Lincoln Street. She was home from KU, on break between rotations. That was lucky for Mac and lucky for me as I had exhausted what I knew to do.

Molly blessed herself and then pried Mac's eyes open with her fingers. "Mac, can you hear me? Come on, little man, talk to me." Molly was focused on her brother and paid no attention to me. I took her lack of comment as tacit approval for what I was doing.

Most people on the block were at work or running errands. Nevertheless, Henryjuner had gone for his mother and Mrs. Rousters arrived just as Lindy came running up.

"Step aside, Billy!" Lindy said, as she knelt where I had been aside Mac.

I withdrew my blood stained hands, leaving behind my handkerchief, shirt, and baseball glove. Mac's broken glasses lay at his feet. I picked them up, folded them, and handed them to Carolyn Rousters who nodded thanks.

"What happened here?" Mrs. Rousters demanded. Clydene heaved more sobs. Carolyn went to her aide. I quickly explained the biker/van door collision which prompted Mrs. Rousters to exclaim, "Oh my God! Lindy, is he going to be alright?"

Mac was beginning to focus his eyes and wince from his head and leg pain. Molly had continued to exhort him to wake up and speak to her.

"I think he'll be alright but he needs to be treated right away. He may have a concussion. Billy has done a good job of staunching the bleeding, but we need an ambulance here. Mrs. Rousters, would you please call for an ambulance and give Henryjuner a blanket I can put over Mac?"

"Of course, dear!" Mrs. Rousters said as she headed for her house to call for help. "Henryjuner, come with me!" she barked.

"Owww!" Mac was awake and alert. "What happened?" He lifted his head. "Owwwww. Molly, what happened?"

"You ran into the flower van's open door and flipped over it. Now, lie still and let Lindy check you out."

Henryjuner arrived back with the blanket which Lindy draped over Mac except for leaving his right leg exposed so that she could continue to press my snotty handkerchief upon the wound to stop the bleeding. We could hear a siren in the distance.

"Owww." Mac pushed Lindy's hand away. "I'm going to throw up," he said. He rolled up onto his left elbow and, true to his word, barfed right on top of my fielder's mitt.

Hugh III, Mac's twin, showed up just as Mac's gurney was being placed into the rear of the ambulance. Molly climbed in to ride to the hospital with her brother. She told Hugh III to take Mac's bicycle back to the house and to stay there with Lindy who would wait with him until Molly or her dad arrived. Molly gave Mrs. Rousters her dad's office phone number.

"I don't think Daddy will be there. He does his sales calls in the afternoons," Molly said. "But he has an answering service so you can leave a message. Thank you so much for your help," Molly said to Mrs. Rousters before the ambulance door was closed to make the one mile run to Coffeyville Memorial Hospital.

I walked Mac's bicycle along with Hugh III and his bike back to their house. Mac's Schwinn English Racer had bent handlebars, a twisted seat, and a mashed front fender that was abrading the front tire. The front wheel seemed to be intact.

"We were racing up to Ise Field," Hugh III said. "When I saw he wasn't behind me, I thought he'd cut through a backyard to take an alley. I waited for him at the athletic field. When he didn't show up, I thought he'd just gone someplace else to fool me. He thinks he can mess around with me 'cause he's older."

"Older? You're twins."

"Yeah, we're twins, stupid. But he popped out six minutes before I did. He claims he's my 'big brother.' I say he's a dope."

With that, we laid the bikes down next to the Madigan's front porch steps. Hugh III pulled open the screen door and walked through the open living room door into the house.

I walked back down the street to retrieve my ball glove, torn shirt, and handkerchief. I now had blood stains on my undershirt, hands, arms, and face. I grabbed a stick and stuck it under the backhand strap and into one of the glove fingers so I didn't have to get any of Mac's barf on me. I took it into the backyard and hosed it off. I didn't like soaking my leather glove—a Ralph Kiner autograph model—but I figured the cow had stood out in the rain plenty of times. I hung my handkerchief and shirt over our clothes line and soaked them, too but none of the blood came out.

When my mother arrived home, she commended me for tending to Mac but she wished I hadn't used my shirts to sop up his blood. The shirt was already in the trash, bound for the incinerator. Mom said to do the same with the undershirt and then go take a shower.

The hospital ER made quick work of Mac's injuries. The bleeding was staunched once and for all. X-rays were taken of his right leg and head. No bones were broken. He most likely had a mild concussion.

Less than an hour after Mac and Molly showed up at the Emergency Room, their family physician, Dr. Soeldner, arrived to confirm what the ER staff had found. Dr. Soeldner, in practice in Coffeyville for more than thirty years, repaired Mac's scalp with nine stitches and the cut on his right leg with five stitches. After a tetanus shot, Mr. Springer, the Negro orderly that everyone called "Cobbie," wheeled Mac, followed by Molly, to the children's ward on the third floor. Cobbie said Dr. Soeldner wanted him to spend the night at the hospital "under observation" but Cobbie said he was sure Doc Soeldner would send him home the next day.

Mac asked if there was anything he could eat. As the nurse tucked him into his hospital bed, she said it would be another hour before supper trays were delivered. Five minutes later, Cobbie showed up with two grape popsicles, one for Mac and one for Molly.

When the supper tray of salad, meatloaf, green beans, applesauce, a slice of bread with margarine, and glass of milk showed up, Mac had just begun to complain about the meatloaf that Molly was making him eat when Hugh Madigan II arrived.

Mr. Madigan immediately began berating Cormac for foolishly running into a van door. When Molly attempted to intercede, Mr. Madigan told her to "zip it." He said he would deal with her later to find out why she hadn't just used some gauze and adhesive tape instead of having an ambulance called. "I can hardly wait to get the bills for all this mischief," Mr. Madigan growled.

He would have continued to rant if Head Nurse Elaine Battaglear had not intervened. She unhesitatingly shushed Mr. Madigan and told him that Dr. Soeldner had given strict orders that Cormac should rest without being disturbed or upset, even if Mr. Madigan was his father.

Mr. Madigan reluctantly held his tongue. He looked at Cormac and said, "Eat your food, then go to sleep! I'll fetch you tomorrow. Let's go, Molly."

Bruised, bandaged, and slightly concussed, Mac was indeed fetched the next day. Physically, he made a complete recovery and had his stitches removed a week after the accident.

Four days later, I was lying on the sofa in our backroom watching *"Our Gang"* comedies on KOTV, channel six in Tulsa, the clearest of the four channels we received via rooftop antenna. The front doorbell rang. When I pulled the front door open, there stood Molly Madigan on the other side of the screen door.

"Hi!" I said.

"Hi!" Molly said. "My dad wants to talk to you."

"Your dad—Mr. Madigan wants to talk to me? What did I do?"

"Don't be dense, Billy! My father is on the front porch. He wants to talk to you. Are you coming peacefully or shall I rip this damn screen door off its hinges and drag you there?"

"I-I'm coming. I-I'll go," I stammered.

Molly stepped back. I pushed the screen door open and pulled the front door closed behind me. Molly was already on her way back to her house and I followed a few yards behind, tucking in my shirt and running a hand over my hair.

Sure enough, Mr. Madigan was sitting on the front porch in a wicker arm chair. Like Captain Jack, he had a table beside him. On the table was a drink—probably not lemonade like Captain Jack served. Mr. Madigan was puffing on a cigarette.

Molly walked up the steps. I planted myself at the bottom of the steps. "Daddy, this is Billy Howard. Billy, this is my father, Mr. Madigan."

With those introductions complete, Molly opened her screen door and went inside.

"Hello, Billy," Mr. Madigan said. He squished out the stub his cigarette in an ashtray. "How long have you been on Lincoln Street now? A year? Two years?"

"Uh, hello, Mr. Madigan. A year—I mean it was a year last June, so I guess that's a little more than a year. I guess I'm not exactly certain." Wow! How pea-brained was I going to be with Mr. Madigan sitting on his throne and peering down at me over his reading glasses?

"Come up here, Billy."

I climbed the stairs. I wasn't thrilled about moving into closer proximity. *"What does he want?"* I wondered. *"I bet he's mad about the accident. I'm going to get creamed by Molly's father!"*

Mr. Madigan sipped his drink and then said, "Billy…"

"Yes, sir," I said, as if I were a defendant before a judge. *Other kids' parents can't give me swats,* I reassured myself.

"Billy," he continued, "Molly and Lindy across the street have both told me that you were Johnny-on-the-spot to help Cormac when he smashed into the delivery van. As you know, Lindy has almost completed her nursing degree. She said you did a good job of stopping the bleeding on Cormac's leg and head. She said it probably would have been better if you had not moved his head but she noted that Cormac was bleeding from both his head and leg. She said you used your ball glove and shirt as pillows and your handkerchief and shirt to put pressure on the bleeding. Is that right, Billy? Is that what you did?"

"Uh…y-yes sir," I replied, beginning to relax a little but, nevertheless, trying to keep my guard up.

"Where did you learn to do this first aid, Billy?" Mr. Madigan asked. "Did they teach you that in the public schools? Holy Name doesn't do any first aid teaching. I guess the scout pack does some training. Anyway, Billy, how did you know what to do?"

"You mean about putting some pressure on a bleeding cut?" I said. Mr. Madigan nodded "Yes." "Well, I guess it was *Reader's Digest*. Yeah, I read a story about how to do some first aid in an article in *Readers' Digest*. My folks subscribe to it. Then we give it to Captain Jack with some other magazines." I thought, *"Dope! He doesn't care a wit about us giving magazines to Captain Jack! Shut up!"*

"Readers' Digest! Now if that don't beat all! I may have to get a subscription myself, Billy. Hah! *Readers Digest*. Wait'll I tell my bridge buddies out at the Country Club about this." Mr. Madigan just kept chuckling to himself. *"Can I go now?"* I was thinking to myself.

"Billy…," Mr. Madigan began again.

"Yes, sir," I interrupted.

"…Billy, after what Molly and Lindy told me, I wanted Molly to invite you over here so I could thank you personally for helping Cormac. His mother would have baked you a cake but I don't cook."

I was flabbergasted. "Thank you, sir," I said. "I mean thank you for thanking me. I'm glad Mac's going to be okay."

"Yes, he'll be fine," Mr. Madigan said as he took another sip of his drink. "But if he wants his bike fixed, he'll have to do it himself or pay to get it done out of his allowance. I still have no idea what the ambulance and hospital bills are going to be. I've got insurance through my company, but I'll still have a fifty dollar deductible. And I don't think any insurance covers broken eyeglasses. Dang fool kid!"

"Yes, sir," I said again for no reason except that I couldn't think of anything else to say. I was still thinking, *"Can I go now?"*

Mr. Madigan reached to the side of his chair and picked up a grocery sack and placed it on one knee. "Molly said that you ripped your shirt and bloodied your hanky to help Cormac. Lindy said he made a direct hit on your ball glove when he threw up. Is that right?"

"Well, yes sir," I replied, "but I hosed off my glove and it'll be fine. My mom said the bloody handkerchief and shirt had been used for a worthwhile purpose and she didn't mind burning them to ashes."

"I figured as much," Mr. Madigan said. He reached into the sack and pulled out an envelope that was sealed. "Billy, here's an envelope with a five-dollar bill inside. Give it to your folks with my thanks. Use the money to buy a new shirt. Get one you like. And get another handkerchief, too."

"Oh, you don't have to do this, Mr. Madigan..." I said.

"No, I don't suppose I have to do it, Billy, but gratefulness is as much a duty as is coming to the aid of someone in distress." With that, he handed over the sack. "Pull it out," he said.

I looked into the brown paper bag and was dumbstruck!

"Take it out, Billy."

I pulled out a brand new baseball glove—a Stan Musial autograph first-baseman's mitt. "Wow, Mr. Madigan!" I exclaimed. "I play first base on my Pony League team but I've never had a real first-baseman's glove. Thank you, sir!"

You're welcome, Billy! Have a good time with the glove," Mr. Madigan said with a subdued smile. "Now you won't have any lingering scent of Cormac's vomit. Leather and vomit just don't mix well, do they—certainly not like scotch and soda."

The accident broke the ice for me and Molly. From that point forward, I was not hesitant to approach her. Of course, my approach never meant that she would necessarily pay any attention to me, she being a girl and older and whatnot.

One of the largest elm trees on Lincoln Street was in the Madigan's front yard. It had towering branches, including those that draped to the center of Lincoln Street to tease the tips of the elms growing up from Lindy's side of the street.

One sturdy branch of the Madigan's elm did not reach as high as some of the other tree branches, but it did jut out over the sidewalk and parking. When the Madigan kids were younger, Mr. Madigan had attached two swings to the jutting branch. One swing was a one-rope pendulum tied to an old tire that had been fitted with a plank to sit on. The other swing was a two-rope wooden-seat swing. They were side by side.

Swingers could hold hands if they wanted, something that Molly and I rarely did. The swings swung across the parking into Lincoln Street and back across the sidewalk into the Madigan's yard. It was in those swings under the elm tree that Molly Madigan and I would banter and build our friendship. I came to cherish those dangling conversations.

Chapter 9

The Duplex

Next door, to the east of our house on Lincoln Street, was a two-story duplex. It was divided vertically. Unit A was the two-story mirror image of Unit B. The residents who rented one side or the other of the duplex were transitory. Often the duplex was the first place a family landed when they moved to Coffeyville. Sometimes, if personal finances were in decline, the duplex was the last place a family lived before moving on to greener pastures. No fewer than a dozen families called the east or the west of the duplex their home during the time I lived on Lincoln Street.

A young married couple—Rod and Delia—who were in their mid-twenties resided in the duplex for a few months. They were not far removed in age from some of the high school students of Lincoln Street.

The duplex had no porch chairs. When Delia wanted a cigarette, she would often lean up against the couple's two-door Studebaker Champion and puff away. One summer day, Delia and Carolyn Rousters were both on the street side of the parallel parked Studebaker when I rode up on my bicycle to say "hi."

Delia immediately dropped her cigarette into the street, snuffed it out with her foot, and began lambasting me for scratching their Studebaker with my bicycle fender. Delia was at least ten years older and sixty pounds heavier than I. Arms akimbo, standing in the street, she nodded her head at the purported scratch which she said must have occurred sometime during the previous night or that morning.

I didn't think I had done any such thing but she was insistent. Other kids began to gather around the Champion.

"It's going to cost some money to get that fixed. I need to talk to your parents. We're not like you, poor little rich kid living in a big house. We have to work for our money." With that, she turned in a huff and went inside the duplex.

I was straddling my bicycle. I backed up and rode away, saying not a word to the onlookers.

As concerned as I was about Delia seeking reimbursement from my parents for something I did not believe I had done, I was more stunned to be called "a poor little rich kid." My parents both worked hard at their jobs and around the house. Even I was earning my own pocket money in the summer by mowing lawns.

Rich kid? Nah, it couldn't be. (And it wasn't.) When I was growing up on Lincoln Street, I wanted for little. As an adult, as I began to garner some wealth because of my writing, I realized that while growing up on Lincoln Street, my family was very middle-middle-class.

Despite Delia's ire, nothing more came of the matter once she had vented at me. The next day, when I thought no one was around, I dashed out to the parked Studebaker to take a quick peek at the driver's door where the scratch had been cited. Whatever the scratch's origin, someone had been able to buff it away.

Unburdened, I went back to our carport, lifted up my bike's kickstand, hopped on, and rode away. Sailing a bike under tall elm trees is a happy remembrance. I did, however, keep my eyes peeled for angry Studebaker owners.

Chapter 10

Dance Lessons

During World War II, Clement Hedley of Coffeyville was the driver for an Army light colonel at RAF Lakenheath, not far from Norwich, East Anglia, in the United Kingdom. The colonel was the community liaison officer whose assignment was to keep relationships between the Brits and the Yanks cordial.

For their part, most of the Yanks liked the British countryside with its quaint villages and the natives who spoke the King's English. Most of the Brits, on the other hand, had mixed feelings about the Yanks. They were glad the Americans were on hand to fight the Nazis. However, they were not thrilled with how the Yanks rumbled through their communities like bulls in a china shop. Thus, the classic summation of the Brits' perspective during the war was that the Yanks were *"Overpaid, over-sexed, and over here!"*

Be that as it may, the Americans were a hit with the U.K. women. LTC Orville Cain facilitated community dances to encourage the locals to mix and mingle with the soldier boys of both nations. Often, Colonel Cain delegated various aspects of the dance preparations to his driver, Sergeant Clement Hedley.

By fortuitous coincidence, before enlisting, Hedley had been the bus driver for *"Clarinet Cal and the Sunflowers,"* which was a twelve-member band that performed from Kansas City to Wichita. As a result, Clem was well-versed in pop music and popular dance.

There is a segment of British culture that is big-time into ballroom dance. One such person was Winifred Embody. Winnie and her partner Boland Pierce-Noth had won the East Anglia Ballroom Dance Trophy in 1940. But Pierce-Noth had reported to the Royal Air Force a week after winning the trophy in Norwich.

Winnie worked days in a munitions factory near Bury St. Edmonds. She also did her bit by teaching ballroom dance at the various military clubs and community centers. Always on hand for the weekly dances, Winnie rarely found a Brit or Yank who could match her ballroom skills. That changed when she met SGT Clem Hedley over a punch bowl at Lakenheath, in early 1944.

Following war's end, in November 1945, three days before SGT Hedley and LTC Cain boarded a troop ship to return to the U.S., Clem and Winnie were married in a ceremony conducted by U.S. Army and RAF chaplains. The couple had a one night honeymoon before Clem headed for the coast and embarkation from Southampton. Not until April 1946 did war bride Winnie arrive in Kansas City via New York, Chicago, and the Santa Fe Zephyr. Clem met her at Union Station and they dined at a bistro in Kansas City's famed Plaza. After three days in a small hotel, Clem and Winnie drove the 160 miles from KC to Coffeyville.

Winnie had traded fields of barley for fields of wheat. Among her culture shocks was the fact that post-war unemployment meant that Clem was struggling to find steady work. He was then working two jobs—farmhand and linoleum installer.

Fast forward ten years: Clem had used the G.I. Bill to finish college at Pittsburg State Teachers College. He majored in accounting and eventually became senior bookkeeper at the SEKAN Refinery on the east side of Coffeyville. Clem and Winnie had two children, Winston and Isadora. Winnie found time to bake scones and hot cross buns that she sold to individuals, bakeries, and a couple grocery stores at Easter, Thanksgiving, and Christmas.

The couple's frugality and a V.A. loan allowed the family to move to a small house in Edgewood, west of the paint smelter. The house that they purchased, modest by American standards, was three-times as large as the Embody cottage in Lakenheath.

A year after their move to Edgewood, Clem hired a couple of buddies to work with him to build an extension on the back of the house. The extension was not an additional bedroom. They built a dance studio. Two sides of the room were mirrored with barres.

For more than a decade, the Hedleys instructed elementary and junior high school students in ballroom dance and the rudiments of ballet. Fifth and sixth grade students attended on Tuesday nights. There were two hour-long sessions each Tuesday and Thursday night. On Wednesday night, Winnie instructed ballet students.

Originally, I went to the dance lessons because my parents had heard about the classes. They enjoyed dancing at the Moose Lodge and VFW, so they encouraged me to learn some social grace. I overcame my fears of looking like a fool with two left feet because I had noticed that the people who took dance classes were among the *"in crowd."*

Each lesson cost fifty cents. Winston would open the front door for us. As we passed through the living room and kitchen, we were to drop payment into a coffee cup watched over by Isadora. We proceeded through the kitchen and out to the backroom where dancers were assembling, boys on one side, girls on the other. A 45 r.p.m. record player was at the ready.

Clem and Winnie would demonstrate the steps for the night. We studied waltz, fox trot, and jitterbug, over and over, with more sophisticated steps layered into the routines for those who could handle them.

Boys and girls were taught how to hold one another for a proper turn around the dance floor. Bodies were appropriately separated, girl's left hand upon the boy's right shoulder; girl's right hand held by the boy's left hand with both hands being at a height just below the boy's left shoulder; boy's right hand around the girl's waist with his right palm hovering the small of her back so that the tips of his fingers and the heel of his hand would firmly be able to direct the girl around the miniature ballroom.

In a seemingly more innocent time, it was only then dawning upon pre-pubescent children that there might be reason for boys and girls to interact. Alas, most fifth and sixth graders were in those days puzzled as to why this should be or how to go about it.

In the seventh grade, I began attending school dances. Virtually all of the seventh grade boys and girls stared at one another across the gymnasium floor. Half of the eighth grade students did the same. The rest of the eighth graders and nearly all of the ninth graders actually moved about the dance floor.

Then there were parties that were usually hosted by girls whose parents would permit a rug to be rolled up, furniture rearranged, and lights dimmed so that the kids could talk, dance, and eat. Some boys were members of *DeMolay International* and some girls were *Rainbow Girls*. As such, they could use the Masonic Hall for dances. I received my share of invites. They were usually good times. Sharon, Dixie, Mary Ann, Cathy, and Kathy were among the lasses to whom I was able to apply lower-back hand pressure in an effort to figure out how I might apply hand pressure elsewhere on their lovely bodies.

Anyway, I am indebted to the Hedleys for making me a more than sufficient dancer. I enjoyed dancing. I may not have been *Fred Astaire* but I did have my *Ginger Rodgers*. My Ginger's real name was *Carla Delgreco*.

Chapter 11

Captain Jack

Captain Jack Daugherty was one of the people I had met through my parents when they went to the VFW. He was an Army Air Force veteran from World War II. He was tall, lean, and looked like cowboy movie star Randolph Scott. Captain Jack used a cane because of shrapnel that was still present in his right leg. He lived a block away from us, to the west, on the north side of Lincoln Street.

Like many other veterans, Captain Jack was patched up as best as possible, loaded up with medals and mustered out. Captain Jack could walk, but not too far in one effort. He always used his cane. His right leg was stiff, but he still maintained a military bearing. I never heard him complain about his personal lot. He would complain about politicians and the New York Yankees and the high price of steak but never about his wounds.

Captain Jack had his veteran's benefits but he also had family money stemming from oil leases in the four-state area which he managed. He was partially disabled but he wanted for nothing. He had a well kept house and a rocker on the porch with a table beside the rocker.

On the table, Captain Jack kept his books, magazines, and pipes. Among the books I noticed him reading were *The Robe, Quo Vadis, Animal Farm,* and *The Postman Always Rings Twice. Life* and *Popular Mechanics* seemed to be his favorite magazines. He was a voracious reader and rarely was without Meerschaum pipe in hand or clinched between his teeth.

Knowing his reading habits, Captain Jack's friends would send some of their books and magazines to him, a form of salute to the veteran. So it was with my parents. Every couple of weeks, my mother would gather a stack of *Mechanix Illustrated, Reader's Digest, Colliers, Look* and whatever else had been read at our house to send over to Captain Jack. He was more than capable of paying for his own subscriptions but enjoyed the care packages he was sent.

Despite all the duplicates he received, he enjoyed his magazine manna as it showed him what other people were reading.

People liked to see Captain Jack coming. He was modest and soft spoken but when he spoke, people listened. He could have exploited the respect he had accrued to run for political office, serve on a board of directors, or otherwise share his hard-won wisdom. But he was content with a life of ordered routine among the tiers of Coffeyville society.

Saturday nights, Captain Jack watched TV. He watched sports and then *Have Gun Will Travel, Gunsmoke, and The Millionaire.* Sunday mornings, he attended the Presbyterian Church and was a confidant of Pastor Basso. Sunday afternoons, he read the Coffeyville, Kansas City, and Tulsa newspapers. Sunday nights, he watched the *Ed Sullivan Show.*

Tuesdays and Thursdays, Captain Jack read. His Bible first, then he would move on to magazines and books. He couldn't manage the steps at the Carnegie Public Library so he ordered regularly from the *Book-of-the-Month Club.*

Monday nights he dined at the Coffeyville Country Club. Afterwards, while sipping Scotch whiskey, he played bridge with Mr. Richards, the newspaper publisher, Mrs. Richards, and Dr. McGinnis, the superintendent of schools. Many Tuesday nights, he would dine and drink with the Madigans who lived on the other side of my block on Lincoln Street. Wednesday nights, Captain Jack went to Scully's Bar. He sat in the corner booth like a righteous Mafia Don. For two hours, various patrons would rotate through the booth to offer the Captain an evening greeting. Over *Pabst Blue Ribbon Beer,* they'd discuss crops, baseball, politics, the executions of Russian spies, Julius and Ethel Rosenberg, serial killer Caryl Chessman, and the prospects for the *Golden Tornado* in the upcoming football or basketball seasons.

Friday nights, Captain Jack was at the VFW. He'd eat the buffet. He'd have a few Highballs and mainly talk about the war with his fellow vets. But at 9:00 p.m., the captain turned his focus to the VFW's television set to watch with others the Friday night fights.

Once, Captain Jack was sitting with my parents at Scully's. He mentioned to the barkeep that he needed his gutters cleaned and was looking for a handyman. My dad piped up and said, "Forget it, Captain. I'll take care of it." So, the following Saturday at 10:00

a.m., Dad and his Moose Lodge friend Herschel Shoaf arrived with ladders in hand and cleaned the gutters. Captain Jack wanted to pay them but Dad refused, saying he and Herschel were just being neighborly.

In the years following, Herschel became an occasional drinking buddy with Captain Jack. But Herschel had been a Navy enlisted man and Captain Jack an Army Air Corps Officer so their war experiences didn't have a lot of commonality, other than seeing some of their peers turned into mincemeat.

Captain Jack found out that my parents sold insurance so he took out car and house insurance with them. My parents became his friends for life. And he was never short on magazines from our house.

I twisted the door bell ringer twice. Mrs. Patterson came to the door.

"Hello, Billy," she said. "Come right in. Captain Jack will be glad to see you and your batch of magazines."

Captain Jack was at his dining room table with a cup of coffee. "Hi, Captain Jack. Mom said she hopes you haven't read all of these."

"Billy, that is a mighty fine stack," Captain Jack said. "I seriously doubt that I've read them all. Right here on top— this *Reader's Digest* I have not seen. I'll get into it this afternoon. Mrs. Patterson, how about a piece of your fine pecan pie for Billy."

"Right away, Captain Jack. Please sit at the table, Billy."

"Did you hear the *A's* game last night, Captain Jack?"

"I heard the tail end of it, Billy, after I got back from the country club. Quite a comeback. That was only Talbot's second homerun of the season. Comebacks always taste good, Billy, like our boys' wins in Europe and the Pacific during the war."

"You're right, Captain Jack."

"Enjoy the pie, Billy," Mrs. Patterson said, as she placed the plate, fork, and paper napkin before me. "Here's some milk to wash it down."

"This is great, Captain Jack. Thanks, Mrs. Patterson." I dug in. After a couple of big forkfuls and a drink of milk, I said, "Captain

71

Jack, did you hear on the radio about Khrushchev banging his shoe at the United Nations? Do you think there'll be another war?"

"Wars and rumors of wars will always be with us, Billy. Yes, I heard the reports about Khrushchev pounding away. Nikita Khrushchev is a windbag. Somebody should stick a pin in him. Billy, I wouldn't lose any sleep over him, at least not at this point," Captain Jack concluded.

After another couple of bites, I said "I have a friend—his name is Jim—his parents have built a bomb shelter. What do you think of that, Captain Jack?"

"I think they'll get good use of that bomb shelter as a tornado shelter, but I don't believe they'll need to use it to hide from any bombing runs or ICBMs. Coffeyville is about as much in the middle of the U.S.A. as one can be. Those Russian planes or missiles would have to get past a lot of other states before their troops, planes or missiles were much of a threat to us. Still, some idiot like Khrushchev can always push a button just to see what happens. Life's a risk—all of life's a risk, Billy. I'm carrying around a handful of Nazi shrapnel in my leg, but life's still worth the living— especially when there's Mrs. Patterson's pecan pie."

"Captain Jack, thank you for the compliment. I'll see you on Friday." With that, Mrs. Patterson was out the front door of the house to her car, an old Plymouth coupe.

"Fine woman," Captain Jack said. "Widow. Her son fought in Italy. Wounded. Now he works as a porter on the *Santa Fe* out of Kansas City."

Chapter 12

Walking Home from School: The Sexual Peril of Coke

When the dismissal bell rang at Roosevelt Junior High School and Field Kindley Memorial High School, nearly two thousand students fanned out in all directions from the combined campuses. Bicycles, student driven cars, parental pickups, and a few motor scooters or cycles were involved in the daily comings and goings. The vast majority walked home, to the grandparents' house, or to a part-time job.

Lincoln Street dead-ended to the west at Cherokee which was alongside the junior high school, home of the **Rough Riders**. My walks to and from school were usually solitary. But from time to time, I was joined by a classmate.

One day, Scott Brentano was walking with me. Scott had been a buddy through the elementary grades. He was going to spend some time at my house to play chess. We were fairly evenly matched. The elm trees were budding and it was one of the warmest days of the early spring. The start of the baseball season was only weeks away. But Scott's mind was not upon chess or baseball.

"Sammy Trotter has to be the *King of the Dorks,*" Scott said.

"What do you mean?" I asked.

"A bunch of us were standing in the school yard at lunch time. Everyone's jawing under the elm tree. Sammy taps me on the shoulder says, 'Scott, I need to talk to you.' I turned away from Jennifer Bartovich who was telling us about her slumber party last Saturday and said, 'What the hell, Sammy? Can't you see I'm in the middle of something.'"

"'Sorry, Scott,' he says. 'Maybe you can clue me in on something. This is serious.'"

"Okay," I say. "What's so serious?"

Sammy looks around, like he don't want nobody listening or even watching. He grabs my arm and moves us a few feet farther from the crowd."

"'Look,' Sammy says. 'It's like this. Yesterday, I stopped at the A&W for a *Coke* and carried it with me back on campus.'"

"I said, 'So what? Ain't nothing wrong with that.'"

"'Yeah, yeah, I know,' Sammy says. 'I was just standing here with my *Coke* when Vicki Strasberger walked right up to me. She says, "May I have a sip, Sammy?" Before I knew it, she takes the cup out of my hand and takes a big draw on the straw.'"

"Again, so what, Sammy," I say. "I'm surprised Vicki Strasberger even knows your name. With her stack, you should be thrilled she wanted to suck on your straw."

"'But,'—again Sammy looks to the left and right—'that's what I'm a little confused about. You know how in science class, Miss Clough has been talking about plants and how they, how they reproduce.'"

"Yeah, yeah," I said. "Come on, Sammy. The bell's gonna ring. Is there a point to this?"

"'Don't get sore, Scott,' he says. 'With the plants, the boy plants get their stuff mixed up with the girl plants' stuff and then there are baby plants. My mouth had been all over my *Coke* straw. There had to be some of my spit in the straw when Vicki sucked on it. Would that be enough spit to make her have a baby? I wouldn't want that!'"

"Billy boy—right then and there—I fell down on my knees laughing," Scott said. "I roared! Sammy pulls me up and says, 'Don't laugh, Scott. This is serious stuff. What am I missing here?'"

"Just then the bell rang. So I put my arm around Sammy's shoulders, pull him to me, put my other hand up to his ear and whisper, 'Sammy, not until you put the straw you've got between your legs into the cup Vicki Strasberger has between her legs will you be at any risk of fathering her children. Celebrate, Sammy! The rabbit lives!

"Sammy looks at me and says, '*What rabbit?*'"

Chapter 13

Dusty and Vonda Lang

One Saturday, a new family moved into the duplex unit that was closest to our house. They were husband, wife, son, and daughter. I walked up to the two men who were taking furniture pieces off the back of a flat-bed truck.

"Hi," I said. "I'm Billy Howard. I live next door. Can I help?"

"Hello, Billy Howard. I'm Dusty Lang and this is my friend Emory Hulsey. Sure, we can use some help. Pick up any of those small pieces or boxes there by the tree and take them inside to my wife Vonda. She'll tell you where to put them. Please be careful!"

"Yes, sir," I said to the tall blond man in a t-shirt. Both men were sweating heavily.

I picked up a table-model radio and headed for the porch. The screen door and front door had been propped open. I walked right in. A barefoot woman in blue jeans and a yellow top walked into the living room from the kitchen. "Who are you?" she asked, blowing back some errant hair that dangled in front of her face.

My name is Billy. I live next door. I asked the man named Dusty if I could help. He said to pick up any of the small stuff and take it to you and you would tell me where to put it."

"Well, alright then, Billy. Take that radio and put it anywhere on the kitchen counter," Vonda said, moving toward a floor lamp that she moved to the other side of the living room. As she did so, the Lang's children, Eddie, 5, and Lois, 3, marched into the room banging away on two toy drums. Vonda relocated the kids to the front yard, warning them to stay out of the pathway of the furniture movers.

Among the things I learned about the Langs on that moving day was that Dusty had been hired as a salesman at *Carter's Men's Wear* on West Ninth Street in downtown Coffeyville, across from Klein's Drug Store. Vonda was a stay-at-home mom.

As I moved boxes back and forth, I thought I was merely doing my good deed for the day to impress my parents who had gone shopping. But then the bombshell exploded! In our bits and pieces of conversation, Dusty Lang revealed that he was a former major league baseball player! *Hallelujah!*

In the years that the Langs lived next to us, I learned that Dusty had played for the *Cleveland Indians*. Those were the days when the American and National Leagues had only eight teams each. Competition for the *bigs* was fierce!

After five years in the minor leagues, Dusty's major league career consisted of only two games played in September of 1955. In that year, the *Indians* were fighting for the pennant against the New York Yankees. On September 1, when rosters could be expanded for the home stretch, Dusty was among the hopefuls who were welcomed by *Indians* manager, Al Lopez.

Dusty was a left fielder but the Indians were full up with outfielders. His major league moments of glory came as a pinch hitter on successive days during a series in Detroit. Dusty hit for the pitcher as a leadoff man in the top of the ninth in the first game. With two strikes, he was hit by the next pitch, a curve ball that didn't break in the cold wind blowing off of Lake Erie. The next batter hit the first pitch to the second baseman who began a 4-6-3 double-play. Dusty was 0 for 1.

The next day, a light rain was falling when Dusty was sent up as a pinch hitter for the catcher in the top of the ninth. Two were out. Dusty worked a 3-1 count and then popped up to the shortstop. The game was over. Dusty was .000 for his Major League career.

The *Indians* finished second that year, three games behind the *Yankees*. The *Yankees* then lost to the Brooklyn Dodgers who won their only World Championship as an East Coast team. One week before Thanksgiving 1955, Dusty was back in Missouri working as a farmhand till it was time for spring training again. Unfortunately, it was that week that Dusty received a one page letter from the *Indians*, giving him his unconditional release. He was free to sign with anyone but no team invited him to the grapefruit league in Florida the following spring. Therefore, Dusty regrettably concluded that it was time to pack it in, suck it up, and deal with reality. In this case, reality meant finding work anywhere but on a farm.

Dusty's family farm had been sold by his folks when he was 13. The family moved into Aurora and Dusty's dad was employed as a mechanic for the *Oklahoma Tire and Supply Company* franchise. Vonda's family was still farming. She had three brothers who reluctantly were helping Pop in what Vonda was convinced would wind up in an auction. Dusty and Vonda were open to most anything but not life on a farm.

Dusty was a people person. He figured he could get himself a sales job. Salesmen made the world go around, didn't they? Of course, he had never sold a thing in his life. But he was prepared to learn. "I didn't go to college, but I'll learn what needs to be learned about selling, whether it be selling combines, aluminum siding, or shoes," he told family and friends.

Dusty figured that Vonda would be his cheerleader in this new chapter of their lives. He figured wrong. Until that point, Vonda's main interests had been to get away from the farm, to get away from minor league motels, and to get her husband and kids relocated into a big house in Cleveland. As it turned out, Vonda had a long and painful period of adjustment from Cleveland to Coffeyville. The two burgs had nothing in common except that they each began with *"C!"*

Chapter 14

Young Love I

"Young love, first love,
Filled with true devotion,
Young love, our love,
We share with deep emotion.
"Just one kiss from your sweet lips,
Will tell me that your love is real,
And I, I, I can fe-el that it's true."

(#1 Hit 1957 - Sung by Tab Hunter)

My *"young love,"* my *"first love,"* was Carla Delgreco. Everyone called her *"Carly."*

We met when we were taking ballroom dance lessons at the Hedley's studio. Carly attended Edgewood Elementary School. I was at Garfield. When she was about to enter third grade, Carly's family moved to Coffeyville from Hartford, Connecticut, a huge cultural shift. Carly's dad was a department manager at the Continental Can Company plant, east of town. She had a brother, Marco, who was three years younger.

To begin our dance instruction each week at the Hedley's, Clem and Winnie, the instructors, would demonstrate a new step for a waltz, fox trot, or jitterbug. To observe Clem and Winnie glide around the dance floor, the boys and the girls lined up on opposite sides of the dance floor, backs to the walls. Following the demo, the boys were instructed to invite a girl to dance with them.

None of the boys was overly eager to enlist a partner lest rumors spread around school the next day that the couple had reached *"item"* status. Of course, a few of the girls did want to achieve *"item"* status. I considered "item status" to be a far-fetched social accomplishment for me. Therefore, I held back from approaching a potential partner until I spotted the girl or girls who were the last to be picked; then I gallantly offered an invitation to one or the other of the wallflowers in training.

Carly Delgreco was never the last girl invited to dance. She was short with a perfectly proportioned body that was in the early stages of blossoming. She had black hair and dark brown eyes. Indeed, she was one of those girls whose smile would light up the room. All the guys were attracted to her. Carly was even popular with the other girls, none of whom could match her looks or winsome personality.

Week after week, our class of dancers would meet. Then, one night, an amazing thing happened. Clem Hedley called the group to attention and said, "Tonight and for the last few weeks leading up to our summer break, Winnie and I are going to try a dance instruction experiment. We want to pair two of you as partners for these final sessions. Winnie and I believe these two dancers have shown themselves to be leaders of the pack and we would like to determine two things from this experiment:

"First, we want to see if these two dancers will pay attention, learn together, and take their current skills to a higher level. Second, we want to find out if these two can be an encouragement to the rest of you, to inspire you to persevere, and take your own dancing to the next level.

"Something Winnie and I find amusing about this pairing is that neither of us can recall these two ever dancing together. So, let's see what will happen with this grand experiment. Please come to the center of the dance floor, Carly Delgreco and Billy Howard."

"Take me now, Lord!" I thought to myself. "Nothing could be better than this!"

My male classmates pushed me to the center of the dance floor. Carly walked right up to me and, to my delight, took hold of my hand. Our classmates followed Clem and Winnie's example by applauding and shouting a couple of whoops. Carly smiled. I blushed.

Winnie said, "The rest of you gentlemen, please invite a young lady to dance with you. We're going to jitterbug."

I turned to Carly, still holding her hand. "May I have this dance, Carly?"

"Yes, you may, Billy," she said with that smile. "I would love to dance with you!"

In the Mood by Glenn Miller began to blare. Carly and I began to dance. We were able to put it together. Indeed, both Carly and I were *in the mood!* When the song was nearly three-quarters done, the rest of the class spontaneously backed off into a circle and we had the floor. We were not Fred and Ginger but both Carly and I knew how to play the moment. We finished with a flourish. Applause! Clem and Winnie were laughing because their experiment seemed to get off to a promising start.

Over the remaining five weeks, I lived for those dance lesson nights. I didn't have the nerve to call Carly on the phone. We did not see one another any other time during the week. When we were together, we happily talked, laughed, and realized that we were actually improving as dancers. We knew nothing about dance contests. If we had seen one during those weeks, we would have immediately recognized that most of the competitors were way out in front of us. But that would not have mattered at all. At that point, I was thrilled merely to be with Carly. In the Hedley's ballroom, she was the dancing queen and I was her king!

I was a member of the junior high school's Choral Reading Choir. The choir, comprised of sixteen members, male and female, recited well known poems or song lyrics. I don't believe choral reading choirs survived the '60s. Our group regularly performed at elementary schools, nursing homes, and service clubs. We rehearsed each Tuesday night from 6:30 to 7:30 p.m. The Choral Reading Choir's rehearsal slot was at the same time that the *Rough Riders'* cheerleaders practiced.

One Tuesday night around 7:40 p.m., I exited the back door of the school and headed for Lincoln Street. Fifteen yards later, I heard the unmistakable voice of cheerleader Carla Delgreco, "Billy, wait for me."

With a smile, I turned to greet Carly. This was long before the day when students routinely hugged one another in greeting. Such a public display of affection back then was rare.

"Hi, Carly," I said with a broad smile. "Where are you headed?"

"I'm walking down to the Tackett. My parents and brother are there for the double-feature. I'll arrive in time for the second show. It's a musical, I think, something about brothers and brides."

"May I walk a ways with you, Carly?" I asked. "My house is about three blocks from here on Lincoln Street."

"I know where it is, Billy. Yes, please walk with me."

On that cold winter's night, both of us were bundled in warm coats and gloves. We were more than a year removed from our final dance lessons with the Hedleys. Despite our dance floor success, my shyness and self-consciousness thwarted any thoughts I had about courting Carly. Besides, I had heard through the grapevine that Carly's parents said she could not date until she was sixteen.

Actually, we had little occasion to spend time together. We had different class schedules. We did not live in the same neighborhood or attend the same church. At pep rallies and sports events, Carly was always up front or down front with the other *Rough Riders* cheerleaders. Recurring hallway "Hi's" were pretty much the extent of our social interaction. But if she was ever anywhere near, my Carly radar went off and she would be the object of my attention.

Carly continued to mature physically in the most wonderful way! As a beautiful girl, a cheerleader, good student, and genuinely kind person, Carly was esteemed by the in-crowd, the out-crowd, the faculty and administration.

As we began our walk, Carly said, "I'm mad at you, Billy Howard!"

I stopped in my tracks and looked at her. I could not believe what I had just heard. A stake had pierced me! "Good golly, Carly! What did I do? What have I done?"

Carly smirked and began walking again. I quickly kept astride.

"You've ignored me, Billy! That's what you've done!"

"Ignored you?" I stammered. "Carly, there is no one that I'm happier to see than you!"

"Do tell, Billy! Well, actions speak louder than words!" she huffed.

"What's that mean, Carly?"

"It means, Billy Howard, that in the nearly two years we've been in junior high, you have never danced with me—not once, despite all the school dances there have been."

"Oh, wow, Carly!" I said, dumbfounded at her avowed interest in me. I was aghast that I had missed golden opportunities to be close to Carly. "I guess maybe I didn't think you'd want to dance with me. I mean, you never seem to have a shortage of guys that want to dance with you, especially upperclassmen."

Carly stopped in her tracks and stared at me. "You can't be serious, Billy! I like dancing. But, the truth is that I have never danced with any boy, including upperclassmen, who dances as well as you do. In fact, I rarely see you on the dance floor at all. Are you so conceited that you think we girls should line up to ask you to dance?"

"I—I—I,..a,..that is,…. I—I mean…"

"Shut up, Billy!" Carly said, slipping her arm through mine. "You fouled up—which my mother says is what boys do! But I forgive you, Billy. Now, just keep your mouth shut and walk."

In the silence of our stroll along the brick sidewalks of Lincoln Street, I marveled that in only three minutes my emotions had fallen off a cliff and then skyrocketed beyond the orbits of Russia's *Sputnik* or America's belated *Explorer!* Then, we arrived in front of my house.

"It's been great to walk with you, Carly," I said. "I can't wait for the next school dance."

"Neither can I, Billy. Don't you dare ignore me again! Here's a little something to help you remember." Carly grabbed my jacket lapels and pulled me toward her. Then, SHE KISSED ME!

"Goodnight, Billy. See you in the hallways," Carly said as she walked away, headed for the Tackett Theater.

I stood speechless and motionless on the sidewalk as I watched Carly walk away in darkness till she came under the glow of the corner streetlight. She turned right to reach Eighth Street and walk the remaining seven blocks to the theater.

Most people remember their first kiss. Carly's was my first romantic peer-kiss. I had no idea how girls reacted to such an occasion but I was over the moon. My euphoria was not merely because it was THE first kiss but mainly because it was a CARLY KISS and she would always, always be that wonderful, special person! As I headed into my house that night, I had to suppress the grin on my face, lest my parents wonder what was up. And I also had to suppress what was up in my crotch!

Carly's kiss was a breakthrough moment for me, a confidence-builder that fostered my courageous entry into the *"dating scene."* Truth be told, I was not very assertive. Part of this hesitancy was because I did not enjoy having to be chauffeured by my parents if I actually invited a girl to a dance. Sometimes I tried to get a date with a girl who lived within walking distance of me and the event venue. The couple of times that I did this, there was no objection. There was never any risk of being hassled on the streets as we walked along, except for shouted harassment by fellow students driving by.

One girl I dated at least three times—putting me on the brink of *"going steady"*—had a friend who regularly had backroom dances at her house. Her parents would greet eight or ten persons, all couples, and then send them to the back of the house where a small-bedroom-sized room had been turned into a dance space with subdued lighting. A 45-rpm record player provided the music. The party room was next to the kitchen which opened into the living room where the parents of the house would make their presence known every fifteen or twenty-minutes.

I even kissed two or three girls of my own initiative.

"...of my own initiative." That was the only glitch I had regarding the Carly kiss. *She* kissed me. I loved it! Always will! But I wanted a return match wherein *I* would initiate the kiss. It was a guy-ego thing.

So, I began plotting how and when I might accomplish a Billy-initiated *super lip-lock!*

"I think Heaven will be like a first kiss."

The Sugar Queen
Sarah Addison Allen

Chapter 15

Holy Moses!

Classes at Roosevelt Junior High School began at 8:00 a.m. On this fall day, all students reported first to their homerooms. At 8:10 a.m. the ninth grade students began pouring out the front doors of the junior high school. They were led down to the sidewalk that paralleled Eighth Street. Each of the home room teachers instructed the students to form a two-by-two line that went perpendicular from the sidewalk back to the imposing school building. Talking was permitted and everyone seemed to be in a good mood except for a few skinny girls who were shivering under the partly cloudy skies.

At 8:20 a.m. the eighth grade classes poured out the front doors and formed another two-by-two line just east of the ninth-graders. At the same time, marching from the rear of the junior high school, came the itsy-bitsy seventh-graders who also fell into line parallel to Cherokee Street.

Principal Rutledge and Vice Principal Vesco were on the sidewalk checking out the lines. Homeroom teachers were to walk aside their classes as faux-platoon sergeants.

At 8:33 a.m., merely three minutes past Mr. Rutledge's intended departure time of 8:30 a.m., the boys' and girls' phys-ed teachers—Mr. Calvin and Miss Mitts—took the lead to cross Cherokee and head the mile to downtown Coffeyville. The seventh-graders followed them. To the dismay of the faculty and staff, Spit Corner was drenched.

We were on our way to see the motion picture, *The Ten Commandments,* during school hours! How sweet was that?

"Do you think we'll be able to buy popcorn?" Evan Furnas asked.

I was on the outside, to the right of Evan. "Dunno," I replied. "I don't know that I want to eat popcorn at nine o'clock in the morning. I'd like to have a *Coke* if the vending machine is working. What I'd really like are *Jujubes*. But my parents told me never to have them again. Some *Jujubes* got stuck to one of my molars and I lost a filling."

"Are there enough seats at the Midland to hold us all?" Evan wondered.

"Us and more," I said. "Mr. Bass said that Holy Name was sending its seventh and eighth graders to this showing. Their elementary kids will come later."

"Was Moses Catholic?" Leland Carpenter asked from behind.

"No, dimwit!" Evan said. "He was a Jew. Catholics didn't exist back then. Neither did Protestants."

"So, this is a Jewish movie?" Leland said. "As far as I know there are only a dozen or less Jewish kids in the entire school. Why are they making all of us go?"

"I don't give a hoot why they're making us go as long as I don't have to sit through history and math!" Evan responded.

"I thought the Jews killed Jesus. My Uncle Olan told us that on Easter," Leland chimed in.

"Give it a rest, Carpenter. Don't you know anything about the Bible? The movie is about how God used Moses to lead the Jews out of Egypt to *the Promised Land*—that's *Israel,* in case you didn't know."

"What? Was it like a land grant program?" Leland asked. "My grandpa got a government homestead of 640 acres out by Hays. He's a wheat farmer."

"Now you've got it, Carpenter," I said, shaking my head. "It was God's little homestead plan just for the Jews."

"Wow! I didn't know the Jews were farmers. My Uncle Olan said these days most Jews are bankers or actors. But I don't believe Mr. Murphy over at First National is Jewish."

Thankfully, the conversation was ended abruptly when Mr. Vesco passed by, urging everyone to tighten up the line. "The Midland Theater is not going to hold up the start time of the movie. Let's keep moving right along!" Mr. Vesco shouted like a Drill Sergeant. We were just passing Karbe's grocery store. Karbe's entrance opened without hands thanks to an *electric eye,* the electronic wonder of the town. Miss Clough was positioned alongside the eye to make certain it was not triggered scores of times by the passing students.

"Do you know the Ten Commandments?" Evan asked me.

"What do you mean? I know what they are," I replied. "God gave them to Moses on stone tablets."

"So what are they?" Evan continued.

"They're rules, regulations. Things we're not supposed to do or that we are supposed to do to keep God from getting mad at us."

"Yeah, yeah, I get that. But what are the ten specifically?"

"Don't worship other gods. Don't steal. Don't lie. Honor your parents," I said.

"God helps those who help themselves," Carpenter said. "Be clean like God is. And don't be an *adult*...but I've never understood that one."

"Sorry, Carpenter," I said with a snort. "What you just said must be on somebody else's list."

"Maybe they'll give us a list of the commandments after the movie's over," said Dale Hall who was walking beside Carpenter. "Do you think we'll get tested on the movie? I didn't bring anything to take notes with."

"God may test us but I don't think the school will. But if the school does test us, maybe the teachers will hand out Bibles for an open book test." Furnas laughed at his own joke. No one else did.

"Who's paying for all this?" Carpenter asked. "I mean the high school saw the movie yesterday. The rest of the week the elementary schools are going to attend. At $.40 a ticket, that adds up. All the tickets gotta stack up to more than a thousand bucks. That's heap big wampum."

"The preachers are paying for it," Furnas said.

"No, they're not," I said. "Preachers don't make much money. I think all the churches chipped in."

"My dad is in the Lions Club," Hall said. "My dad says the Coffeyville ministers association is paying for some of the tickets. Then the Lions Club, the Rotary Club, and the Kiwanis Club all chipped in."

"Why? What's in it for them?" Carpenter asked.

"Nothing," Hall asserted. "It's just their good deed for the year. You know, so we don't become thugs or ruffians. Hah! Maybe they think seeing the movie will keep us from going beltless, wearing black leather jackets, or ducktails. Fat chance!"

"I still don't care," Furnas said. "I'm just grateful to the Good Lord for getting me out of history and math!"

We made it to the movie house and our seats with eight minutes to spare. The seventh and eighth grade students sat downstairs, separated by the kids from Holy Name. The ninth-graders were ecstatic to get the balcony. Some on the back row may have seen little of the film due to napping or necking. Two ninth-graders were removed for bad conduct.

The Midland Theater did not sell popcorn, *Coke, Jujubees* or anything else to eat or drink. *The Ten Commandments* was two hours-and-twenty-minutes long with an intermission. The intermission was supposed to be fifteen minutes but went thirty because of the backup at the girls' restroom.

In that day, no one thought it odd that a movie based on the Bible should be shown to students during the school day. As the newly opened Broadway musical *The Music Man* exhorted the townsfolk of River City, Iowa, *"[You] gotta figure out a way to keep the young ones moral after school!"* The elders of Coffeyville agreed with *Professor Harold Hill.*

Chapter 16

The Hound from Hell

When I was a kid, there were few ways for a pre- or early-teenage boy to earn money. However, mowing lawns was one way to get some spending money, provided you could work out a deal with your father to use the family mower. Usually, there was no problem in negotiating with dear old dad.

I had one negotiating point: "I want to use the mower to make some bucks." Dad had a handful of negotiating points: "1. Mow our lawn for which you will not be paid though you may continue to eat and sleep in our house. 2. Pay for the gas. 3. Keep the mower clean. 4. Keep the blade sharp. 5. Repairs are at your expense."

"Whatever you say, Dad."

Mowing lawns was hot, sweaty, and poor paying work. I was not meticulous in my mowing. Unfortunately for me, my few clients were fastidious about how they wanted their lawns to look when the mowing was done. *"Do it again"* was very much a part of their lawn care vocabulary.

The largest lawn I mowed—the lawn that earned me the most money—belonged to Mrs. Whitfield. For mowing her lush and fast-growing lawn, I was paid the handsome sum of $1.50, no matter how long it took to give the grass its weekly haircut.

Mrs. Whitfield had a half-acre of lawn that surrounded her house. It was a corner lot on Lincoln Street, across from the Rousters. I despised mowing that lawn. Frankly, I despised mowing any lawn in particular and manual labor in general. The best thing that mowing lawns did for me was to motivate me to become a writer who doesn't even callous his fingers.

Anyway, Mrs. Whitfield had surrounded the perimeter of her house with odd-shaped flower gardens. While these gardens cut down the amount of lawn to mow, mowing close to their edges without hitting a brick divider or cutting down flowers was a challenge to my precision (of which I had little).

As if the heat, humidity, thick Bermuda grass, and the irregular gardens, were not enough of a problem for a slacker groundskeeper, there was also the challenge of confronting *Van Gogh.* Mrs. Whitfield's pet dog named *Van Gogh* was a *schipperke,* a small, chunky dog with a thick double coat and a ruff around his neck. To be AKC certified, the schipperke must be black. *Van Gogh* had a black coat and a black heart!

A schipperke's body is short, compact, and looks like a square from the side. A well formed schipperke has the head of a fox and erect ears. They grow to be a foot tall and weigh up to eighteen pounds. Make no mistake: Schipperkes are *little Napoleons!*

Vincent Van Gogh was a brilliant Flemish painter who, in a moment of personal pique, sliced off his own ear. *Van Gogh* the dog, Mrs. Whitfield's hound from hell, shared two things with Van Gogh the artist. Both had Flemish origins. Each suffered gross mental instability!

In naval parlance, the Dutch derived word *"skipper"* means the *"captain"* of a ship. Thus, a *"schipper-ke"* is a *"little captain,"* often found on canal boats in Belgium and Holland. The dogs are *"ratters,"* fearlessly committed to search-and-destroy missions against rodents that would dare come upon a schipperke's vessel.

Alas, there were no Flemish narrowboats within five thousand miles of Lincoln Street. Van Gogh was a malcontent as the little skipper of a backyard that had nary a waterway in sight. Van Gogh was a schipperke with a massive superiority complex equaled only by his loathing of foolhardy teenage humans who brought lawnmowers into his territory.

Some weeks, I would be lucky in that Mrs. Whitfield had taken the small dog into her house. From time to time, I would see Van Gogh poking his head through the curtains to peer out at me. He knew better than to bark inside the house but he always bared his teeth to me at the window. I gave him the finger a couple of times till I realized that Mrs. Whitfield might be watching. Unfortunately, at least two-thirds of the time, Van Gogh was outside. Usually, he would be tethered to a spike in the ground with a fifteen-foot chain. While the stake was positioned aside the garage, the range of the chain protruded well into the area of lawn I was to mow.

One hot summer day, I had been pushing the mower over Mrs. Whitfield's lawn for only ten minutes, accompanied by Van Gogh's cacophonic bark. He was working himself into a lather. Suddenly, over the roar of the lawnmower's engine, I heard something *snap.* As I looked around, it took only an instant to realize that Van Gogh had broken his chain and now was in hot pursuit of my heels. I launched into a run around the house, trying to gain distance on the mutt, and figure out how I could escape his fangs. I had just begun my second revolution of the house when the front door opened and a voice yelled, *"Van Gogh, come here!"* From a safe distance, I saw Van Gogh halt, turn around, and trot over to a teenage girl who picked him up and began to stroke his head. The girl carrying the dog walked toward me.

"Sorry about that!" she said. "He's doesn't care for strangers and schipperkes don't like to have their space invaded." She continued to stroke Van Gogh who appeared as if he had neither care nor enemy in the world. He glanced at me and then looked away as if I had no relevance to the routine of his day.

I was still panting from the run. "Yeah, well, no problem. He didn't catch me!" I said, wiping sweat off my brow.

The girl shifted Van Gogh to her left arm and stuck out her right hand to shake. "My name is Harriet Whitfield. I'm Mrs. Whitfield's granddaughter from Kansas City. I'm going to spend the next few summers with her because my parents are traveling."

"My name is Billy Howard. Nice to meet you. Why don't your parents take you with them?"

The girl with blonde hair and blue eyes laughed and said, "My parents are missionaries. They are traveling in Thailand. I was actually born in Thailand. But these days there are some troubles in Thailand and my parents don't want me to be traveling with them. They'll be back before school starts and we'll all go back to Kansas City."

"I kinda know where Thailand is." I replied. "Southeast Asia, right? Didn't it used to be called 'Siam?'"

"Wow, you're right, Billy!" Harriet replied. "Not many kids know beans about Thailand."

"Yeah, well, I saw that movie about *The King and I* and *Reader's Digest* had an article about those brothers who were the Siamese twins," I said.

"Well, Billy, I'll let you return to your mowing. I'll take Van Gogh inside the house. He won't bother you anymore."

"Thank you, Harriet," I said. "I appreciate that."

As she turned to go she said, "When you're done with the mowing, check here on the front porch table. I'll leave you a glass of ice water."

"Thanks, again," I said.

I continued to mow the lawn, paying a little more attention to the difficult spots than I usually did as I wanted to impress my new acquaintance, Harriet. When done, as I drank the ice water, I marveled at having had a conversation with a girl who did not call me a *"dweeb."*

Chapter 17

Brodie Frenk

To restate, I was nearly twelve when my parents and I moved onto Lincoln Street. For the next nine years, I roamed the neighborhood, meeting the neighbors, young and old, and watching the comings and goings of various families whose lives had intersected with the elm enshrouded neighborhood.

Brodie Frenk was one who went and came back to the neighborhood several times before he finally left again for good....or, if not for 'good,' then to excel in rakishness. When he left the third time, he did not leave alone. That departure became one of the little scandals about which the folks on Lincoln Street and elsewhere in Coffeyville would gossip for years to come.

The Frenk family lived on Eighth Street, the main drag through town that, until the Eleventh Street bypass was built, was also U.S. Highway 166. The Frenk's house was on the corner of Eighth and Washita. Between the house and alley, what had once been a detached garage for the house had been converted into a shop for the repair of lawnmowers and small engines. Walt Frenk, Brodie's father, was owner and chief mechanic. He had a storefront entrance facing west on Washita plus an alleyway entrance to roll in mowers or motorcycles to be repaired. This repair facility was directly south of the Rouster's Lincoln Street property, specifically their garage. The alley in-between was the primary venue for the neighborhood kids' renditions of *Kick the Can*.

Thelma Frenk was Walt's big-boned wife. She was usually pleasant to the neighborhood kids with the exception of two, her own. Brodie was the eldest. He had a sister, Geraldine, who was my age. Often, Thelma would come out her backdoor, stand on the top step of the small porch, and survey the scene to see if she could spot her kids. Whether she could see them or not, she would start yelling vitriol at Brodie or Geraldine or both as to how or why they had or had not accomplished their appointed chores according to Thelma's standards. Easily, Thelma could be heard four houses away. She would have made a great drill sergeant.

When I first met Geraldine, she was as meek as a mouse. As she grew into teenage, she transformed from mouse to shrew. Assuredly, the last person on the earth Geraldine wanted to emulate was her mother, but Geraldine had been daily and deeply imprinted by her mother's preferred style of close interpersonal communication. Geraldine could have been president of the local Junior Bitch Society. Happily, she eventually outgrew her bitchyness.

By the time Brodie was sixteen, he had developed immunity to his mother's bluster which, of course, infuriated Thelma. Brodie had learned how to ignore his mother by paying attention to his father. Though no one knew for certain what went on behind closed doors, no one had ever seen Thelma yell at Walt. No one had ever seen Thelma address an endearment to Walt or any compliment for keeping the family fed, clothed, and sheltered. Apparently, they had negotiated some sort of cessation of hostilities agreement far in the past.

This truce was facilitated by Thelma never setting foot in the lawnmower shop and Walt remaining in the lawnmower shop as many hours as possible each day. Walt was always in the shop by 6:30 a.m. He always left the shop at 5:50 p.m. That's when he would go into the house, wash up, and sit down in front of the television. He'd pull a TV tray in front of him and wait for Thelma silently to bring him his evening meal which he ate while watching the news and the beginning of primetime programs. If the kids were around, they and Thelma watched what Walt wanted to view. In those days, there were only four channels that could be received via antenna in Coffeyville so everyone at least had a one-in-four chance of seeing what they wanted.

Beginning at 8:00 p.m., Walt would have the first of three Highballs. He rarely finished the third, usually falling asleep sometime after 9:30 p.m. Thelma would retire at 10:00 p.m. Walt would wake up by 11:00 p.m., undress and roll into bed where he would remain until 5:45 a.m.

Brodie had learned ample mechanical skills from his dad. Brodie was happy to put them to good use on a series of motorcycles he paraded through the neighborhood and around town over the years. Marlon Brando's motorcycle gang movie, *The Wild One*, had been produced nearly a decade previous. It appeared that Brodie regretted being born too late to be a member of the Brando entourage. Brodie was a wild thing who wanted to be part of a wild bunch!

Of course, Brodie had a black leather jacket, biker boots, and a red kerchief which he wore over his head. He had classy sun glasses. When he was younger and had smaller cycles, Brodie looked stupid trying to imitate Brando. But as he grew to adulthood, he looked the part. However, the leather jacket, boots, and sunglasses couldn't conceal the fact that Brodie was pretty much a big jerk!

I would often try to talk to Brodie—after all, he was a *"big kid."* Many a night, Brodie would be tinkering with his current bike in the lawnmower shop. Sometimes kids would gather to watch what Brodie was doing. He rarely spoke. We rarely spoke to him for fear he would toss us onto the alleyway's gravel.

Nevertheless, one night I spotted Brodie at work and no other kids in sight. I walked into the shop but remained a sufficient distance away so that I would have a good head start if I had to vamoose.

"Whatcha working on, Brodie?"

"What the hell does it look like I'm working on, dogface?"

"A chain," I said.

"Brilliant!" Brodie said. "You now know all you need for getting into third grade next year."

"Come on, Brodie. I'm just interested in what you're doing because one day maybe I can buy myself a motorcycle."

"Then go get a job, dogface. Don't spend all your pay on women and you'll be able to get your ride."

"I've got a job—well, I've got a job in the summers. I mow lawns."

"Out-fucking-standing, dogface. Do that for the next three years and you'll have yourself a ten-year-old used motorbike."

I could see that this conversation was going nowhere. I looked around the shop. Same old, same old. The calendar picture of a topless Marilyn Monroe still hung over the parts sink. All of her interesting body parts were covered with greasy fingerprints.

"Good night, Brodie," I said.

"Good night, dogface. Feel free never to come back!"

When Brodie was nineteen, he enlisted in the U.S. Army. The last thing Brodie wanted was to labor in his father's lawnmower repair shop. Mainly, Brodie wanted to get the hell away from Coffeyville and the Army seemed just the ticket.

Joining the military in the late 1950s was not an unusual thing. America was less than twenty years removed from WWII and less than a decade away from the Korean Conflict. The Vietnam Conflict had yet to raise its ugly head.

The Frenks had a backyard farewell party for Brodie. People mingled on all four sides of the Frenk house and lawnmower building. Liberally spiked punch and cake were served along with beer and chips. Well-wishers came and went. The neighborhood adults and kids also passed through. Kids had to take punch out of a non-spiked bowl. Dang!

Brodie sat on the back step with some blonde. Allegedly, she was from South Coffeyville, Oklahoma. Being from South Coffeyville immediately implied the blonde was a loose woman. Those who resided in South Coffeyville said the same about the women north of the state line. Anyway, this particular blonde was all over Brodie.

Geraldine Frenk knew where her parents were stashing the booze in the days leading up to the party. She had siphoned off more than a fair share and was serving it to two of her girlfriends as they sat in Geraldine's darkened bedroom with the revelers just outside.

Thelma sat in a lawn chair, receiving salutations from friends who commended her for rearing a son who would bravely put service before self. Thelma kept grinding her nails into the palms of her hands. She was mad as hell that Brodie was finally going to be out of her grasp. She was not concerned about him becoming a combat casualty. That thought never even occurred to her. No, she was bent out of shape because Brodie was probably going to wind up on another continent, ordered around by lifer sergeants, fed too much food, and be surrounded by too many foreign bimbos.

Folks saw little of Walt at the bash. He was in the shop with two of his drinking buddies. The trio was working their way through some *Jim Beam* that Walt had hidden for that purpose. The buddies had brought him two new calendars. One was another of Marilyn

Monroe. But this one had a plastic overlay that showed Miss Monroe clad in a clingy red dress. Lift up the plastic and the red dress went away. There was Miss Monroe in her birthday suit! The other calendar was of some starlet named Bettie Page who was also buck naked. I had never heard of Bettie Page. Her calendar picture had no plastic covering.

After I had a second piece of cake, I headed home. I walked to the front of the Rousters' house and then over to my house. As I passed the Rousters' front porch in the dark, I noticed Carolyn Rousters making out with her jock boyfriend, Vern Cunningham.

During his three year Army enlistment, Brodie Frenk only made it back to Coffeyville twice. Once was right after basic and advanced training which he had endured at Ft. Leonard Wood (*"Ft. Lost in the Woods"* as it was known to the troops), Missouri. He went all over town on his motorcycle while wearing his uniform. Brodie had no trouble finding some girl to hitch up her skirt and hop on the bike behind him.

After basic and advanced training, Brodie expected orders for Korea. Rumor had it that he was able to collect several sexual favors as going away presents. It's always good to treat a serviceman well!

Brodie's sister Geraldine grudgingly thought he looked *"spiffy"* in his uniform. Thelma saw in Brodie's eyes that he had forever passed into male adulthood which she did not understand or appreciate. She knew such sway as she ever had over Brodie was now a phantom of the past. For the first time in her life, Thelma began to drink in excess.

Walt Frenk, who had been a cook on a U.S. Navy Oiler during WWII, had three bits of advice for Brodie: "Don't be a fool with your money. Don't be a fool with women. Don't be a fool in war."

"Whatever you say, Old Man," Brodie replied.

The second time Brodie returned to Coffeyville was twenty months later when Walt nearly died from an infection he had contracted after cutting off three fingers of his left hand while repairing a rototiller. As Walt was at death's doorstep, the Red Cross was able to secure compassionate leave for Brodie who was freezing in a mountain outpost in South Korea.

Geraldine reported later that she thought her father had rallied by seeing Brodie. But Thelma had been by Walt's bedside throughout the ordeal. When Brodie's presence was credited with bolstering Walt, Thelma began a slow burn like a smoking peat bog. The only thing that ever lessened the intensity of the heat upon her psyche was gin. She eventually died of cirrhosis of the liver. Walt outlived her by nine years.

Chapter 18

Study Hall by the Eastern Wall

"If I were rich, I'd have the time that I lack
to sit in the synagogue and pray.
And maybe have a seat by the Eastern wall.
And I'd discuss the holy books with the learned men,
several hours every day.
That would be the sweetest thing of all."
"If I Were a Rich Man,"

Fiddler on the Roof
Jerry Bock and Sheldon Harnick

Cheerleader Toni Weinstein was a senior when I was a junior at Field Kindley High School. Toni sat in front of me in Mrs. Ballard's Spanish class. We also shared study hall fifth period. From time to time, we would practice our Spanish dialogues and vocabulary together. As Toni was blonde and gorgeous, I reveled in such joint study opportunities.

One day, Toni and I were seated at the farthest table on the east side of the study hall so we would not disturb other students while practicing out loud. Mr. Misch, the study hall monitor, departed the classroom as he often did. Therefore, Toni and I began to discuss everything but Spanish. I have no recollection of how Toni and I got onto the subject of *Judaism* but we did. Among the bits and pieces I remember:

"Why are you wearing a wine emblem?" I asked.

"What in the world are you talking about, Billy?" Toni asked.

"I watch that quiz show *Treasure Hunt* with Jan Murray. The sponsor is *Morgan David* wine and you're wearing—what do they call it—oh yeah, its *logo*. Why?"

"I can't believe you, Billy!" Toni hissed. "Pull your head out of the ground! The name of the wine is *'Mogen David'*—not *'Morgan David.'* *'Mogen"* is Yiddish for *shield—the Shield of David.* Most people call it *the Star of David.* Think about it, Mr. Christian: *Star*

99

of David. You think that's what appeared over Bethlehem when your Jesus was born. Good grief, Billy! Lots of Christian girls wear cross necklaces. I'm Jewish, as you very well know. That's why I'm wearing a Star of David. It's *not* a wine logo!"

"Sorry! Sorry, Toni. I meant no offense. I get it now. Yes, I know you're Jewish but I don't always know what all that means," I said.

"Go ask your church pastor," Toni replied, calming down.

After a couple of minutes went by, I said, "So you don't have a Jewish church in Coffeyville?" I asked.

"'*Synagogue!*'" Toni said. "We don't call it a church. Our place of worship is a synagogue. And there is not a synagogue in Coffeyville."

"I knew that," I said. "Sorry. Why don't you have a synagogue here?"

"For a synagogue to be formed, there must be at least ten Jewish men in the town who want to do so," Toni said.

"You mean there aren't ten Jewish men in all of Coffeyville?"

"Yes, there are plenty more than ten Jewish men in Coffeyville. But for whatever reason, they have never gotten together to organize a synagogue. I asked my dad once why this was. He said, 'It's because when you have ten Jewish men together in the same room you have eleven opinions as to what should be done.' He said he didn't believe the Lord was pleased that a Coffeyville synagogue had not been created yet."

"So, you don't worship? And you don't have anything like a youth group or choir?" I asked.

"We don't have a youth group or a choir, Billy," Toni said. "But we certainly worship. Some Friday nights we have a Sabbath ritual where we begin our meal a few minutes before sundown. My mother usually lights candles and recites a blessing in Hebrew. Then, we really limit what we do Friday night and until the sun goes down on Saturday. Among other things, our family's Sabbath celebrations mean no television, movies, or dates."

"Wow," I said. "No '*Rawhide*' or '*77 Sunset Strip.*' I never knew that. But what about when you're cheerleading at football and basketball games on Friday nights? And what about dances? I've seen you at all the dances with dates and the dances are always on Friday nights."

"What can I say, Billy? I have sinned. When I do, I ask God to forgive me. My family is Jewish but we are not *Orthodox* Jews, the Jews who have long beards and cover-up dresses. My father says God knew what He was doing when he put a teenage Jewish girl in Kansas and God is not a *'kill-joy.'* My daddy says that even *Miriam*—the sister of *Moses*—loved to dance. 'So go have fun,' my daddy says. He's a happy Jewish man. He's happy to be in Coffeyville. He's happy I'm a cheerleader. He always tells me, *'Go have fun, Toni!'"*

"Well, your dad sounds like a nifty guy," I said. "I'm glad you're a cheerleader! You're great with the jumping splits you do!"

Toni chuckled and continued: "Our family drives to Tulsa or Wichita at least one weekend a month to attend a worship service at a synagogue. In Tulsa and Wichita, those synagogues do have youth events and singers. The main singer is called a *'cantor'*—like the comedian *'Eddie Cantor.'"*

"I like Eddie Cantor!" I said. "I didn't know he was Jewish."

"Lots of people in show business are Jews, Billy," Toni said. "Elizabeth Taylor, Eddie Fisher, Danny Kaye, and Judy Holiday, to name just a few. Billy, if you'd like to come to one of our Sabbath meals, I'm sure my parents would be happy to have you join us. You'd enjoy it and my mother is a great cook."

"Would I have to wear one of those beanies?" I asked.

"They are called *'yarmulkes,'* Billy. "Yes it is customary for men to wear a yarmulke for a Sabbath meal. Not to worry, my father has extras and he would be happy to loan you a yarmulke."

"Well, that's very nice of you to ask," I said. "Sure, I don't think my parents would have any problem with that. Then maybe you could come to one of our church potlucks."

Toni laughed and said, *"Muy bien! Como no?"*

Chapter 19

Spit Corner

WARNING: *Do not cross Spit Corner without spitting or….*

"Spit Corner" is located on the northeast corner of Cherokee and Eighth Street in Coffeyville. The name and practices pertaining to *Spit Corner* have their origin in brick-making.

Located upon the Kansas-Oklahoma border in southeastern Kansas, Montgomery County has an abundance of shale, limestone, and building stones. Thus, Coffeyville—the largest community in Montgomery County—was home to a number of brick plants in the late 1890s and early 1900s. When Coffeyville's brick factories were operating to capacity, nearly 765,500 bricks were produced *every day!* They were shipped not only across Kansas and the United States but also around the world. Today, Coffeyville bricks have become collector items which are often found at antique sales or road shows.

In the 1900s, according to the Coffeyville historical records, bricks were in great demand for sidewalks and street paving. Also many railroads used bricks for their passenger platforms. Each brick factory would imprint its brick with a company name or special design.

The *"biggie"* of Coffeyville's variously designed bricks was the *"Don't Spit on Sidewalk"* brick.

This admonishing brick came into being because of the lobbying of Dr. Samuel Crumbine, a member of the Kansas State Board of Health. The good Dr. Crumbine encouraged the Kansas legislature to pass several laws pertaining to public health.

In the first-half of the Twentieth Century, tuberculosis was still a major problem around the world, including the United States. Various means were used to instruct the public on how to avoid the contagion. (At Garfield Elementary School, I read *Huber the Tuber,* a children's book written by Dr. Harry Wilmer, to explain the disease and how to avoid it.) Dr. Crumbine focused on regulating public drinking cups, roller towels, and spitting on sidewalks. It was during such public awareness campaigns that the *"Don't Spit on Sidewalk"* brick was manufactured and used for construction across the land.

To this day, Coffeyville sidewalks and streets have an abundance of well-worn brick. The deep-throated whir of tires on brick streets remains evocative of my youth. Of course, there are an abundance of tree roots that have buckled brick sidewalks throughout the town.

Back in the day, at the corner of Cherokee and Eighth Street, two brick sidewalks came together in front of a laundromat. Both of those sidewalks featured bricks manufactured by the *Yoke Vitrified Brick Company* of Coffeyville. Not surprisingly, that company's bricks featured the imprimatur of a yoke for horses or oxen.

But the two sidewalks—one going north and south, the other east and west—were joined at the corner by an arc-shaped corner-piece whose bricks all featured the *Don't Spit on Sidewalk* imprint.

From day one after the *Don't Spit on Sidewalk* bricks were laid, students crossing at the intersection to arrive upon the campus of the junior high school and high school cheerfully defied the exhortation of the bricks and spat at will. There was so much expectorant rained daily on the bricks that an hour after the schools were dismissed, the attendant at the laundromat splashed a bucket of soapy water across the corner bricks, no doubt in an attempt to protect the attendant himself from contracting tuberculosis or the common cold, however far-fetched that possibility may have been in reality.

It should be remembered that when the bricks and sidewalks were constructed, many bars still had spittoons. Not everyone carried handkerchiefs. Snot was often blown into the wind and onto the ground Japanese-style by sealing one nostril with a pressing finger and unloading the other nostril with a huff. So there was, in fact, some risk of contamination but, as later medical studies reported, not to the extent to justify the need for so many *Do Not Spit on Sidewalk* bricks. But the brick manufacturers recognized a windfall when they saw one and were happy to produce the now legendary blocks.

Spit Corner was not on the campus of the secondary schools. Nevertheless, every once in awhile, a faculty member would stand in front of the laundry at lunchtime or after school in an attempt to deter spitting. When influenza hit the town, the school nurse—Miss Pahmeyer—would put in an appearance in her white uniform and cap. Not to be outdone, sometimes a police car would park beside the laundry with the cop eyeballing the corner as public expectoration was a misdemeanor. However, more often than not, one of the school jocks would engage the officer in some discussion of sports and students with spitting aforethought got a free pass.

One day, Scott Brentano, Tom Shaney, and I were walking along Eighth Street, heading back to school after lunch. We were talking about who knows what when we arrived at *Spit Corner* and paused to ponder the bricks. We dutifully spat and laughed as we checked out the corner bricks to see how much spittle had yet to evaporate.

Scott Brentano said, "Frankly, I think spit gets a bad rap. Look in the Bible: Jesus used spit to heal guys who were blind. All the pro-athletes spit. If Mickey Mantle or Stan Musial put their spit in a bottle, I bet they could make big bucks selling the stuff."

"Just last week," I said, "I saw Buster Mahaney and Tim Hollyfield *'spit-shake'* to confirm their agreement that they were going to hitchhike to Colorado come summer. I also read in *TV Guide* that funny guys like Milton Berle and Danny Thomas are always doing what they call *'spit takes,'* you know, where they start to take a drink of water, someone else says something funny or shocking and Uncle Milty spits out the drink—a *'spit take.'"*

"My dad and uncles always play *'Spit in the Ocean'* poker when they get together," Scott Brentano said. "They love it!"

"We all saw the movie *To Kill a Mockingbird,"* I said. "The kids in that were always doing spit-shakes."

"I got another one," Tom Shaney said. "You've heard of Coach John Wooden, haven't you—you know, he coaches the UCLA Bruins?" I had never heard of Coach Wooden at that time, but both Scott and I nodded that "Sure, we know Wooden."

"So, Wooden has been coaching for more than ten years at UCLA and he's got a handful of pregame rituals he and the basketball team go through. Like, the players have to eat the same food before each game, exactly four hours before the buzzer goes off. All the players have to wear two pair of fifty-percent cotton socks, all smoothed out so they don't get blisters. And before every game Coach Wooden spits on the floor and rubs the spit with his foot. Then he's good to go."

"Who told you that, Shaney?" I asked.

"I read it in *Sports Illustrated*. You can go to the library and read the story for yourself," Tom replied.

"No, no, I believe you," I said. "But I don't recall all that spitting getting UCLA a national championship."

"You're right," Shaney said. "But *Sports Illustrated* says this might be the year the Bruins go all the way. I mean, all that spitting has got to pay off sometime!"

"It'll never happen!" Brentano said. "UCLA will have to play the Jayhawks or Kentucky to get a national championship. I will *spit-shake* on UCLA never winning a national basketball championship."

Neither Tom Shaney nor I had enough vested interest in UCLA to spit-shake. Obviously, the three of us were clueless about the ultimate basketball fortunes of Coach Wooden and the UCLA Bruins. Live and learn!

WARNING: *Do not cross Spit Corner without spitting or..."*

"you'll dry up and blow away!"

"your saliva will go sour!"

"your tastebuds will melt!"

"you'll get dandruff on your crotch!"

"your children will all be green!"

"you'll never be able to French kiss!"

"your boobs will explode!"

Chapter 20

The Invisible Man

Usually, when I walked up to anyone, I would be acknowledged. "Hi, Billy." "Hiya, Howard." "How you hanging, Billy?" "Hey, dork!" So it was most of the time when I walked onto the Madigan's property. Mr. Madigan would say, "Hello, Billy." The twins would say, "Hi, deadhead." Molly would usually greet me with her brown eyes and say, "Hi, Billy. Park your butt and let's talk."

However, many times when I walked onto the Madigan property, I suddenly became *The Invisible Man,"* or at least the invisible teenager. Molly and whoever else was there simply ignored me. They didn't say "hello." They didn't say "goodbye." They just ignored me.

They weren't mad at me. They weren't illustrating contempt that I was a year or two younger than most of the kids assembled. They weren't ignoring me because I was a dweeb, dork, twerp, or prick. They just flat out ignored me. My reaction to this evolved over time.

At the beginning, I was hurt and ticked. "What did I do? Is there an issue here? Did I do something to somebody? What? What?" Of course, I never asked any of these questions. I sat quietly in my annoyance and bewilderment.

But with the passage of time, I realized that I was being given access to my potential life one or two years into the future. With Molly's friends, I was able to observe some of the native rituals of older teens in a little speck of a place called Coffeyville. I took mental notes. (If I hadn't taken such notes, this memoir wouldn't be here.) As strange as it was at times, I came to enjoy being invisible.

One afternoon, I knocked on Molly's door. Through the screen door I heard Molly yell, "Who is it?" "Billy," I said.

"Come in and park it."

As I had so many times before, I walked into the house and into the den. On the sofa by the front window were Molly and J.D. Lemon, a junior in high school. They were locked in a tight embrace and necking. I sat down in an easy chair opposite the sofa, presuming that the afternoon love fest would come to an end now that an additional guest had arrived at the Madigan home. I was wrong.

For the next five minutes, Molly and J.D. practiced their kissing techniques. Mouths didn't open too wide. I saw no tongues. Hands did not wander much. Every few minutes, J.D. would start to massage Molly's butt, beautifully clad in short-shorts. Rather than slapping his hand away, Molly just turned her body. Female breasts were not manhandled but Molly showed no hesitancy in pressing herself against J.D. He reciprocated.

I diverted my eyes but Molly and J.D. were like magnets, drawing my gaze back to them at least once per minute. At that time, I had enjoyed only a few kisses and had yet to enjoy the pleasure of a neck-fest. When they would open their eyes, J.D. and Molly would look at me. But I evoked absolutely no reaction from them. I could have been a part of the upholstery.

Actually, on this occasion, it was Molly who began to get a little hot and bothered. I did not sense that I was inhibiting either her or J.D. but then my denseness regarding social interaction had, by that point, been well documented. Unless one of them spoke up and told me to hit the road, I would just sit there. During their embraces and osculation, they never said a word to me. *"Am I really this irrelevant?"* I wondered. *"Or was I just invisible?"*

After the aforementioned five minutes, J.D. had to go to work as a box boy at Karbe's Super Market. J.D. gave Molly one last kiss and walked out of the den and house. "So long, Billy," he said. Through the den window, Molly watched J.D. drive away. She stood up from the sofa, tracked down a cigarette, lit up, and sat back down on the sofa.

"So, Billy, how you hanging? Had any new women lately?"

On another occasion, Carolyn Rousters was sitting with Molly on the front steps of the Madigan house. I rode up on my bicycle. I dismounted, put down the kickstand, and walked closer to the steps where the two girls were talking. I stood right in front of them. For the next ten minutes, the two of them continued to talk about various subjects, most of them related to school, school homework, and teachers. They would turn and look at me but, in effect, looked right through me. Once again, I was invisible.

When I realized that I was not really there, I walked up the steps right between the two girls and sat down in the porch rocking chair. As was the case on other occasions, I had a ringside seat for their conversation.

Carolyn asked, "How do you think your dad has been doing since your mom died?"

"He's become a drunk," Molly said. "He drank before, but not like he does now. I think he drinks on the job. I don't know that for sure, but I've smelled alcohol on his breath sometimes when he's come from the office. I asked him about it once. He got mad and said he had taken clients out for lunch and it was routine to have a drink or two."

"Does he drink at night?" Carolyn asked.

"Hell, yes," Molly replied. "I fix dinner with virtually no help from the twins or Dad. He drinks coffee or tea at the dinner table. But as soon as dinner is over, he goes into the living room, pours himself a drink and starts reading. He reads and drinks, reads and drinks until he just drinks. After three or four drinks, whiskey or Highballs or straight gin, he falls asleep in his chair. We never talk. The twins and I go to bed. Sometime around midnight, Daddy comes up the stairs. No matter how much he drinks, he always leaves at 7:45 a.m. to go to work. He's back every night at 5:15."

"We might move," Carolyn said.

"You're kidding me!" Molly said with alarm. I was again in the rocking chair and my invisible ears perked up. "Where would you move?" Molly asked with alarm in her voice. Carolyn was Molly's best friend.

"Somewhere here in town. Mom and Dad want another bedroom. I've been arguing for my own room for the last three years. I've been sharing with Melinda. Henryjuner and Ricky share a room. When I leave home, Henryjuner will get my room, presuming we find a house with four bedrooms. There might be something in Edgewood, but I don't know if my folks can afford that neighborhood."

"Shit!" Molly said. "I want you to have your own room. But if you move, who the hell will I have to talk to? Besides, I've heard that the smoke from the paint smelter causes the paint on the Edgewood houses to peel."

"Yeah, we've heard the same. Thanks to the smelter we always know which way the wind is blowing. How many bedrooms do you have?" Carolyn asked.

"Now, we have three. There is a fourth, small bedroom on the first floor that Grandmother used when she was staying here. But it's become a storeroom since she died. Upstairs, we have a bathroom and three bedrooms. The twins have a small room with bunk beds. You've seen my room. At least I can fit a small desk into the room. Then there is Daddy's bedroom."

"How do you think the twins are doing since your mom died?" Carolyn asked.

Molly was silent for a moment. "They're not doing well. They were only ten when Mom passed. Then Grandmother died within a month of Mama. Two weeks after Mama was buried, the twins woke me up in the middle of the night. Mac said, "Please, Molly, can we get in bed with you?" I said, "Yes." Two or three nights per week, they are still there."

Carolyn sat up. "Molly, are you saying the twins still sleep with you?"

"Yep."

"Do you think that's wise, Molly? Two boys and a girl? They're not little boys anymore."

"Don't break my chops, Carolyn. Our mom died. The twins were only ten. We sleep. That's all we do. We sleep. They're good boys. Damn! I can't believe the crap this family has gone through."

Molly blew her nose. "Hey, Carolyn, I'm glad to hear about your move. Invite me over when you're in the new homestead."

Carolyn and Molly hugged. Carolyn left. Molly remained sitting on the steps. She did not acknowledge my presence. I was not offended. I was used to being invisible. But I was sad about what Molly's family had to endure. As young as I was, I was old enough to know that life is often good but it is mostly hard. Harder for some than others.

Chapter 21

"Traveling Companion of the Earth"

Two momentous events occurred Friday, October 4, 1957:

Leave It to Beaver debuted on CBS, a run that concluded in 1963.

Sputnik was launched into earth orbit by the Union of Soviet Socialist Republics (USSR). *"Sputnik"* meant *"traveling companion of the earth"* and was the first artificial satellite to circle our globe. While the eighty-pound satellite beep-beeped smoothly through the dark void of space, *Sputnik* set off shock waves across America.

With Europe and much of Asia devastated following World War II, the United States became pre-eminent in virtually every arena of life. At the end of the *"Great Patriotic War,"* as the Russians called WWII, the United States controlled fifty-percent of the known wealth in the world. As war-torn nations progressed in their economic recoveries, America's percentage of the pie of wealth diminished.

Be that as it may, throughout the 1950s, the United States seemed to have the upper hand in the *"Cold War,"* a term coined to describe the state of relations between the U.S. and the U.S.S.R. following WWII. The launch of *Sputnik* sent a collective chill up the American spine, and that included the spines of students, faculty, and administrators of schools across the land.

Earlier in 1957, two U.S. Vanguard missiles had failed in their launches. These were Inter-Continental Ballistic Missiles (ICBMs) that were attempting to put American satellites into orbit. But the *Sputnik* rode atop a Soviet R-7 *Semyorka* missile and won the first heat of the space race.

The satellite itself was one thing but the missile system was quite another. Earlier in the year, the Soviet Union had fired a missile over six thousand miles. With the *Sputnik* success, it was plain for the world to comprehend that the Soviet Union had the military might to deliver a nuclear missile to any continent within a half-hour's time. The U.S. capability was not as advanced at that point and, thus, the threat of guided missiles increased global tensions as the United States and Soviet Union continued with their Cold War brinksmanship.

On the Monday following *Sputnik's* launch, my third period class was Science taught by Miss Gertrude Clough, one tough teacher with whom I had negotiated a mutual dislike. As was the case with everyone else in the class, my focus was upon *Sputnik*, ICBMs, the Russkies, and whether global thermonuclear war was imminent.

When the class bell rang, Miss Clough entered her room from her hall duty position. Our class was silent. Miss Clough sat down at her desk, clasped her hands in front of her, surveyed the lot of us, and then said, "As I am sure you all are aware, the Soviet Union has placed an artificial satellite named *Sputnik* into orbit around the earth. This is a very significant scientific accomplishment that has never before occurred in the history of the world. The power of the rocket that launched *Sputnik* carries with it many diplomatic, political, and military implications.

"Miss Dornan, please go to the blackboard, take the chalk, and write down the answers the class will now give to my first question of the day: Class, what are the various scientific subjects or disciplines which the Soviet scientists had to master to place *Sputnik* into orbit?"

At first, no one spoke up. But then Danny George, one of the students who seemed adept with matters scientific, said, "Physics."

"You are correct, Mr. George," Miss Clough said. "Who is next?"

Slowly but steadily, our class began to list various scientific disciplines: Trigonometry, biology, metallurgy, calculus, aerodynamics, jet propulsion, and so on.

After awhile, Miss Clough said, "Thank you, Miss Dornan. You may be seated."

"Now class, I trust that you are aware that the United States has also been attempting to place a satellite into orbit around the earth. Our nation's efforts to do this have thus far failed. I do not have any knowledge of why we are trailing the USSR in this regard. But, for the sake of discussion, please give me your thoughts on why the United States with its vast resources has not been the first nation to orbit an artificial satellite."

Miss Clough had called for an unprecedented discussion! At that point, I had no recollection of ever being asked to join into a conversation about why the United States had *failed* at something. I had been growing up in an era of American *successes*. I was mindful that life in these United States was the envy of the world. I understood that our military had proved to be the deciding component in accomplishing Allied victories in both world wars. We had the best cars, the best televisions, the best women's stockings, the best lawn fertilizers, the best hair tonics. *Pan American Airlines* had announced that it would launch inter-continental jet service from New York to London next year. General Dwight D. Eisenhower, who was then President Eisenhower—the Commanding General of D Day—was at the national helm. Who could ask for more? America was the leader of the world—first in everything...*except space.*

What didn't we do? What didn't our scientists do right? Are we now behind the Soviet Union, not just in satellites but in ICBM capability? Was the global balance of power beginning to shift? Would the U.S.S.R. *"bury us"* as Khrushchev predicted? Would our children be reared as Communists under a flag of hammer and sickle? Children? Hah! None of us in Miss Clough's science class were concerned about our potential offspring. For the very first time in our American lives, we began to wonder if we would make it to adulthood.

Chapter 22

The Hearse

I was walking home from a Saturday matinee at the Midland Theater. As I was strolling by the Post Office, *"the Hearse"* pulled up alongside me.

"Hey, Billy Howard, what's up?"

The voice belonged to *the Hearse*'s driver, Brillo Stubblefield.

"Hi, Brillo," I said as I walked to curbside. "I just finished the matinee. On my way home."

"Hop in," Brillo said. "I'll give you limousine service."

"Great, Brillo! Thanks!"

When Brillo finished junior high school, he celebrated by using some money that he had saved and more money that his *"bucks-up"* grandmother gave him to purchase the wrecked pearl white Ford station wagon that was known around town as *"the Hearse."*

Its former owner was gunning the engine up U.S. 169 for the sake of experiencing speed when the engine blew. The driver reacted by swerving onto the shoulder of the highway. Then the driver had the opportunity to experience flight. The Ford flew off the highway near the entrance to the Skyline Drive-In Theater and landed in a wheat field, soggy from the previous day's rain. The soggy soil saved the driver's life who, nevertheless, was hospitalized with two broken legs, numerous contusions and bruises, along with a concussion. The Ford required last rites.

"Brillo," was born Lester Eugene Stubblefield. As the eighth grade came to an end, some heavy-duty testosterone began flowing through his system. Lester sprouted whiskers as dark as his jet black hair. Within a month, he had a beard. In consultation with Lester's parents and the school nurse, the Principal—Dexter Rutledge—said he could keep the beard as long as it was neatly trimmed. Lester wore his beard as a badge of masculine superiority.

One lunch break on the junior high school campus, Imogene Conover ran her hand over Lester's beard and declared that it felt like a *Brillo Pad,* the popular scouring pad for cleaning pots and pans. Lester wasn't thrilled with his new epithet but, nevertheless, put up with it because of the notoriety it gave him.

In his three years of high school, Brillo had found various ways to earn money. He was not too concerned about his grades, so he spent most of his non-work, non-sleep, non-eating time at his Uncle Bub's muffler shop down by the *Missouri Pacific's* maintenance roundhouse. Uncle Bub had given Brillo sufficient work space and tools to permit Brillo to make dedicated progress in resurrecting, repairing, restoring, and customizing the totaled station wagon. During the restoration process some of Brillo's chums began referring to the station wagon as *"the Hearse."*

The history of the station wagon meant little to me. I was eager to hop into *the Hearse* and enjoy cruising with upperclassman Brillo along Eighth Street.

The moment I sat down at shotgun and pulled the door shut I knew I had made a huge mistake. Instantly, I was hit in the face with the foulest sewer odor I had ever encountered. The rotten-egg, dead body stench was up close and personal.

"Don't worry, Billy-boy! You'll get used to it in a minute," Brillo said. "Your nose will turn it off. Trust me. And don't fight it!" Brillo eased back into traffic and headed west.

"My gosh, Brillo," I gasped. "What is this smell?"

"It's offal," Brillo replied.

"I know it's awful! But what is it?" I leaned my head out the window.

"It's *'offal,'* not *'awful.'* 'Offal—*o-f-f-a-l*—offal!'"

I pulled my head back inside and pressed back into the seat, surrendering to the sewer gas as a drowning man finally relents to water pouring into his lungs. With watering eyes, I asked, "What the hell is *'o-f-f-a-l?'*" That's when I noticed Brillo was wearing hip-waders.

"'Offal' are guts, Billy. Cow guts, pig guts," Brillo explained. It's everything that's left over after slaughtering and dressing an animal. I work at Sunflower Packing Company—SuPaCo. Just got off work."

"What in the world do you do there? Swim in the guts?" I asked.

"Almost," Brillo replied. I jerked my head around to stare at him. I noticed that he was sitting on a tarp, apparently to protect the seat covers from slime.

Brillo chuckled as he glanced over to me and said, "Billy, all the offal gets tossed onto the floor by the cutters, the butchers, and the packers. The offal then gets hosed off the rendering floor by me and another guy. We also use push brooms and a huge squeegee-like tool to get the guts into a slough that feeds sort of a square funnel with grates at the bottom. The offal has to be small enough to pass through the grates. When it passes through, it goes into a good size sewer pipe and out into the Verdigris."

"All that blood and guts get dumped into the river?" I asked with widened eyes.

"Billy, packing companies have been doing that for centuries," Brillo said as we passed the Carnegie Public Library. "Why do you suppose the Verdigris has such fat carp and catfish?"

"Oh lordy," I groaned. "So all of this stink comes from just pushing a broom and squeegee around the slaughter house?"

"No, Billy," Brillo said as he waved to a buddy working at the Skelly station. "The stench comes from the funnel or chute. You know, the place where the offal has to pass through the grates. Every day—two or three times—the grates clog. When they do, I climb down a ladder with a large spade and start chopping. I slice, dice, and mince the offal until its small enough to pass through the grates and begin its trip to the Gulf of Mexico. Sometimes the gunk comes above my knee. That's why I wear these rubber waders. Another guy hoses off my waders but the goop has sunk into the rubber and won't come out. That's why the stink. But, like I said, you get used to it. I suppose it must be like the places where they do autopsies. So, has your nose turned off yet?"

"Yeah, Brillo, it's off," I said. "I don't know if it will ever turn on again."

"Sure it will, Billyboy. Just take a shower. If you sense any lingering stink, just put a little *VapoRub* under your nostrils for awhile. It'll clear up and you'll be as good as new."

"How long have you been doing this?" I asked.

"For more than a year now. I work twenty hours per week and I make good money--$1.65 an hour. And all my profit goes right into my little *ZoZomobile,"* Brillo said as he lovingly patted the dash.

"'ZoZomobile? I thought this was *'the Hearse?'"*

"You local yokels call it *'the Hearse.'* That's a terrible name!" Brillo said. "That's why I call it my *'ZoZomobile."*

"Holy cow, Brillo! What's *a 'ZoZo.'*"

"Ain't telling, Billy-boy—least not yet. But it will all come out when that chicken-heart Paulie Pyle agrees to race. Then the whole town will know what a '*ZoZomobile*' is."

As we approached Karbe's market, Brillo said, "Excuse me, Billy-boy. I'll get you home in two shakes but first I need a couple bucks of gas."

Brillo turned into the Sinclair station across from Karbe's. Regular gas was $.28. For most teenage drivers, $2.00 would cover a weekend's worth of cruising while $5.00 would fund an entire week. When *the Hearse* or *ZoZomobile* rolled over the compressed air bell, Delmer Tyrell, son of the station's owner walked quickly from the service bay. He was clad in Sinclair's off-white long-sleeved shirt, black necktie, cap with the Sinclair dinosaur emblazoned above the brim, and a coin-dispenser attached to his belt.

"Hey, Brillo! Good to see you," Delmer said. "What can I getcha?"

"A deuce of regular will do, Del," Brillo replied. As a courtesy to the nostrils within in a three-block area, Brillo and I remained seated in the car.

Delmer cranked the pump numbers back to zero. After 7.14 gallons of gas were dispensed, Delmer replaced the nozzle that had no anti-pollution stopper attached, and began washing the windows, three on each side plus front and rear.

As Delmer reached the windshield, he said, "Paulie Pyle was here about an hour ago. He had the top down on his T-Bird. Said he was going over to Independence to impress some of those *Bull Dog* women. I think he was probably just going out to see his grandma in Tyro. I asked him when he and you were going to have your drag race of the century out on the runways. Paulie just laughed and said he had no idea if or when he would have any time for such a small matter with such a huge expectation of his victory."

As Delmer moved to checking the tire pressures, he continued, "I gotta admit, Brillo, most of the talk I hear thinks Paulie would cross the line two or three lengths in front of your Hearse."

Brillo shook his head in disgust. "Delmer, people think a lot of things. Please note, however, that I am the one who is ready at any time to take on Paulie. Hell, I may even give him a car-length advantage. As you can tell, I've got my baby moon wheels and only 10,000 miles on my recapped Goodyears. Once, I beat Paulie, I'm going to lower the car. You gotta remember, Delmer, Paulie's driving with one of those prissy Ford engines. My Ford is packing a 327 small block Chevy engine—Edelbrook intake, Holley carb, and dual exhaust. I've even ordered me a hula girl for the dashboard all the way from Honolulu, Hawaii—*Aloha!*"

"Brillo, there's no doubt you turned a sow's ear into a pretty good looking purse—maybe not a silk purse, but no one can say you haven't done a mighty fine job. But to me, what you've done to your White Knight here has simply drawn you even with Paulie's T-Rex of a T-Bird. What's your gimmick? Where's your advantage? I mean a quarter-mile drag course is a mighty short distance to get it all together."

Delmer popped the hood to check the oil, radiator water, battery water, belts and hoses. A couple minutes later he returned to Brillo's window to take payment. "It all looks good, Brillo. Thanks for the business."

"You betcha, Del." Brillo started the car and slipped it into gear.

Before he pulled away, Brillo said, "Delmer, I'll tell you what my competitive edge is and you can tell anyone you want 'cause if it gets back to Paulie Pyle it will never sink into his thick skull. *Maintenance.*"

"Maintenance?" Delmer said. "What about maintenance?"

"Simple, Delmer," Brillo said. "I do maintenance. Paulie don't. I bet every piece of that T-Bird is original equipment and he's put more than 50,000 miles on that pissant sports car with the same tires if you can believe it! Almost everything on my rebuilt juggernaut is brand-spanking new. That's my edge, Del! Keep your jockstrap tight and have a good weekend!"

We drove the few remaining blocks to my house on Lincoln Street. I said, "Brillo, I've never had much interest in working on cars but it sounds like you've done a bang-up job. Any race between you Paulie will probably be remembered longer than the Dalton boys trying to rob our banks."

"You're right about that, Billy-boy. Well, here we are," Brillo said stopping the station wagon headed in the wrong direction in front of my house. Brillo put the car in park and reached into his pocket for a cigarette.

I hesitated in getting out which was counter to my initial reaction when I first entered Brillo's car. "Hey, Brillo, they say you'll never get what you don't ask for. So, here goes: I'd really, really like to know what a *ZoZo bird* is. I promise I won't say a word till after the race."

Brillo took a deep draw on his *Old Gold* and then blew out the smoke. He looked up and down Lincoln Street to see if there was anyone who might overhear this secret of secrets.

"Okay, Billy-boy. But if you say a word before the race, I'll stuff you down the offal chute. Understand?"

"Yes, Brillo," I said. "Tick-a-Lock!" I mimed zipping my lips and turning the key.

"So," Brillo began,

"It's World War II out in some sweltering jungle in the Pacific. A marine spots one of his buddies holding a bird with a huge beak and brightly colored feathers.

'What are you doing with that bird?' he asks.

'This is no ordinary bird,' the buddy replies. 'This is a ZoZo Bird.'

'What the hell is a ZoZo bird?' the other guy asks.

'Watch this,' the guy with the bird says. 'You see that coconut over there,' he says pointing to a spot on the ground about ten yards away.

'Yeah, I see it. So what?'

The marine with the bird says, 'ZoZo Bird: Coconut!' Immediately the bird flies to the coconut and with one bite dissolves and swallows the coconut. Then the bird flies back to the first marine.

'Bullshit,' the other marine says. 'No way! What's the trick?'

The marine says, 'It's no trick. Watch again. See that monkey over there eating a banana?'

'Yeah, yeah,' the other marine says.

'ZoZo Bird: Monkey!' The ZoZo Bird flies directly to the monkey. In one bite, the bird dissolves and swallows the monkey, leaving the banana intact. Then the bird flies back to his marine handler.'

'I can't believe that happened,' the other marine says.

All of a sudden, the marines' platoon sergeant walks up to them. The platoon sergeant says to the guy not holding the bird, *'You can't believe what, bootbrain?'*

The marine replies, 'I can't believe this here ZoZo Bird!'

The sergeant says, *'ZoZoBird, my ass!'*"

I burst out laughing! "I won't tell a soul, Brillo! That is so funny!" I continued to laugh as I opened the door and exited the *ZoZomobile*.

Brillo leaned over to the passenger side and whispered through the open window. "Now, you understand, Billy-boy. My *ZoZomobile* is gonna eat Paulie Pyle's ass!"

Brillo's tires squealed as he pulled away. As for me, I could not get to a shower fast enough! And yes, I also needed the *Vick's VapoRub!*

Chapter 23

Spring Breaks and Easter Assemblies

From time to time, Coffeyville students heard reports or rumors from other schools about activities that differed from ours. Some Coffeyville students would visit cousins in other towns over the Christmas break. Back in Coffeyville, they would report their findings.

"Did you know that in Topeka, the high schools have what they call a *"Senior Trip?"* Ross Gossard reported."

"What's that," someone in the lunchtime campus huddle asked.

"It's where the kids save money in a class fund from the time they're freshmen or sophomores by doing car washes and bake sales and whatnot. Then, in the spring of their senior year, depending on how much money they've collected, the whole class takes a train trip to Chicago or St. Louis or Washington, D.C."

"Do the kids get to go by themselves?" Archie Rush asked.

"No, no, they don't get to go alone," Ross continued. "They have teachers and parents who are chaperones. My cousin at Topeka Central High said her class was going all the way to Atlanta. She also said that they would keep the boys and girls in separate train cars."

"Why don't we have senior trips?" Rush asked.

No one had any idea why not. Indeed, most of us had never heard of the concept.

"Listen to this, comrades," Buster Mahaney spoke up and moved to the center of the group, better to be seen and heard. In Salina—and I was told also in McPherson—the schools don't have Easter vacations."

"How do they get by with that?" Shirley Chronister, the editor of the high school *Tornado Times* student newspaper asked. "I thought everywhere had Easter vacations. I bet the preachers didn't like that."

"No, see, it's a whole different deal up there. When we have Easter vacation, we're out of school on Friday—what do you call it—oh yeah, *Good Friday*—Saturday, Sunday, and Monday. So we miss two school days. But in Salina, they don't call it Easter vacation. They call it *'spring break'* and the kids are out of school from Palm Sunday through Easter Sunday. That's five whole school days!"

"Man, if that's true, we all are getting the shaft!" Rush bemoaned. I'm gonna talk to my old man about this. He plays Pinochle with the superintendent of schools. A whole five days and we only get two! That can't be right. The Coffeyville school district can spring break my ass!"

Indeed, we never had a senior trip or a whole five days called spring break. But we always had an *Easter Assembly.*

In the ninth grade, I had been tapped to do a reading from the *Old Testament* at the Easter assembly which was always held during the final class hour on the day before Good Friday.

When it came time for the assembly to begin, I was backstage at the junior high school auditorium, an excellent auditorium with a proscenium stage, backstage, wings, loft, and stage lights. It was a bona fide theatrical auditorium, not a multipurpose gym or *cafetorium* which is neither fish nor fowl.

The Mixed Choir was already standing on risers with Miss Richards, the conductor, to the side. When Vice Principal Vesco gave us the cue, Student Council President Seaton Lake, and the rest of us who were participating in the program, filed on stage and stood in front of six folding chairs down stage left. Then, Seaton approached the lectern microphone.

"Welcome to the Easter Assembly!" Seaton said. "Leonard Coyle will direct the *National Anthem* and Lois Perry will lead the *Pledge to the Christian Flag*. But first, please stand and let us recite the *Pledge of Allegiance to the American Flag."*

So let it be said. So let it be done.

When we were again seated, Sylvester White, a handsome Negro student with a deep voice walked to the standing microphone a few feet to the right of the lectern. With Miss Richards accompanying on the piano, Sylvester sang, *"Were You There When They Crucified My Lord?"*

I had been warned by Miss Richardson that after Sylvester sang, I was not to wait for applause because she said applause is not appropriate in a religious service. Indeed, there was no applause and

I stepped forward to read. I had practiced reading the passage aloud every day for a week. Wearing a suit and tie, I was in a heavy sweat.

I looked out over the packed auditorium. I began, "Eight hundred years before the birth of Jesus, the prophet of the Lord wrote in…

"Isaiah 53:1-9

"Who hath believed our report?
And to whom is the arm of the LORD revealed?
For he shall grow up before him as a tender plant,
and as a root out of a dry ground:
He hath no form nor comeliness; and when we shall see him,
there is no beauty that we should desire him.
He is despised and rejected of men;
a man of sorrows, and acquainted with grief:
And we hid as it were our faces from him;
he was despised, and we esteemed him not.
Surely he hath borne our griefs, and carried our sorrows:
Yet we did esteem him stricken, smitten of God, and afflicted.
But he was wounded for our transgressions,
he was bruised for our iniquities:
The chastisement of our peace was upon him;
and with his stripes we are healed.
All we like sheep have gone astray;
we have turned every one to his own way;
and the LORD hath laid on him the iniquity of us all.
He was oppressed, and he was afflicted,
yet he opened not his mouth:
He is brought as a lamb to the slaughter,
and as a sheep before her shearers is dumb,
so he openeth not his mouth.
He was taken from prison
and from judgment: and who shall declare his generation?
For he was cut off out of the land of the living:
For the transgression of my people was he stricken.
And he made his grave with the wicked,
and with the rich in his death;
because he had done no violence,
neither was any deceit in his mouth."

I made it through the passage with only a slight slip on *"iniquity."* When I sat down, student Pam Reese accompanied on the piano while Miss Richards directed the choir in singing *"Fairest Lord Jesus."*

Following the choir, Amy Kathleen Donovan read from the New Testament:

"Mark 15:33-39

"And when the sixth hour was come,
there was darkness over the whole land until the ninth hour.
And at the ninth hour Jesus cried with a loud voice, saying,
'Eloi, Eloi, lama sabachthani?'
which is, being interpreted,
'My God, my God, why hast thou forsaken me?'
And some of them that stood by, when they heard it, said,
'Behold, he calleth Elias.'
And one ran and filled a spunge full of vinegar,
and put it on a reed, and gave him to drink, saying,'
'Let alone; let us see whether Elias will come to take him down.'
And Jesus cried with a loud voice, and gave up the ghost.
And the veil of the temple was rent in twain
from the top to the bottom.
And when the centurion, which stood over against him,
saw that he so cried out, and gave up the ghost, he said,
'Truly this man was the Son of God.'"

Sandy Schaub and Gracie Truman, members of *The Madrigals* at the junior high school, sang a duet of *"Beneath the Cross of Jesus."* Sandy was a lovely pearl white and Gracie was a beautiful russet brown. Skin color was always noted in those days whether anyone would admit to it or not.

Gracie Truman and Sylvester White had been featured in the Easter Assembly. To my recollection, that was the first time that any colored students had had such prominence in any non-sports school assembly.

When the duet was over, Seaton Lake said, "The closing prayer will given by Denton Widmer. (His father was the local Assemblies of God pastor.) The prayer will be followed by all of us singing *"Up from the Grave He Arose!"* After the hymn, we will be dismissed.

We wish everyone a meaningful Good Friday and a happy Easter! Please stand."

I understood then and now that such a service as portrayed above was discriminatory against non-Christians—*like me*. I did not become a Christian until my sophomore year in high school. But I had attended such Christian services since elementary school. They didn't bother me at all, probably because, even though I was not a Christian, I was at least a *God-fearer*.

Non-Christians did not have to attend such services. They could pass the time in the library or study hall if they so chose. I never opted out.

However, by the time I was graduated from high school, prayer and any sort of religious assemblies were no more in Coffeyville public schools. Court rulings, school districts' fear of being sued with the attendant legal fees, and the near universal American misunderstanding of what Thomas Jefferson actually meant when he opined that there must be "*a wall of separation*" between church and state all brought an end to what in reality were Christian assemblies in public schools.

Such Easter services did not celebrate religious diversity, only the sacrificed and risen Christ. Indignant liberal judges ruled that such religious oppression and political incorrectness could not continue. As a result, most school kids today have little idea of how integrated Christianity once was in the routine of public education.

"He who troubles his own house will inherit the wind."

Proverbs 11:29a

Chapter 24

Young Love II

Fred Astaire and Ginger Rodgers were not married to each other. They never dated. They were business associates with a close personal bond that developed by enthralling the American movie-going public with their amazing footwork on a dance floor. Carly Delgreco was my *Ginger!*

To understand the exhilarating relationship I had with Carly, draw two side-by-side circles that overlap one another's volume by ten percent. Fill in the overlapped portion with deep purple, an intense and wonderful overlay that manifested itself on dance floors and rarely any place else.

The depiction of our own close bond with one another was hardly by design. That's just the way it was. We were not aggrieved when we were not together, but we hit all our marks when we did have occasion to talk with one another or dance together.

One such occasion was the first ever *"Yearbook Dance."* Another miraculous event in my life was that, at the end of the eighth grade, I had been chosen by the school administration to be the first Editor-in-Chief of the first-ever Roosevelt Junior High School yearbook, *The Rough Rider.* I was on cloud nine regarding this extra-curricular position. As it turned out, I sweat bullets as the yearbook staff and I sought to meet our deadlines with copy and photos submitted to the publisher long before the digital age was even a gleam in the eye of some unborn geek

However, the *Yearbook Dance* worked out well. We named a Yearbook Queen—Tonya Conway—who was crowned during a break at the dance. With the pomp completed, we returned to the dance. Two guys who counted their prospects for real live dates as *"slim"* and *"none"* took solace by being DJs. They spoke no *between-platter-patter*. They merely stacked up the forty-fives on a record player. There was not a jacked-in unified sound system so a free-standing microphone was placed in front of the record player's speaker and, voila, music was in the air.

Faculty and parental chaperones were posted by the gym exits. They were also positioned in the balcony.

The play list for the night included such now golden oldies as

Theme from "A Summer Place"
Smoke Gets in Your Eyes
The End
Chances Are
Lonesome Town
Rock Around the Clock
Barbara Ann
Only the Lonely
Jail House Rock
Peggy Sue
Sleep Walk
Wake Up, Little Susie!

And more!

Following the coronation ceremony, as the dancing resumed, I was gabbing with Rayburn Brogan when Carly Delgreco walked up, grabbed my hand, and led me onto the dance floor. The DJs had just launched *Sing! Sing! Sing!* featuring the Benny Goodman Orchestra and drummer Gene Krupa. Like Glenn Miller's *In the Mood, Sing! Sing! Sing!* was a solid gold swing tune that went on for more than five minutes. The dance floor was packed.

At first, Carly and I just smiled at each other as we began to dance. Then she began to giggle because she knew what was coming. Most of our classmates knew a few basic jitterbug or swing steps. No one knew as many steps as did the Hedley's experimental dance couple.

We were content to blend into the throng for the first half of the song. But then we turned up the dial and it happened again—the other dancers began to back off to the edges of the dance floor as they continued to dance. Then, they all stopped and began to clap in tempo as Carly and I burned the floor in the center of the gym. Just as *Sing! Sing! Sing!* came to a crescendo-ing climax, so, too, did our dancing. Carly and I were swinging and whirling dervishes.

On the final notes, I unreeled Carly so that we concluded our dance at arm's length, side-by-side, holding hands, ready to take a bow. Our fellow students were quick with their applause. We bowed to one side and then to the other. AND THEN, IN THAT *MAGIC MOMENT,* I reeled Carly back to my side, looked down into her radiant face AND *I* KISSED CARLY! She actually held that moment for an instant and then unreeled herself feigning shock.

The crowd went wild! A public kiss?! Everyone knew that Carly and I were not an item, but they also knew that we were best buds on the dance floor, like Fred and Ginger. Carly and I were separated by the congratulatory students and we were happy to bask in the limelight.

Osa Fields, one of the school's best athletes, patted me on the back and walked away. He appeared to be the last of the well-wishers. I used my handkerchief to wipe my brow. As I turned to head to the restroom, I found myself face to face with Mr. Vesco, the vice principal.

"Billy, I need to have a word with you. Hear me now, Billy," Mr. Vesco said. "You should have known better than make a public display of kissing. That is not acceptable conduct at a school dance. You knew that, didn't you, Billy?"

I gulped. My eyes widened. My chest tightened. I fought for a breath. "Yes, sir, Mr. Vesco," I blurted. "Yes, sir, I know that—I mean, uh..well..yes, I knew that about kissing."

"That being so," Mr. Vesco said, staring directly into my eyes, "what have you got to say for yourself?"

"Sa—say for myself?" I stammered. "I…I..uh..I suppose nothing, Mr. Vesco. I hadn't planned on kissing Carly—I mean it just sorta happened at that moment."

"'It just sort of happened at that moment,' did it, Billy?" Mr. Vesco said. "Well, Billy, you'd best learn how *to control your moments,* especially in a public place like a school dance. Take my meaning, Billy?"

"Yes, sir, Mr. Vesco. Absolutely!"

With that, Mr. Vesco turned to walk away. But before I could exhale a sigh of relief, he turned back to me. I braced myself again.

"By the way, Billy," Mr. Vesco said. "You and Carly really danced well. Really well!" He left. I resumed breathing. My blood began to circulate again.

That night, I had difficulty falling asleep. Truth was that I didn't want to fall asleep. I relived the night over and over, even the part with Mr. Vesco. *I kissed Carly!* Maybe it wasn't planned to go that way but EVERYONE saw me kiss Carly! Can life get any better than this?

Moments before I finally fell asleep, I remembered the movie *South Pacific* with Mitzi Gaynor and that foreign guy, Rossano somebody. To me, the *Yearbook Dance* had been *"Some Enchanted Evening!"*

"God match me with a good dancer."

Much Ado About Nothing!
William Shakespeare

Chapter 25

The Pig Stand Accord

The *Pig Stand* was a café/diner/beer joint south of U.S. 166, across from Walter Johnson Park on the east side of Coffeyville. It was famous for its *"pig"* sandwiches. It was a great place to grab a few beers and shoot the breeze. Of course, high school students could not purchase alcohol legally. Nevertheless, the Pig Stand was a great place to enjoy sandwiches, fries, and ice cold pop with friends any night of the week.

One Tuesday night near the end of the school year, Paulie Pyle and his pal Hap Barber were cruising in Paulie's Thunderbird following their DeMolay meeting. Hap suggested a burger at the Pig Stand and Paulie said, "Amen to that!"

As was the custom of many Pig Stand patrons, Paulie did a loop around the café to check out the parking lot. Paulie and Hap were eyeballing cars to get an idea of who was inside the joint. There weren't more than a handful of cars, typical for a mid-week night. On weekends, the gravel parking area was always full to overflowing.

As they were finishing the inspection loop, Hap spoke up and said, "Look at that, Paulie. There's *the Hearse*. Brillo must be having dessert."

"Yep," Paulie said. "Brillo is chowing down. Hap, tonight is going to be a history making occasion." Hap said nothing in reply as he suspected what Paulie had in mind.

Paulie parked his convertible. Paulie and Hap entered the Pig Stand through the door on the east side that was next to the ahead-of-its-time drive through window. Across the room, Brillo was munching cheesy fries, drenched in catsup, while holding court with Dirk Blackett, Allen Helkenberger, and Johnny Wishall. Brillo and his entourage saluted Paulie and Hap.

All these guys were classmates who had been friends for years. The car rivalry was serious but it did not obliterate the shared history the group had with one another. Paulie and Hap went up to the counter to give the dishwater-blonde waitress Addie their order. Then they sat down in a booth at the opposite end of the café from Brillo.

At a table in the center of the café, two geezers wearing coveralls and Farm Bureau caps were nursing beers while puffing on nubby cigars. That was the Tuesday night crowd at the Pig Stand.

Brillo had the latest issue of *Road and Track Magazine* in front of him. As he leafed through the pages, he and his buds were talking about car engines, upholstery, steering wheel knobs, automatic transmissions, and anything else vehicular.

Paulie and Hap were talking about their summer plans and when they would depart for college. Paulie had been accepted by KU on a golf scholarship. He expected to major in business and accounting. He could not wait to pledge a fraternity and enjoy the good life of wine, women, and song—and, oh yes, a little study thrown in to keep the parents happy.

Hap said he would leave for California on August 1 by train from Kansas City. He was going to live with his grandparents in La Mirada and attend Biola College, formerly the Bible Institute of Los Angeles (B.I.O.L.A.) which Paulie had never heard of. Hap said he wanted to be a pastor.

Before Paulie and Hap could discuss what they anticipated the reality of campus life to be, Brillo Stubblefield pressed his ample belly against the booth's table.

"Paulie, two things before our little group sails into the night," Brillo said with a grin, a toothpick poking out the left side of his catsup stained mouth.

"First, since the word on the street is that you always stiff the help, we put down enough bucks to cover what you ought to leave tip Addie. Count it as our graduation present to you and Hap."

Paulie finished chewing a bite of his *Pigzilla Sandwich*. Looking up at Brillo, he said, "How kind of you, gentlemen. When Hap and I are off at college in the fall, we will miss your generosity and smiling faces. Now, Brillo, Hap and I don't want you to miss your curfew so what's your second point?"

Brillo was used to Paulie's retorts. "Number two is the usual, Paulie. Before you and Hap head off to your new alma maters, when are we going to race? Or are you just going to slink out of town and let the dear hearts and gentle people of our sweet little hometown draw their own conclusions as to why you wouldn't put that worn-out T-Bird up against my beauteous rod? Set a date, Paulie!"

Without hesitation and without looking up from the onion ring he was twirling on his index finger, Paulie said, "June 10 at 9:00 p.m. at the airport. Now, if you have nothing else, I wish you a good night, gentlemen."

Brillo and his bunch took a step back in astonishment when they heard Paulie set a firm date. Brillo responded by saying, "June 10 at 9:00 p.m. at the airport. I'll be there with bells on. But, just one more thing. With this collection of witnesses, good men tried and true, I want your hand on this, Paulie."

Paulie tossed his napkin onto the table, slid out of the booth, as Brillo's pals backed off further. Brillo repositioned his toothpick. Then he spit on his hand and stuck it out. Paulie laughed, spat on his own hand and they shook. The onlookers cheered.

Brillo said, "Come on boys, we've got some fine tuning to do." With a nod to Hap and Paulie, Brillo and friends left the Pig Stand. Paulie and Hap ordered lemon meringue pie and continued their conversation about their college fantasies.

"Some people get an education without going to college.
The rest get it after they get out."

Mark Twain

Chapter 26

The Swinging Nurse

Lindy Lundquist was in her porch swing reading. She held a good size hardback book in her lap, pressed open by her left hand as she held a small, nearly empty, *Coca Cola* bottle in her right hand. She did not look up when I walked onto her porch but she did say, "Hi, Billy."

"Hi." I leaned against a porch pillar and riffled the short stack of baseball cards I was carrying.

She was silent for a full minute. I figured she was finishing a chapter. If she didn't speak up, I'd just wander along. Presently, Lindy pulled a nail file from the back of the book and placed it as a mark for where she stopped reading. She looked up with a smile. "So, what's new with you, Billy?"

"Not much. The *Cardinals* and *A's* are both off today so there's nothing to listen to. What'cha reading?"

Dr. Zhivago.

"Medical book for school?" I asked.

She smiled. She was never condescending to me.

"*Dr. Zhivago* is a novel about a Russian doctor named 'Zhivago.'"

"Is he a commie?" I asked.

She laughed as she put the book beside her. I sat on the porch rail still holding my cards. "No, he was not a 'commie.' The story is set before and during the Russian Revolution when the Soviet Union was being established," Lindy said. "Dr. Zhivago was trying to stay out of the fighting."

"Was he a deserter or coward?"

"No, not at all," Lindy said. "Actually, the man who wrote this book—his name is Boris Pasternak..."

"Like Boris Karloff?"

"...Yes, like Boris Karloff. Anyway, because of what he writes about, Boris Pasternak is not liked by the Communists. His book had to be smuggled out of the Soviet Union and he's in hot water in Russia."

"Are they going to shoot him?" I asked.

"I don't know. I doubt it," Lindy replied. She finished her *Coke*. I looked at one of the three BoBo Newsome cards I had. Nobody would trade for BoBo.

"Are you home for the summer?" I asked.

"I'm home for good. I graduated—two weeks ago," Lindy said. "I packed up my things in Lawrence, visited a friend in Kansas City for a week, then took the train from KC to Coffeyville. It took forever. We stopped everywhere and then it was after midnight when the train arrived here."

"So, what do they call you now? I mean, you've got a degree, right? What's the degree?"

"I have a Bachelor of Science Degree in Nursing from the University of Kansas. In September, I'll take my boards for my license and—if I pass—I will officially be an R.N.—*'Registered Nurse,'* but you, Billy, may still call me 'Lindy.'"

"I'm glad you're done, Lindy," I said. "That's swell about your degree. Nobody in my family—my aunts and uncles and cousins— none of them has ever graduated from a college. One or two may have taken some classes at a JC."

"Well, William Howard, I hope you are the first in your family to get a college degree. Right now, less than ten percent of Americans have a four-year college degree. If you get a bachelors degree, it can be a big help to you in earning your way. I recommend it. You'd love a college campus. What do you like to do? What would you want to study?"

"Oh, I don't know." I was silent for a moment, deciding whether to reveal something to Lindy but, if a guy couldn't trust Lindy, who could a guy trust?

"Actually, I like to read," I said. "Sometimes I think it would be great to write a story that got made into a book. Did you ever read *Twenty Thousand Leagues Under the Sea* by Jules Verne?"

"Why, yes. I think it was the summer before the ninth grade. It was awfully slow at the beginning but then it became quite a tale."

"Wow! You're the first girl I ever knew who read *Twenty Thousand Leagues Under the Sea.*" I studied BoBo's stats, momentarily annoyed that the *Cardinals* and *Athletics* weren't going to play until tomorrow night.

"So whatcha gonna do now, now that you're a Registered Nurse or gonna be?"

"Look after my mom. My aunts have taken turns watching her while I was in college. Now, I'm back. Maybe I'll do some part-time work at the hospital or in some doctor's office. But taking care of Mom is my first concern."

"Is she getting better?" I had no idea of her illness or injury.

"She seems to stay the same. She's paralyzed because of a stroke."

"What causes that? My dad said my grandpa died of a stroke."

"Many things can cause a stroke," Lindy said. "In simple terms, it's a blood clot that gets on the brain and damages it." She drank the last of her *Coke*. "I think my mom's stroke was caused by stress."

"What kind of stress?"

Lindy turned her head and looked right at me. *"You don't want to know, Billy. You don't want to know."*

I couldn't believe it. What had I done? What nerve had I hit? There was actually a tear rolling down her cheek. I jumped off the porch rail and stuck my baseball cards in my back pocket.

"Gee, Lindy, I'm sorry. It's none of my business, the stress I mean. My dad tells me all the time to mind my own business. I'll go."

"Hang on, Billy." Lindy pulled a Kleenex out of her pocket and blew her nose.

"What I meant, Billy, was that some really rough things have happened to our family that no one would want to happen to them. I didn't mean to be rude." She wiped her nose again.

If something happened on Lincoln Street that was really bad or even really good, pretty much everyone heard about it quickly. I hadn't heard anything about something really rough happening to the Lundquists since they moved here and they had moved onto Lincoln Street after we did.

"These rough things happened before you moved to Coffeyville?" I caught myself. "I'm sorry, Lindy. There I go again. You have a nice night."

"Billy." I stopped.

"Sit down on the swing. I'll be back in a minute. I need to check on Mom." She took her book and *Coca Cola* bottle. I sat down. It was still twilight but I thought I saw a lightning bug across the street near the Madigan's house.

After about five minutes, Lindy returned carrying two bottles of *Coke*. She handed me one. "Thanks, Lindy," I said. *"Migh-ty fine,"* I thought.

Lindy sat down next to me on the swing. She crossed her legs, smoothed her summer dress, and pulled out another Kleenex. I gave the swing a push with my legs.

"We owned a farm. We still own the farm, a thousand acres west of Caney. My dad and mom worked the farm from the time they were married. Dad inherited it from my grandpa. Grandpa was a nice man. We grew wheat mostly, some alfalfa, a few feeder cattle, and free range chickens." She sipped her *Coke* and then looked into middle distance.

"One Saturday, my Mom and Dad drove to Coffeyville to get some groceries and supplies. We kids played on the farm while our parents were away. In Coffeyville, Daddy put a load of feed bags in the back of the pickup. When they got back to the farm, Daddy honked the horn for us kids to come help Mom unload the groceries.

With the tailgate down, Daddy backed his pickup to the barn to unload the feed. He got out of the pickup, walked behind it to open the barn door, when the pickup's brake slipped. There was just a slight slope. He must have heard the truck start to roll because he was turned around facing the bed when we found him. The tailgate smashed Daddy into the barn door. The tailgate pierced his belly. The feed bags slid and crushed his chest. It must have been over quickly."

"When he didn't come back to the house, Mama walked outside but couldn't see anything except the pickup in front of the barn. When she got there, she saw daddy. He was already dead, of course. But the impact of the truck had caused his right eye to pop out and rest on his upper cheek. Mama screamed—I heard her from the kitchen. Then she walked right up to Daddy and gently pushed his eye right back into the socket. She was staring at him staring back when I got there. He was only forty-seven."

The words caught in my throat. Finally, I said, "Gosh, Lindy. That's terrible! I'm so sorry! Is that when you moved into town?"

"No, Billy, no. That didn't happen until more than a year later. After the funeral, after we all calmed down a little, Mama called us to the table, my sister, my brother, and I."

"I didn't know you have a brother and sister."

"I don't..or..that is, I have a sister but I no longer have a brother."

I was puzzled. "How's that?"

"Billy, you wanted to know what happened to my mother. I'm telling you. Sometimes it helps me to talk about it but it's not easy. Just let me tell the story. There's not much more to it. Then maybe I'll answer your questions...or maybe not."

"Sorry, Lindy. Go ahead. I won't interrupt."

"Tilly—that's short for 'Matilda'—is my sister. She's three years older than I am. When Daddy died, she was seventeen. I was fourteen. Our brother Tim was nine."

"Mama called us together. We talked. We prayed. We talked. We prayed. We decided we'd stay on the farm. It wasn't just for Daddy's sake or because we had to for the money. Mama figured we could lease the land if we had to. We kids didn't know anything about whether mama and daddy had much money or not. It never came up. We had clothes, food, the farm, movies and radio. We didn't have television because we were too far out in the country. But we had everything we needed—except Daddy, of course. So we decided to stay. We divvied up the chores. Mama hired a fellow to do the heavy lifting. Despite how sad we were that daddy was gone, we felt better doing what he loved."

"And it was working out. We planted wheat. The rains came. The harvest came. We prayed for a good price per bushel. Mama said we made some money and that Daddy would be real proud of us all. I'd go out behind the barn and cry that Daddy wasn't there to see us...or that he wasn't there so we could see him and he could hold us."

"Anyway, after the harvest, it came time to harrow the fields. Tilly was the best of us with all of the farm equipment. She drove the pickup. She drove the combine, the tractor, and she had pulled the disc harrow for years. One day she went out to harrow. At lunchtime, Mama sent Timmy out to call Tilly to lunch. She was down in the south quarter. Timmy ran after her. Mama and Tilly and I had all warned Timmy about trying to jump onto a moving

141

tractor. Daddy would just grin when Mama told him of Timmy's death-defying antics."

"On more than one occasion, Timmy would run up beside the tractor, jump up on the pull bar and just shinny up behind Tilly as she was driving. Apparently he tried to do that again. But he didn't make it or he slipped—we don't know what happened. He just fell."

"Tilly didn't hear him scream over the engine noise. We don't even know if he did scream. She hadn't seen him. All Tilly was doing was harrowing the field as she had done many times before. She drove to the end of the quarter, turned around, and headed back with the next pass. Then she came upon Timmy. He was torn up bad. She knew he was gone. Tilly went wild. She ran back to the farm house hysterical.

"She and Mama jumped into the pickup and Mama drove across the field to the tractor and saw Timmy. Tilly stayed in the truck and shrieked and cried. Mama stood looking over Timmy for awhile. Then she got back in the pickup, drove back to the house and called for help. I had gone to a Four-H meeting in Coffeyville. They couldn't track me down. The first I knew was when my ride turned onto the farm drive and we saw lots of cars and two sheriff's cars with their lights flashing." Lindy paused, took a deep breath, and wiped her eyes with the Kleenex.

My throat was dry and I was biting my lip.

"I'm going on too long," Lindy said. "Sorry, Billy. The accident was not Tilly's fault but she's had some very serious psychological problems since then. Mama and several doctors we saw said she should go to the State Hospital at Osawatomie. She's been there eight years now. I don't know if she'll ever be able to leave permanently."

"When Tilly went to Osawatomie, that's when Mama and I came to Lincoln Street. A year later, the day after Tilly's birthday, Mama had her stroke. She's been bedridden ever since. I don't know that she knows me or knows anyone but we talk with her every day. I became a nurse to help her and other people like her. Maybe one day they'll figure out how to fix these things."

When I could speak, I said, "Do you see Tilly? Does she ever get to visit you?"

"I see her once or twice each month. She recognizes me. We talk. She can do most things but she needs to be in a place that is very safe for her."

Groping for words, I said, "She must be very nice if she's anything like you." I meant what I said but I realized how forward my comment was. I blushed.

I'm sure Lindy noticed but expressed no concern. She went on. "Billy, you've actually seen Tilly. Maybe no one told you or we didn't properly introduce you to her."

"When did I see Tilly? I'm sure I would have remembered."

"It was a few months ago. You were walking home. Maybe you had been to the movie or at the *Journal*. You turned the corner and there were all sorts of people on the porch and in the front yard."

"Oh, yeah, I remember that. Wasn't it a family reunion or party? You asked me if I wanted some cake. I said yes."

"Yes, it was a party, a birthday party. It was Tilly's birthday. Did you see me sitting here on the swing with a girl?"

"Yeah, I did. She had long brown hair, right? White dress?"

"That was Tilly, Billy. *'Tilly, Billy'*—that's funny." Lindy chuckled. "Tilly made it through the day. But events like that with lots of other people are very hard for her. The human mind is a very tender thing, Billy. People are…well, people are fragile. Like the sign says, 'Handle with care.'"

Silence.

Then—I can't believe I had the sensitivity or the courage to ask her—I said, "Lindy, how have you made it through? I mean this has been—what you've told me—I mean…that really is rough stuff, really rough. "Are you"—I paused—"are you all right?"

Lindy   stood   up.   She   picked   up   the   two empty *Coca Cola* bottles. She smiled at me and said, "Billy, no one is *all* right. Lots of other people have endured worse than what has hit the Lundquist family. Just think of World War II and Korea and the *Gold Star* parents and the amputees and the shell-shocked. If tomorrow morning you can get out of bed and know what day it is and be able to walk to town to see a movie at the Midland Theater or shout at a football game, then you are *'all right'* enough to make it through the day and even the next day and perhaps even do it with a smile. Daddy used to call me a *'cock-eyed optimist.'* It's from a play, I think."

Holding a bottle in each hand, Lindy leaned over and pecked my cheek. I flushed. This had been one heck of a porch talk!

"Go home, Billy. I'm glad we talked. It's actually been a help to me. Now, go write the world a best seller! I want to see your name on a book cover and a movie screen!"

"Life is difficult.
This is a great truth, one of the greatest truths.
It is a great truth because once we truly see this truth,
we transcend it.
Once we truly know that life is difficult
—once we truly understand and accept it—
then life is no longer difficult.
Because once it is accepted,
the fact that life is difficult no longer matters."

The Road Less Traveled
M. Scott Peck

Chapter 27

"What's the City Got to Do with This?"

In those days, the *Coffeyville Journal* published six days per week, taking Saturdays off. The weekday editions were delivered in the late afternoons. As soon as paperboys finished the school day, they pedaled their bicycles to the *Journal* and then descended into the basement pressroom. There, they would roll or fold the newspapers that were literally hot off the presses. When they completed enough for their routes, they bagged the papers, placed the newspaper bags across their bicycle handlebars, and headed out to every corner of the town.

But the Sunday edition of the *Journal* was delivered by 8:00 a.m. This meant the editorial staff worked throughout Saturday afternoon and evening to prepare the Sunday newspaper, usually the largest paper of the week in terms of pages. My routine was to show up around 3:30 p.m. and do as I was told in the newsroom until around 11:00 p.m. The hot-type presses would usually begin to rumble by 11:00 p.m. with the first copies being circulated in the pressroom and newsroom, with two or three copies taken over to KGGF next door.

Because of my Saturday schedule, I often picked up Tom Shaney for lunch. Tom worked at an auto supply store on Ninth Street. One summer Saturday, I parked in front of the store and went in to see if Tom was ready for his lunch break.

He was helping a customer so I began to stroll around the store. Mr. Bowser, the owner, knew why I was there and did not approach me as a prospective client. Then I noticed that Tom had a cast on his left forearm and hand. He was not using a sling. I also noticed that he had a bandage on the back of his head and it appeared that the area had been shaved, presumably for the sake of inserting stitches. *"This should be an interesting lunch,"* I thought.

A couple of minutes later, Tom's customer left with a bundle of garden hose. Tom nodded to Mr. Bowser and headed my way. "Let's do it, Billy," he said and we headed to the car. We drove a few blocks over to the Dale Hotel, named after a local man who died in WWI. Our usual lunchtime haunt was the Dale Hotel Coffee Shop. We parked ourselves at the counter. I ordered a club sandwich and Tom got his usual chicken fried steak.

"Break it to me gently, Tom-O," I began. "How did you mangle yourself?"

Tom sipped his *Bubble Up.* "Big Hill," he replied. "Went swimming Wednesday afternoon. I was having a good time. Really a great day to be at the pool and the crowd wasn't too large.

"I swam a few laps. Then I did a few dives off the low board. Sparky Weeks was there and he was diving mainly off the high board. I did the high board once and nearly did a belly-buster so I figured I should stay with the low board."

Sparky Weeks had been on the high school swim team. Now, he was attending Coffeyville Junior College.

"So, you hurt yourself diving?" I asked as our meals were delivered.

"Nope. I didn't hurt myself diving," Tom said. "I hurt myself *sliding.* "

"Good grief, Tom!" I said. Sitting to his left, I tapped on the cast that wrapped his left forearm and hand. "What happened? Did the slide fall on you?" I snickered.

"Really funny, Billy! Thanks for feeling my pain," he said, sprinkling salt on his fries.

Following another drink of *Bubble Up,* Tom said, "After he had spent some time diving, I noticed that Sparky had gone over to the slide. He went down feet first a few times. But then he did a headfirst slide on his back. I was surprised the lifeguard didn't blow his whistle but I suppose the guard figured that Sparky was experienced enough to know what he was doing.

"Anyway, I thought a few slides looked like fun. I did a few. Sparky took a break to take a leak. Some ten-year-old girl and I were the only two using the slide for awhile and then she went back to the shallow end. That's when Sparky came back.

"So, I asked him what I needed to know before making a headfirst slide on my back. Sparky said, 'No big deal. At the top, lie down so that everything from your waist to your head is lying on the slide. Keep your butt and legs on the platform so you can push off. Put your arms on top of your body with your hands over the

146

family jewels. Tilt your head back till it touches the slide and then push off.'

"I told Sparky that I thought I could handle that. But then Sparky said, 'Remember this, Shaney, my friend: Keep your arms over your body and away from the sides of the slide. Also—and make certain you do this—the moment you hit the water tilt your chin all the way forward so you don't bang your head on the bottom of the pool. Got all that?'

"'Piece of cake,' I told Sparky. So up the ladder I went. No one was behind me. I took my time. Laid out just as he said with my butt and legs on the platform. I pulled in my arms, covered the jewels, put the back of my head on the slide, and pushed off."

"Is that when it happened?" I asked.

"Yep. That's when it happened alright," Tom said. He put his knife and fork down, took another swig of *Bubble Up* and swiveled on his counter stool to face me.

"My push off was just as it should have been. But I barely got my legs off the platform when I felt my body wiggle or I thought I felt my body wiggle. Somehow I thought I was at risk of popping over the side and falling onto the concrete. That, of course, was a really stupid thought because that would not have happened. Unfortunately, in my inexperience, I moved my arms and hands out to stabilize myself against the sides of the slide. In so doing, I got my arm and hand under the steel tube that is clamped onto the vertical part of the side. It was like they had cut away twenty-percent of a steel pipe and pressed it down onto the vertical side to make a smooth top. But the underside of the clamped-on pipe was not smooth. There was no weld to seal it and I got myself caught under it."

"Ouch!" I said. "That hurts just hearing about it."

"But wait, there's more." Tom turned back to his chicken fried steak and poured some more catsup onto it. After he carved himself another bite, Tom said, "Remember Sparky said that when I hit the water I should tilt my chin forward so that I didn't bonk my head on the bottom of the pool?"

"Sure, I remember," I said. "Don't tell me you…"

"I'm telling you," Tom interrupted. "I forgot all about tilting my head when I was getting sliced and diced. I hit the water and then I torpedoed the bottom.

"Sparky saw what happened. When I popped up from under the water, he pulled me out of the pool by my right arm. The life guard also saw me crash and burn. He blew his whistle and came running over.

"Out of the water, I was bleeding all over the place. The lifeguard wrapped a towel around my arm to staunch the bleeding there. He had me pull my forearm to my chest, so he could stretch the towel to the back of my head to do some mop up work there.

"That's when Celia came running out from the concession stand with the first aid kit and a couple more towels. They smeared some ointment on the cuts and applied a couple of bandages. They put gauze over the cuts and scrapes and then wrapped my arm in an Ace Bandage. They wrapped another Ace Bandage over the back of my head and then under my chin. I looked like one of those cartoons of some guy with a bad toothache."

"Did they call for an ambulance?" I asked.

"Nah!" Tom said. "The lifeguard, a guy named Freddy, said I should get the cuts looked at but he had done all he could and I was good to go. Celia gave me another towel to take with me but she asked that I would bring it back after I bleached and washed it. I said I would.

"So I went back to the locker room and changed out of my trunks. I got dizzy once when I bent over. But then I left and drove back to the farm. My mom was there. She's a nurse and I knew she'd know what to do.

"When I walked in the back door of our house, Mom was at the kitchen sink peeling potatoes. She took one look at me and said, 'Sit down at the table.' She washed and dried her hands. I said nothing. She walked over to me, put her hands on her hips, and said, 'Someday, I suppose we'll all laugh about this, but today isn't that day, Thomas James Shaney!'

"She quickly took a look at the bloody mess as I began to explain what happened. She cut me off and said, 'I'm not going to have you bleed all over my kitchen. You can hemorrhage all you want at the emergency room. Now, go on back to the pick-up. I'll drive. But first I need to turn off the stove and grab another towel. This is why I have gray hairs, Thomas!'

I was done with my club sandwich. I ordered a slice of chocolate cake and another *Coca Cola*. In those days, a waitress would refill your coffee, tea, or water free of added charge, but if you wanted more pop, you paid. "To go cups" were unheard of.

Looking at his watch, Tom put down his napkin onto the counter. "Bottom line: I sliced muscles in my arm and hand. I was lucky I didn't slice a tendon or nerve. I had thirty-two stitches on my arm and hand. I have to wear this cast for another week so everything can get a good start at mending. I have a bald spot and twelve stitches in my head. I had x-rays that said I did not have any broken bones or a concussion. Everything itches but I can't scratch any of it. Our insurance covers all the expenses except the sixty bucks deductable which Dad says I'm going to pay. Our doctor said everything should be good as new in a month. Other than that it was a great day at the pool."

As I was driving Tom back to work, I asked, "Is the city going to pay for any of your expenses since you hurt yourself at the municipal pool?"

"I asked my dad that question," Tom said. "Dad said, 'Hell no, boy! What's the city got to do with this? You're the one who stuck his hand under the edge when you were told to keep your arms over your body. Gotta learn to be responsible for yourself, son. Why should the good people of Coffeyville pay for some kid's folly? It'll be a sorry day in the U.S.A. if a city were ever to pay a bill like that!'"

Chapter 28

Walking Home from School: Measuring Up and Down

"Let me tell you how you can figure out the size of a girl's boobs." Scott Brentano was a fount of sexual knowledge and I was a very thirsty eighth-grader.

"Look, you're in class," Scott said. "You're sitting behind some girl. She's leaning over her desk writing, or reading, or who gives a hoot what. Just look at the outline of the brassiere strap that runs across the middle of her back. Measure it with a pencil or with a ruler if you can."

"Which way am I measuring, left to right or up and down?"

"Crap, Billy! Don't you know nothing? Up and down, up and down, vertically! Why the hell would you want to measure side-to-side? *Dope!"*

"Up yours, Brentano! Just tell your dang story!" I demanded.

"This is not just a story, Billy-boy. This is science!" Scott declared. "Okay, here's the deal: You measure her strap up-and-down. The base number in this little formula is twenty-four."

"Why twenty-four," I asked.

"Shut up, Howard. This is how the formula works. The engineers that work with the astronauts must have figured it out. Who knows? Who gives a rip? I'm telling you the base number is twenty-four!

"Now, listen carefully, Billy: For every one-eighth inch of her strap, she's got an extra inch of *boo-zoom* to add to the base number of twenty-four. So, if she's wearing a half-inch brassiere strap, that's only four-eighths. Add twenty-four and you got twenty-eight inches. Way too small. Throw her back in. If she's got a one inch strap—up and down, remember—then that's good for eight-eighths. Add eight to the 24 and the tittie total is up to thirty-two inches. Now we're getting somewhere."

"But listen to this news flash," Scott said as he stopped at the corner of Lincoln and Washita. "In math class, I sit behind Connie Smoot. I swear on my not-yet-dead-mother's grave, yesterday Smoot was wearing a strap that was two inches—not left to right,

151

man—but up and down. Do you realize what that adds up to? Twenty-four plus sixteen! *Forty!* Can you believe it? *Forty inches of ecstasy!* I would so love to give her a milk shake!"

The next day in history class, I was so entranced by Norma Dubwig's 1.5-inch strap that I failed to hear Mrs. Hendrix call my name three times to answer a question about *Sun Yat Sen.* I spent thirty minutes after school prying gum from under the student desks. As I scraped, the same thought kept running through my mind:

$$24 + 12 = 36$$

Would I ever lay my hands on such treasure?

"Snow and adolescence are the only problems
that disappear if you ignore them long enough."

Earl Wilson
Newspaper Columnist

Chapter 29

Disease Under the Elms?

One fine day, I was riding my bicycle back from the *Journal* when I spotted a City of Coffeyville cherry-picker truck parked in front of our house. The arm of the cherry-picker was fully-extended. In the bucket was a city worker who was using a chisel to chip bark off of the elm tree on our parking. He was placing the bark pieces into a brown paper sack.

Another worker aside the controls of the cherry picker was in the process of using a brace and bit to drill into the lower trunk of the elm tree. He had another brown paper sack to hold what the drill extracted.

I parked my bicycle under the carport and then walked out to the parking.

"Hello!" I said. "I live in this house. Whatcha doing, mister?"

"Hiya kid," the city worker said. He stepped away from the tree for a moment, pulled off his hardhat, and wiped his forearm shirtsleeve across his forehead. He looked up at his colleague in the bucket and then over to me.

"We're checking for beetles—*bark beetles,*" the city worker said. His sweaty uniform shirt had the name "Burt" stitched over the left pocket.

"What are bark beetles?" I asked.

"They're like *Typhoid Mary.* You know who she was, right?"

"Yeah, sure," I replied. "She was the carrier who started the typhoid epidemic. She didn't get sick but people she came in contact with did and most of them died. Am I right?"

"Sounds right to me, kid," Burt said. "Bark beetles don't get sick either unless we poison them. Bark beetles are moving across the country from the east carrying *Dutch Elm Disease.* That contagion will kill an elm tree every time. They've got the scourge over in the Joplin area now, maybe already into Kansas at Chetopa or Pittsburg. That's bad news. Now, we're going around town looking for the dang insects, drilling core samples, and chipping away bark samples so the arborists—arborists are tree experts—so the arborists can determine if we have any infestation in Coffeyville."

"You said, '*Dutch Elm Disease,*'" I said. "Aren't these *'American Elms?'*"

"Correcto-mundo, kid!" Burt said. "But the word 'Dutch' in this case means where they discovered what kind of disease the bark beetles were carrying. They figured it out over in the Netherlands—you know, Holland. The people there are called *'Dutch,'*" Burt said as he returned to his drilling. "Unfortunately, knowing just exactly what the disease is doesn't mean we're able to do anything about it. We can't vaccinate an elm tree like we give polio shots to people."

"So have you found any bark beetles in Coffeyville or here on Lincoln Street?" I asked.

"I haven't seen any of the bugs yet. Burt said. "Me and my buddy Jose up there are just beginning to pull samples. We'll label these sacks as to where we found the samples and then the city will send them off to Kansas State University in Manhattan for analysis to see whether the creepy crawlers have already been here. Don't know when we'll hear back from K-State."

"If you do find *Dutch Elm Disease* in Coffeyville, what happens to the infected elms in town? There must be hundreds, maybe even thousands," I said.

"Not much you can do, kid, except mark the elms with a big 'X' and cut them down. The wood can't even be used in your fireplace. They've gotta burn it all with kerosene in some gravel pit to keep the bark beetles from moving on down the road."

"Yo, Burt, bring me down," Jose said from above.

"Coming down," Burt said as he maneuvered the levers on the side of the city truck.

"And just so you know, kid—you might want to tell your folks this—if we do find evidence of *Dutch Elm Disease*, the city will only remove the trees that are public, like this one here on the parking. If the tree is on your own property, the city will give you thirty days to take it down and burn it up. If you don't, the city will do it and add it to your property tax."

"*Wow!*" I said. "We've got two elm trees in the backyard."

"Well, nobody's gonna cut down anything anytime soon," Burt said, climbing into the truck cab to drive away. "But, just in case, I suggest you enjoy the shade and your hammock while you can. See ya, kid!"

Chapter 30

Young Love III

"The course of true love never did run smooth."

A Midsummer Night's Dream
William Shakespeare

As we moved into our junior year of high school, Carly Delgreco attained her sixteen candles. She was allowed to date. There was a line of would-be suitors. Carly's reputation had only been enhanced as she topped out at 5'4" and popped out to a 34C (according to Scott Brentano's scientific calculations).

I had not sought to ask Carly out on a date. With work and extra-curricular activities, I was challenged with my homework. I had finally admitted to myself that I wanted to be the first person in my family to achieve a college degree. Belatedly, I had learned that admission to the college of my choice would require good grades. Such grades were not a hallmark of my academic career but I was improving.

As our junior year came to a close and I began to consider my senior year at FKHS, Carly kept coming to mind. There was no connection between Carly and my studies. We only had one class together which was *Stage Production.* Finally, one evening as I was walking along Lincoln Street, it occurred to me that *I missed Carly.* That evening, as I did a couple of exercise loops of Lincoln Street, I hatched a grand plan of attack. I was going to ask Carly out on a date and then ask her out on more dates, if she would have me.

I was pretty certain that my request for a date would not impair the friendship that we had already built. If she said no to going out with me, I would be disappointed. But Carly would always be an honored icon on the mantel of my mind.

The Hillcrest Country Club on the way to Big Hill had a banquet room and patio that could be rented by Coffeyville residents. Geraldine Frenk's parents anted-up the bucks to rent the place for an end of the school year party. Though Geraldine and I had less and less in common as the years passed, she graciously included the Lincoln Street gang on the invitation list. I responded affirmatively to the invitation, but said I would be late due to my work at the *Coffeyville Journal.*

It was the Saturday night following graduation. All former juniors such as I rejoiced in our new status as *"seniors,"* finally the *top dogs* of FKHS! I pulled into the country club parking lot an hour after the soirée had begun. My parking spot was the farthest away from the club due to my tardiness. As I walked past the other cars, I spotted Carly coming out of the clubhouse with her purse in hand and apparently heading for her car. I jogged the short distance to her.

"Hi, Carly! I hope you're not leaving. I just got here," I said. "I had to work late at the paper."

We met behind her car. "Hi, Billy! I have to leave early. I promised my mom I'd help her with the packing."

"Packing?" I said. "Where are you going?"

Carly placed her purse on the trunk of her car. She reached out and took my hands. "We're moving, Billy. We're moving to the Chicago area within the next two weeks. My dad is already there."

I could not believe what I was hearing. *"You're moving to Chicago!* Why? What's happened?"

Carly pulled my hands behind her back for me to hug her. She wrapped her arms around me. She pressed her cheek upon my chest. "Oh, Billy, it's so terrible. We just got word three days ago. Daddy says Continental Can may close the Coffeyville plant sometime in this next year. They want him at their headquarters in Schaumburg to help make the decision. If they decide to close down the Coffeyville plant, he will have to decide which workers are offered a transfer and who will be laid off. My dad's not happy about this either, but he has no other job prospects. This came as a surprise to all of us."

"Oh God, Carly. I can't believe this. Who could ever equal you as a dance partner? What am I saying? *To hell with the dancing!* I'd give up our dances if it meant you could stay here, Carly. You've been so, so nice to me! With all my foul ups with my parents and at school, you've been a very bright light for me! You're a great girl, Carly! Illinois doesn't know what it's getting!

Carly began to wipe back tears. "Don't make me cry, Billy. You're the person that I will miss most—you, the most! I've prayed to Jesus and Mary but there has been no change. Oh Billy, promise me you'll write to me. I'll send you my address in Illinois as soon as we get one."

"Absolutely, Carly. I'll write to you. Please write back to me. Carly, we'll see each other again. I'm sure of it! In a year, we'll be out of high school. Who knows? Maybe we'll go to college close to one another. We could show up at some college dance and wow the crowd there. They'll cheer for us just as they have here."

She looked up at me. With tears streaming down her cheeks, Carly smiled and said, "Oh, Billy, we must be the greatest dancers in the history of Coffeyville!" I laughed. She laughed. We both knew we were merely two big dancing frogs in a small Kansas pond!

Then our eyes locked. In unison, we pressed into each other and kissed. It was a long, long, wondrous kiss. She finally stepped back and took my hands again.

"I must go, Billy. I promised my mother. Let's not make this any harder than it is. I'll write to you soon." She picked up her purse.

I said, "Carly, I will so miss you. I'm already aching!"

Carly snapped away to open her car door. She quickly backed out and pulled away. I stood watching as a cloud of dust and numbness began to envelop me. Carly's car was nearly to the parking lot exit when it stopped. Carly put the car in park with the engine running. She stepped out of the car and stood between the door and the driver's seat facing me.

With a shout, Carly said *"I love you, Billy Howard!"*

With that, she re-entered her car and drove away.

I don't know how long I had been sitting on the bumper of my car.

"Billy Howard, is that you?" The voice belonged to Axel Blair, the steady boyfriend of Geraldine Frenk.

"Geraldine was wondering where you were. She knew you'd be some late. Now, she'll be glad you're here. I just came out to the car to get Geraldine's sweater. Let's go, Billy. They've still got hot dogs and cold tater tots."

I went to the party. I remember none of it. I don't think I was there more than thirty minutes before I left. I cruised around town till nearly midnight. When I got home, my parents were already in bed, thankfully. I sat in the dark of the family room till 3:30 a.m. before finally going to bed.

"Ever has it been that love knows not its own depth until the hour of separation."

The Prophet
Kahlil Gibran

Chapter 31

What a Drag!

June 10 was the second Friday following graduation from FKHS. Paulie Pyle had chosen the post-graduation date so that any parental problems that might accrue from the event, however onerous, would not impinge upon his final days in high school. Paulie's parents had no interest in blocking his matriculation to Kansas University. They were resigned to the fact that their oversight leverage with their only child was quickly waning.

During the time following the Pig Stand accord, Paulie did little to enhance the racing mettle of his Thunderbird. He had changed the oil. He personally checked the air pressure in his tires. With the running of the Memorial Day *Indianapolis 500* race only days past, Paulie thought the bald spots on his Michelins would give him an Indy car competitive advantage over Brillo. The drag race would be a fitting finale for his present tires. He knew he would have no problem convincing his father to install a new set of tires for him before heading off to KU and golfing fame. Paulie also checked his radiator water, washed the T-Bird, and squeegeed his windows. He would race with his ragtop down. Graduated *Golden Tornado* cheerleader Toni Weinstein was going to be Paulie's date for the night, though she would not race with him. Paulie was looking forward to his post-race private celebration with the beautiful and savvy young Jewess.

Brillo Stubblefield went about his race preparations very differently than Paulie. He had actually given some thought to lifting the engine, but he concluded that was not necessary in light of Uncle Bub pronouncing the *ZoZomobile* to be in excellent shape. However, he did replace plugs and points, the water hose, and fan belt. Every day prior to the race, he checked the timing and the air pressure in his tires. Brillo thought his baby was purring!

Brillo and his Uncle Bub had collaborated on overlaying the white station wagon with the *ZoZomobile* design. Emblazoned on the side panels in gold and black lettering was *"Zozomobile"* with flames coming off the tail of the name. *"ZZ"* was painted on the

161

hood and back door panel. Brillo was convinced that no one with a nickel's worth of sense would thereafter think of his beast as *"the Hearse."* The resplendent *ZoZomobile* was an *"I'm Going to Eat Your Ass"* hot rod!

Four days before the race, Brillo began cruising around town with his new *ZoZomobile* colors. Brillo was delighted and proud of the attention the newly decorated station wagon received. Public acclaim was a good thing, Brillo concluded.

Brillo sent a buddy to South Coffeyville, Oklahoma, to purchase a discounted stash of beer to be used at the post-race party he was planning at Uncle Bub's garage. Brillo had no date for the night of the race but good buds, good *Budweiser,* and the thrill of victory would be more than sufficient to warm his heart.

The Friday, June 10, drag race venue was *Harold C. McGugin Field*, named after the late Congressman from nearby Liberty who had practiced law in Coffeyville. During WWII, McGugin Field was established as a training site by the U.S. Army Air Forces. Following WWII, the airfield was converted to an industrial park. For many years, the industrial park's largest client was Continental Can Company.

McGugin Field had two runways. Runway 4-22 ran southwest to northeast. The main runway, 17-35, went south to north. Daytime air traffic was generated by private civil aviation and corporate planes that ferried industrial park executives and technicians in and out of Coffeyville.

From time to time over the post-war years, weekend, daylight drag races had been sponsored on the south/north runway of McGugin Field. There were also reports of unsponsored night-time drag races staged by Coffeyville youth. The police or sheriff rarely reached the airfield prior to the conclusion of such impromptu races.

The main entrance to McGugin Field was from two west-facing gates along U.S. 169. Those gates were locked at night. However, nearly every Coffeyville native knew that you could gain access to the industrial park by taking U.S. 169 approximately one-half mile north of McGugin Field and then turning right on Angola Road. A half-mile east on Angola Road, anyone could enter McGugin Field by turning right on the gravelly Second Street. The airfield was large enough to have a grid of named and numbered streets that crisscrossed the industrial park. Some roads were paved. Some were not.

The first street to intersect Second Street was a perimeter road. A left turn and then a right turn would put a driver parallel to Runway 17-35. Forty yards east of the perimeter road was a drainage channel that was only ten yards off the runway. The drainage channel had a small berm on the west side. Drivers put their front tires on the berm so that their headlights would illuminate a portion of Runway 17-35.

People began showing up at the airfield around 8:30 p.m., just as a full moon was rising. At the intersection of Angola Road and Second Street, Axel Blair stood sentry with a flashlight. Anytime a car turned off U.S. 169, the Axel would blink his flashlight at the oncoming car. People headed for McGugin field would recognize the signal and slow to turn onto Second Street. Drivers doused their headlights and navigated with their parking lights only. Other sentries with flashlights were posted along Second Street and the perimeter road.

At the berm, cars were spaced out to provide full high-beam headlight coverage of the portion of Runway 17-35 that would be used for the race. Most drag race courses are one-eighth of a mile or one-quarter of a mile. No sticklers for drag racing protocol, both Brillo and Paulie agreed to a course that was approximately one-third of a mile. Each felt the longer course would best illustrate the quick start and rapid acceleration capabilities of their rides.

Tom Shaney and I had driven to the event in Tom's pick-up. We parked on the berm about five or six yards to the left of the already positioned Volkswagen driven by Carolyn Rousters with Geraldine Frenk at shotgun. On the other side of the beetle were Carly Delgreco and her cheerleading colleague Toni Weinstein, Paulie Pyle's post-race squeeze. Beyond Carly's Mercury were Scott Brentano and his date Audie Rice. Scott was driving his Packard, a car no longer manufactured. Nevertheless, Scott said it ran well. He was especially proud of the Packard's white sidewall tires.

Spectators were invited onto the tarmac to walk the course and toss any litter, stones, or other debris to one side or the other of the runway. As Tom and I headed toward the tarmac to take our turn at trash removal, I nodded a "hi" to Carly and Toni. Carly and I locked eyes for a moment. We waved at each other and then she turned away to talk to Toni. I hoped to talk with her before everyone left the airport after the race.

As Tom and I walked the tarmac, Brillo and Paulie slowly cruised their vehicles up and back the course, revving their engines to impress and annoy the crowd.

"Hi guys!" Brillo said as he eased along side of us. "I hope you've got other plans for the night. This little race ain't gonna take long—at least, it's not going to take me long."

"Good luck, Brillo!" I said. "The hype is over. Now, we'll see what's really what!"

"Don't blow your engine, Brillo!" Tom said. "Nobody in the crowd wants to mop up streaks of oil and STP!"

"Chevy engines don't blow, Mr. Shaney!" Brillo said. "Stop by the garage when the race is done for a little liquid afterglow, if you catch my meaning."

"We catch your meaning, Brillo. See you there. I hope you'll still be in one piece!" Tom said.

"That's right, Brillo, be safe!" I said. "You don't want Mrs. Bryant, the KGGF safety lady, to get on your case." Brillo laughed and pulled away.

As Tom and I were making our return walk on the runway, Paulie Pyle and his black Thunderbird matched our pace. "Evening, gents," Paulie said. "Did you get yourselves a good vantage point to see this race of the century?"

"Yeah, we did, Paulie. Just past the mid-point. We'll see it all, from start to finish. You are planning to finish, aren't you?" Tom teased.

"Don't be a smartass, Shaney, or I won't autograph your jockstrap," Paulie replied.

"Looks like you really spiffed up the shine of this bird," I said. "Did you shine up anything on the inside?"

"Oh, I did a little of this and a little of that," Paulie said. "Don't tell Brillo, but I actually fed my gas tank with some *Gumout* and mothballs. But really, my little chickadees, there was not all that much to do. I regularly get this baby up to one-hundred-twenty on U.S. 166. On a short course like this, my black beauty won't even break a sweat."

"I thought about bringing out some ten-penny nails from the store and laying them down on the track to see how you boys would do on your rims," Tom said.

"You should have done that," Paulie replied. "These Michelins would fly right over them. You'll notice that I have smoothed out the tread so that I am essentially running on *Formula One* tires. Tomorrow, I'm going to ship these victory tires to the *Hot Rod Hall of Fame.*"

"Whatever you say, Paulie," Tom replied. "Just keep everything together for a third of a mile and we'll all go home happy, no matter who wins."

"'No matter who wins?' I can't believe you just said that, Shaney. With the bucket of junk, Brillo's driving, it wouldn't surprise me if I'm the *only* racer to cross the finish line tonight. Don't bet against me, Thomas!"

As Paulie pulled away, I said, "Well, it seems they're both confident. Maybe it will be a photo-finish."

"I really don't care who wins," Tom said. "I figure that Brillo will still be serving that liquid afterglow at Uncle Bub's garage no matter what happens."

As we arrived back at Tom's pickup, Scott Brentano passed by saying that Paulie and his T-Bird were three-to-one favorites. But Scott, always the contrarian, had put five bucks on the *ZoZomobile*.

By 9:00 p.m. the tarmac had been cleared. Harley Powell, one of the three finish line judges, told the spectators to turn off their lights to save their batteries as the race was being delayed ten minutes merely to permit latecomers to see the spectacle. We were also told to put some sort of cover over the taillights so that as little attention as possible would be drawn to the site from cars passing on U.S. 169.

It was interesting to see how folks configured their viewing sites for what was going to be less than a thirty-second race. Tom and I were seated on the front fenders of his pick-up with our feet resting on the bumper. Carolyn Rousters and Geraldine Frenk had taken a blanket closer to the drainage ditch and plopped down, hugging their knees. Carly and Toni were on top of the Delgreco's Mercury with their legs resting on the windshield. Scott and Audie were standing between the line of cars and the drainage ditch. Audie was in front of Scott who had his arms wrapped around her waist, pulling her to him. Others had left their cars to sit in lawn chairs. Many people were sipping pop bottles, maybe even a beer bottle or two.

Then, from the finish line end of the row of cars, came the signal to *light 'em up*. Runway 17-35 was flooded in moonlight and car lights. By that time, the entire one-third mile course was well lit.

Rick Hulsey had volunteered to serve as the race starter. A three judge panel of Harley Powell, Hap Barber, and Johnny Wishall were at the finish line to determine the victor. Hap Barber positioned himself on the far side of the track while Harley and Johnny were on the near side. Harley waved his arm to affirm the judges were ready and set.

Paulie honked the Thunderbird's horn and Brillo followed with the *ZoZomobile's aahh-oooga* horn. Brillo was in the near lane and Paulie was to his left. They were racing from north to south. There was only the slightest of breezes from the southwest.

The two drivers revved their engines. Twin brothers Micah and Malachi Stover stepped to the outside of each bumper to assure that the two cars were evenly positioned at the start line. Rick Hulsey, the flagman, walked south, down the center of the runway, some twenty yards or so. He then stepped off the runway to the far side. He was carrying a three-foot length of one-inch dowel that had a white dishtowel tacked to it. The only sound was the idling of the race cars. The crowd began to hold its breath.

Slowly, the flagman lifted the dowel in his right hand while holding the dishtowel close to the pole with his left hand. He did not trifle with the drag racers. Almost as soon as the arcing pole reached its zenith, he released the dishtowel and furiously waved the start flag.

Immediately, the engines of the Thunderbird and *ZoZomobile* roared. Tires squealed as they peeled forward. The two racers were even for the first three-hundred yards. Then Paulie's top-down T-Bird began to pull away. As they were approaching the mid-point, the T-Bird's back wheels were even with the *ZoZomobile's* front bumper. The spectators were leaning forward or standing, everyone screaming their support for Paulie or Brillo.

It is true. Life does go into slow motion when the unspeakable rushes toward you.

Paulie's bald right-front tire blew out with a huge bang. With tread flying into the air, the T-Bird immediately veered right and crossed the *ZoZomobile* which slammed into the right rear-end of the Thunderbird. As Brillo slammed on his brakes, the *ZoZomobile* whirled down the track, performing three three-sixty spins. The finish line judges bolted away from the track. In a cloud of white smoke and with the screech of straining brakes, the station wagon crossed the finish line just as its radiator blew, spewing steaming water through the grill. Neither Brillo nor Paulie were wearing helmets but Brillo did have on a waist-belt, a relatively new automotive accessory. Despite the belt, Brillo's head had smashed into the windshield, cracking both head and glass. Blood began to gush. Finish line judge Hap Barber was quick to his side.

While the *ZoZomobile* remained on Runway 17-35, Paulie's Thunderbird did a right-angle turn off the track. Brillo's collision with the T-Bird's right rear momentarily caused the black car to tilt into the air, with only the left side tires on the ground. When the T-Bird banged back down to all four wheels, the right front rim had virtually no tire remaining. Still moving at a high speed west toward the spectators, the T-Bird nose-dived into the drainage ditch and Paulie flew out the driver-side door, his arms flailing. When the driverless T-Bird hit the drainage ditch, it rebounded twenty feet into the air and sailed into a trajectory that targeted the row of headlights. With both doors open, the crumbling T-Bird descended toward the screaming onlookers.

I stood straight up on the pickup's bumper. Tom Shaney leapt onto the pickup's hood and crouched, looking at the diving T-Bird. The VW next to us was empty. At the Delgreco's Mercury, Toni Weinstein jumped off the roof and crouched between it and Scott Brentano's old Packard.

Carly stood up on the hood of the Mercury, frozen. She looked up and saw the T-Bird's hood fly away. The empty driver/passenger compartment was coming directly toward her. She thrust both arms into the air as if she were going to catch the errant Thunderbird. As she reached up, Carly screamed "JESUS!"

The crash of the Thunderbird onto the Mercury was thunderous! At the impact, I immediately jumped down from the bumper to climb across the Volkswagen in an attempt to rescue Carly. I barely placed my knee on the VW's hood, when the Thunderbird and Mercury exploded in a fireball. Tom Shaney, who was coming right behind me, and I were blown off the VW whose windows were shattered. When I hit the ground, I felt my left wrist crack. Then I felt the heat from the flames. Something had hit me in the head. Something worse had hit me in the heart. As I struggled to get up off the ground, all the lights went out.

Chapter 32

A Dark Night of the Soul

*"Sometimes it takes darkness
and the sweet confinement of your aloneness
to learn."*

Sweet Darkness
David Whyte

Removed as I am in time and space from the events at McGugin Field on that full-moon June night, I still wince whenever I reflect upon it. Yet, I've realized over the intervening years that everyone has races, collisions, and explosions strewn throughout their lives. Such events make us or break us. Either way, they shape us. Here is the reckoning for that long day's journey into night:

When disaster strikes, some people are immobilized, others are *galvanized.*

Harley Powell was running away from Brillo Stubblefield's whirling station wagon when he saw Paulie Pyle ejected from the Thunderbird. Paulie landed on his back in the drainage ditch which had been softened by a trickle of rainwater from earlier in the day. When the Thunderbird and Mercury exploded, Harley and several others in proximity were knocked to the ground by the blast. As Harley regained his footing, he spotted the Stover twins, both of whom, Harley knew, were working toward becoming Eagle Scouts.

"Micah! Malachi! Tend to Paulie!" Harley yelled.

Scott Brentano told his knocked-down date Audie Rice to stay on the ground while he ran toward his car that was five or six yards from the burning vehicles. The left side windows of his blue 1950 Packard Custom had been blown out and the windshield cracked. Flying debris from the explosion caused the left side of the Packard to look as if it had been strafed by a machine gun. Amazingly, his tires were intact. Scott entered the passenger side of the Packard and then slid behind the wheel to drive it forward, away from further damage from the inferno.

On the other side of the fire, Tom Shaney picked himself up off the ground and saw that I was unconscious but breathing. Tom jumped into Carolyn Rousters VW. The keys were in the ignition and Tom quickly backed the bug away from the burning cars. Then he leapt out and barked, *"I need some blankets and a Boy Scout over here now!"*

Harley spotted Hap Barber, Paulie Pyle's cruising mate and witness to the Pig Stand accord, running to him from the *ZoZomobile*. He had been on the far side of the finish line and was the first to reach Brillo Stubblefield when the station wagon had come to a halt.

"How's Brillo?" Harley asked.

"He's dizzy," Hap replied. "His head hit the windshield but he was belted so he didn't go through. He's got a gash on his head but Rick Hulsey will stop the bleeding one way or another and stay with him. How bad is Paulie?"

"Don't know. He's breathing. The Stover twins are working on him and others are holding him down. I don't think he's conscious but I also don't think he's dying. Thank goodness for soggy drainage ditches!"

"Listen, Harley," Hap said, "I'm going to go lay hands on Paulie and pray for him. Then I'll round up as many kids as I can and move 'em down to the end of the row. I'll calm them down and we'll start praying."

"Pray that God will turn the clock back thirty minutes," Harley said.

Hap headed for the drainage ditch and Paulie Pyle. Scott Brentano, driving his Packard, wheeled up to Harley who was pulling a small fire extinguisher from the cab of his pickup. As Audie Rice ran to get into her date's Packard, Scott yelled, "Harley, I'm going to the payphone in front of the aviation office to call for help." Audie was still pulling her passenger door closed as Scott peeled away.

Harley Powell quickly joined two other guys who had small fire extinguishers in their cars. They ringed three sides of the burning crash scene and spewed CO_2 onto the mangled Thunderbird and Mercury. Despite the risk of a flare-up or another explosion, the flames were knocked-down moments before the fire extinguishers exhausted their contents.

The fire-fighting trio avoided the right side of Carly Delgreco's car where Toni Weinstein had taken worthless cover. They did not attempt to peer between the layered cars to find Carly. They had no interest in imprinting the death scene any deeper into their psyches than was already the case. The volunteer firemen dropped the extinguishers and moved elsewhere to help.

While waiting for the ambulance, Micah and Malachi ministered to the unconscious Paulie Pyle. After noting that Paulie's breathing was steady though labored, the brothers sought to immobilize the injured racer. Johnny Wishall and Alice Lightstone held Paulie's arms while Carolyn Rousters braced his head.

Despite the fact that he was lying in a wet drainage ditch, the twins did not want to move Paulie. Micah used his pocket knife to slice open Paulie's pant legs. Paulie had an obvious compound fracture of his left leg as part of the fibula protruded through the skin. Sight of the fracture caused both Johnny and Alice to gasp and wince but they maintained their hold on Paulie's arms. Paulie's nose looked broken and he had a scalp wound whose bleeding was clotting due to the pressure Malachi was applying to it.

Rick Hulsey, the flagman, had raced down the track to help Brillo. He was conscious but his stomach was aching due to the restraint of the seatbelt. More seriously, Brillo had a bleeding gash on his forehead where he had banged into the windshield despite his waist restraint. Brillo was also massaging his neck which doubtless had whiplashed. Rick helped Brillo into the back seat of the *ZoZomobile*. Rick pulled off his t-shirt and used it to staunch the bleeding from Brillo's head wound.

Suddenly, Brillo lurched his upper body past Rick to vomit out the door, splattering Rick's shoes and pants. Brillo said he felt dizzy, so Rick had him lie down. He kept Brillo talking in an attempt to keep him conscious. Brillo's speech was slurred and sometimes incoherent. The *ZoZomobile* sat atop the finish line with one flattened tire. A slow stream of steam oozed out of the grill and from under the hood.

Seventy to eighty people had gathered for the drag race. There were probably thirty-five to forty vehicles that cast their lights upon Runway 17-35. After the collisions, explosion, and fire, half the cars quickly left the airfield.

The industrial park's civil security was divided between the Montgomery County Sheriff's Office and the Coffeyville Police Department. Scott Brentano had reached the CPD. Others called the sheriff's office. Within twenty minutes of the accident, a dozen sets of flashing lights from both jurisdictions were on scene to untangle what had transpired.

Tom Shaney had not a scintilla of interest in those who had left the site. He was concerned about those who were left on site. In particular, he was laboring to get me to the hospital emergency room ASAP.

Tom was using his handkerchief to staunch the wound over my left eye and telling me to wake up. Porter Downey ran up to the driver's side of Tom's pickup. Porter actually was an Eagle Scout.

"What do you need, Tom?" Porter asked as he saw me moaning on the ground.

Without looking up, Tom said, "In the bed of the truck, there's a tarp and a blanket underneath it. Put the tarp on the bed with the blanket spread out on top. See if you can get two more blankets and some sort of head rest. We've got to get Billy away from Carly and Toni before he wakes up. We'll take him straight to the ER. You can ride with him in the back of the pickup. I have no idea how long it will take an ambulance to get here. But when it does get here, the attendants can deal with Paulie and Brillo."

Porter was already unfolding the tarp as Tom finished his instructions. "Sounds good to me," Porter said of Tom's plan.

Geraldine Frenk ran up to the side of the pickup carrying two blankets which Porter took from her. "Thanks, Geraldine, he said. "Now find some sort of pillow or head rest."

Geraldine raced to Carolyn Rousters scorched VW. In the back seat, Carolyn kept a sofa pillow which she hugged when she went to a drive-in movie with one of her girlfriends. (If she had a date with a boy, no pillow was required as she could hug him.)

Geraldine returned to the pickup and tossed the pillow into the bed. Meantime, Tom had ripped his handkerchief in two and tied the ends to make a pressure bandage for my head wound.

"That should hold till we get to the ER, Tom said. "Help me put Billy in the back."

Tom and Porter lugged me like a sack of potatoes to the back of the pickup. Tom placed my upper body onto the tailgate. Then Tom jumped onto the bed to pull me across the pallet that they had manufactured. He placed my head on Carolyn's pillow and covered me with a blanket. As Tom hopped over the side to get into the cab, Porter jumped into the bed, pulled the tailgate shut, and sat down beside me.

"Geraldine, we're going to Fourth Street and across to the hospital if anyone wants to know. Thanks for the help" Tom said as he put the pickup into gear and pulled away.

Harley Powell stationed sentries around Brillo, Paulie, the skid marks, and the burnt cars so that investigators would be able to examine a relatively undefiled accident scene.

It didn't take long for Hap Barber to round up those students who were not working the accident. He led them to the finish line end of the row of cars. On the grass between the cars and the drainage ditch, two groups had formed.

The first group, the smaller of the two, contained the inconsolable—all girls—who were sobbing and occasionally screaming. Most of those girls had boyfriends with them who were trying to comfort their dates. But the guys had also been shaken to the core by the events of the night. One set of grieving sophomores departed the circle and drove away.

The second group, the larger of the two, contained students standing, kneeling, or lying face down on the ground, praying to God. They were astonishingly calm and measured in their prayers, continuing to lift their petitions to the Lord long after the emergency workers were on scene.

I will always be grateful that I did not regain consciousness next to those charred cars and bodies.

As Tom Shaney crossed the Verdigris River back into town, the police cars, fire truck and ambulance passed us going the other direction. The sirens woke me up for a moment. All I could think of was *"why is my bed bouncing?"* I was really puzzled when I saw

Porter Downey hovering over me and pulling a blanket up under my chin. That's when I blanked out again.

The *Journal's* staff photographer—Grady Brunger—arrived to document the venue for the police and for the newspaper. Since the drag race was on a Friday night, there would be no edition of the *Journal* until Sunday. The staff would have plenty of time to prepare their reports. KGGF, however, was able to break the story Saturday morning. As the news spread, a pall descended upon the town.

Carly Delgreco and Toni Weinstein were killed instantly by the impact of the Thunderbird upon them. The explosion of the T-Bird and Mercury rendered their remains unrecognizable. Identification was via dental charts.

Brillo Stubblefield sustained head lacerations, a brain concussion, plus numerous cuts and abrasions. He was hospitalized for a week because of his head injury. Cobbie, the hospital orderly, regularly delivered Popsicles to Brillo.

The *ZoZomobile* sustained comparatively minor damage. The radiator had blown and a tire was ruined. The right-front fender and the bumper would have to be replaced. The station wagon was towed the next day to Uncle Bub's garage.

Paulie Pyle had a brain concussion. His head wound required nineteen stitches. He had three cracked vertebrae, a broken collarbone, a broken pelvis, a ruptured spleen, and a broken left leg. After twenty-four hours at Coffeyville Memorial Hospital, Paulie was taken to Wesley Medical Center in Wichita where he remained for three weeks.

Tom Shaney pulled into the emergency entrance to Coffeyville Memorial Hospital. He dashed into the waiting room to solicit help which was quickly forthcoming. The medical team assessed me as having a broken left wrist, a punctured left eyebrow that needed to be cleaned out and sutured back together, and most likely a concussion.

As the technician was positioning my left hand for the x-rays, I came to. "What's happening?" I asked, attempting to sit up. A nurse pushed me back down on the gurney. She gave me a brief report as to where I was and why. She also asked if I knew where my parents could be contacted. "Your friend Tom tried your home phone but there was no answer."

I said, "Try the Moose Lodge." There, my parents were located and said they would be at the hospital within ten minutes.

I was hospitalized for three nights. I was released in time for the funerals.

That first night at the hospital, no one said anything to me about Carly and Toni. No one said anything to me about Paulie or Brillo. Everyone knew what had happened. I knew what had happened. None who had gathered around me were in denial. I was not in denial. But I was numb—not merely from the medications—but mainly from the horrible events at the airfield that had battered all of us present for the drag race..

On that beautifully moonlit night, Coffeyville cried itself to sleep.

Chapter 33

Truths and Consequences

"How strange it is to view a town you grew up in,
not in wonderment through the eyes of youth,
but with the eyes of an historian on the way things were."

Marvin Allan Williams
Novelist

When the all-grown-up Dr. Scott Brentano and I savored nightcaps at the Willard Hotel in Washington, D.C., he exhorted me to flesh out our lives growing up in Coffeyville, Kansas, our hometown. Tell the story of the way it was, the way we were, and the manner in which *"the way we were"* influenced the way we now are. One of my skeptical responses to Scott was that readers of the mid-1980s and later, would be challenged to believe the collective small town naiveté, mores, and worldview perspectives that were extant in southeastern Kansas *a mere* twenty-five to thirty years prior.

The following description of the aftermath of what in Coffeyville became known as the *"airfield disaster"* illustrates my point. The sum of the aftermath can be disclosed in one two-sentence paragraph:

> *"The 'airfield disaster' with its deaths*
> *and injuries, happened because of a couple*
> *of cocky, competitive drag racers and a*
> *bunch of dang fool kids who egged them on.*
> *Well, the whole lot of them, sure-as-shootin,'*
> *learned a bucket-full of life lessons that*
> *moon-for-the-misbegotten night!"*

Here are the truths and consequences that emanated from that *"misbegotten night:"*

177

Legal

The only two persons prosecuted for the evening's events were Paulie Pyle and Brillo Stubblefield.

Following a six week investigation by local, county, and state agencies, Paulie Pyle was charged with trespassing, reckless operation of a motor vehicle, unauthorized racing, reckless endangerment of others, and two counts of vehicular manslaughter. A week before the trial date, in a plea bargain agreement, Paulie pled guilty to reckless operation of a motor vehicle and the two counts of vehicular manslaughter. Judge Abraham Lincoln Sappenfield rendered the agreed upon sentence: Six months in the Montgomery County jail at Independence, five years probation, a one thousand dollar fine, plus court costs.

Paulie began serving his sentence a week prior to Thanksgiving. While incarcerated, he had a steady stream of visitors. He was released from jail the following April, one month earlier than scheduled, due to good behavior. Upon discharge, Paulie moved to Russell, Kansas, west of Salina to reside upon and work on his grandparents' farm. His golf scholarship to Kansas University was revoked. As summer arrived, Paulie enrolled at Fort Hays State College. He did not join a fraternity. Fort Hays State did not have a golf team.

Thereafter, Paulie did not return to Coffeyville, except to visit his parents. When he did so, he did not contact any of his friends, nor did he cruise the streets.

Lester "Brillo" Stubblefield ultimately accepted a deal whereby he pled guilty to the two counts of vehicular manslaughter. He was sentenced to four months in the county jail, three years of probation, a one thousand dollar fine, plus court costs. He, too, had many visitors and was released two weeks ahead of schedule due to good behavior. Brillo returned to Coffeyville, working at Uncle Bub's and taking classes at Coffeyville Junior College.

Brillo never drove the *ZoZomobile* again. He spray-painted over the *ZoZomobile's* art work. Before he began serving his county jail sentence, Brillo and his Uncle Bub hauled the station wagon to a junked car dealer in Fayetteville, Arkansas. Brillo figured he would never see any part of the vehicle again.

Despite the circumstances by which Carla Delgreco and Toni Weinstein died, no civil suits were filed by either family. The community impression was that the families believed the girls were where they wanted to be—as foolishly fatal as that turned out to be—and like a fan attending a baseball game at risk of being bopped by a foul ball or hit by a thrown baseball bat, there is the concept of *"assumed risk."* The same assumption of risk applied—whether they understood it or not—to the kids gathered for the drag race that Friday night in June at McGugin Field.

In retrospect, I find this perspective of personal responsibility and a willingness to accept consequences of one's own actions to be remarkable in light of the fact that, were such an accident to occur today, numerous law suits would stem from the unfortunate event.

Community

The Coffeyville City Council meeting two weeks following the accident lamented the deaths and injuries and offered its condolences to families and all involved.

The city council instructed municipal staff to make certain that the areas patrolled by the Coffeyville Police Department at the industrial park and airfield were secure and would discourage trespassing. This included erecting a locked gate at the intersection of Angola Road and the airfield's Second Street.

Several Coffeyville residents appearing before the city council called for the city to facilitate organized drag races to permit *"cocky drag racers and a bunch of dang fool kids"* to vent their need for adrenalin rushes in a safe venue. By the following summer, various groups had joined with the city in establishing a season of six drag race weekends that took place, not at McGugin Field, but at the other municipal airport on Big Hill. That season resulted in no serious injuries.

It should be remembered that at the time of the accident, anyone over the age of thirty had been impacted in some way by World War II and the Korean Conflict. If someone walking the residential streets of Coffeyville paid attention, they would spot many front door window panes that displayed one or more gold stars that

179

indicated a household that had suffered loss due to military combat. Individuals and communities never *"get used"* to sudden death but the citizens of Coffeyville understood that grim stuff happens. Rather than crawling under the covers into the fetal position, they took a necessary time out to recharge and then got back into the game of life, striving to do something that meant something for the greater good.

(Hell! I can't be certain that is the way it was. That's the way *I* thought it was. For the moment, I have no reason to disbelieve myself. Happily, I have not yet fallen that deep into cynicism!)

School

The drag race took place following the end of the school year. Summer school (typing, Driver's Education, English, History, and one or two other courses) began the Monday following the accident. I was told that unless a student raised the issue, not one word was said by any of the teachers about the deaths and injuries. There were no announcements by the administration regarding the accident.

By Wednesday, students were concerned about attending the funeral services. There was no provision made by the administration for students to be away. Individual teachers told the students that they could be away from class if the students thought it necessary. But the students were told they would have to make up their work as would be the case if they were absent due to an illness.

During the six years at Roosevelt Junior High School and Field Kindley Memorial High School, other students besides Carly and Toni died in drownings, car accidents, or due to illness. There was little change in this *laissez-faire* coping routine over the years. In contrast, as I write this memoir in the mid-1980s, I know that these days, following some student or campus tragedy, trained *"grief counselors"* arrive on the school grounds to comfort students and assist them with the grieving process.

When anyone suffers a serious personal loss, they have experienced the equivalent of an emotional, physical, spiritual, social, and mental head-on collision. Grief symptoms of shock, anger, dismay, lack of appetite, numbness, resignation, depression, bottoming-out, and restoration of equilibrium play out over a six-month to two year period in a healthy recovery from grief. Thus, I support school districts providing grief counselors to students when necessary. But such intervention was nowhere to be found at Field Kindley High School following the accident that stole away Carly Delgreco and Toni Weinstein.

Frankly, I was concerned that my recollection of no intervention by counselors was in error. So I corresponded with classmates to ask if I had missed something. Their responses are telling regarding how things were then as compared to now:

"You are being facetious, aren't you?"

"Don't remember any help to help us cope."

"I don't remember any counseling.
Of course, back then, we were supposed
to take responsibility for the things we did
and own our own feeling
about what happened around us."

"Counselors? What counselors?"

"There wasn't any. We weren't pampered
like the kids are today."

"Back then we girls tended
to talk to our best friends about everything,
probably more than our parents, ministers,
or teachers."

"Back then, the kids that went to the Boys
Club was like family."

*"Our parents weren't too busy to ask about
our feelings and we all ate supper together
and discussed our day."*

Everyone that was close to Carly or Toni needed a little help from their friends to make it through the grieving process. As far as I know, we all were successful in accomplishing the long march through the valley of the shadow of death. Fortunate are those anywhere who can say of their hometown that it was populated by *salt-of-the-earth* folks who lovingly cared for one another. Such was my experience with Coffeyville.

Family

The fatal crashes had set off shock waves of consequences for the families involved.

The Delgreco and Weinstein families were understandably devastated by the deaths of their beautiful and talented daughters. To me, each girl had been a classmate and friend.

Toni Weinstein's funeral service took place in *Congregation Beth Shalom* in Tulsa on the Friday morning following her death. There was a caravan of vehicles that trekked from Coffeyville to Tulsa for the service which was presented in English and Hebrew. The Coffeyville gentile contingent did not follow all that was said or sung. But they all understood that they had lost a friend and that God's peace should be invoked.

Carly Delgreco's family was in the midst of job-related tumult attendant to preparing for a quick move to the Chicago area when the cheerleader was killed. During the time the Delgrecos had been in Coffeyville, they had become well networked through work, at Holy Name Catholic Church, Rotary, the Knights of Columbus, and the Hospital Aid Association. There was also Carly's network of student friends.

The crowd for Carly's Friday afternoon funeral included standing room only. Following the mass, Carly's remains were sent by train to Chicago with her parents and brother as escorts. A Delgreco family plot in a Catholic cemetery was established near Schaumburg, Illinois, headquarters of Continental Can Company. Mr. Delgreco remained a member of the management task force which did, indeed, shutter the Coffeyville CCC plant the year following, a severe blow to the local and regional economy.

My parents were uncertain as to how to deal with me.

They were not pleased that I had put myself in harm's way at the drag race but, of course, none of the kids thought we were in harm's way. My parents were grateful that my injuries were not more severe. My wrist fracture was a simple one and healed without incident after eight weeks in a cast. The small shrapnel that had punched a hole into my head above my left eye could have been much worse. Fortunately, my concussion was mild, the scar nearly invisible, and I had no subsequent eye or vision problems.

My parents understood that I—like many others—had lost two friends. Though they had never met either Toni or Carly, they had heard much about Carly. On the rare occasions when my parents attended a football or basketball game, they had seen the cheerleaders in action.

The bottom line was that my parents kept a tight rein on my comings and goings for a month or so. To say that things then returned to normal would be a distortion of the difficult reality that I and other friends of the deceased and injured were confronting.

Six months following Carly's death, on a wintry day of the new year, I received a note from the high school office to contact Mrs. Voelzke, one of secretaries, at the end of the school day. I had no idea what the note was about but I took comfort in knowing that I was being called to see a secretary, not the principal.

After the final bell rang, I stuffed what I didn't need for that night's homework into my locker. Then I retrieved my winter jacket and the books and notebooks I would need that night. With the books bouncing on my hip, I headed toward the first floor school office. As I entered the office, Mrs. Voelzke nodded in my direction but had two students ahead of me. When she finished with them, Mrs. Voelzke walked over to her desk to pick up an envelope.

As she came to the counter, she said, "Billy, Mrs. Delgreco—Carly's mother—has sent this letter for you. As you know, the family is in the Chicago area now. Mrs. Delgreco did not have your family's address so she sent the letter here to the office requesting that we pass it along to you." She handed me the letter.

"Thank you, Mrs. Voelzke," I said. I placed the envelope inside my history book and headed to Lincoln Street and home.

That night, I took care of my homework and such chores as I had. When I finished with the homework, I still had time to watch *"The Garry Moore Show"* on TV and the first fifteen minutes of the news with anchor Cy Tuma on KOTV, Tulsa. Heading off to bed, I said my good nights, grabbed my history book and went to my room.

The letter was addressed to "Billy Howard, c/o Field Kindley High School, Coffeyville, Kansas. In neat handwriting, it said:

"Dear Billy,

"Mr. Delgreco and I hope you and your family are in good health and spirit. Also, we hope your school year is progressing well. I'm sure you realize that high school is a special time in everyone's life.

"As I am certain you understand, Carly's passing has been and still is a tragic blow for our family to endure! I don't know that time will ever heal this loss but I am not presently as helpless as I was when this wound was so fresh and raw.

"I realize that you have also grieved for Carly. From the registration book, I am aware of your attendance at her funeral mass. Thank you for being there!

184

"My purpose in writing to you is to affirm that Carly truly counted you as a cherished friend. I know that you met at the Hedley's Dance Studio. Carly told us all the girls said you were the best dancer. She was frustrated that you never danced with her. Of course, when the Hedleys teamed the two of you, Carly was thrilled!

"I don't know if you knew that, on the occasion of the *Yearbook Dance,* Mr. Delgreco and I were chaperones, viewing the proceedings from the gymnasium balcony. We saw the two of you triumph with the *"Sing! Sing! Sing"* swing dance. And then we were stunned by your bold kiss of Carly! Though we said nothing to Carly at the time, Mr. Delgreco and I just laughed and laughed at the two of you and your success before your classmates. We also saw Mr. Vesco have a man-to-man chat with you afterwards. Such a happy night!

"Carly kept diaries. I have only recently allowed myself to read her diaries. The diaries do not record each of her days. She focused on events or people that were dear to her.

"Her final entry in her diary was from the night of the Hillcrest Country Club end-of-the-school year party. I had asked her to return from the party early enough to help me with some of the packing we had just begun for the move to Illinois. Carly was undecided about whether to go to the party because she was upset that this would be the last time she would see some of the kids who had been her friends for years. (She so loved living in Coffeyville!) I encouraged her to go to the party and she did.

"When she arrived back home, her mood was decidedly improved and she told me it was because of you. She said that the two of you had met as she was leaving. When you heard about the move, she said, you were shocked and sad. But then you said you would write her regularly. Also, you suggested that when you were both in college, you might be able to get together and show those other college kids how to dance. Billy, your conversation made a positive difference to Carly that night. Her diary entry for that night was only one line: *"I love Billy Howard!!! xoxoxoxo"*

"Oh Billy, this is such a difficult letter to write, but I know Carly would want you to know these things.

"The night of Carly's passing, the only reason she went to the airfield was because she expected you to be there. She told me that she didn't think she could bear talking with you as that would be painful for both of you. But she just wanted to see you, even if from afar.

"Mr. Delgreco and I may have given you a carpool ride home one night after a dance lesson at the Hedleys. If so, that was our only personal contact with you. Over the years, Carly filled in many details about you. Now, Carly is gone and you must continue with your life.

"As you attempt remarkable things in the years ahead, Billy, please know that the surviving Delgrecos join with Carly in affirming that you are a very special young man! With the help of the Father, you must pursue challenging tasks in your life. You have the pluck to accomplish great things! As you do, every once in awhile, please give

a happy thought to the Delgreco family and
your forever special friend, Carly!
May the saints preserve you, Billy!

Angelina Delgreco
(Mrs.Anthony Delgreco)

-----

*"Acceptance of what has happened is the first step
to overcoming the consequences of any misfortune."*

William James
Physician/Psychologist/Philosopher

Part III

Chapter 34

The Power of Racing Down Steps

In an attempt to win favor with my peers and elders as I began junior high school, I adopted a strategy of *"go along to get along."* In truth, I did not know all of the dynamics of this course of action, but I was attempting to fly under the radar of any schoolyard or classroom confrontation whatever the issue at hand might be.

Essentially, I was attempting to hide in plain sight. There was no one thing I could single out as a reason to blend in other than my self-perceived deficiencies of height, weight, complexion, and lack of social grace. I later realized that my methodologies would only work so long and then I would be found out.

An example of this involved Blanton McCoy from Long Hollow, Kentucky. His family moved to Coffeyville when Blanton's daddy and uncle found work at the local paint smelter. Blanton was proud of his *Bluegrass State* origins and alleged that his great-grandpappy had been one of the surviving belligerents in the infamous *Hatfield-McCoy* feud.

Blanton and I were both in the eighth grade but had experienced very little interpersonal contact. One lunch hour, awaiting the resumption of classes, many of the students who were part of the in-crowd or wannabes were gathered around one of the campus elm trees. Blanton and a couple of his buddies walked up to join the

189

group when Blanton tripped on a projecting tree root and went splat in front of everyone.

We all laughed in derision. I joined in the laughter and then, stupidly outspoken that I was, said a little too loud and a little too late, *"Stumblebum!"*

Blanton, who had already developed a sugar belly, picked himself up, dusted his pants and hands, replaced his *John Deere* hat, and turned to stare at me. The crowd recognized Blanton's upset at his fall, the laughter, and especially towards me. Blanton walked to me and, with his three-inch height advantage, looked down and said, "Billy Howard, I don't much cotton to pop-offs. You need to learn when to keep your yap shut and I'm gonna be your teacher. Today, Billy-twerp, right after the closing bell rings, I'm going to be at the bottom of the front steps. Unless you are a milksop, you and your yellow belly will meet me right there. I will take you out with one punch. And if you don't show up, everyone at this school and everyone in this town will know that you are a chicken-livered coward." With that, Blanton and his buds stormed away.

Fortunately, the bell rang and our group began to disperse. Of course, two or three guys drew alongside to taunt and question:

"Whatcha gonna do, Billy?" Damon Neese asked.

"Blanton may tie his right hand behind his back and take you down with his left hand—maybe not even a punch, just a slap," taunted Aaron Alderman.

"You really stepped in it this time, Howard. You gonna run and hide or show up? We'll all be there, Dumbo!" chortled Vic Bilderback.

With those discouraging words and the report of the impending fight spreading around campus, I could not concentrate during my fifth and sixth hour classes. Let me rephrase that: The only thing I could concentrate on during English and Algebra was the fact that two choices confronted me: (1) By 3:15 p.m. I'd be limping home with a bloody nose, blackening eyes, and a torn shirt or (2) I would flee to fight another day (Hah!) and be deemed a wimpy chicken by all inhabitants of the known universe.

In fifth hour English, rather than reading the short story, *"The Man without a Country,"* I debated in my mind what to do. As the class was about to conclude, I had finalized agreement with

Shakespeare or the Bible or some general that said something like *"A brave man dies but once, a coward many times!"*

Throughout Algebra, instead of determining the values of *x, y,* and *z,* I accepted that the upcoming Blanton bruising as inevitable. The Algebra problem I was trying to solve was how to get it over with as fast as possible, take my lumps, lick my wounds, and return to school tomorrow to say—if my jaw were not broken and I still had my teeth—"Well, I tried." Maybe my peers would give me some E-points for effort.

If I could rush into the fray, I wondered, the blows that would come my way might dissolve into a blur. While I decided this would be my best plan of attack (Hah!), I also recalled comments by people whose lives were threatened who said upon survival that during the near-death experience, everything slowed down. I did not want what was about to befall me to slow down!

Fifteen minutes before the end of the school day, I began to pump my hands from open to closed, opened to closed, opened to closed to prepare my fists. I began to tap my feet and take deep breaths. Tony Womack whose desk was next to mine looked up from his reading to glower, "What the heck is wrong with you, man?"

When the closing bell rang, I bolted upright and grabbed my books. But I waited at my desk which was near the back of the classroom until everyone had exited. Then I strode purposefully out the door to head for my locker which was one floor above at the other end of the school building.

My eyes were fixed on finding an expeditious route through the maze of students who were talking with one another, depositing or retrieving books and jackets from their hallway lockers. As I moved rapidly, I heard various comments:

"So long, sucker!"

"Good luck, Howard!"

"Don't go, Billy!"

"Do you have an icepack with you?"

When I reached my locker on the third floor, I had to dial my lock combination twice, not because I was nervous but because I was stoked. I challenged myself to cry out to Blanton and all assembled, *"You want me, Stumblebum? Well, here I am! Let's do it!"* I considered that for a millisecond and then concluded I would be best served by keeping my mouth firmly shut.

With my books in my locker, I slammed the door and refit the lock. The hall crowds had thinned. I began to roll up my sleeves as I went down the stairs to the second floor.

Roosevelt Junior High School is a stately, four-story brick building. It sits in the middle of a large campus. Sidewalks coming from various directions lead to the wide front entrance of the building. To get inside RJHS, one has to climb six wide steps to the first exterior landing. Then another six steps takes one to the entrance landing. There are two sets of double-doors to pass through to the interior entrance landing. Then there was one last flight of twelve steps to the second floor level with the school offices to the left.

Walking fast, I reached the second floor landing and halted. At a distance, I peered through the door windows and spotted Blanton and his dunderhead sidekick, Ollie Mobus, joking with a small circle of students. I was relieved to observe a *"small circle"* of people. Though news of the impending fight had reached the far corners of the school, when the opponents were identified, most persons probably concluded this train wreck was far too predictable and there was no point in wasting time on what most of my peers would have considered the foregone conclusion of my painful defeat.

Taking a deep breath, I silently said *"Geronimo"* and plunged down the interior steps. I banged through the doors and stopped on the exterior landing. Despite my resolve to keep my mouth shut, I surprised myself and everyone else there by shouting, *"Hey, Stumblebum: Here I am! Let's do it!"*

I lunged down the steps, taking the final six two at a time. My eyes were fixed on Blanton McCoy and he was staring back agape. "Oh, merciful Lord, please let this be over quick." I prayed as I raced to within arm's length of Blanton with my dukes up.

I began to circle. I was heaving breaths so hard that I thought I might hyperventilate. As I began to circle Blanton, he began to back up slowly, doubtless so he could take his windup and pitch me to the stars. In a repeated stage whisper—though I didn't realize it at the time—I was growling, "Let's do it, Stumblebum! Let's do it!"

Suddenly, Blanton moved quickly and I braced myself for the punch. But there was no punch. Blanton's quick move was to grab his cohort Ollie Mobus and pull that fat dweeb in front of him.

"What the hell are you doing, Howard?" McCoy said, still backing in a circle holding Ollie by the scruff of his neck. "You want a fight, Howard? Well, the fact is, I was gonna give you a real hillbilly stomping. But then I realized that I wouldn't get any meaningful satisfaction by stepping on such a sweetie-fart goony-bird like you. So, back off or I'll send in Ollie to clean your plow."

Blanton stopped circling, still holding Ollie by the scruff of his neck and his right arm. Ollie had suddenly turned ashen. "Now, are you going to calm down, Howard, and let us all go our separate ways or is Ollie going to have to whip your puny little butt?"

I couldn't process what Blanton was saying. Why wasn't I wiping muddy blood off my face? Why wasn't my shirt torn? I took a step back and looked around at the circle of students. They were snickering and whispering and pointing at Ollie and Blanton.

"Wake up, blockhead!" I thought to myself. "You don't have to fight! You don't have to be smacked to oblivion. *Get the hell out of here!"*

I looked again to the crowd and then back to Ollie and Blanton. Ollie's eyes were opening wider and wider. I was still heaving breaths and my fists were still up and ready to engage. I feinted with a quick half-step forward that caused Ollie and Blanton to hop backward a step. Then, after a pause, I dropped my still clenched fists to my sides, turned and walked away without looking back.

I was about to cross from the campus onto Lincoln Street when Tom Shaney raced up and threw an arm over my shoulder. *"Way to go, Billy! Way to go!"* he repeated as he slapped me on the back.

I kept walking. As we began stepping along Lincoln Street my breathing began to ease. With my eyes still full front, I said, "Tom, what just happened there? Why am I not wiping blood from my nose and trying to see through swelling eyes?"

Tom laughed. "You scared the shit out of him, Billy! Blanton beats up on all sorts of kids but I bet not one of them ever came charging at him saying, *'Let's do it, Stumblebum! Let's do it!'* You were fantastic! What you did to McCoy will be all over town by this time tomorrow."

I stopped and turned to Tom. "Shaney, listen to me!" I said. "I was the one who was scared. The only reason—*listen to me*—the only reason I ran down the steps was to get my beating over with as quickly as possible. I had no thought of throwing a punch or actually landing a punch and I didn't. Why did Blanton back off?"

We began to walk again. "I have no idea why that bozo McCoy did what he did, Billy," Tom said. "He's a jerk! But Coach Mayfield always says, *'The best defense is a good offense!'* Maybe your charge down the steps was like Teddy Roosevelt's charge at San Juan Hill. You apparently convinced McCoy that you were a force to be reckoned with, whether true or not. How funny, Billy! The town will be talking about this for years. Come on! Let's go to *Pert's Variety Store* and I'll buy you a *Coke* to celebrate."

"Assume a virtue, if you have it not."

Hamlet
William Shakespeare

Chapter 35

Student Counsel

One spring afternoon before school was done for the year, I finished my work at the *Journal* and headed back to Lincoln Street on my bicycle. When I got there, rather than stopping at my house, I kept riding toward no place in particular. Then I noticed that my friend Harley Powell's pickup truck was parked in front of Captain Jack's.

Harley was a BMOC, a *Big Man on Campus.* He was a year older than me. I met Harley in our church youth group. We hit it off as friends. Harley's parents had moved from Coffeyville to California and the aerospace industry when Harley began high school. He pleaded to stay in Coffeyville for his high school years and his parents acceded because Harley's grandparents also lived in Coffeyville and would put him up in their back bedroom.

Harley was always on the Honor Roll. He was the Junior Class President and, in a couple of weeks, he would stand for election as President of the Student Council for the next school year. He was built somewhat like a trim fireplug. He wasn't stocky or fat. Indeed, he was a 6' tall athlete, playing varsity football and tossing shot in track and field. In football, he could have been a linebacker or a fullback, but he was insistent that he wanted to kickoff, punt, and split the uprights for *Points After Touchdowns.* Because of his reliability, the coaches had no problem with his choice.

Harley often gave me a ride home in his pickup. Many times he let me cruise around town with him on the weekends. We had good times together and he was a positive influence.

Since Harley had worked hard to become a real-deal *"all around good guy,"* it came as no surprise that he wanted to gain an appointment to West Point. To that end, Harley enlisted the help of Captain Jack and the good Captain was happy to be of service.

On this day, they were sitting on the porch on either side of Captain Jack's book and drink table. When I pulled up in front of Captain Jack's porch, the veteran nodded to me and said, "Hello,

Billy. Park your bike and sit a spell. Mrs. Patterson has plenty of tart lemonade in the pitcher."

"Thanks, Captain Jack. That would be great!" I replied. "Hi, Harley!"

"Hey, Billy. Finished your day at the paper, have you?" Harley asked.

"Yeah. Pretty quiet day. There are tornado watches for western Kansas and Oklahoma but the fronts are supposed to leave us alone."

"Hello, Billy. Here's your lemonade and a napkin." The voice belonged to Mrs. Patterson who, through the screen door, had heard Captain Jack's invitation for me to sit and sip.

"Thank you, Mrs. Patterson," I replied and sat down on the top step of the porch in front of Harley and Captain Jack.

"Well, Billy, it appears that Harley has nearly all his paperwork in place to file his applications to West Point and to Representative Docking. I've known many a graduate of the United States Military Academy and Brother Powell is just the kind of stalwart young man that West Point wants."

"After you send in your applications, Harley, how long will it be before you hear back from them?" I asked.

"Oh, West Point may want some additional information along the way which should be no problem for me to send to them. But final word won't come until after the first of the year. That's when Representative Docking will publish the names of his Congressional appointments to each of the military academies along with alternates."

"What's your parachute, Harley?" Captain Jack asked. "If, for whatever dang reason, Representative Docking doesn't name you, then what's your Plan B?"

"California," Harley said, as he sipped the last of his lemonade. "That's where my folks are. They have residency and I would qualify as an in-state student. Probably UCLA, maybe Berkeley. Come fall, I'll send in UC applications but that is a small matter compared to all that's involved with West Point."

With that, Harley stood. "Thank you, Captain Jack. I really appreciate your help with all of this. I'll get back to you if I run across some nit that needs to be picked. But I'm pretty sure I'll have the packet in the mail by the end of the month. See you, Billy."

"Bye, Harley," I said.

"So long, Harley. Don't be a stranger!" Captain Jack said, followed by another sip of lemonade.

"Do you think the *A's* have a shot at the pennant this year? And what about the *Cardinals?*" I asked.

Captain Jack did not hesitate to respond. "No, to the *Athletics*. Maybe, regarding *St. Louis*. That Charlie Finley, you know—the owner of the *A's*—is one smart owner and businessman. The Commissioner of Baseball can't abide the man, I hear. But Finley's smart. Playing the World Series and All Star games at night so more people can watch, well, that only makes sense. And he's forked over some big bucks to get the likes of *Catfish* Hunter and *Blue Moon* Odom. But they're not seasoned yet, Billy. In a couple more years, I think the *A's* may be able to make a run for the pennant."

"Now, *St. Louis* is a different story. Boyer. Schoendienst. White. Musial. These boys have been around the base paths a few times. But I'm concerned about *Stan the Man*. I don't think he's got more than a couple more seasons in him. It would be a shame for him not to get in another World Series. Let's see what happens between now and Independence Day."

Despite it being almost 4:45 p.m., nearly two hours after the final bell at school, Carolyn Rousters was just passing by.

"Hello, Carolyn," said Captain Jack. "Come, sit down, and have some of Mrs. Patterson's lemonade with us."

"Hi, Captain Jack!" Neither Carolyn nor I acknowledged one another. She lingered for a moment, perhaps pondering how much time she could spend sipping lemonade before she had to be home to help her mom prepare supper. "Sure. That would be nice." She placed her books and notebook on the porch beside her as she sat down where Harley Powell had been.

Mrs. Patterson's watchful eye and attentive ear had seen and heard the exchange. She came through the screen door with a glass of lemonade and a plate of cookies which she handed to me to pass around. Carolyn smilingly accepted the lemonade with a "Thank you, ma'am."

"You're coming by a little late today, Carolyn. Did one of your teachers make you stay after school?" the Captain chuckled.

My ears perked up. It would be news if the astute and precise Carolyn had become a miscreant.

"No, Captain Jack," Carolyn laughed. "My rap sheet is still clean. This weekend, kids who want to and can pay for it are taking a bus trip up to Lawrence to tour KU. Mr. Alvey, one of the history teachers, is the sponsor. He's going along so he had an orientation for those of us who are making the trip. We have to leave the high school parking lot at 6:30 a.m. and we won't get back till 9:30 at night."

"How many are going?" I asked as I munched on my second oatmeal cookie.

"I suppose about forty. That's a busload, isn't it? We get to go on a new bus, not one of the yellow school buses. Only seven or eight of the students going have ever been to KU."

"Have you been?" I asked.

"Nope. But it's where I'd like to go to college. I like the *Jayhawks*. Plus crimson and blue are great colors!"

"Do you have any idea as to what you'd like to study?" the Captain asked.

"No, not really. Those of us who are going on the trip had to go to the library to look through a KU—what do they call it—oh, a catalog. Mr. Alvey wanted us to read about life on campus, the costs, the scholarships. In the catalog, each of the departments lists its courses. When we arrive at KU, each of us will be given a map of the campus with each of the departments marked. Apparently, there will be someone at each department to talk to us. There are kids coming in from other Kansas schools, too."

"Have you chosen any departments to visit?" the captain asked.

Carolyn looked down at her lap and then away for a moment. She looked back to me and said, "Billy,"—the first time she had acknowledged my presence—"you're sworn to secrecy or you know what will happen." I had no idea what would happen if I blabbed whatever she was going to say but I, nevertheless, nodded that I understood her point.

"Mr. Alvey said everyone would have time to visit at least three departments and still have time to go to the Student Union. They've even got a bowling alley in the Student Union."

"What's a Student Union?" I asked.

Captain Jack intervened before Carolyn could give vent to her annoyance with me. "It's like a big recreation hall, Billy. It is a lounge with tables and some food venders. They probably have a ticket desk for ball games or travel or concerts or other campus events. It's a place where students go to socialize, play cards or other games, and generally relax."

"Sounds like a great place," I opined.

"Anyway, Captain Jack," Carolyn continued, "from what I heard today, almost all the girls are going to visit the Education Department and the Nursing School. Some of the boys may go to the Education Department. It's for those who want to be teachers. I'll visit the Education Department to keep Mr. Alvey happy but I'm not going to the Nursing School."

"Where will you go for your other two visits, Carolyn?" the captain queried.

"Billy, this is the 'sworn to secrecy' part. Captain Jack, I'm going to visit the Engineering Department and the Physics Department."

I laughed out loud. I couldn't help myself!

"Billy!" Carolyn seethed at me. Captain Jack even gave me a look of askance.

"Sorry! Sorry, Carolyn. I've just never heard of girls studying engineering or physics after high school. Does that happen, Captain Jack?" as I sought to recover favor on the porch.

"Can't say that I know, Billy. Maybe somewhere in the big wide USA. I never bumped into any women in the military who specialized in any kind of engineering or physics, but then I was just one little blip in the whole galaxy of that war."

Captain Jack continued: "Carolyn, I think I'd really enjoy—let me say, I believe *Billy and I* would really enjoy hearing about your interest in these departments. Your curiosity is really special to my way of thinking. I have always thought you are very talented and smart."

"Thank you, Captain Jack. I'm interested in engineering and physics but I don't know how interested I am. I think it goes back to *Sputnik*. I can remember when that happened and how lots of people were saying that the U.S. was losing—I guess you call it *'the space race'*—with the Russians. I liked science in elementary school but that was just building a circuit to light up a light bulb or maybe mixing a few things in test tubes. I've gotten more interested in science since then. But, like you, I've never heard of any women really studying engineering or physics as a career other than being a high school science teacher, I guess. But I don't want to teach science like Miss Clough. I want to practice—I want to apply science. But I don't know what all is involved. Saturday, I just want to hear what they have to say at KU. Maybe I'll come back and decide I want to own a ranch and raise kangaroos."

"Carolyn, I think your plan for which departments to visit at KU makes a heap of sense."

"I do, too," Captain Jack." It was Mrs. Patterson carrying a fresh pitcher of lemonade. "I think it's a grand idea, Miss Carolyn. Why there's no reason whatsoever to think that a bright young lady like you could not do well at whatever she put her mind to. 'Course, I know you're gonna do well, too, Billy."

"Carolyn," the Captain said, reaching into his pocket, "here's two-bits. After you've visited all the departments, head over to the Student Union, buy yourself a malt, and chew on what you've seen. It'll be a grand day! I look forward to hearing about your adventure to Lawrence. *Rock Chalk, Jayhawks!*"

Carolyn said thanks to the Captain for the quarter. We finished our lemonade and cookies. Then we both said thanks to Captain Jack and Mrs. Patterson and headed home. We walked away, side by side, to our houses in the next block. Neither one of us said a word.

The following Tuesday afternoon, I rode my bicycle out of our driveway and saw Carolyn Rousters sitting on her front steps. I pulled up before her.

"Hi, Carolyn!" I said. "How was the trip to KU? Did you see everything you wanted to see?"

"I told you to keep your mouth shut, Billy."

"Carolyn, I know that. I haven't told anybody, cross my heart. Anyway, I was thinking that maybe the engineering and physics thing is a cool deal. Why not study it? Who knows, maybe one day there'll be girl astronauts. I know that there are some women who are pilots, so why not an astronaut? Or would they call them *'astronautettes?'*"

"Billy, they would call them *'astronauts,'*" Carolyn huffed.

Carolyn looked around to see if any other person was on the horizon. Then she said, "The trip to Lawrence was great! Everyone was tired when we got back home, but the trip was fantastic! The campus is beautiful, rolling hills, lots of trees—you should see the buildings. Oh my gosh, I would love to go there. They even let us go into some of the women's dormitories. Everyone has at least one roommate."

"But what about the departments, you know, the enginee..." I began, wanting Carolyn to cut to the chase.

"Yes, Billy, I know what you're interested in," Carolyn interrupted. "All the faculty people were very nice, even the professor in the Education Department. But the Engineering Department and the Physics Department people did bang-up presentations. There were all these good looking guys! I saw only one other girl. Her name was *Syrelda*—I've never heard that name before. Anyway, Syrelda is from Shawnee Mission and her dad is a structural engineer and has his own business. She wants to do the same thing and her dad is all for it."

"Did you tell your folks about where you went?"

"Yeah, sure," Carolyn replied. "They don't have a problem, at least, not at this point. Both of them went to the junior college. Mom graduated with her A.A. They said I've got two more years of high school and a lot can happen. Then they said the usual about keeping my grades up."

"You made the Honor Roll again, didn't you?"

"Yep, but I sure had to burn the midnight oil! All of the departments at KU gave us sheets that listed high school courses we should take if we want to major in that subject. When I reached out my hand for the course list in the Engineering Department, a guy who had been introduced as a "Graduate Assistant"—I guess that's some kind of teacher's aide—says to me, 'Is this for your brother, Miss?' I said, *'No! It's for me!'* The moron frowned at me. I grabbed the list, spun on my heels, and left that Graduate Doofus in my dust.

Then I walked over to *Jayhawk Central*, that's what they call the Student Union. I pulled out the quarter that Captain Jack gave me, bought a strawberry malt, and read the student newspaper till it was time to meet Margie Horton and Scarlet Bumpass to go bowling. Dang, I'd like to be a co-ed there."

Carolyn looked at her watch and then stood to go inside. She looked back to say, "It was a great trip, Billy. You should go next year. You can hear all about their writing departments."

I rode away on my bicycle wondering how far away the KU men's dormitories were from the women's dormitories.

Chapter 36

"Twerp!"

I was burning trash one day, long before long before any governmental entity thought about trying to halt the air-polluting practice.

Every house in town had some sort of incinerator. Most, like ours, were located on the alleyways. For many, a 55-gallon oil barrel sufficed. The top end piece was removed. Eventually, the bottom end piece would corrode into nothingness. Just above the bottom of the barrel, a fist-size hole was cut. This was so a barrel full of trash could be lit from the bottom, assuring complete conflagration. Once a week, the trashmen would navigate the alleys. These big burly dudes would manually lift each of the 55-gallon drums and empty the contents into the trash truck. Automatic lifts and OSHA had not been invented yet.

But my family's property on Lincoln Street had an *"upscale"* incinerator, courtesy of previous residents. The incinerator had been constructed out of unreinforced bricks with some cement pasted on the outside to hold the thing together. It had a concrete base. It looked somewhat like an igloo that had a well-punctured top. Our incinerator had an ignition hole on the yard side. On the alley side, there was a rectangular opening which allowed the trashmen to shovel out the ashes and remaining debris since they couldn't lift the non-portable incinerator.

One evening, doubtless the day before the trash trucks drove by, I was watching the fire burn several days worth of trash that I had gathered and dumped into the incinerator as part of my weekly chores. From time to time, I would use the small tree branch I was holding to bat down a not-wholly carbonized piece of newsprint or notebook paper that lifted skyward, powered by the thermals emanating from the incinerator. My parents had given me firm instructions not to allow any errant trash from our incinerator to burn down the neighborhood.

As I marked time, Brodie Frenk roared east to west down the alley on his Harley-Davidson, heading toward the lawnmower shop.

He kicked up both dust and gravel and I dashed inland to avoid the spewing gravel and other airborne pellets. As the dust settled, I walked back to the incinerator where moments later Brodie rolled his almost idling cycle alongside our backyard fence.

Brodie had been back from South Korea for seven months. He had been honorably discharged as a corporal. He liked to brag that he was in the infantry. He omitted the fact that he was a clerk-typist at the Command HHQ and rarely risked frostbite. Nevertheless, he had done his bit for the country, had apparently saved some money, and was spending a year cycling around the country with occasional pit stops in Coffeyville. Despite being awarded an *Army Commendation Medal*, Brodie was still pretty much a big jerk.

"How ya doing, Twerp?"

In the intervening three-and-a-half years since Brodie went away, I had progressed from *"dogface"* to *"twerp."* Despite my disdain for Brodie, twerps needed to demonstrate deference to their elders, whether the elders were jerks or not.

"Doing fine, Brodie," I said. "Where you been?"

"I've been to Galveston. Know where that is, twerp?" Before I could respond, Brodie continued, "Galveston, Texas, right on the coast of the Gulf of Mexico. Lots of wetbacks working in the bars there, but some of those Mexican senoritas have mighty fine asses. Their tits aren't much, but mighty fine rear ends. Which do you prefer, twerp? Tits or asses?"

I started to stammer, poking at the fire. "Well, I, I usually like both." I had no idea what the hell I was talking about. I figured it would be only a moment or two more before Brodie rendered some final insult, peeled out, and left me picking grit out of my teeth.

"Yeah, I like 'em both, too, twerp. But the marketplace is going to force you to choose one or the other one of these days." Now I truly had no idea what he was talking about. But before any of my confusion could be increased, Brodie rolled away. He did not peel out. I did not have to pick tailings out of my teeth. Brodie hadn't even said, "See ya, twerp!" It was probably the best conversation I ever had with Brodie.

While Brodie and I had been having our *tete-a-tete,* Vonda Lang had brought her two kids out to the duplex's backyard. As Eddie and Lois began to play, Vonda walked toward the alley and sat down on a tree stump just a few yards away from the alley. She was making certain the kids stayed between her and the back of the house and did not wander into harm's way. She pulled a pack of cigarettes out her housedress pocket and lit up. Dusty would not be home from Carter's Men's Clothing for another ninety minutes. This may have been Vonda's first real break since she arose that morning.

Brodie cruised back down the alley toward the Frenk's house. Happily, he did not acknowledge me in any way as he passed.

The incinerator fire was out. I stirred the ashes and headed inside to continue reading *The Red Badge of Courage.* As I walked into the backdoor, I could see that Brodie had rolled his hog alongside Vonda Lang. When I headed for baseball practice 45 minutes later, Eddie and Lois were still playing. Vonda and Brodie were still talking.

Chapter 37

The Ham Berger

Michael Berger was one talented dude! His grades were good. He was a starting forward on the Roosevelt Junior High School basketball team. He ran the 440 in track, both individual and relay team. He could sing and he could act. He had the lead in the ninth grade play, *The Inner Willy*. In the annual school musical, *Sing and Swing,* Michael sang *"On the Street Where You Live"* from *My Fair Lady.*

The only slight negative about Michael—who was otherwise counted as an all-around good guy—was that when he was in the public eye, on stage or on the basketball court, he was a *"ham."* He *over-acted.* He *over-reacted.* He milked every moment of performance, whether it was athletic or theatrical.

This *"hamming it up"* could have been a turnoff to various audiences or spectators but, in reality, Michael's *hammy-ness* actually endeared himself to his viewers. Somehow, he always gave the onlookers the impression that he knew what he was doing. Some of what he was doing was *cheesy,* except that he knew he was being cheesy and he knew that everyone in the audience knew he knew he was being cheesy. The whole thing was just one big inside joke for those who were paying attention.

Following the two performances of *Sing and Swing* in my ninth grade year, the director, Miss Richards, arranged for the cast and crew to have a school-day field trip to the *Woolaroc Museum and Nature Preserve* near Bartlesville, Oklahoma, nearly sixty miles away. At that time, I had visited very few museums. Of course, I had been to the *Dalton Defenders' Museum* which was then located above the *New Castle Café.* The restaurant formerly had been the *Condon National Bank* when the Dalton's made their ill-fated robbery attempt in October 1892. My interest in going to *Woolaroc* had more to do with missing a day of classes than my interest in statues of pioneer women.

The trip cost three dollars. That included roundtrip on an air conditioned bus with one free bottle of pop. Everyone was told to bring a sack lunch. We departed the junior high school at 8:30 a.m. I grabbed a window seat on the right side. Moments later, *"Ham"* Berger sat down next to me.

"Hey, Billy!" he said. "Howya doin'?"

"Doin' fine, Ham," I replied. "How you!"

"The name is 'Michael,' if you don't mind. If you do mind, I'll mash your face!" Michael said with mock invective.

"Sure, sure, Michael, my man," I said. "But explain something for me. Why do you not like your nickname? You know everybody thinks you're cool. Is it because you're Jewish and don't like the pig connection?"

The bus pulled away. We would be cruising for more than an hour to reach Woolaroc.

"In response, Billy-boy, two things," Michael said. "First, the reason I don't like 'Ham' or 'Ham Berger' is because of *Perry Mason.* And second, I'm not Jewish."

"Whoa, whoa!" I said with some astonishment. "You lost me there. Let's take them one at a time. How did *Perry Mason,* the TV defense attorney, get caught up in all of this? I would think that *Della Street,* Perry's secretary, would often bring her boss a ham sandwich when he was working late. Clarify, please."

Michael crossed his arms and leaned back as if he were getting ready to doze. But he turned his head toward me and said, "If you watch the credits on *Perry Mason,* you know that the TV series is based on the crime novels of *Earle Stanley Gardner.* I've actually read a handful of the novels. They're not bad.

"But my problem with the nickname *'Ham'* is because Earle Stanley Gardner has already made this joke. The district attorney who always loses to Perry Mason is *Hamilton Burger*—'B-U-R-G-E-R—which is not how I spell my name. In the TV series, they never call him "Ham," always 'Mr. Burger' or 'Hamilton.' But in the books, calling Burger 'Ham' is a running joke. And Ham is always the loser. I'm not a loser and I don't want people to associate me with a loser. *Comprende, amigo?"*

"Si! Si! I get it. Hamilton Burger *is* a loser, now that you mention it. But I don't know that everyone else will get it. Maybe the nickname won't follow you to high school," I said.

"Time will tell, Billy. But at least I won't hear 'Ham' from you again!" Michael said with emphasis added.

"Nah, not to worry, unless I offer you half of the ham sandwich my mom packed for me today. And that brings up the second point. You said you're not Jewish. But in social studies you did a show-and-tell on one of those *minnow* things."

"*'Menorah,'* goober," Michael said. "The Chanukah candelabrum is called a 'menorah.'"

"Right, 'menorah.' And you said in your little talk that your family puts a menorah in the window every Chanukah. So doesn't that make you Jewish?"

"No, Billy. To be a Jew, you have to be born of a Jewish woman or go through a long conversion process. My mother is a Christian, a Presbyterian. I'm a Christian, baptized, catechized, reformed, and confirmed—the whole nine yards. It's my dad who is Jewish. I don't think his parents were all that pleased that he married a non-Jew. But they've been married seventeen years now, so apparently they are still getting along."

"How do you handle holidays and church and synagogues and Sabbaths and Sundays?" I was trying to show Michael that I was not totally ignorant of Judaism.

"My sister and I handle it just fine," Michael said. "So do my parents. Most Sundays we go to First Presbyterian Church for Sunday School and worship. Half the time, Dad shows up for worship. He likes Pastor Basso's short sermons. Once every month, Dad goes to the synagogue in Tulsa. Once every two or three months, the whole family goes along. We lay low for a Sabbath once a month. We celebrate Passover and Chanukah and Christmas and Easter.

"Two years ago, my mother gave Pastor Basso a book on how a Jewish boy is supposed to prepare for a *Bar Mitzvah*—that's when you turn thirteen and become a son of the Mosaic Law. Well, I'm not Jewish but Jesus was a Jew. So to surprise my dad, I memorized some Hebrew verses and we had a special family ceremony and dinner in the church's Fellowship Hall. My dad cried. Later this year, my sister Ally is going to have a *Bat Mitzvah*—'Bat' is Hebrew for 'daughter'—like *'batty!'* Hah! That's a joke Ally doesn't like."

"That's really interesting, Ha...I mean, Michael," I said. "I have an uncle who is Baptist but is married to a Catholic. I don't think they get along as well as your parents. Ann Landers writes about mixed marriages all the time. I don't think she cares much for the idea. But if it works for your folks, that's great!"

"There are lots of mixed couples," Michael said. "You've seen George Burns and Gracie Allen. He's a Jew and she's Catholic. Ed Sullivan has Stiller and Meara, the comedy team, on his show every few weeks. Stiller is a Jew and she's Catholic. Both those couples seem to get along well. Although I think I heard that Meara has converted to Judaism."

"You can do that?" I asked.

"Of course, you can do it. And it's easier for women. They don't have to get snipped, if you catch my meaning."

"Ouch! Yes, I catch your meaning!"

We rode along in silence till we reached Bartlesville. Michael dozed. I watched the rolling plains of the former Indian Territory. Lots of oil business in Bartlesville, thanks to Frank Phillips who founded Phillips Petroleum there. Frank and his wife Jane built *Woolaroc Ranch* in Osage County, southwest of Bartlesville, as their country home.

As our bus drove out of Bartlesville for the final few miles to *Woolaroc*, I asked Michael, "Would you marry a Jew? That would probably make your dad happy."

"Maybe. Perhaps. I don't really know, Billy. I don't know if I could handle the worry."

"What worry?" I asked with yet more astonishment.

"I told you, Billy, that I learned the catechism. I even memorized the first fifty questions and answers of the 1563 *Heidelberg Catechism* to get my *"God and Church"* badge for Boy Scouts. All together there are one-hundred-twenty-nine questions and answers in the catechism. It's number twenty-two that concerns me about my dad. It would absolutely cause me worry about a wife of mine who was Jewish."

"For heaven's sake, Michael, what does this number twenty-two say?" I asked.

Michael looked away, took a deep breath, and then looked back at me. "It says, Billy:

'QUESTION: What, then, must a Christian believe?

210

'ANSWER: All that is promised us in the gospel, a summary of which is taught us in the articles of the *Apostles' Creed*, our universally acknowledged confession of faith.'

"You see, Billy-boy, Dad's a great guy, but he doesn't accept the Gospels as true and he certainly doesn't believe in the *Apostles' Creed*. He just sorta believes *'to each his own.'* That's all well and good, but if number twenty-two is true, that Jesus is the only way to salvation, then Dad's got a problem. And that kind of problem becomes the whole family's problem."

"Wow!" I said. "That's heavy duty! Do you believe number twenty-two is true?"

Michael sat silent for a few moments. We were just turning through the Woolaroc gate.

"Yeah, Billy," Michael said. "I do believe it. Sometimes I wish I didn't. However, my dad always says *'everything will work out in the end.'* I hope he's right, Billy. Eternity is one long, long bus ride."

Chapter 38

Quiet Desperation

One year in high school, I did a report on *Walden* by Henry David Thoreau. I received an *A-* on the paper which was fine with me. By that time, I had learned that a 1,000 word report could be made easier if several quotes were cited and reprinted from the book. One of the quotes I used was

*"Most men lead lives of quiet desperation
and go to the grave with the song still in them."*

In my teens at the time, I didn't fully comprehend the significance of Thoreau's assertion regarding *"lives of quiet desperation,"* even though I witnessed such lives being endured in the duplex next door to our house on Lincoln Street.

Dusty, Vonda, Eddie, and Lois Lang moved into the duplex's Unit A with scant furnishings. The Langs drove a 1954 Chevrolet Bel-Air coupe. It was pretty beat up and Dusty was often seen with his head under the hood trying to hold the body and soul of the car together until the Langs' fortunes improved.

One day only a week or so after the Langs arrived on Lincoln Street, I carried a load of trash out to the incinerator. The Langs' clothesline was alongside our common fence. Eddie and Lois were running back and forth between the clothesline poles. I walked over to the fence.

"Hi, Vonda!" I said. "Have you unpacked all your boxes?"

Vonda pulled a clothespin out of her mouth to affix one of Eddie's shirts to the line. "Hello, Billy. Only about half the boxes have been unpacked. We've still got a ways to go but we're getting there, slowly but surely."

"Where did you move from, Vonda?" I asked.

"Springfield, Missouri, U.S.A.," Vonda replied.

"Does Dusty like his new work at the clothing store?" I asked.

"As a matter of fact, he does. But he's got a lot to learn and a lot of suits to sell to feed four people. Mr. Carter seems like an alright guy and he loves to talk baseball with Dusty. Good for them! I can't abide baseball anymore."

"My dad buys his suits from Mr. Carter. Now he can buy them from Dusty," I said. "I even got a couple suits there to wear on Easter or a special event at school or to a funeral. But my mom doesn't like to buy me suits. She says I outgrow them too fast."

Looking down at the ping-ponging Eddie and Lois, Vonda said, "I can relate. I know all about growing kids."

We talked for a few more minutes till she finished hanging out the clothes. "Have a nice day, Billy," Vonda said. She dropped her bag of clothespins into the empty laundry basket, held the basket on her hip, and called after her kids to lead them back inside the duplex.

Harrison V. Carter thought Dusty Lang was the greatest thing since sliced bread!

Mr. Carter had inherited Carter's Men's Clothing Store from his father, Alexander, who in turn, had inherited the enterprise from his father, Lucius. Harrison Carter's grandfather had begun the mercantile enterprise as a general store in 1872. In the early years, Lucius Carter was in direct competition with Colonel James A. Coffey, the founder of Coffeyville, who operated a trading post. But Coffey moved on to other entrepreneurial pursuits in various Kansas communities and the Carter's general store prospered.

It was Alexander Carter's idea to specialize in men's wear. This occurred after Lucius Carter had gone on to his final reward, shortly before the beginning of WWI. The Carters, Lucius, Alexander, and Harrison, all proved to be capable businessmen. They made good money when the farmers had excellent harvests. They lived off their cash reserves when harvests were bad.

Harrison Carter lived in a big, three story house on Tenth Street, approximately eight blocks from his store. He could be seen walking to work early in the morning and back late at night. At the house, Carter employed a full-time cook and housekeeper and a part-time handyman who also did maintenance at the clothing store.

Harrison Carter had bought the house as a wedding present for his wife, Elsie. They thought the place was grand! Their son, Emory, was born in the third floor master bedroom.

After ten years of marriage, Elsie and Emory died when an engine boiler on a Katy Railroad locomotive exploded near Topeka where mother and son were going to visit her parents. The explosion killed the engineer and fireman but it was the derailment that killed the Carters and six other persons when they were pinned under their coach. Harrison Carter never remarried.

Carter became active in community affairs. He was a member of First Methodist Church and the Lion's Club. He labored long and hard to foster the fortunes of his store and Coffeyville. Carter was never bored by his business but he took no great delight in it either. He viewed the store as a trust that had been passed on to him by grandfather and father. At that time, Carter was already into his 60s. He did not like thinking about what would happen to the family business when he died. The only remaining family member was his nephew, Mort Hollyfield, over in Springfield. But Carter concluded Mort, the driver of a beer delivery truck, didn't have the skill set or interest to manage a menswear store. Only in recent years had Carter begun to think that if anyone ever expressed interest in buying the place, he might actually sell.

Carter's one relief from the burdens of life and work was baseball. As a youth, he had not been an exceptional baseball player or athlete of any sort. He played varsity football and basketball but he was never "All-League" material. He enjoyed all sports but he feasted on baseball.

Hall of Fame pitcher Walter Johnson of the *Washington Senators*, the *"Big Train"* as he was called, had a working farm just outside of Coffeyville. For many years, Johnson pitched a charity exhibition game in Coffeyville's Forest Park which was later named Walter Johnson Park.

Though he could afford New York and Washington, D.C., prices, Johnson regularly visited Carter's store to Harrison's delight. Every November, Johnson would come in and get fitted for two suits. He'd also pick up a couple of pairs of coveralls and three or four flannel shirts.

Carter and the store's tailor, Bernie Weinberg, would drive out to the Johnson farm to deliver the suits and make any final alterations.

That gave Carter additional time to talk to the major league all time strikeout king. It was a sad day in 1930 when Johnson's wife Hazel died and the Big Train moved back east. Behind Carter's office desk hung an autographed picture of Johnson, flanked on either side by framed baseball cards of the legend.

By no stretch of the imagination did Dusty Lang come anywhere near the talent or fame of Walter Johnson. Be that as it may, Lang had been a professional baseball player for six seasons. He had been on a major league roster for three weeks. He had made two appearances at the plate. He grew up with the *Cleveland Indians'* Boyd Benson and he played ball against many other players who became well known in the *bigs*. If anyone ever bothered to ask— and Harrison Carter was quick to ask—Dusty actually had some fascinating stories to tell about the realities of pro ball.

A mutual mentoring relationship developed between Dusty and Mr. Carter. Dusty would teach Mr. Carter about what baseball—at least minor league baseball—was truly like. Mr. Carter would teach Dusty about suits, ties, and shoes, their fabrics, materials, origins, costs, and commissions. Each proved a good student.

Despite Dusty's acceptance by Mr. Carter and his progress as a salesman, Vonda saw little change in her daily routine. Dusty's added income from commissions allowed Vonda to manage life in the duplex without noticeable economic pain. She was glad not to be on a farm. But Vonda felt trapped and desperate for something, though she knew not what.

Truth be told, Vonda was mourning the fact that she was not living in a big house in Cleveland, Ohio, as was the case with childhood friend Diana Kunkel. Diana was the wife of the *Indians'* Boyd Benson. In high school, Dusty, Vonda, Boyd, and Diana double-dated. Boyd and Dusty had both signed minor league contracts with the *Indians* the week after high school graduation. Now, the Bensons were in a ranch-style house in Cleveland and the Langs were in a duplex in Coffeyville. Vonda was not comforted that each town began with the letter "C."

One day in the summer, I was walking down the alley behind our house when I saw that Vonda had laid out a picnic blanket in her backyard. Lois was napping. Eddie was flipping through a picture book. Vonda was sitting on the back steps of her apartment wearing shorts, a blue halter top, sandals, and sunglasses. She had what looked like a glass of *Coke* in her hand.

"Hi, Vonda," I said.

She looked up at me but did not seem to recognize me at first. Then, "Oh, hi, Billy. Guess I was daydreaming." I was five feet away from her and I could smell the whisky. She didn't try to conceal it. She swirled her glass with her finger and took another drink.

"Got a ball game tonight?" she asked.

"No. Tomorrow night. Ya oughta come," I said.

She was silent for a moment as if she were processing the few words I had just said and what they meant.

"Nah, gotta put the kids down. Dusty will be there, I'm sure." Dusty had become a part-time coach for the Pony League team I played on, the Pirates.

"You want some pop, Billy?" Vonda asked as she stood up.

"No, thanks," I said.

Vonda said, "Watch Eddie and Lois for just a minute, Billy. I want to fresh-up my drink."

Two or three minutes later, Vonda returned with a full glass. She plopped herself back down on the porch step. "Awfully hot today, isn't it, Billy?"

"Sure is, Vonda. Well, gotta go," I said.

The next night, Dusty didn't make it to our Pony League game. When I returned home, it was Dusty who was sitting on the back step, smoking a cigarette. I looked across to him. "Hi, Dusty! We won!" I paused. No reply. "Seven to four." No reply. I went inside.

A few days later, after supper, I carried the trash out to the incinerator. It was a warm evening, no expectation of rain. Dusty was working his way along the clothesline, taking down the laundry. It was such an unusual thing to see Dusty dealing with laundry, I blurted out, "Hi, Dusty. Where's Vonda?"

After a brief hesitation, he replied, "She's a little under the weather tonight. Thought I'd give her a hand and take down these clothes."

"Yeah, great," I said. "See ya!" I wondered if I would ever learn to say anything in the right way at the right time.

While life on the home front was hardly a bed of roses for Dusty and Vonda, Dusty's work at Carter's Menswear and his relationship with Mr. Carter were on solid footing. Dusty was improving in his knowledge of menswear and was developing a good rapport with customers. Mr. Carter had invited Dusty to speak on baseball to the Lion's Club one Tuesday and he was well received.

Mr. Carter was judicious in choosing his times to talk with Dusty about baseball. He loved baseball but he was too much of a steward of his family business to risk sinking sales because of frittering away too much time talking about how Ted Williams compared to Stan Musial. But when Mr. Carter did raise an issue of the national pastime, Dusty responded with alacrity. Dusty never condescended in his remarks to his boss. If Dusty had ever had an extended major league career, he would have done well in dealing with fans.

A few years before Dusty was hired in Coffeyville—1955, to be exact—the *Philadelphia Athletics* endeared themselves to the Midwest by moving to Kansas City. Prior to the *A's* arrival in KC, Mr. Carter would drive eleven hours from Coffeyville to St. Louis twice a year to see major league baseball at the venue closest to him. St. Louis was 351 miles from southeast Kansas. Kansas City was a mere 172 miles north of Coffeyville, less than half the distance and half the time to travel to see the *Cardinals*. You could even go roundtrip in a day if you were so inclined.

As a matter of fact, Mr. Carter was so inclined. On July 4, Independence Day, the *A's* would be hosting the newly franchised *Los Angeles Angels.*

"Dusty, I've got a proposition for you, sort of a bonus, if you want it," Mr. Carter said.

"What's up, boss?" Dusty responded.

"You fly. I'll buy. On Independence Day, the *A's* are playing the *Los Angeles Angels.* If you'll do the driving of my car to and

218

from KC, up in the morning and back at night, I'll buy the tickets, the gas, the hotdogs, the beer, the peanuts, and whatever else we need to make a day of it at Municipal Stadium. I know Vonda may not think this is such a great idea and that's for the two of you to decide. But if the two of you say my plan is *A-OK,* I'll give you an extra ten bucks so that Vonda can take the kids to a movie in air conditioned comfort. Or she can get a baby sitter, and have some time to herself. It's your decision. It won't bother me one way or the other. I'm going to KC. I just thought you might like to come along."

"Thanks, boss. I'll talk it over with Vonda and get back to you tomorrow."

Vonda said, "As far as I'm concerned, you can go and not come back. Hell, yes, I'll take his ten bucks. Damn right I'll get a baby sitter. I'll go anywhere that I don't have to smell baby powder."

Independence Day that year was a Tuesday. At 8:00 a.m., Mr. Carter pulled up in front of the duplex and honked. Mr. Carter exited the driver's side and walked around to the passenger side of the front seat. It took only a moment for Dusty to come out of Unit A, slip behind the wheel of Mr. Carter's 1960 black Oldsmobile 98, and drive away.

At 9:30 a.m., Sharon Chambers, a senior at Field Kindley who had been recommended by Carolyn Rousters, showed up at the duplex to babysit. Ten minutes later, after imparting all necessary child care instructions, Vonda walked out of Unit A and drove away in the Chevy. Vonda was wearing a red blouse, pedal-pushers, and sneakers. She also wore a red bandana and sunglasses.

Vonda headed downtown which was deserted on this holiday morning. When she reached Walnut Street she turned right till the street became U.S. 169. Three miles south of Coffeyville was the state line for Kansas and Oklahoma. Vonda drove another mile and then turned left off the highway. Three blocks later she reached the *Southern Club*, a real-deal honky-tonk that served up good food, good booze, and good country music. The gravel parking lot was large as it was shared with the *South Coffeyville Stock Yards.* There was no livestock auction scheduled for Independence Day. A couple of other cars were parked in the lot. When Vonda's parents came to town, they always went to the *Southern Club.* It was the only place Vonda could rely upon for getting a good steak and a truly cold beer.

Vonda rolled down her window and lit up. No living soul could be seen. Only a few cars were traveling north or south on U.S. 169.

At 10:05 a.m. Vonda spotted something on the highway. She flicked her cigarette onto the gravel, rolled up the window, checked her lipstick in the mirror, and waited. Thirty seconds later, Brodie Frenk drove his hog directly at the Chevy coupe. He stopped 10 yards away and revved the bike's engine twice. He made no gesture to get off the bike.

Vonda grabbed her purse and stepped out of the car. She put the purse strap over her head and right shoulder. She locked the car and dropped the keys into the purse's side pocket. Then she walked over to the cycle, put her hand on Brodie's shoulder to steady herself and climbed onto the Harley. She tightened her bandana and placed her arms around Brodie's waist. The cycle roared away, kicking up gravel, some of it pinging the sides of the Chevy coupe.

When they reached U.S. 169, Brodie headed south toward Nowata, or Tulsa, or some country lane.

Vonda was back at the duplex by 4:30 p.m. She paid the babysitter. Then she filled a bucket with soap and water and grabbed some old rags. She took Eddie and Lois to the front yard. Vonda began to wash the dust off the coupe. When she concluded she had done enough with her rags, she grabbed the hose coiled by the side of their unit, turned on the water, and rinsed the car. She used a chamois on the windows and took the kids back inside. The car was dry long before Dusty returned.

The *Athletics* defeated the *Angels* 2-0. *KC* pitcher Diego Segui gave up seven hits but was backed up by a solid defense which was a rare thing for the *A's* that year. Catcher Haywood Sullivan had provided the runs by hitting a fourth inning homerun off of Dean Chance with Jerry Lumpe on base courtesy of a walk.

For Mr. Carter, it was one of the best days he had had in years. He had attended many games, but he usually went alone. To have a commentator like Dusty right at his side was a grand thing for a true baseball fan.

For Dusty, the day was bittersweet. He was grateful for the opportunity to see the game. He appreciated the way Mr. Carter had taken him under wing. Dusty was feeling good about earning his keep at the menswear store. The beer and hotdogs were good. But watching others play professional baseball was not so good. Four players—three from *Kansas City* and one from *Los Angeles*—had played minor league ball with Dusty. Most of them had been in the *bigs* from one or two years after Dusty had been released. *"How the hell are you supposed to be glad for them and not sorry for yourself?"* Dusty wondered. He stopped the beer man for another brew.

It was 8:10 p.m. when Dusty came through the door of the duplex uncertain as to what to expect. He had brought Eddie and Lois souvenir rubber balls imprinted with the *A's* logo. He had brought nothing for Vonda.

When he arrived, Dusty was relieved to find that Vonda was sober. She and the kids were upstairs. She had bathed the kids and was putting them to bed. Dusty said he would finish up with them. Vonda said, "Good. I'm taking a shower."

Dusty read the kids a couple of *Little Golden Books* and then kissed them goodnight. He turned out the light.

Dusty walked into his bedroom, pulled off his shirt, shoes, and socks. He then went down stairs, grabbed a beer from the fridge, and sat down at the kitchen table to read the *Coffeyville Journal.* He heard Vonda exit the bathroom but she did not come downstairs. He figured rightly that she was going right to bed. No more arguments today.

Vonda was asleep that Tuesday night by 9:00 p.m. Dusty came to bed at 10:30 p.m. and was snoring within ten minutes. Vonda remained in bed till her clock radio said 1:00 a.m. Then she rolled out of bed and went into the hallway outside the kids' room. She peered at the children's beds. She stood there for two or three minutes. Then she headed downstairs. She was not concerned about Dusty waking; he never awakened during the night no matter how loudly the children howled.

Downstairs, she walked into the living room and opened the closet. The light of a full moon shone through the windows sufficiently to permit Vonda to see all she needed to see. She took a change of clothes off a hanger and got dressed. She pulled on a jacket and bandana. She double-checked that her sunglasses and wallet were in her purse.

Then she reached to the bottom of the closet and pulled out a rucksack which she had packed after washing the car. She slung one of the rucksack straps over her shoulder and walked into the kitchen. There, she pulled an envelope out of her purse and placed it on the kitchen table. The envelope was addressed with the initial "D."

For a moment, Vonda stood still in the middle of the kitchen. Her moonlit shadow could be seen on the linoleum floor that she so despised. Standing in place, Vonda did a three-hundred-sixty-degree turn to look at the kitchen and what else she could see of the downstairs. Then she spat on the floor and walked out the back door.

Vonda quietly shut the door and screen. She gently stepped off the porch, but then walked briskly toward the alley. She went past the Rousters garage, turned right and walked to where the alley intersected with Washita.

Sitting on his cycle under the street light was Brodie Frenk. He took her rucksack and forced it into his small storage compartment. Vonda zipped her jacket and tightened her bandana. They both climbed onto the bike. Brodie fired the engine, rolled away to the left for half a block, then turned right onto Eighth Street. He was going west on U.S. 166. When they passed the city limit sign for Coffeyville, Vonda squeezed Brodie and whooped. It was nearly two hours past midnight but Vonda still thought of it as Independence Day.

A large cloud moved in front of the full moon.

Chapter 39

Walking Home from School: Be Prepared!

"Let me show you something, Billy-boy." Scott Brentano had pulled out his wallet.

"Whatcha got?" I asked, always playing Scott's straight man.

"Here, look." We stopped on the sidewalk, a block east of the junior high school on Lincoln Street. He opened the wallet. I could see three one dollar bills. "Three bucks. Big deal. Don't spend it all in one place."

"Not the money, dope. Look. Beside my thumb."

I looked again. There was a small plastic packet about the size of an *Alka-Seltzer* pouch. I showed no sign of recognition. Scott was beginning to get a look of incredulity upon his face. "What?" I said in frustration.

"You Dodo. It's a *rubber.*" Scott proclaimed proudly.

Actually, that was the closest I had ever been to a condom, Though at the time I had never heard the word *"condom,"* only *"rubber."*

"You got a big date?" I tried to be matter-of-fact. Of course, Scott knew better. My sexual ignorance was legend.

"No, I haven't got a big date—or at least not tonight. But that's the thing," Scott explained. "You never know when opportunity will strike and like the good Boy Scout I am, I want to be prepared."

"You dropped out of scouting two years ago, Brentano."

"Immaterial!" he said. "Anyway, I've got five of these suckers. I'll sell you one for a dollar."

"Go peddle your wares elsewhere, Scott. Say, where did you get these?"

"Not in Coffeyville, Bozo. Do you want to ask a pharmacist who plays golf with your dad for a six pack of rubbers? I don't think so."

"Fine. So where did you get them?" I asked.

"Iola," he replied.

"Iola? That's sixty miles from here. What were you doing in Iola?"

"My mother has an old aunt who lives there—old as the hills. She made me go along so I could be pinched on the cheek by that biddy. Anyway, after the introductions and after the old aunt starts to make tea, she turns to me and gives me fifty cents. She says, 'We're just a block from the square, Scott. Hopkin's Drug Store is right on the corner. Get yourself a malt while your mother and I visit.'"

"She didn't have to say it twice," Scott continued. My mother was glad to get me away from all the bric-a-brac of auntie's old house. So off I went. You see, you need to take advantage of your out of town trips to secure your supplies of you-know-what. Iola was perfect. No one there had ever seen me before except auntie."

"Right," I groaned.

"I had a chocolate malt, courtesy of great auntie. Then I used my own money for the rubbers. Walked right up to the pharmacist and said, 'Five rubbers, please.'"

"The doc stared at me for a minute. Then he said, 'What kind would you like?'"

"I said, 'Any kind will do.' The doc snorted but he pulled out the rubbers, dropped them into a little brown sack, took my money, handed over the merchandise, and I walked back to auntie's well prepared."

A couple of months later, I asked Scott if he had been able to use any of his rubbers. He said, "Hell, yes. They're all gone."

"All gone?" Now I was incredulous. *"You used all of them?"*

"Yeah," he said. "No big deal. We had a water-balloon fight at youth group. They worked great!"

Chapter 40

The Invisible Man: A Hunting We Will Go

Lindy and her boyfriend Chet were standing on the porch steps of Lindy's house as I turned the corner, walking back from work.

"Hi, Chet. Hi, Lindy," I said. I paused on the sidewalk.

"Hi, Billy," they responded.

Chet said, "Gotta go, hon. Talk to you later." Chet pecked her on the cheek and crossed me to hop into his truck and drive away. Lindy sat down on the steps. "Where have you been, Billy?"

"Work. At the paper. I'm gonna have a couple of stories in Sunday's edition. No by-line, just stuff about who's been traveling and who's had house guests. I don't even see how that's news, but it fills up space."

"You'll have your by-line soon enough, Billy. And big stories to report. Then there'll be no stopping you." Lindy always encouraged me. "Sit down and tell me what's happening with you."

I sat down opposite her on the porch steps, but I had no opportunity to talk as Carolyn Rousters and Molly Madigan walked into the yard and sat down, Indian style, before us.

"What have you ladies been doing on this gorgeous day?" Lindy inquired.

"Trying to keep from losing our minds!" Molly said. "There is never anything to do in Coffeyville. Carolyn and I just got back from cruising Eighth Street and even drove by the junior college and up to Big Hill. We checked out the pool to see if anyone we knew was there. No one. Nothing. Dullsville."

Lindy laughed. I suddenly realized that in the presence of these three females I was going to fade into invisibility within seconds.

Molly asked, "Lindy, when your family lived on your farm, did you allow hunters on your property?"

"Sure," Lindy said. "Most hunters would stop by the farmhouse to check in with us. In fact, I can think of only one time my dad ever found someone shooting on our property without having checked with us first. He heard shots and went to investigate. Turned out to be a couple of college boys. One of them had a cousin in

Coffeyville, borrowed a rifle and drove into the country till they found what they thought would be a good place to shoot tin cans. Dad found them. Told them next time to give notice. They apologized and just drove away. I don't know if they hit any tin cans. At least, they didn't kill any of our cattle. Why are you asking about hunters, Carolyn?"

"Because this weekend, our entire family is driving to Tecumseh, outside Topeka, where my Uncle Floyd has a farm. We do this every year. When we get there, everyone in my uncle's family—he and Aunt Mildred have two boys—and everyone in our family goes hunting for pheasant or quail. For five years I've marched around their south forty carrying one of my dad's old shotguns and I haven't fired a shot yet. I'm not going to. Target shooting live animals just doesn't buzz my bod!"

"Don't get me wrong," Carolyn said. "I like to eat pheasant and quail. I've eaten rabbit. I've even eaten squirrel. That's all fine. I'd just rather meet the game for the first time at the supper table, not out in a wheat field."

Lindy laughed again. "Carolyn, I own two rifles of my own. One my parents gave me on my twelfth birthday and the other one I inherited when my dad died. I guess I'll have to scratch you off my list of hunting partners. As to your family trip to your uncle's, maybe you can develop some cramps and spend the day with a hot water bottle."

"Oh, Lord, they're talking about cramps. I gotta get out of here!" I thought to myself. If I just walked away, I doubt that they would have even noticed. Unfortunately, my legs didn't move, an apparent symptom of invisibility.

"Have you ever been hunting, Molly?" Lindy asked.

"Yeah. Sure," Molly said. "I used to go hunting quite a bit before my mother died. Dad would take me and the twins. Captain Jack would go with us most of the time. Dad and Captain Jack have all sorts of friends who own farms and would let us hunt one thing or another or just target shoot. The twins couldn't hit the broad side of a barn. I was damn good. I literally shot a pheasant through the eye one time."

"But you haven't been hunting in a while?" Lindy asked.

"No. Since the deaths, Dad's not much into anything except work and reading his magazines. He sold most of his guns. I think he has only one rifle left, a .22."

"Tell you what, you choose the Saturday and we'll go out to our farm and shoot something to smithereens. Are you up for it, Molly?"

"Absolutely, Lindy!" Molly said. "Next Saturday's good for me. Just let me know when you want to leave. I've even got a red flannel shirt and a *John Deere* cap."

"Splendid!" Lindy said. "You can use one of my rifles and I have plenty of ammo. Maybe Chet will join us. Would you like to come, Billy?"

I magically reappeared right before their very eyes. "Yeah, Lindy, that would be great but I don't think my folks will go for it. A couple of years ago I was out to hunt with my dad and two of my uncles. I aimed at a squirrel that was running across my sight line. I fired. I missed the squirrel but I shot out my uncle's left front truck tire. My other uncle laughed his head off. My dad and the uncle who owned the truck were not happy campers. You all have a good hunt."

"Yeah, Molly, have a good hunt!" Carolyn said. "Maybe the taxidermist will stuff the soup can you kill!"

Chapter 41

How to Encourage an Apology

The school day was complete. Harley Powell and I had walked east behind the high school and junior high school toward Cherokee Street. As we approached the street, we were standing just north of the service alley that ran between the schools and Ise Athletic Field. Tom Shaney was going to pick us up when he finished his *Key Club* meeting. Then we were going to my house for hamburgers as a prelude to listening to the radio broadcast from Miami Beach, Florida, of the heavyweight championship boxing match between Floyd Patterson and Ingemar Johansson. Les Keiter and Howard Cosell would be the ringside announcers.

As Harley and I were talking, Blanton McCoy—who in junior high school had backed out of a fight merely because he was intimidated by me racing down the school steps to get my whipping over with—and his idiot sidekick, Ollie Mobus, walked past us on the sidewalk without a nod by them or by us. About ten yards past us, the two stepped onto the parking, presumably to continue their conversation without blocking the sidewalk.

A few other students strolled by. Then I noticed that Patsy Spencer, a Negro girl, was coming along the sidewalk on her long trek along Fifth Street to the predominantly Negro populated northeast side of Coffeyville.

Patsy was in the eighth grade. When she was in Cleveland Elementary School, her family drove to Oswego to visit Patsy's uncle, aunt, and cousins. On the way home, the Spencer's car was struck by a drunk driver. The five members of Patsy's family all survived the accident but with serious injuries.

In Patsy's case, she had only one serious injury. She lost her left eye. As a result, when Patsy returned to school, she wore a black eye-patch, the kind allegedly sported by pirates. Patsy adjusted well to her handicap (as such an injury was called in those days). She had good grades and a pleasant personality.

Ollie Mobus' earthly hero was the dolt Blanton McCoy. Blanton was big, brash, and a blowhard. Alas, his bluster was sufficient to intimidate boys smaller than Blanton. When Blanton sensed fear, he was uninhibited in his bullying tactics. Ollie Mobus was not the hulk that Blanton McCoy was. Blanton was tall and fat. Ollie was short and fat. Ollie was not good at bluster, but, he, too, was hesitant to pick on anyone his own size. However, he was not afraid to pick on girls, particular one petite, one-eyed, Negro girl named Patsy Spencer.

As Patsy approached, Ollie went into his song and dance:

"Why looky here, Brother McCoy. It's the little pirate girl— *Patsy the Pirate*. Where's your parrot, Patsy the Pirate? Would you like to come over to Ollie's house and walk the plank with me? I think you know what I mean. *Aaahhhrrrggg!* Won't you say *aaahhhrrrggg* for me, Patsy darling? I hear that pirate girls are real outstanding when it comes to cuddling and cooing. What's more, Patsy the Pirate, I heard tell that pirate girls of color— especially those with only one eye—are really good at making whoopee—*chocolate whoopee!* Maybe I can add some whipped cream to your pudding, Patsy the Pirate. Why won't you answer me, Patsy? Dang, girl! You done hurt my feelings. One of these days I may just follow you home. How'd that be, Patsy the Pirate?"

"That would be really stupid, Ollie!" The voice belonged to Harley Powell who was standing right behind Ollie.

Ollie's taunting had immediately caught Harley's and my attention. Patsy was wise enough to walk on by and ignore Ollie. But as Ollie moved to his climactic comments, Harley had had enough. Ollie had taken a couple of strides toward Patsy and as he did so Harley and I advanced behind him.

Ollie turned on a dime when he heard Harley's voice. He backed off a step. But, since his mentor Blanton McCoy was watching, Ollie screwed up his courage and said, "What's that you said about *'stupid,'* Harley, my friend?"

Harley advanced a step. "Ollie, you are not now, never have been, and never will be my friend. What I said was that you would be really stupid if you ever tried to threaten Patsy Spencer by following her. What's more, I just heard your taunting of a girl who is half your size. I know you can't pick a fight with some dude your own size so now you're trying to get your rocks off by troubling girls?"

"Oh, no, no, Brother Powell. Patsy's not just any girl. She's my cute little one-eyed Negress pirate girl—*Patsy the Pirate.*"

"That's enough, Ollie. Shut your trap. You owe the girl an apology!"

"Well, *shiver me timbers*, Brother McCoy. I can see clearly now! Harley, you've got your own crush on Patsy the Pirate. You really like that little ninny. Who knew? Harley Powell loves ni……"

If Harley had punted a *Wilson* brand football instead of Ollie's groin, the spheroid would have had a four second hang time and travelled at least forty yards. As it was, Harley's size twelve foot lifted Ollie at least six inches off the ground. The pitch of Ollie's voice traveled much higher. He landed in a heap, writhing and screaming in pain. As most students had already departed campus, Ollie's moans and groans drew little attention except from Blanton McCoy who was attentive but from a distance.

Just then, Tom Shaney drove up in his pickup.

"Billy, help me with this tub of lard!" Harley said.

Harley and I picked Ollie off the ground and dragged him still whining to the back of Tom's truck. We pushed him into the bed and Harley hopped in with him. Harley said to Tom, "Drive over to Fifth Street and head east till we spot Patsy Spencer. This lummox has some apologizing to do."

I was riding shotgun. We only had to drive two blocks east on Fifth Street to catch up with Patsy. She was walking with a girlfriend. Tom pulled to the curb a few yards ahead of Patsy. Tom jumped out of the cab to help Harley with Ollie. I walked toward Patsy and her friend. When Patsy and her friend spotted the four of us, they started to run, but I leapt in front of them and said, "Patsy, don't run. Ollie has something he wants to say to you."

The two girls were holding on to one another when Harley and Tom dropped Ollie to his knees in front of the distressed girls. Harley said, "Say your piece, Ollie!"

Ollie winced, still in pain from the punt. He looked up, directly into Patsy's eyes. "I'm sorry, Miss Patsy. What I said about pirates and all was not...nice. I know it was rude of me. And I'll never follow you home. So, I'm apologizing to you now. It won't happen again. I promise." Then Ollie looked to the ground, mindful of his own humiliation, and hoping he didn't get Harley's boot again.

Patsy released her friend. She walked over to Harley who was on the right flank of Ollie. She put out her hand for Harley to shake which he did. "Thank you, Harley, for what you've done," Patsy said. Then to Tom, "Thank you, Tom." And then to me, "Thank you, Billy. You're all special to me."

Then Patsy leaned over and looked into the face of Ollie. She said, "I accept your apology, Ollie. I forgive you." Like heaping coals onto his head, Patsy reached out and patted Ollie's cheek. Then she and her friend continued their hike across town. Ollie slumped over on his side.

Harley, Tom, and I returned to the truck. We pulled away as Blanton McCoy arrived to assist and berate his vanquished pal. We picked up some drinks at A & W, cruised for awhile, didn't say much, and then headed to my house.

That night, Floyd Patterson retained his heavyweight boxing crown via a sixth round knockout of Ingemar Johansson.

One week following Ollie Mobus' teachable moment, the high school student elections were held. Harley Powell was elected President of the Student Council with eighty-three percent of the vote.

Chapter 42

PEZ

One summer day before our junior year in high school, I was cruising with Tom Shaney in his pickup. As we came down Central, we spotted Scott Brentano coming out of *Leo's* neighborhood grocery store with a bottle of pop. Scott saluted us and said, "Hiya! Come have a drink with me!"

Tom parked. We went into *Leo's* where I pulled a *Pepsi Cola* out of the pop cooler that was filled with ice and cold water. Tom grabbed a tall *Bubble Up* which indicated he'd spend most of the remaining afternoon burping. We each added some penny candy to our orders and then joined Scott outside.

"Let's go around here," Scott said, leading the way to the north side of Leo's which was in the shade at that hour. Since it was over ninety degrees, shade made a lot of sense. We sat down on an old wooden bench that was aside Leo's brick building.

"Where ya been, Scott?" I asked. "I don't think I've seen you since school let out."

"That's because I've spent nearly a month in Hays and Kansas City," Scott replied. "Cousins in Hays. My grandma on my mother's side in Kansas City. It's good to be back in Coffeyville! Got back yesterday afternoon."

"What's to do in Hays?" Tom asked, slurping his *Bubble Up.*

"You gotta be kidding," Scott replied. "The most action my cousins and I got was trying to fry an egg on the hood of my uncle's rusted out tractor. It was over 110 degrees for the entire week we were out there. My uncle and aunt and my three cousins have a wheat farm—five thousand acres. They're so far out in the boonies, they don't have television and the radio crackles with static. We swam in their pond which was fine if you didn't mind muddy banks and an occasional water moccasin to shoo away.

"My uncle plays on a slow pitch softball team so we went into Hays and saw a game. Man, those farm boys can hit for distance! But because it was still so hot at game time, I could only tolerate the heat by buying two or three dishes of homemade ice cream from the concession stand. At their farmhouse, they have no air conditioning, only a big attic fan that sounds like a *TWA Constellation* taking off. I could barely sleep at night."

"Was Kansas City any better?" I asked.

"Lots better, Billy! Grandma's house is air conditioned. There's a city pool a few blocks away. A library was nearby. And we saw an *A's* game. The *Athletics* actually won. Beat *Detroit* 5-0 and Dick Howser hit a two run homer."

"I may have heard that game on KGGF," I said. "Anyway, it sounds as if your summer is off to a better start than ours. My Pony-Colt team is a game below .500. I've been swimming once. Mostly, I've been hunkered down in our air conditioned back room watching TV."

"I ain't done squat," Tom said, "other than chores on the farm and mucking out the barn. Billy is my entertainment director. We take turns cruising our vehicles along the blistering hot streets of Coffeyville."

"Okay, my fine feathered friends, bring me up to date," Scott said. "I have been out of touch. No phone calls with anyone in Coffeyville—my dad won't let me make long distance calls because of the cost. No *Coffeyville Journal*. I tried picking up KGGF but that didn't happen in Hayes. In Kansas City I didn't try because I could listen to the top forty on WHB. So give me the skinny, guys. What's juicy? What have I missed?"

Tom and I looked at one another in silence. After a moment, Tom belched and said, "Scott, you have not missed a thing, unless you count watching the grass grow or bumpers rust. These lazy, hazy days of summer are passing real slow."

"That's about it," I said. "Of course, summer school is underway. I'm taking typing from Mr. Kreutzer who would have made a great Nazi. But I'm up to twenty-five words a minute now."

We sat in silence, taking sips of our pop. I handed around some banana-flavored *Kits* taffy squares.

After a minute or so, I said, "Well, I suppose one thing that happened while you were away was that Leila Rutter had her baby— or I guess I should say, Mrs. Leila Rutter Drenner had her baby. It's a boy but I don't know any names."

"Son of a gun!" Scott said. "You mean Charlie Drenner manned up and married Leila? Amazing! So what's Charlie gonna do now, work as a soda jerk down at Klein's Drug? I don't think they're going to be able to live in much more than a cardboard box."

"I don't know. I haven't seen either Charlie or Leila. Apparently, they got married by a JP in Independence. Of course, the parents had to sign for them to get a marriage license since they're both under twenty-one."

"I'll be back in minute," Scott said as he headed back into *Leo's*. I figured nature had called to him. Tom and I stoically stared at the rays of the sun pelting the street through the branches of the elm trees. The summer heat and humidity in Coffeyville discouraged movement.

Scott reappeared carrying another round of *Coke, Pepsi,* and *Bubble Up*.

"Here you are, gents," Scott said. "If you two are going to catch me up to date on the exciting events of Coffeyville, the least I can do is keep your tongues well lubricated."

"Bullcrap!" Tom said. "I'll take your pop—thank you very much—but what you really want is for us to gossip like three old biddies. That's what my mom, sister, and my aunts do. That's when I go upstairs to read in my room."

I laughed. Scott shook his head at Tom's mock indignation. Tom drew another big gulp of *Bubble Up*.

Silence.

"I'm puzzled about something," Scott said to break the silence. Tom and I nodded to Scott to continue.

"I don't know why it is, but some people think I'm the phone company's central switchboard. Instead of people dialing *'Information,'* they call me—you know, for what's going on around campus. Usually, everyone fills me in on who has a new car or who wrecked a car or who's broken up or who started dating or who's grounded and all of that."

"Maybe you should write a gossip column for the *Tornado Times*," I said.

"Fat chance the administration would ever let any of my stuff appear in print," Scott said. My prose is too hot to handle. But I don't care about that. I like being the "go to" guy for the latest buzz."

"So what's the problem?" Tom asked. "What are you puzzled about?"

"Four!" Scott said.

"Four what, Scott?" I said. "Four Kings? Four horsemen? Four-score and seven years ago? Don't play games with us."

"Look guys, I'm puzzled by four knocked up seniors: Leila Rutter, Becky Coughnauer, Earlelynn Williford, and Barbara Grauerholtz. Something's wrong with this picture and I don't know what," Scott said.

"My brother is five years older than I am," Scott continued. "When he was in high school and I was still at Garfield, he told me that every school year some girl in high school or even junior high school and sometimes both—some girl would get knocked up. So what's the tally since we began junior high school? By my count until this past year began, the *knockups* have averaged one-point-four per year and most of the *knockees* were between eighth grade and eleventh grade. The only senior was Norma Updegraff, two years ago, thanks to Jeff Funk. But this year, four senior girls killed their rabbits. Was it something in the water?"

"The something was not in the water, Scott. But a *'hose'* was involved!" I joked.

"That's bad, Billy!" Scott said. "Another thing that puzzles me is those four girls were not lowlifes in any way. Leila was editor of the yearbook. Becky was the captain of the girls swimming team. Earlelynn was Vice President of the Student Council. And last but not least, Barbara Grauerholtz was a cheerleader for heaven's sake. They were all friends with one another, too. Were these four unplanned stork deliveries coincidence or conspiracy?"

"Conspiracy?" I said. "What the hell are you talking about? What high school girl would conspire to have her reputation ruined, her future destroyed, and her bank account at a perpetual zero? I'll give you a dime. The payphone is in front of the store. Go call Leila Rutter Drenner and ask her if her bouncing baby whatever is the result of a conspiracy?"

Having finished his *Bubble Up* to quench the *Fireball* he had crunched, Tom Shaney mashed the bottom of the bottle into the dirt in front of the bench. As he began to make circles in the dirt, he said, "It wasn't a conspiracy. It wasn't a pregnancy pact. It was stupidity."

"Yeah, they were all four too stupid to keep their knees together," Scott said.

"There was more to it than that," Tom said. "They all got pregnant because—as bright as that quartet was and is—they were stupid, naïve, and ignorant."

"'Stupid, naïve, and ignorant?' My, my, those are strong words!" Scott said. Scott and I leaned forward on the bench to get a good look at Tom. Scott asked, "You know something, Shaney?"

"I know the whole story!" Tom said, dusting dirt off his hands.

Scott stood up and walked in front of Tom. "You? You, of all people, know the full story? Come on, Tom, 'fess up. If I believe you, I'll buy you a pack of sunflower seeds." With that, Scott plopped down on the grass, crossed his legs, and waited for Tom to continue.

Tom leaned back onto the brick wall. "Listen up, then!" he began. "I'm only going to tell this once.

"A week or two after school was out, my mom, dad, and I went over to my Uncle Dexter and Aunt Charlene's in Pittsburg to spend a Friday and Saturday night visiting. My dad and uncle had gone off to a liquor store to buy some booze for the weekend. I was upstairs in the small bedroom they had put me. I was reading a Robert Heinlein sci-fi book, *Red Planet.*

"My mother is a trained nurse but quit to work the farm with dad. My Aunt Charlene is a nurse at the Pittsburg hospital. A woman named Eileen is another nurse who works with my mother in Pittsburg but Eileen lives in Altamont.

"Cowtown," Scott interjected, referring to Altamont's nickname that rudely pertained not just to bovines but to Altamont's women as well.

"Right. *'Cowtown.'* Now, don't interrupt," Tom said.

"Eileen came by to give my aunt some green beans and spinach she had canned," Tom continued. My aunt says, 'Stay for coffee.'

"Turns out that the little bedroom where I was reading was right over the kitchen where my mom, my aunt and Eileen were sitting. The bedroom had a floor register to let heat come up from downstairs. It was open and I could hear everything they said.

"I'm not going to give you their conversation verse by verse. But here's the sad story about how naïve and ignorant Southeast Kansas girls suddenly get *'in a family way.'"*

"We're all ears," Scott said.

"Eileen, the nurse from Altamont, is Becky Coughnauer's aunt. When Becky had to leave Field Kindley because she was prego, she went to live with her Aunt Eileen. Altamont high school let her finish her senior year there. Eventually, Becky told her aunt the whole story. Becky's aunt tells the story to my mom and aunt and here I am telling the story to you. This is communication at its finest!

"Anyway, Eileen tells my aunt and my mom that the whole family is Catholic and that the priests and nuns have told the faithful to have nothing to do with birth control pills," Tom continued. "Not only that, but sex had never been a topic of discussion between the parents and the Coughnauer girls. Of course, the nuns never gave them any facts either. The girls were flying blind.

"Then Glenda, the older sister goes off to KU. When Glenda is set to begin her senior year at KU, Becky is about to become a senior at Field Kindley High School. The night before big sis goes back to school, she tells Becky that she's been on the pill since her junior year. Other than making that revelation, Glenda apparently didn't go into to much detail about how she used the pill. But Becky probably had no problem putting two and two together.

"A week after Glenda goes back to the Lawrence campus, Becky is emptying Glenda's dresser drawers so that she can use them till Glenda comes back. While rearranging stuff, Becky discovers a full packet of birth control pills and she decides to throw a party. She invites her chums Leila, Earlelynn, and Barbara over for a backyard swim and slumber party. A good time is had by all.

"Finally, these four babes are in their nighties, all gathered around Becky's bed, swapping stories. But before its time to rack out for the night, Becky puts a small paper sack in front of them and says, 'You've got twenty questions to discover what's in the sack.'

"These clueless girls exhaust their twenty questions and demand to know what's in the sack. Becky reaches in, pulls out the packet and opens it up for the girls to see. Barbara immediately asks, 'What's that?' while Becky, Leila, and Earlelynn all begin to giggle. Finally, Becky says, 'They're birth control pills!'

"Barbara jumps up and says, 'Oh, wow! Can I hold them?'"

"You mean, none of them had seen a pack of birth control pills before?" Scott asked.

"Have you seen a packet of birth control pills?" I asked Scott. "I haven't."

"No, I haven't seen them," Scott said. "I know that my sister-in-law uses them. How big are they? Like Tums or Alka-Seltzer?"

"No, dipstick!" Tom said. "They're small, smaller than an aspirin. And the packet isn't much larger than a cigarette pack."

"So what happened," I asked. "Did Becky start using the pills?"

"Yes and no," Tom replied. "Remember, that these pills have only been available for less than two years now. Those chicks were clueless and there was no paperwork with the packet. Eileen said the pill pack had twenty-one pills in sort of a circle configuration. The woman is supposed to take one pill a day until she comes to her time of the month and then she stops until that's over and then she starts again on a new packet of pills."

Scott said, "So, are you saying that Becky used up the one packet, couldn't get another, but still wanted to whack and that's how she got knocked up?"

"No, Scott. Let me finish—I want those sunflower seeds." Tom continued his tale: "These girls all knew how babies get made but they didn't know beans about how to use the birth control pills to keep a baby from being made. Bottom line, when they were all about to call it a night, Becky gave each of the other girls an empty PEZ container. She dropped five pills into each container and she kept six."

Scott laughed. He said, "You mean to tell me those girls were walking the hallowed halls of Field Kindley while they were carrying birth control pills in Pez containers?"

"Eileen told my mom and aunt that the girls actually believed they were supposed to swallow one pill every night they thought they might get laid. Three of them thought they had five free bangs and Becky had a six pack. One by one by one by one they all conceived to make it a banner year of unwed mothers for the *Golden Tornado!*"

Again, we were silent for a minute. Then Scott said, "That is the most amazing tale of tales I have ever heard! Man, Tom, you were in the right place at the right time. Talk about scoop of the century! But what's the rest of the story? The babies? Anyone else get married besides Leila?"

I spoke up. "I heard that Earlelynn went to a convent in Topeka. Apparently she gave up the baby for adoption. What I heard is that they wouldn't even let her see the baby after it was born."

Tom said, "When word got out about Becky being pregnant, she moved to Altamont to live with her Aunt Eileen. Apparently, Becky is going to marry Taz Downey in September or October. Taz is spending the whole summer with a harvesting team to get some money together. Becky was allowed to transfer to Altamont High School to finish her senior year but the school wouldn't give her a diploma. They told her to take the G.E.D."

"And what about Barbara Grauerholtz?" Scott asked.

"She flew the coop!" I said. "Dillon Shade said he'd marry her, but Barbara said, 'No way, Jose!' She was really pissed at the whole situation. She turned eighteen in February. She took her savings from working at *Dairy Queen* and teaching little kids to play the piano and combined it with some money her grandparents gave her. Barbara's parents pretty much disowned her. So, off to California she went with the baby. She has an older cousin in the San Fernando Valley who is gonna help her settle in."

Scott said, "None of the four could walk across the platform. No diplomas. But the guys were able to walk."

"That's right. As long as you aren't pregnant or aren't married, you can pick up a diploma."

"Okay, it's bad enough for the couples involved and I would not want to be in their shoes," I said. "But what frosts me is that every time news circulates that some girl is pregnant, my parents start lecturing me not to get myself into *'that kind of trouble.'* Shucks! I can barely get a date! I'm not likely to *'go all the way'* for some while now."

Tom Shaney said, "I took Jill Grimm on a date last Friday. I was going to take her to the drive-in but instead we wound up on Big Hill watching the Roosevelt Drive submarine races. When we came up for air, we started talking about one thing and another and then I raised the topic of the pregnancies. We were both in the mood for some heat but neither one of was interested in turning the big-belly quartet into a quintet.

"Jill told me that when she heard about the pregnancies she remembered having two emotions—'feeling so sorry for them.' She said, 'To me, it seemed they were at "the end," living in a tiny apartment, no social life—not even a movie—and their friends slowly moving on.' Also, she said she was making a list of things she wanted to do before she got married. Getting knocked up was not on the list. She said she didn't want to reach her fortieth birthday and be depressed about all that she hadn't done because of stupid mistakes she'd made."

"Wise chick, Tom!" I said. "And she's got great eyes! You may want to stay in touch."

"So that's it, Scott. That's the whole shebang. Now you owe me," Tom said.

"I never welsh on a bet!" Scott said. *"Sunflower seeds all around!"*

Chapter 43

And Then There Were Three!

Dusty Lang awakened to the sound of Eddie and Lois squabbling. That was unusual, not the squabbling, but that Dusty should be awakened by such a fracas. What also was unusual was that he did not hear Vonda's voice arbitrating the kids' dispute. Dusty checked his watch. It was 7:45 a.m. Most mornings, Vonda would have had the kids downstairs for at least an hour by now. "What now? Dusty groaned to himself as he rolled out of bed.

Before entering the kids' room, Dusty ducked into the bathroom to urinate. Drip drying his hands, he came out of the bathroom and walked into the kids' room. Eddie was playing with a truck on the floor. Lois was jumping up and down in her crib yelling at Eddie to let her join him. Eddie was talking but mainly to the truck.

"Hey, what's happening here, kids?" Eddie asked.

"Hi, Daddy!" they cried.

There was no indication that Vonda had been there.

"Where's your mommy?" Dusty asked.

"Don't know, Daddy," Eddie answered. "She told us to stay in our room until she came in to get us."

"Sounds like a good plan," Dusty said as he lifted Lois out of her crib. "Go potty and come downstairs. We'll get you some breakfast."

As Eddie and Lois proceeded to the bathroom, Dusty went down the stairs. He heard no sound of Vonda. She wasn't in the kitchen. She wasn't in the living room. He looked out back. Then he went into the living room and looked out to the front. The coupe was where it had been left. The only thing out of the ordinary was that the living room closet door was open. He closed it and walked back into the kitchen.

Then he spotted the envelope with the initial "D." He picked it up and pulled out the note. It was short but not very sweet:

Dusty—

I'm gone. Don't try to find me. I don't even know where I am going except away from this damn little town. I suppose we both tried. It didn't work. Tell the kids whatever you want. This hellhole has overwhelmed my love for them. God have mercy on us all!

V

Dusty slumped into a kitchen chair. He had been slammed in the stomach. Eddie came down the stairs. Dusty had to gasp for air.

"What are you doing, Daddy?"

Dusty said nothing. He refolded the note and replaced it in the envelope.

"What are you doing, Daddy?" Eddie repeated as Lois joined the guys.

Dusty stood and placed the envelope on top of the fridge. Then, he turned to Eddie and Lois. He smiled, "Sorry!" he said. "I was just reading a letter. Now I've read it. So let's have breakfast. Who wants Frosted Flakes?"

The kids were so fascinated with Dusty rummaging through the cupboards to construct breakfast that it wasn't until Eddie had taken two spoonfuls of cereal that he asked, "Where's Mommy?"

Dusty was tying a bib onto Lois. "She had to go somewhere. She'll be back. She'll be back!" he said. He thought to himself, *"What the hell am I saying? I hate that bitch!"*

At 9:30 a.m., Dusty called Mr. Carter.

"Good morning, boss," Dusty said.

"Yes, it was a great trip. Really fine, boss. ... Right. Sullivan hit that curve ball on the screws .... Listen, boss. Something's come up here with the family. I'm not gonna be able to make it in today.

... I'm sorry, boss, I can't really get into it now. I'll be there tomorrow. ... Right. Sorry again. I'll see you tomorrow."

Dusty knew that there was some likelihood that Vonda would be back home before the day was out. The note may have been just a scare tactic, an illustration of the hate and contempt she harbored against him. However, over their years of in-fighting, Dusty had learned Vonda's moves, her jabs and feints. This note did not bespeak routine sparring. The little tragedy of their marriage had descended to a new low. *"Suck it up, Dusty"* he thought to himself. *"It may be a long winter."*

Indeed, necessity is the mother of invention. Dusty loathed the state of his marriage—if he still had a marriage. Fortunately, he did not loathe his kids. Mrs. Ida Schwell, a retired widow, lived in Unit B of the duplex. She had always gotten along well with all members of the Lang family. She was slightly hard of hearing but not so deaf that she hadn't heard Vonda's rants or the children crying. Nevertheless, she always dealt graciously with the Langs and had babysat a few times.

Before sunset July 5, Dusty had made arrangements with Mrs. Schwell, Carolyn Rousters, and Sharon Chambers to take care of the kids when Dusty was at work. He had told them, "Vonda's had to go away for awhile, so I need some help with the kids." None of the caregivers asked any questions. The environs of Lincoln Street were too small a neighborhood for the Lang's marital reality not to be quickly deduced.

The kids would eat well but, if Vonda truly was a thing of the past, Dusty would be dining on just a little more than bread and water in order to afford the childcare. He knew that at some point he could probably enlist support from his mother or sisters back in Aurora. But he was not presently prepared to report yet another failure in his life.

A couple of times, Dusty thought he was painting too black a picture of the situation. Surely, Vonda would be back. Maybe she would be gone a few days. But she had been *"gone"* when she was on some of her drinking binges inside her own four walls. They had worked their way through those episodes, why not this one? Dusty would think about that for a few moments and then say to himself, *"Dusty, you are the world's biggest fool!"*

Eddie and Lois did not understand their mother's absence. For two weeks straight, each of them cried themselves to sleep. Tantrums and weeping repeated during the day, according to the babysitters. Finally, the kids began to adjust and adapt to Vonda's absence. Dusty had no illusions as to how searing was this circumstance upon the children. *"God help us!"* he prayed throughout the day.

Help came through Dusty developing newfound resolve to confront his pitiful lot which he acknowledged was mainly of his own design. A week after Vonda had left and not returned, Dusty shared, with great embarrassment, the state of his marriage and his new home front reality with Mr. Carter.

Dusty's boss listened stoically to what his employee had to say. When Dusty finished, Mr. Carter leaned back in his desk chair.

"I'm sorry to hear this, Dusty," Mr. Carter said. "I hope things will work out for your family. I know you'll do what's right for the kids. Let me know if I can ever be of help to your personal situation."

"Thank you, Mr. Carter," Dusty replied. "I'll do my best not to let any of this affect my work."

"I'm sure you will, Dusty," Carter responded.

Whatever awkwardness the two men may have felt for a few days regarding Dusty's home situation, they did not discuss particulars. This was not because Mr. Carter was indifferent or that Dusty was defensive, it was because the day-in, day-out working together had engendered a mutual respect between the two. Each believed the other to be a person of integrity who could be trusted to do the right thing or, at least, strive to do the right thing. Dusty continued to do good work. Talking baseball returned to its normative state at Carter's Menswear.

Dusty still loved baseball. He would still play catch with me and now little Eddie as well. Occasionally, he would show up at a practice for our Pony League team. Eddie and Lois loved running around the bases.

Yet, for all his love of baseball, every night when he collapsed into bed, Dusty wished he had never met his high school pal—now of the *Cleveland Indians*—Boyd Benson.

Chapter 44

A Matter of Debate

The school year at Field Kindley was coming to an end. There were only three weeks left before I would become a junior, no longer a sophomore, lowest rung in our three-year high school of nine hundred students. As the fourth hour lunch bell rang, I headed toward an exit and the ten minute walk to our house on Lincoln Street where my mother would have a couple of bologna, cheese, lettuce, and tomato sandwiches on *Roman Meal Bread* waiting for me.

As I was about to cross Cherokee over to Lincoln Street, Sylvester White caught up with me.

"Hey, Billy!" he said.

"Hi, Syl. How you doin'?" I replied.

"Fine. Mighty fine."

"So, what's up?" I asked.

"Billy, do you have anything going on today right after school?" Sylvester asked.

I thought for a moment. "Don't think so, Syl. What can I do for you?"

Sylvester said, "Gracie Truman and I would like to talk something over with you and Harley Powell. Shouldn't take long. I've already spoken to Harley and he's available."

"Sure, Syl. No problem," I said. "Where do you want to meet? Library? Study hall?"

"Gracie and I thought maybe we could meet with you at Captain Jack's. You know he's just a few minutes down Lincoln Street," Sylvester said.

I was surprised at the venue. "Captain Jack's? Fine with me. I didn't know you knew Captain Jack."

"Mrs. Patterson who does Captain Jack's housekeeping is my auntie," Sylvester said.

"I didn't know that, Sylvester," I said. "She's a nice lady and, man, can she bake great pies."

"You're right about that, Billy. Okay, then, we'll see you at Captain Jack's whenever you can get there. Who knows, maybe Auntie Gladys will have some pie ready for us."

"My mouth's watering already! See you then, Syl."

When school was dismissed for the day, I met Harley Powell by his locker and we then headed for Captain Jack's.

"What do you think this meeting is about, Harley?" I asked.

"Haven't a clue!" Harley said. "But it's interesting that we're meeting with Captain Jack."

"And probably Mrs. Patterson, too," I said. "I never knew that Sylvester was related to Mrs. Patterson."

"Nope. Neither did I," Harley said.

"In light of your election as next year's Student Council President, maybe the east side of town is going to name you an *'Honorary Negro,'*" I joked.

"I could go for that," Harley said, "if it meant I could get discounts on barbequed ribs and southern fried chicken."

Harley knocked on Captain Jack's door. With cane in hand, Captain Jack himself answered the door, a task which was more often performed by Mrs. Patterson when she was working at the house. Once inside, we were greeted by Mrs. Patterson, Sylvester White, and Gracie Truman. Mrs. Patterson was dressed as if she were headed for church, not adorned in her housekeeping dress and apron. Even Gracie and Sylvester were spiffed up more than what was usual for a school day. I suddenly realized that neither Harley nor I were *"spiffed up"* and I became self-conscious about my attire. Now I was really wondering about the purpose of this get-together. For his part, Captain Jack appeared to be in his usual casual clothes.

Captain Jack said, "Harley and Billy, why don't you sit at either end of the sofa. You'll notice that we have prepared for your arrival by placing pecan pie and ice tea at your disposal." The others appeared to be nearly finished with the pie they had been given. Captain Jack sat down in his recliner and took a sip of his coffee.

"I don't know if I have ever been so fortunate to have four talented and gifted students enjoy such excellent pie with me in the confines of my own home," Captain Jack said. "Thank you for the pie, Mrs. Patterson. Thank you all for coming.

"Harley, you and Billy are here to learn about a situation that involves all of the students at the high school" the Captain said. "Earlier this week, Mrs. Patterson asked if I would hear some concerns that are on the hearts and minds of Sylvester and Gracie. I believe you know that Sylvester is Mrs. Patterson's nephew. Mrs. Patterson and her sister Jacqueline—that's Sylvester's mother— attend the Zion United Missionary Church that Gracie's father— Pastor Ezra Nehemiah Truman—pastors on East Third Street.

"Mrs. Patterson, would you like to continue?" the Captain asked.

"Thank you, Captain Jack," Mrs. Patterson began. "Harley and Billy, an incident that involved the two of you gave impetus to our request for this meeting. Gracie, you have something you wish to say to Harley and Billy?"

"Yes, Mrs. Patterson. Thank you. Harley, you probably do not know that Patsy Spencer is my cousin. Patsy is a dear girl who has dealt with the loss of her one eye with courage and a positive outlook. We all know that there are and always have been unfortunate issues between Negro students and white students. Blanton McCoy and Ollie Mobus are two white students who have harassed Patsy and others. Recently, you observed Blanton and Ollie's abuse of Patsy and you came to her aid. I cannot tell you how much your defense of Patsy and rebuke of Ollie Mobus has meant to Patsy, our entire family, and frankly to most of the Negro people who live in Coffeyville."

Sylvester then spoke up. "Harley, you and me have done a lot of sports together. We've done a lot of jawing together. We've done a lot of laughing together. But we've never talked about black and white. In fact, I don't know that anyone does—I mean Negroes talk among Negroes about whites and I suppose white folk talk about colored folk amongst themselves. But we don't talk between one another—or at least I haven't."

Gracie said, "It's the same for me. I have many white people who I honestly believe are my friends. I like them and it seems they like me. But we've never talked about black and white. My daddy almost did not accept the call to pastor at Zion United Missionary Church because he said he had been told by many of his fellow pastors that Coffeyville is one of the most racist towns in Kansas."

Captain Jack spoke up, "Gracie, your family has been in Coffeyville for more than ten years now. What's your daddy's opinion of race relations in Coffeyville today?"

"Captain Jack, my daddy would say that dealings between the colored folks and the white folks are not good. But he would not say that Coffeyville is the 'most racist' town in Kansas. Things aren't good but no one is fighting about it. But there is very little conversation about these issues, though Daddy does say that the Ministerial Association has had a few talks on these matters."

Harley finished his pecan pie and placed the plate and fork on the end table. He said, "Captain Jack, this conversation so far is not what I expected when you invited Billy and me to stop by. I was hoping for pie and we got that. Thank you, Mrs. Patterson.

"As to the topic you've been addressing, I know full well that this is a concern in our town. I laugh when I hear some white guy say, 'Some of my best friends are Negroes.' But in truth, I would like to think that some of the Negro boys and girls that I've gone to school with truly are my friends. I haven't invited any Negro guys to my house but I live with my grandparents in their back room. The truth is that only Billy and one or two others have ever been in the house where I live. So, Captain Jack, how do Billy and I fit into this picture?"

"Well you might ask, Harley?" Captain Jack said. "For the moment, let Sylvester continue."

"Harley, you and Billy and even Tom Shaney fit into the picture because you all stepped into the picture frame when you stepped up to bat for Patsy Spencer," Sylvester said. "When word got passed around about that encounter, my own conscience hit me up on the side of my head. Gracie and I have been bothered 'bout something for a year now. You all helping Patsy has encouraged Gracie and me to seek your advice so that we can finally settle an account."

I said, "You want advice from us? How can we be of any help?" I had a look of surprise on my face.

"Give Syl a little more time, Billy," Gracie said. "Before we asked to talk with you, we spoke to Mrs. Patterson and Captain Jack. They both thought it would be a good thing to hear what you might have to say. Syl, share with them some of the background."

"Sure, Gracie," Sylvester said. "We all have been taught about *Brown v. the Topeka Board of Education.* Segregation was allegedly struck down. The notion of *'separate but equal'* facilities got struck down. That was almost a decade ago.

"I know that there has been some progress in race relations across the country and even here in Coffeyville. Most Negro kids don't have a problem walking the streets of Coffeyville. But we know enough to stay on the northeast side of town after the sun goes down. But Gracie and I are concerned about a situation that came upon us at Field Kindley.

"You know, I did some research over at the library and I found out that black folks make up about fifteen percent of Coffeyville's population. But there is not one black teacher at the high school or junior high school. I can't vote so I have no influence on the Board of Education. But I do have a vote sometimes at the high school—I mean regarding student matters. Harley, I'm proud to say that I voted for you as Student Council President!"

"As I did!" Gracie said.

"And as I did!" I chimed in.

"Thank you all!" Harley said with a smile. "Go ahead, Syl."

"At the high school, there are Negro athletes in all the sports and they are often the best of the bunch," Sylvester said. "But there are no Negro girls on the swimming team. 'Course I don't know what Negro girl is really a great swimmer. I do know many Negro students who make great music. Gracie and I sing in the choir. You know, we've done solos. But there are no Negro girls in the *Drum and Bugle Corps* and you don't even have to play all that well to be selected for the corps because the members are taught what they need to know.

"You know we all turn out for the basketball and football games. But there is no black cheerleader. Even in the pep squad, the *Tornado Tillies* have no Negro members. That just don't make sense and it don't seem right."

Harley asked, "Gracie, do you want to be in the *Drum and Bugle Corps?"*

"No, not really," Gracie said. "I do have some friends who would like to be in the corps."

"Did they try out?" I asked.

"No, Billy," Gracie said. "They all know better."

"What's that mean?" I asked.

Mrs. Patterson said gently, "It means, Billy, that we know where we're welcome and where we are not welcome."

Harley said, "What you both say is true. Though no one has ever spoken to me about this, I agree with your description of how things are. So, have you reached the point where you can tell me how Billy and I fit in to this situation? Do you want the Student Council to address race relations?

"No!" Gracie said. "That would probably create more problems. Wanting to talk with you two doesn't have anything to do with the Student Council."

"Then what?" I asked.

"You are both members of the Debate Team," Sylvester said.

"Now, you just lost me, Syl!" Harley said. "Sure. We're both on the Debate Team. Love it! Do you want us to debate someone?"

"No, Billy," Syl said. "Gracie and I want to be on the Debate Team."

"Why not?" I said. "The two of you would be great!"

"Thank you! Gracie said.

"But the problem is we both signed up for Debate last year," Sylvester said. "But when the school year began, Debate was not on our schedules. Both of us were put into Stage Production with Mr. Burchinal. That was a good class, but it wasn't what we wanted."

"Why didn't you try to get your schedules changed? That happens all the time," Harley asked.

"We did try, Harley," Gracie said. "Mr. Thorne, the Vice Principal, is in charge of scheduling. When we spoke to him, he said it would be difficult to make the switch with the school year already underway. He said he would talk with Mr. Collie, the debate coach to see if he could handle another two students in light of how crowded the debate class was already."

"Crowded? Debate wasn't crowded!" I said. "I don't think there were more than fourteen of us in the class. I can't believe that Mr. Collie wouldn't have been able to handle another two students."

"So then what happened?" Harley asked.

Syl said, "Mr. Thorne said he would get back to us in a couple of days. He told us that on a Thursday during the noon hour. I waited till the following Monday afternoon and went to Mr. Thorne's office to find out if Mr. Collie had approved the schedule change. The secretary said that Mr. Thorne had left that morning for the Kansas

State P-TA Convention in Topeka and would not be back until the following Monday."

"We waited till the following Monday," Gracie said as she continued the story. "We went to see Mr. Thorne. When we went into his office and he asked how he could help. We told him that we had come back for an answer. He said he was sorry but the administration's policy was that no switches could be made after three weeks into the new term. Sign up for next year when it's enrollment time again," he said.

"Interesting," Harley said. "What do you think Billy or I can do?"

"The first part you just did," Sylvester said. "We wanted you to hear what we had to say."

"Listen, guys," I said. "Not that I would have absolutely known this, but if the Debate Team had heard about the two of you wanting to join, I believe everyone in the class would have said, 'Right on!' But I never heard any such thing."

"Nor I," Harley said. "So, what do you want to do next?"

"We want to talk with Mr. Brixton, the Principal," Sylvester said. "We've each put down Debate as an elective for next year. We don't want to show up here in late August and go through the same rigmarole as we did this year. We also wanted to know if the two of you would sit in with us at a meeting with Mr. Brixton."

Before either Harley or I could answer, Captain Jack said, "Folks, let me speak a little about your meeting with Mr. Brixton. I think that's a real good idea. I hear he is a very fair man. However, over the years—especially in the military—I've had more than my share of confrontational meetings with commanding officers. May I suggest that your visitation committee consist of Gracie, Sylvester, and Harley. No offense, Billy. I just think you need to avoid the appearance of ganging up on Mr. Brixton. I'm sure Harley will be able to well represent Billy, if necessary."

"That's not a problem for me," I said. "Let me know what time is your meeting and I'll say a prayer for you."

"You and me both, Billy," said Mrs. Patterson.

"Count me in, too," Captain Jack said. "I'm happy to say the Almighty and I are still speaking to one another."

The meeting with Mr. Brixton took place three school days later at 3:10 p.m. Mr. Brixton listened to everything Syl, Gracie, and Harley had to say. When they finished, Mr. Brixton said this was the first he had heard about the matter. He said he understood why Gracie and Sylvester were trying to avoid what had happened for the current school year. He said he would consult with Mr. Thorne and Mr. Collie. When his examination of the matter was complete, Mr. Brixton said he would get back to Gracie and Sylvester. He told Harley that he appreciated his willingness as incoming Student Council President to stand by his friends in this matter. Mr. Brixton concluded by saying he had participated in Debate in high school and college and believed the experience he gained in the subject had served him well since he had become a teacher and administrator.

Gracie, Sylvester, and Harley all believed Mr. Brixton had given them a fair hearing. The waiting game began again.

Mr. Brixton's investigation revealed that Debate Coach Collie had never been aware of Gracie and Sylvester's interest in Debate. Coach Collie said he would welcome the two to the class and predicted they would do well as debaters.

Mr. Brixton learned that Vice Principal Thorne purposefully did not speak to Coach Collie because he believed the addition of the Negro students to the Debate Team would be detrimental to class morale and overall school morale. Mr. Brixton advised Vice Principal Thorne that he should never again practice such obstructionism.

The day after the school year concluded, the *Journal* reported that Vice Principal Thorne had resigned his position at Field Kindley. During the summer, Mr. Thorne moved his family to Arkansas where he became a Vice Principal at Pine Bluff High School from which he eventually retired.

Nine days before the end of the school year, Gracie Truman and Sylvester White had notes waiting for them at the beginning of their first period classes. The notes were from Mr. Brixton and said,

"Your enrollment in Debate this fall is confirmed. I expect to see your name on several trophies! Good luck!"

After the school year concluded, one week or so before Independence Day that year, I received a phone call from Gracie Truman. She said that on the Sunday before Independence Day, her father—The Reverend Doctor Ezra Nehemiah Truman—would appreciate Harley Powell, Tom Shaney, and I attending the worship service at Zion United Missionary Church. She said her father wanted to meet the three of us and thank us for what we had done for Patsy Spencer and in support of Gracie and Sylvester getting onto the Debate Team.

On Sunday, July 2, Tom, Harley, and I arrived ten minutes before the 10:00 a.m. worship service. Sylvester met us and led us down to the second row in front of the pulpit. Also seated on the second row were Mrs. Patterson and Captain Jack, Mrs. Patterson's sister Jacqueline and her husband Leroy, Sylvester, Gracie and her mother Mrs. Truman. We four Caucasians stood out like drops of *Wite-Out* on a sheet of carbon paper! Again, I was underdressed.

The worship service went on for two hours and fifteen minutes. I enjoyed it, especially the music and the preaching by Pastor Truman. After completing his sermon and the subsequent altar call, Pastor Truman asked everyone to be seated. Then he said,

"This week we will celebrate Independence Day. Negro Americans know that independence is not enjoyed equally by the people of America. But since the Fall, the Lord has said all peoples will struggle over one thing or another until Jesus returns. Nevertheless, we can be grateful to people of every color who seek after

*righteousness in how all God's people deal
with one another.*

*Today, I want to introduce to you seven
Coffeyville residents who have courageously
taken stands to protect and provide equal
treatment to others no matter their color or
background. Let me introduce Captain Jack
Daugherty, Mrs. Gladys Patterson, Mr.
Harley Powell, Mr. Billy Howard, Mr.
Thomas Shaney, Mr. Sylvester White, and
Miss Gracie Truman."*

The congregation stood with lingering applause. Amazing!

During the new school year that began in late August, Sylvester and Gracie along with their respective Debate partners, did, indeed, add to the trophy hardware collected by the *Tornado Tonguesters!*

However, when the Debate Team travelled to another city for a Friday/Saturday debate tournament, Gracie and Sylvester each had single hotel/motel rooms while the rest of the squad doubled-up by gender for the night.

Chapter 45

The Birthday Present

"Come in!" Molly said. After responding to my knock, Molly immediately turned and went back to the piano.

I let myself in and followed her into the den. I sat down on the sofa and flipped through pages of *The Scarlet Letter* which I rightly deduced was being read for an upcoming English report. At the moment, Molly was practicing some classical piece for her school's spring concert.

She played and replayed for several minutes, then stopped. She stood up, picked up a stack of music from the top of the upright and stuck it under her arm. She then lifted the piano top, reached in and pulled out a pack of *Chesterfield* cigarettes, a small ashtray, and some matches. She took out one of the cigarettes. She turned to me, waving the fag in the air and asked, "Want one?"

"No, thanks." The fact that I didn't or wouldn't smoke was amusing to her. She replaced the cigarettes, closed the piano top, and replaced the music. She carried her unlit cigarette, matches, and ashtray over to the sofa where she sat down opposite me. She lit up, blew the opening drag back toward the ceiling, and stuck the match book into her jeans pocket. The ashtray rested on her thigh. She had on a turtleneck sweater and was barefoot.

As Molly drew her feet under her, I asked "What were you playing?"

"Tchaikovsky's *Piano Concerto Number One.* It's what Van Cliburn won the *International Tchaikovsky Competition* with in Moscow."

"Is Cliburn a Communist?"

"No, silly. He's a Texan. It was a big deal. He went to Moscow and beat the Russians at their own game. He got a tickertape parade in New York, for God's sake. Don't you know anything?" She blew smoke my direction.

I waved the smoke away. "Give me a break, will ya? I don't play musical instruments. I thought you played that—whatever—Russian concerto thing good."

"Thank you, Billy."

"Are you going to play that in Moscow?"

"Billy, I'll be lucky if Sister Mary Claire lets me play the damn piece in Wichita. I still haven't got it completely memorized and the fingers on my right hand are as stiff as a corpse's. I'm also supposed to play *"Bumble Boogie"* which, as I'm sure you know, is based on *"The Flight of the Bumblebee"* by Rimsky-Korsakov, another Russian. Lest you be concerned, Rimsky-Korsakov also was not a Communist."

"Don't make fun of me, Molly, or I'll stomp your bare feet."

"You don't scare me, white-boy prick."

"Nice talk, Molly."

Molly looked at her watch. "Oh, shit!" she said. She mashed out her cigarette in her hide-away ashtray and sat up. She said, "Listen, Billy-boy, I hate to be rude, crude, and unsophisticated, but I need to get back to my book. I gotta find out whether *Hester* kills her bastard husband or not. We'll talk another day."

"Not a problem," I said as I stood up. "I gotta go change anyway."

"Big date?" she asked facetiously.

"No. It's my birthday. My family is going out to eat, probably to Bones."

"Today's your birthday!" Molly exclaimed. Why didn't you tell me sooner? How old are you? 35? 40?"

"You know dadgum well it's 14!" I said.

"Ah, yes, well you always come across much older when we chat on the swings," Molly said. "Well, I've got good news for you Billy-boy. I actually have a birthday present for you."

"You're kidding me!" I said, getting ready to be the butt of another of Molly's jokes.

"Now who is being rude, crude, and unsophisticated, pickle-head? I said I have a birthday present for you and I damn well do." She stood in front of me. "Now, listen. Follow my instructions exactly. Got that? Exactly!" I nodded my head in assent.

Molly continued, "If you don't follow my instructions to the letter, I swear I will kick you in the balls. Do you understand me?"

"Yes, Molly, I understand you."

"Good. Now close your eyes!" she said.

"What?"

"Damn it, Billy-boy, I said close your eyes. Are you getting deaf in your old age?"

I closed my eyes.

"Now give me your hands," she said as she reached out and pulled them to shoulder height. I knew I'd be lucky to escape with only one broken arm.

"Relax your arms," she said as she shook my arms. "Now, I'm going to give you your birthday present. But you must not open your eyes. You must follow my every instruction. Do you understand me or should I just kick you now?"

"'Good golly, Miss Molly,' I understand. My eyes are closed," I said. "I'll do what you say. Just do whatever you're going to do to me. I've got a steak waiting for me."

"Okay, birthday-boy, here we go."

Silence.

Nothing.

She was still holding my hands up in the air. Then she drew my hands toward her and down. She pressed my hands upon her *breasts!* I didn't open my eyes but I opened my mouth in astonishment! It was not a glancing blow. She held my hands in place for four or five beats, caressing the back of my hands with hers. Then she flung my hands down. "Don't open your eyes!" she nearly shouted. "Now keep your eyes shut and turn around."

I turned around.

"When I say so," Molly said, "you will open your eyes and walk straight out the door without looking back. If you don't do what I say, I will kick you in the butt and in the balls. Do you understand me?"

"Y-y-yes," I said, as adrenalin and a hard-on rushed within me.

"Turn around." I turned around. "Open your eyes and go home, birthday-boy!"

I opened my eyes, opened the door, and headed across Lincoln Street. *Wow! Wow! Wow!* Now that was a gift that would keep on giving!

Chapter 46

Morro Bay

Morro Bay is a resort community on California's central coast. It is only a few miles south of *Hearst Castle* and the hippie enclave of Cayucos. The tourist bureau happily informs visitors that:

> *"Morro Rock is a large geological formation called a 'morro' that is located a few hundred feet off the shore from the city of Morro Bay. The rock stands 576-feet tall."*

Climbing the rock, as noted by numerous signs at the base, is strictly prohibited. Attempting to climb the rock is a foolish endeavor because, while a few hearty souls may make it to the top, all of them will need assistance returning to the base. When they are restored to sea level, they are handed a bill for rescue services.

Brodie Frenk, Vonda Lang, and their new drinking buddy, *Griff,* skinned and scraped their hands, knees, and shins the day before as they attempted to climb Morro Rock. They hadn't gotten more than five feet off the ground before sliding back to the gravel. They were stoned, no pun intended. They thought their inability to climb the rock was the funniest thing in the world.

They were all in need of bandages of some sort. Griff said he had gotten sand into one of his shin scrapes and needed a beer to wash it out. Brodie and Vonda affirmed the medical wisdom of such a proposal and off they went to the *Sea Lion Bar.* Vonda was especially delighted at how quickly a few beers would wash away the stings of life.

They hit three bars before returning to the *Pacific View Motel,* $4.00 per night, paid in advance. At the last bar, the trio bought two six packs of beer and some pulled pork sandwiches. Back in room 107, the three continued to laugh, drink, eat, and smoke a few joints that Griff happily shared. Vonda was having a wonderful time as the haze in the room grew thicker and thicker.

It was ten months since Brodie and Vonda had ridden away from Lincoln Street in the early morning of the day after Independence Day. On the day following their attempt to climb Morro Rock, it was a little past 7:00 a.m. when Brodie and Griff stepped out of room 107. Brodie quietly closed the door behind him. In one hand, he held the *"Do Not Disturb!"* door hanger. He placed it on the doorknob.

Tucked under his arm was Vonda's purse. He walked over to a trash bin and began rummaging through the purse contents. He retrieved $13.25 in cash, Vonda's driver's license, and Social Security Card. He stuck them all into his back pocket. Comb, brush, lipstick, one stick of Juicy Fruit, sunglasses, a post card of Hearst Castle, three loose cigarettes and a book of matches, Brodie tossed separately into the trash, followed by the purse itself.

Brodie walked over to his *Harley-Davidson* motorcycle. He put on his sun glasses. He nodded to Griff who was standing by his cycle. The two walked their bikes away from room 107 by about fifty yards. Then they roared away, north, toward Cambria and Hearst Castle. Most likely their target was well beyond the central coast of California. A couple of fellow boozers at the *Sea Lion Bar* said that Vancouver weed was *primo deluxe.*

Room 107 looked as if it had been ransacked. Such was the result of last night's revelry. The mattress of one of the twin beds was leaning up against the wall for no apparent reason. Blankets had been placed on the box springs in lieu of the mattress. The other bed had blankets in a jumble. Pillows were on the floor. The room had at least eighteen beer bottles strewn around, none broken, none unopened. The light over the sink was on. A sliver of sunlight came through the window by the edge of the pulled curtains. The sliver of light was beginning to cross Vonda's right cheek.

Vonda was face down on the floor. She was wearing jeans. She was barefoot. She was topless. Her brassiere hung over the floor lamp that had no bulb. Her t-shirt was lying atop her shoes below the window.

Vonda's left cheek was pressing down on a pillow made of pulled pork, mustard, onions, and butternut squash bread. Shards of what looked like coleslaw were matted in her hair.

She began to stir. The beer and the marijuana caused her re-entry to consciousness to be very slow. The first thing she noticed was a dull pain but she couldn't pinpoint the pain's location. Then she realized that the ache was emanating from her groin. She was unable to move her body. Her face remained upon the goo of the pulled pork sandwich. She was able to move her right arm. She slid her hand under her pelvis. *"God, what is that?"* she wondered, still in a fog. Then she realized what she felt was a beer bottle. She had been lying on a beer bottle.

Vonda slowly pulled the beer bottle out from under her and her groin felt immediate relief. She began to open her eyes, blinking against the sliver of sunlight that was still upon her face. As was usual to her morning waking routine, she at first had no idea of where she was.

"What's happening? Where am I? Why am I here? Why can't I see anything?" were questions that were a routine part of her passage from drunken stupor to a semi-lucid state of wakefulness. In this case, she couldn't see because she hadn't opened her right eye all the way, her left eye was resting in mustard, and the room was dark.

Slowly, ever so slowly, Vonda lifted her head. Her neck was sore. She realized she was on the floor. She did not realize she had been lying in a deli sandwich or that she was topless. Though her head was ringing and her tongue was parched, Vonda pushed herself up to her knees and lifted her upper body to survey her whereabouts. Then she remembered. "California, Brodie, some other guy— *Grits,* or was it *Griff?"*

As her eyes looked about the semi-darkness of the room, she realized that the place was a dump. She slumped her back against one of the beds. That's when the deli sandwich began to fall off her cheek. Pieces of pulled pork, onion, and pickle dribbled down upon her left breast and the floor. Vonda was startled by the garbage. She jerked forward which caused sandwich fixings to go flying across the room. She picked the mush off of her left cheek and finally recognized that it had once been a part of the butternut squash sandwich she had ordered. She groaned as she pulled slaw and perhaps some potato salad out of her hair.

As she began picking food off her breast, she realized she had been topless. That was not unusual attire for her partying. Brodie liked her tits. But as she peeled a mayonnaise covered cucumber off her nipple, Vonda suddenly became nauseated. She snapped out of her torpor and lunged for the waste paper basket. Most of her vomit made it inside the canister.

When her heaving was done, she crawled up the wall to a standing position. She stood there for a moment, catching her breath, and testing her legs. She edged her way into the bathroom. The light caused her to wince. Her appearance nearly caused her to barf again.

She splashed cold water onto her face, washed off the residue of sandwich and vomit, pulled more debris from her hair, realized that she needed to pee and shower ASAP. Holding her head in her hands as she sat on the toilet, she realized that Brodie and the other guy were not around. She flushed and went out to the window, carefully pulling back the curtain so her half-naked state would not be displayed. The sunlight again caused her to wince and drawback. When she was finally able to peer outside, she saw no sign of the motorcycles. They probably went to get some food. Vonda's empty stomach was growling out cries for protein. Or maybe a *Bloody Mary.*

Vonda picked up her t-shirt, pulled her brassiere off the lamp, and sat down on the bed which still had a mattress. Next to the bed was her rucksack. She pulled out a pair of panties and went into the bathroom to shower. A half-hour later when she emerged towel-drying her hair, she was again wearing the rank t-shirt and jeans. The shower had returned her from the dead to the near dead.

She pulled her watch from her rucksack. It was 9:50 a.m. "Where the hell are those dickheads with the food?" she snarled to herself. She put on her shoes and opened the window curtains enough so that she could inspect the carnage inflicted upon the room. "This is truly a pigsty!" she thought.

"What day is it?" It took Vonda several seconds to get her brain to cough up that it was Monday. The room had been paid for in advance through Tuesday. *Then where will we go?* With that thought, Vonda sat on the edge of the bed as if she had been stricken. *"God, how long can I go on like this?"* Her head hurt. She thought of Eddie and Lois. She wrapped her arms around herself and began to rock back and forth. Her bones ached. Her soul was trying not to drown.

Vonda busied herself by cleaning the waste basket, filling it with beer bottles, placing the extras alongside it. She was able to tip the mattress leaning upon the wall back upon the box springs. She had no recollection of the mattress being lifted up during the drinking of last night. She was clueless as to why Brodie or Griff had thought it was necessary.

As noon approached, Vonda had sobered up enough to be really hungry and really pissed. She ranted silently. "Where the hell are those bastards? I've got to get out of here. This place needs to be aired out and the maid needs to do what she can to restore order. Hell, those jerk-offs are probably already drinking. I'm going to lunch."

With that, Vonda looked around the room for her purse. She looked under the beds, inside her rucksack, inside the bathroom cabinet beneath the sink. Nothing. "Shit, I'm losing my mind," Vonda thought. "Where the hell did I put that damn bag?"

She repeated her search, twice. For want of any better idea, she pulled the door open and stepped outside. Most of the motel guests had left for a day of area sightseeing or for yet another destination. Vonda looked around the parking area in front of 107. Nothing. She walked past 108 which was the end unit. She peeked around the corner. Nothing but the dumpster. She started to walk back to the room but then stopped. She paused, thinking. Then she said aloud, *"No! He wouldn't!"*

Vonda dashed around the corner and peered into the open dumpster. Some refuse had been recently dumped but Vonda immediately spotted the strap of her purse. *"That son-of-a-bitch!"* she yelled. She began sorting the trash, quickly retrieving her meager possessions. Then, as she rummaged some more, she realized what was missing. *"The cash. My driver's license. My Social Security Card. Shit! Shit! Shit! Shit!"*

When she was satisfied that there was nothing more to be found, Vonda returned to 107. Her hands and arms were black to the elbows. She had gotten the grime onto her face as she was trying to wipe perspiration away. She walked into the motel room and left the door open. She sat on one of the room's two chairs again placed her head in her hands.

"Maybe they'll come back. They're probably just screwing with my head," Vonda thought. Almost immediately she dismissed this idea as being absurd.

"You've been dumped, babe! You're on the edge of the damned Pacific Ocean and the only people you know are three bartenders, a deli cook, and a motel maid."

That night, Vonda upended the furnishings of Room 107 all by herself. This time she was not wrestling with Brodie or Griff. She was wrestling with herself and with God. She screamed, tumbled, and pounded. A little before 3:00 a.m. Vonda finally collapsed on a bed. She and the sheets were drenched. She slept deeply.

She awoke at 10:30 a.m. She knew she had to be out of the room by noon. She put everything back into place, removed the sheets for the maid, and even cleaned the bathroom. At noon, Vonda picked up her purse and rucksack and walked out of the Pacific View. She knew where there was a bench and she just wanted to sit down and stare at the Pacific.

As she slowly trudged along, she became aware that her hip was hurting. She began to limp. "Swell! Just what I need, a pulled muscle." Sitting on the bench eased the pain. But the limp never went away. She limped the rest of her days—*"An old wrestling injury,"* she would tell friends.

Later in her life, Vonda was not hesitant to talk about the errors of her ways in hopes that someone might actually learn from her mistakes. But while she told many sad and sometimes funny stories, she told only two people about what happened during the soul rending darkness of Morro Bay.

Harrison Carter's housekeeper and cook, Mrs. Gatchel, had served tomato slices, green beans, fried potatoes, and broiled catfish for supper. No dessert. Desserts were only served on Tuesdays, Thursdays, Sundays, and holidays. Mr. Carter thanked Mrs. Gatchel for the fine repast and carried his second cup of coffee to his easy chair in the living room. He was half-way through the newly arrived *Esquire* when the phone rang. Mrs. Gatchel answered it.

Moments later, Mrs. Gatchel walked into the living room, wringing her hands in her apron. "Mr. Carter, you have a long-distance, person-to-person, collect call."

Mr. Carter closed the magazine. He looked up with amazement. "Who on earth from?" he asked.

"From Vonda Lang, Mr. Carter."

Chapter 47

Cruising, Bushwhacking, and Postage Due

In the 1960s, fourteen-year-old kids, provided that they had taken a driver's education class, could secure a learner's permit to drive. *Fourteen!* To this day, that is still the threshold for garnering a learner's permit in the Sunflower State. Kansas teenagers rejoice and are glad!

With a learner's permit, a Kansas fourteen-year-old could drive anytime there was a licensed adult in the right front passenger's seat. Additionally, farm kids could drive by themselves to and from school by the shortest route or to and from town for farm errands, again to be accomplished by the shortest route.

I can well remember my first forays onto the streets of Coffeyville and the highways and byways of southeastern Kansas. I held the steering wheel in a vise-like grip, afraid that any momentary relaxation of my hands would result in me swerving into a loaded school bus or off a precipice into the Verdigris River.

Of course, by the time we reached sixteen, despite what insurance companies might assert, all of us counted ourselves to be well-experienced, emotionally stable, hormonally balanced drivers. One's sixteenth birthday was a rite of passage for various reasons, the main one being that the learner's permit could then be traded in for an unconditional driver's license. Is life sweet or what?

One spring Friday night, Harley Powell was driving his pickup up and down Eighth Street. I was along for the ride. We had stopped at A & W for hamburgers and cokes. Every few blocks, Harley would honk at one of our friends driving by. Some cars would have four, five, six girls or guys packed in. They were just cruising. Some cars had a boy-girl couple in the front and a boy-girl couple in the back. They were double-dating. Some cars had only two persons, a guy driving and his sweetycakes hugging him from the middle of the front seat. Such couples were probably going steady and looking for a place to park. Most cars had no seat belts.

"I'll say this," Harley said, "those Jew boys didn't waste any time. When his appeal was turned down, they hung Herr Eichmann and stretched his neck good. I hear they cremated him and tossed his ashes into the Mediterranean."

"If ever some bastard deserved to die, he was the man!" I said. "Have you seen the newsreel footage of those camps? Man, I don't know how any of those suckers survived. If Hitler hadn't taken the easy way out, they should have hanged him a half-dozen times. Still wouldn't have made up for what he and the dang Nazis did. I've got an uncle who still has screaming nightmares about being a paratrooper this long after the war's been over."

By this time, we had wended our way up to Big Hill, site of the city water tower, swimming pool, Pfister Park, and a landing strip for small planes. The park was interlaced with access roads. Some of these tree-lined roads provided excellent parking areas to permit students to enjoy *"the submarine races."*

Harley decided to do some bushwhacking. We saw the Nash Rambler that Vern Cunningham drove. We figured he was with Carolyn Rousters. When they pulled down a side road, Harley turned out his lights, pulled over, and turned off his car engine for a few minutes. We wanted to give Vern and Carolyn time to become fully engaged in whatever they were going to become fully engaged in.

After an appropriate amount of time passed, Harley started his car but left his lights off. He pulled back onto the main road and then turned onto the side road where Vern and Carolyn had parked. Harley slowly moved toward the rear of the Rambler. When he was about ten yards away, he turned on his high beams, illuminating the Rambler and its fogged up windows.

The window fog was not so thick that we couldn't see two heads pop up from the front seat. Then Vern and Carolyn—who had no idea at that point who had bushwhacked them—presented their middle fingers to us. A few weeks before this, Zachery Witherspoon and Becky Barndollar had similarly popped up with middle fingers raging. Unfortunately for them, it was a deputy sheriff who was the bushwhacker. They were cited for loitering.

In our case, Harley simply drove past Vern and Carolyn's car and we shouted *"bushwhacked"* out our open windows. As we moved on through the park, it occurred to me that I had never been bushwhacked, mainly because I had rarely ever found someone who would park with me.

We were almost to the west entrance of the park when I said, "Wait a minute, Harley." He slammed on the brakes. "Go around the loop again!" I said. "I think I just saw Lenny Wilkus's old Pontiac down by the bandstand."

"Wilkus is not dating anyone, is he?" Harley queried. "I thought he and Sudi Cannady broke up at Christmas time."

"They did!" I replied.

Lenny Wilkus was a year ahead of me. He was a *National Merit Scholar*. He probably had the highest IQ in his class.

As we began to loop the park for another pass by the bandstand, I said, "Kent Coble said he has to punch Lenny to get him going on his lit tests."

"What do you mean?" Harley asked.

"I mean—according to Coble who sits right behind Lenny in Miss Walterscheid's honors class—when she hands out a test paper with the questions, Lenny just stares at it. He's reviewing the questions, maybe to decide where to start. But Coble says Lenny locks up, sort of freezes, chewing on his pencil and staring at the questions. The class will have been writing for five or ten minutes but Lenny hasn't moved. Coble says he always has to reach forward and poke Lenny a couple of times to get him to move. When he starts up, he's fine. Usually aces his papers. I wonder what would happen if sometime Coble just let Lenny sit there like a statue."

Harley had driven the loop and he turned toward the small amphitheatre or bandstand. We pulled alongside the old blue Pontiac. The windows were down but it didn't appear anyone was in the car. Harley and I got out of his pickup and peered into the Pontiac. Nothing. Then we heard a muffled pop and the sound of glass breaking.

"The bandstand!" Harley said.

We began walking down the center aisle of the audience benches, a WPA project. There was Lenny sitting on the front row. Bottles, cans, and books were lined up on the front of the stage. Some had been broken or thrown into disarray. We turned and looked at Lenny. He was holding a pellet gun in one hand and a beer can in the other. He was drunk.

At his feet were five empty Budweiser cans. "Hi, guys!" Lenny said. We sat down on either side of him. "Have a beer," he offered as he fired the pellet gun at a beer can on the stage. He missed. Harley and I looked around for the beers. It appeared that Lenny was holding the last live brew.

"Great night for shooting something, right guys?" Lenny gulped more beer.

"Sure is a great night for shooting something, Lenny. Whatever you say," Harley agreed. "What are we celebrating?"

"Celebrating? Celebrating? Why we are celebrating the fact that I am the biggest, dumbest fuck-up that ever walked the earth!" Lenny said. He fired again and blew a paperback book across the stage."

"What happened, Lenny?" I had never seen Lenny drinking before, let alone appear soused.

"'What happened, Lenny?' you may very well ask. But I answered you. I fucked up!" he said.

"Could you be a little more specific, please?" Harley said.

"Sure. I flunked!" Lenny said.

"You flunked? You flunked what?" Harley asked. We were incredulous and the thought that Lenny could flunk anything.

"I flunked mailing a letter!" Lenny said and took another swig. Most of what he attempted to drink rolled down his chin and onto his shirt.

"How do you flunk mailing a letter?" I asked.

"Real easy, Billy-boy, if you're a dumb duck like me. Here take a look." He reached into his right front jeans pocket and pulled out a crumpled ball of paper. "That's how you flunk mailing a letter, Billy-boy."

I unrolled the paper. It was an envelope. Harley flicked on his lighter to give us some light. The return address said,

Mr. Leonard K. Wilkus
2201 West Sixth Street
Coffeyville, Kansas

The letter was addressed to:

Stanford University
Office of Undergraduate Admission
Montag Hall
355 Galvez Street
Stanford, California

There was no postage stamp on the letter. Instead of a stamp, there was a U.S. Post Office rubber stamped message:

"Return to Sender.
First Class Postage Due: 4¢"

Harley closed his lighter. "Lenny, you flunked how to mail a letter because you left the stamp off? Good grief, man, it happens all the time. Here, let me give you a nickel. You can buy a stamp, put it on the letter, mail the letter, and I'll even let you keep the penny change."

"How very kind of you, *Harlequin*." Lenny cocked and fired. Another beer can ricocheted across the bandstand platform. "You are a gentleman and a scholar, Mr. Powell. I'm touched by your compassion. But there's just one little problem. *It's too duckityfamn late.*"

"What are you talking about, Lenny? What do you mean *'too late?'* What's the letter about?" I asked.

"The letter is about me saying *'Yes,'"* said Lenny.

"You saying *'Yes'* to what?" Harley asked with exasperation.

"Damn it!" Lenny said. "The letter is about me saying *'Yes'* that I will accept Stanford's acceptance of me to attend Stanford University as a freshman this fall. My acceptance of their acceptance had to be in California last Monday, the thirty-first. I mailed this letter in plenty of time. Today is Friday, April 4. I only got this back from the frigging U. S. Post Office today."

"Hellsbells, Lenny, just call Stanford! Surely they won't dump you because of postage due."

"The bells of Hell you say, Harley." Lenny drank the last of the beer and tossed the empty can onto the stage. "I was on the long-distance line with the Admissions Office all afternoon. So was my dear old dad. But, sadly, because they had not heard from me by the thirty-first, the management of the *Leland Stanford, Jr. Farm* gave my spot away. My dad went bonkers. The Director of Admissions—Dr. Oswald R. Plotkin himself—finally said to my dad,

> 'Mr. Wilkus, it is not our practice at the Stanford University to accept students, no matter how qualified otherwise, who do not know how to affix proper postage to an envelope!'

"He hung up on my dad."

Lenny fired three more rounds. They all missed.

"So, gentlemen, I will now become Field Kindley's first National Merit Scholar to begin his higher education at Coffeyville Junior College. I believe I shall eventually secure a Master's Degree in Screwing Up."

Harley took the pellet gun away from Lenny. We hoisted him up and dug his car keys out of his jeans. We put him into the backseat of his Pontiac. I drove him home and left him in the back seat asleep. I left the keys in the ignition. Harley dropped the pellet gun onto the front passenger seat and then gave me a ride home.

Because of Lenny Wilkus, to this day, I double and triple check all my letters to see that they have sufficient postage securely affixed. Some have accused me of being obsessive about this. *Tough rocks!*

Billy's Believe It or Not!

For the period 1957-1963, as a *worldly-unwise* junior high to high school student on the fringe of or actually a part of the in-crowd and as an employee of the local newspaper, this is what I recall:

> Students who tapped into
> their parents liquor cabinet
> 2

Students who from time-to-time
nursed a can of 3.2% beer
10

Students who used marijuana
0

Percentage of students clueless
regarding marijuana
80%+

Swordsmen or Sluts
1

Chapter 48

The Invisible Man: The Finch Family

I was invisible again. I was sitting in a porch chair at the Madigan's. Carolyn Rousters and Molly were talking about classes.

"Mr. Brighten, my trig teacher—he used to work for Boeing in Wichita until he and a jillion others got laid off—he has this pocket pen holder. He must have ten pens stuck in there," Molly said. "I have no idea what he could possible do with them all. He's got this huge slide rule and he keeps pulling out the middle bar. Honestly, the slide rule looks like it's giving the class the finger."

"What do you have to read for lit this semester?" Carolyn asked.

"Oh, I don't know what all. I know we have to read and report on three of Shakespeare's plays, one each, comedy, tragedy, history. I'm going to do *As You Like It, Romeo and Juliet,* and I don't know what for a history—maybe *Richard II* or *Richard III.* In the dorm, we call them *'Dick 2'* and *'Dick 3.'* Nixon is *'Dick 1.'* What about you?"

Carolyn stood up, gave a tug to her shorts, then sat back down. "We have to choose four Twentieth Century American novels. I've already finished *Catcher in the Rye.* Great book! I wouldn't mind if Holden Caulfield caught me in the rye. Now I'm reading *To Kill a Mockingbird,* almost done. It's also great! Miss Walterscheid said *Catcher in the Rye* and *To Kill a Mockingbird* are the first books Salinger and Lee ever wrote. I wish I could write like that right out of the box."

Molly pulled off her right tennis shoe and shook it out. Then she brushed off the sole of her foot. "I wish *Atticus Finch* would adopt me. He talks to *Scout.* My dad reads his magazines, drinks scotch, and farts."

Carolyn said, "I thought of you when I started reading *Mockingbird* and realized that *Scout's* mother had died. *Scout's* got a younger brother. You've got two younger brothers."

"*Jem* is a gem!" Molly said. "I'd trade both Hugh and Cormack for one *Jem.* Honestly, my family doesn't talk to one another or deal with one another the way *Atticus, Scout,* and *Jem* get along. Since my mother and grandmother died, this house on Lincoln Street is a sullen place. I so want to get away from here. I'd sign the papers myself if *Atticus Finch* wanted to adopt me. Maybe one day I'll change my name to Finch just because I'd like to be a part of the Finch family. *'Alas and alack,'* as that Shakespeare guy says, the Finches aren't real. But I'm here to tell you that the Madigans are all too real."

Carolyn was running her hands through her hair as if she were shaking out a dust mop. "Gregory Peck is going to play *Atticus Finch* in the *Mockingbird* movie," Carolyn said. "You can have *Atticus Finch.* I want Gregory Peck to adopt me."

Chapter 49

Peyton Place

Now as to the matter of sex education: *HAH!*

Fly-over country high school students of the late '50s and early '60s certainly knew there was this thing called *"sex."* But most of us knew little of its intricacies. Few parents bothered to have an official *"birds and bees"* conversation with their kids. The schools hoped to communicate something of human sexuality by giving emphasis to the pollination of plants. But *stamens* and *pistils* were not all that helpful in illustrating the alleged *joy* of human sex.

The Carnegie Public Library had everything that Coffeyville youth needed to learn about sex if they would bother to search the card catalogues and stacks. They were denied access to the *"Adults Only"* section (which had nothing to do with pornography but yet was counted as too advanced for youth. Remember, *"adult"* in those days meant age 21, not 18.) But the instructive prose of available books just didn't have the *"zing,"* the *"pop,"* or the *titillation* that teens were searching for as they began their own explorations of topics pertaining to sexuality.

Movies and television weren't much help, either. Both pushed the cultural limits regarding sexual innuendo and explicitness. But the *"limit"* at the time would have permitted nearly all the TV and motion picture fare to be suitable for a Sunday School party.

In newspapers, *Dear Abby* or her sister *Ann Landers* provided some oblique insight into sexual matters. But teens still viewed the subject as through a glass, darkly.

Playboy magazine was first published in December 1953. But when the class of '63 was still in school, getting your hands on a copy of *Playboy* in Kansas was difficult due to sale and distribution obstacles established by many states and communities. It was into this context that *Peyton Place* was published in 1956.

To the chagrin of critics, library boards, and school administrators, *Peyton Place* sold twenty million copies. The tome was written by an alcoholic New Englander named Grace Metalious. *Peyton Place* was a fictional community, but many believe that some villages north of Manchester, New Hampshire, inspired the setting for the novel.

Grace Metalious was born in poverty, married in squalor, and created an international bestseller. Metalious couldn't handle her success. She died of alcoholism just seven years after the book was published.

It took a while for things to move from the left or right coasts of the United States to the Midwest. It took still longer for new ideas, new fashions, new movies, and new books to reach Coffeyville and Lincoln Street.

Not until 1959 and 1960 did *Peyton Place* paperbacks begin showing up surreptitiously at Coffeyville slumber parties or back rooms at local pool halls. A copy of *Peyton Place* was true contraband, a precious commodity that could generate rental income or a goodly lump sum if one had a copy to sell.

I had ridden my bicycle over to Scott Brentano's house on Spruce Street. I knocked at the front door. Scott answered and said, "Quick! Come in! I've got it!"

"Got what?" I asked. "The clap?"

"No, fool! I've got my cousin Caralee's copy of *Peyton Place*," Scott said. "I found it in her headboard and kyped it. She won't squeal because she's not supposed to have the thing. Let's go to my room. My folks won't be back for more than an hour."

We went to Scott's upstairs bedroom. He closed the door and we both plopped down on his bed, lying on our stomachs, propped up by our elbows with *"the book"* between us. We started to leaf through the well worn pages.

Grace Metalious had written a novel of three-hundred-seventy-two pages. Most of us felt that at least three-hundred-sixty-five of those pages were superfluous. In those days when *Peyton Place* paperbacks were such hot tickets, I recall no student who actually read the entire book. No need. The passages that piqued our interest were on dog-eared pages, highlighted in the margins, and underlined.

Here's a sample of the text that tantalized from page one-forty-nine, an exchange between school administrator *Tomas Makris* and shop owner *Constance MacKenzie*. *Tomas* says,

> "'Untie the top of your bathing suit,' he
> said harshly. 'I want to feel your breasts
> against me when I kiss you.'"

Well, that was direct and to the point, but would seem pretty tame stuff twenty years later. However, teenagers of that era were not used to reading any dialogue that was so explicit. As book sales of *Peyton Place* rose, as a movie with the same name was produced a year later, and as the television series *Peyton Place* began its six year run, critics excoriated Grace Metalious. So it was no wonder that libraries and school districts debated whether it would be possible to keep the young ones moral after school if impressionable minds had access to *Peyton Place*.

As far as the students were concerned, let the school board be damned. We wanted to read this stuff. Years later I concluded that if students had actually bothered to read *Peyton Place* they may have liked it even more than they did. After all, more than half the book focuses upon such characters as *Allison, Selena, Ted,* and *Norman* who are in junior high school as *Peyton Place* begins to unfold. It tracks these students through high school and into adulthood. Certainly, it was a soap opera and I don't associate the phrase *"great literature"* with *Peyton Place*. Nevertheless, as an author, anyone who can sell twenty million copies of anything deserves acknowledgement. Today, there are many '60s teenagers who will acknowledge Grace Metalious as someone who helped them secure a glimpse of routine human sexuality which was veiled at that time.

In light of all of this, I decided to cash in and ride the coattails of Grace Metalious' success. The weekend following my visit to Scott Brentano's house, I had a debate trip to Kansas State College at Pittsburg. During some free time, I headed for the college bookstore and quickly found what I was looking for, paperback copies of

Peyton Place. I had enough money to purchase four copies at fifty cents each. I placed the brown paper bag with the books into my briefcase which all debaters carry with their note cards et al. I figured I would be able to sell these copies at two dollars each when I got back to Field Kindley on Monday. I'd make a 400% profit in three days. *Move over, Rockefeller!*

By Monday I had appropriately marked up one copy of *Peyton Place* which I was going to use as a *"demonstrator"* to prospective buyers. In light of the word already on the street, I expected to have little difficulty in divesting myself of the books at an excellent price.

I figured that study hall would provide a good venue to transact business. The class dismissal bell rang and I stood up from my hour in Geometry to head for study hall. Out into the hallway I went. I was again counting my profits when Vern Cunningham, Carolyn Rousters' hulkish boyfriend, crashed into me, mainly because he was an uncoordinated oaf. Happily, I had no bruises or broken bones. I quickly bent down to pick up my notebook when I realized my *demonstrator copy* had bounced away.

"Is this yours, Billy Howard?" The voice belonged to Home Economics instructor, Miss Eunice MacComber, the *Queen of Old Maid School Teachers*. She was holding *Peyton Place* in both hands.

"Yes, ma'am," I said.

"I can't believe you'd carry this filth onto this campus or even think about reading it!" she hissed. "Follow me, Billy Howard!" she said and began marching toward the school office. My heart raced. I turned white. My stomach sank. My bowels began liquefaction.

In the comings and goings of the hallway where dropped books were not unusual, apparently none of my peers saw my book's title. But they did see me striding behind Miss MacComber with a gait that students immediately recognized as *the gallows shuffle*.

Clark Brixton was then principal of Field Kindley Memorial High School. Like the WWI ace the school was named after, Mr. Brixton had been an Army Air Corps pilot. Mr. Brixton had seen aerial combat in the Pacific. When WWII ended, he used the G.I. bill to secure a teaching credential and later the necessary administrator papers. He had been principal for seven years. He had another ten years to go before retirement. He didn't like surprises.

He didn't like folks making waves. He didn't like Elvis. I was pretty certain he wasn't going to like *Peyton Place* either. And he wouldn't like me because of my association with the previous.

We entered the outer office. Miss MacComber motioned me to sit down with one hand and carried the book in the other. She went behind the reception counter and over to the small alcove where Mrs. Watson, Mr. Brixton's secretary was seated. Mrs. MacComber continued to hiss to the secretary. She clutched the book to her minute breasts. Then, with a flurry, she placed it before Mrs. Watson who audibly gasped. Mrs. Watson stood and with Miss MacComber and the book in tow, walked into Mr. Brixton's office.

A couple of minutes later, Miss MacComber walked back through the outer office, apparently indignant that she had to share air for breathing with the likes of me. *"I shall now surely die!"* I thought to myself.

Mrs. Watson came out to me. She said, "Mr. Brixton said you are to go to your class. He wants to see you here at 3:00 p.m. today.

I didn't bother to ask if I could have my book back.

At 3:00 p.m. I was again seated in the school office. Mrs. Watson was aware of my presence but gave me no instructions. Ten minutes passed. I was standing on the trap waiting for it to spring, clearly cruel and unusual punishment. At 3:20 p.m., Mrs. Watson's phone buzzed. She picked it up. As she heard the voice on the other end, she looked across to me. "Yes, sir. I'll tell him," she said and hung up.

Mrs. Watson crossed to the counter. I stood up as I was the only one waiting and figured my number was up. She said, "Mr. Brixton said he will deal with you Monday. He said you should be back here at 3:00 p.m. Monday. Do you understand his instruction, Billy?"

"Yes, ma'am," I said and walked out of the office in a daze. On the one hand, I had dodged a bullet. On the other hand, my digestive tract was going to be knotted for the entire weekend. I was going to do my best to lose myself at double-features at the Midland and Tackett theatres. Perhaps Burt Lancaster or Tony Curtis would show me a way to save my bacon.

The following Monday I walked into the school office at the appointed 3:00 p.m. Before I could take a seat, Mrs. Watson, who was shuffling papers at the reception counter, looked at me to say, "Mr. Brixton is waiting for you, Billy. You may go right in."

"Oh, Lord, he's *waiting* for me. *I'm toast!*" I thought. My stomach knots cinched themselves again.

I tapped on Mr. Brixton's door and opened it. As I peered in, Mr. Brixton said from behind his desk, "Come in, Billy." I entered and closed the door behind me. I stood in front of the principal's desk. He reached down to his lower right desk drawer. "Here comes the paddle!" I thought. Instead he withdrew my copy of*Peyton Place* and placed it on the desk before him.

Mr. Brixton looked up at me. "This book is not exactly classic literature, is it, Billy?"

"No, sir."

"Have you read *Silas Marner*?" the principal asked.

"Yes, sir."

"What about *Wuthering Heights* or *The Adventures of Huckleberry Finn*?" he asked.

I was sweating profusely. "I'll read *Wuthering Heights* this year. Yes, I have read *Huckleberry Finn*."

"Now, *Huckleberry Finn* had some strange language and some unusual situations, wouldn't you say, Billy?"

"Yes, Mr. Brixton."

"*Peyton Place* also has what some would call strange language and unusual situations. What do you say to that?" the principal asked.

"Yes, sir. I suppose so, Mr. Brixton."

"You suppose? You 'suppose? But they're really *not* unusual, Billy. What this book describes is pretty common. Some of it is petty and trite. Much of the book has a ring of truth, Billy, but it is a very common, the lowest common denominator kind of truth. Are you understanding what I'm saying to you, Billy?"

"Yes, Mr. Brixton."

"Well, if you understand me so far, then you must also understand that this book has set off a whirlwind of controversy since it was published. This happens to be the first copy of the book that has landed on my desk. I suspect it won't be the last."

Mr. Brixton picked up the book and fanned through the pages. "As a principal, I don't like things that distract students or teachers from the main reason they are here. You are here to get an excellent education, the best education the taxpayers of Coffeyville and the State of Kansas can provide for its young people. Regarding literature, this is where *The Grapes of Wrath, Of Mice and Men,* and *Tale of Two Cities* come in. Those books are also true, Billy, but they are not common. I don't like what's common when what's common could be excellent if it wanted to be. Are you still with me, Billy?"

I was barely still with him. My head was spinning with all that he had said and I had yet to discern where he was going with his comments. The only thing I knew for certain was that I hadn't been administered swats yet.

"I'm still understanding you, Mr. Brixton. *'Common'* is okay but *'excellent'* is better."

"Good, Billy," he said. "Good!" He picked up the book and again riffled through it.

"I've done some digging, Billy. I know that several students have personal possession of copies of *Peyton Place* whether their parents know it or not. You seem to be the first student brazen enough to carry a copy onto our campus or at least the first student to have the misfortune of having his copy of this hot little book confiscated by Miss MacComber. I asked around and as far as I can tell you were not using the book to lead your fellow students down the primrose path of mediocrity. Perhaps you wanted to show off. If you had been caught hawking your wares, my perspective of this matter would be different. Still with me, Billy?"

"Yes, Mr. Brixton," I replied. *"Where the hell is he going with this? Surely, I shall pee my pants!"*

"Listen to me, Billy. Cultures get themselves into deep trouble when they start censoring books, banning books, or burning books. I'll countenance none of that here and I believe the Superintendent and School Board would back me on that. Here, you can have your book back."

Mr. Brixton held the book in his outstretched hand and I took it from him. Now I truly was befuddled as to what was going on.

"I want you to put *Peyton Place* deep inside your notebook and carry it off campus without the book being seen by anyone else on this campus, especially Miss MacComber. Don't bring it back on campus. Do you understand me, Billy?"

"Yes, Mr. Brixton," I said.

Good," the principal said as he picked up a letter opener shaped like a knife. "But there is a problem here, Billy, with which we must deal." He began to tap the letter opener on his desk pad. "You distracted me, Billy. You distracted Miss MacComber. You've been a good student and this is the first time we've had to have any disciplinary chat. But I think it is important to keep the main thing the main thing and you have caused my administration some distraction. Comprende, Billy?"

I didn't speak Spanish well, but I figured, "Yes, sir!" would be the right answer.

"So, this is what we will do. You have two weeks to bring me a five hundred word report on either *White Fang* by Jack London or *The Scarlet Pimpernel* by Baroness Orzcy. I presume you have not read either of these books. Is that so, Billy?"

"Yes, sir. I mean no, sir, I have not read either."

"Well, you'll have to get crackin' with your reading if you're going to meet my deadline. The school library has each of these books. Don't let your other homework fall down as you do this. And don't miss my deadline, Billy. I want your report two weeks from today. Do you still understand me?"

"Yes, sir," I replied. I began to feel some unknotting of my guts.

"Now, there is just one more thing, Billy." The guts began to reknot.

"Do you know why I asked you to come back today rather than dealing with this matter last Friday?" the principal asked.

"No, sir."

"I wanted you to come back today so I would have time to read your copy of *Peyton Place.*"

I groaned.

"Frankly, Billy, I found your underlining to be a distraction. If what you have underlined are the only parts of this book you've read, then you have truly fallen to the lowest common denominator of literary criticism. I don't suggest this book be burned. I suggest you put it on a shelf for ten years. In the meantime, read the classics. They will help you to understand better the dilemmas of life and how to deal with them. Then, if you should choose to pick up *Peyton Place* again, you'll see it from a very different perspective. You may then conclude there are other portions of the book more worthy of underlining than the ones you have presently selected."

Mr. Brixton stood up and pushed his desk chair in. He walked to the wall on his right, my left.

"Do you know what I did during WWII, Billy?" he asked as he perused the frames on the wall.

"No, not really, Mr. Brixton," I said. "I know you were a pilot, in the Pacific, I think, but that's about all."

The principal said, "For this conversation, Billy, that's all you need to know. Come, look at this frame. This is the certificate I was given in October 1944 when I had my wings pinned on me."

"Yes, sir," I responded, trying to digest all that was written on the certificate.

"Look at the bottom of the certificate, Billy. It tells where the ceremony took place."

I read aloud, "Grenier Field, Army Air Corps, Manchester, New Hampshire."

"The principal explained, "I deduced from reading your book that the fictional *Peyton Place* was probably based on two or three villages north of Manchester. I spent nearly a year there as I learned to fly. Whenever I could, I would head north from Manchester to visit those villages, talk with the people, and absorb the culture. I grew up in Garden City, Kansas, Billy. Big differences from Kansas to New Hampshire."

"Yes, sir," I said.

"*Peyton Place* existed just like *Brigadoon, Shangri La*, and *Neverland*. Those New England villages had their problems, just like Coffeyville. But my experience with those *Yankees* is that they went out of their way to treat me right and provide a home away from home. They had lots of dances for fly-boys like me to attend. Who knows? Maybe I even danced with Grace Metalious.

"You can go now, Billy," the principal said as he returned to his desk. "But I suggest you steer clear of Miss MacComber."

I still have that copy of *Peyton Place* on my book shelf. I did sell my extra copies of the book. I sold and delivered the copies off campus. I also sold them for what I had paid for them, fifty cents per book. I learned to choose my profit centers judiciously.

Chapter 50

A Rude Awakening

*"The most dangerous word in any human tongue
is the word for 'brother.' It's inflammatory."*

Tennessee Williams
Playwright

It was 12:30 a.m. Friday had come and gone. Hugh Madigan II could be heard sawing logs. His scotch-induced torpor caused him to hear nothing.

Molly was asleep on her left side, half covered, in the middle of her bed. She was clad in her usual nightdress, panties and a man's dress shirt with only two middle buttons closing the *Van Heusen*. At her fingertips was the paperback copy of *Madame Bovary*. She had drunk one of her father's beers before going to bed and was sleeping soundly.

Silently, the twins entered Molly's room. Hugh III slid onto the bed in front of her. Cormac lifted the covers and slid in behind her. Hugh III moved *Madame Bovary* out of the way and grabbed her left wrist. Mac spooned her and grabbed her right wrist. The boys were holding her lightly, grinning at each other. Molly continued to sleep. Her right breast peeked through the opening of the shirt. Hugh III began to caress her breast. Molly immediately awakened and saw Hugh III in her face.

"What the hell..." was all she got out before Hugh III slapped his hand over her mouth. *"Quiet, Molly!"* Hugh III said. Hugh III and Mac had each draped a leg over one of Molly's legs. She was pinned. "You don't want to wake Daddy!" Hugh III continued.

"Don't try to kick us, Molly. You're pinned—1, 2, 3 and out. You lose." Molly was struggling to grab hold of her senses, putting off the sleep, the beer, and the shock of what was happening to her at the hands of her bastard brothers.

"We need you, Molly," Hugh III continued as he stroked her hair. "Like Daddy has so often said, now that Mom and

289

Grandmother are gone, you're the woman of the house. You're the mother;. You're the wife. You're the big sister."

Mac chimed in, "We're getting older, Molly. We have some questions about sisters. We're just curious, Molly." And we heard you take a bath, so you must be all spic and span."

Molly squirmed, eyes glowing with anger. She tried to lurch out from under the evil that was upon her. Her movements were to no avail. Now she fully comprehended what the Cretans were about.

"Molly, relax," Hugh III said. "We're brothers and sister. We're family. Mac and I just want to be *closer* to you, *real close* to you. You understand."

"Now, I'm going to take my hand away from your mouth. Don't say a word. Don't scream. Don't fight us. Just lie there and love us like a big sister should."

Ungagged, Molly, at first, said nothing. She looked back and forth at each of her brothers. Then she spit in Hugh III's face. She seethed, *"I'll see you rot in hell. Now let me go!"*

Mac slapped her. *Hard!* Blood began to trickle from her nose.

From that point until a few lucid moments at the end of the attack, Molly was in and out of consciousness.

When the boys were done they collapsed on either side of Molly. Each of the brothers still held one of her wrists. Hugh III rose up on his elbow and looked into Molly's face.

"You awake, Molly?" Molly heard his voice, opened her eyes and turned her throbbing head toward Hugh III.

"That was good, big sister. Really good. Now we know why you've got so many jocks chasing after you. But the Sisters of St. Theresa's would be so ashamed of you, big sister, *so ashamed!* What kind of penance will you have to do?"

"Now, here's the thing, Molly. Don't even think of saying a word about this to Dad or anyone else. No one will believe you. How could two little brothers who have suffered such family losses do any bad thing to their slutty big sister? Don't say anything to anybody or we'll hurt you *bad*. You know, don't you, that if you say anything to Dad, he'll blame you, if he believes you at all. You're the oldest. You're the big sister. You're the big sister who, *really, really cares* for her brothers!"

The brothers released Molly. As the twins left her bedroom, Hugh III said, "Goodnight, big sister. Love ya! Like Mama used to say, *'Don't let the bugs bite!'"*

The next day, Molly never left her room but for the bathroom. Around 6:15 p.m., Mr. Madigan passed through the hallway to get something from his bedroom before *Perry Mason* began. As he was about to go back down the stairs, he knocked on Molly's door. *"Molly! There are dishes to be done, girl!"* Then he headed for the TV.

Chapter 51

Homecoming

It was a Wednesday evening around 6:30 p.m. Dusty Lang's parents had picked up Eddie and Lois the night before to take them to their Missouri farm for a week. *Carter's* store closed at 6:00 p.m. Dusty was home by 6:10 p.m. Twenty minutes later I knocked on the Lang's back door. I had my glove and ball in hand. Dusty came to the door munching a sandwich.

"Hi, Dusty. Got time for some catch?" I asked.

"Sure, Billy, why not?" Dusty responded. "Let me finish this sandwich and put on some different shoes. I'll be out in a couple of minutes."

When Dusty came outside, he had one of his gloves. He stood by the back door of Unit A. I stood seventy or eighty feet away in the alley. We loosened up and began talking about the week in baseball. The *A's* were slumping. So were the *Cardinals*. Dusty started throwing curve balls. The ball thwacked in our respective gloves. What better way to spend a summer's eve?

The *Continental Trailways* bus arrived at 5:45 p.m. Eight persons got off. The seventh person off the bus was Vonda Lang. She was wearing the same t-shirt, jeans, and shoes she had on in Morro Bay when she realized that Brodie Frenk had dumped her. She was carrying only her rucksack.

Vonda entered the bus station, headed for the restroom and sought to perform cosmetic surgery on her puffy, haggard face and bird's nest hair. She was *The Wreck of the Hesperus*. After ten minutes of mostly futile efforts, Vonda walked out of the restroom, through the waiting room, and out onto Eighth Street. She began to walk west.

Not many passersby took note of Vonda. If any had stared, it would not have fazed Vonda. Her pathetic antics with Brodie had given countless people occasion to stare at the weird couple who, like *"beat generation"* author Jack Kerouac, were on the road with little patience for conventional behavior.

She had not eaten in twenty-four hours. But it was not hunger that was gnawing at her stomach. She knew that she was less than half an hour away from the duplex. As she limped along, she was steeling herself against the likelihood that Dusty would spit in her face and declare to the world, once and for all, *"Throw the baggage out! Never darken this doorstep again!"*

The walk along Eighth Street to Beech took fifteen minutes. She was sweating heavily, from exertion and nerves. To Vonda, her body odor was exceeded only by the stench of her prodigal folly which she feared would never wash away.

She turned north onto Beech. She turned left into the alley between Lincoln Street and Eighth Street. Her worn shoes scrapped along the gravel. She hoped she would make it to the backdoor of the duplex before she collapsed from exhaustion.

Standing at the other end of the alleyway behind the duplex, I stopped my windup and squinted at the woman limping toward my end of the alley. I dropped my hands to my side.

"Come on, Billy!" Dusty said. The game's called *'catch,'* not *'watch.'* Throw me the ball."

I was transfixed by what I thought I was seeing. I kept staring down the alley.

"Dusty!" I said without turning toward him, "you gotta come see." I pointed. *"It's Vonda!* She's coming down the alley."

Like a bat out of hell, Dusty dropped his glove and raced past me and down the alley. I dropped ball and glove and went in hot pursuit of Dusty. Vonda saw Dusty running toward her and spooked. She knelt into a defensive posture and put her hands up to fend off Dusty's blows. *"Please, Dusty!"* Vonda screamed. *"Don't hit me! I'm sorry! I'm sorry! Please don't hit me!"* She began to sob.

Dusty pulled up in front of her. He towered above the ragamuffin. *"Hit you!"* he shouted. *"What the hell are you talking about, Vonda? I've prayed day and night that you'd come back. I love you!"*

Vonda let loose a blood curdling scream and fell face down on gravel, wracked with sobs. Dusty reached down, rolled her over onto her back, and lifted her into his arms. Vonda wrapped her arms around his shoulders as if she were clinging to a ledge on the twentieth floor of a skyscraper. She burrowed her weeping face into the nape of Dusty's neck. Dusty began to walk back down the alley to the duplex.

Vonda had dropped her right shoe and rucksack. I picked them up and followed Dusty and Vonda. Dusty went straight to the backdoor and carried the still sobbing Vonda into Unit A. I picked up Dusty's ball glove. When I reached the screen door, I started to knock to hand over the rucksack, shoe, and glove. Instead, I simply placed the items on the backdoor steps. Finally, I had done the right thing in the right way!

I reversed direction and went to pick up my own glove and ball. That's when I noticed that the homecoming had a larger audience. Carolyn Rousters and Lindy Lundquist, side by side, had witnessed the return of the prodigal. None of us said a word. We just turned one way or the other and walked back to our homes.

My grandmother would have called this an *"angels-in-Heaven-rejoiced"* moment.

Chapter 52

Daddy, Dearest!

Hugh Madigan II was sitting in his living room chair. After dinner, he had removed his dress shirt and now was trying to keep cool in his *"wife-beater"* undershirt, as they were called. Hugh II had peeled his suspenders off his shoulders and they drooped at his sides. Sweat beaded on his neck before it rolled down into the frizzy gray chest hair that protruded out of his sleeveless undershirt. He was on his second scotch. With cigarette in hand, he was reading the *Farm Equipment Journal.*

Molly came down the stairs. She had on a *Van Heusen.* The tails were tied around her waist. She was wearing her short shorts, appearing tighter than ever, and her tennis shoes. She walked to the front door that was open and peered through the screen, seemingly debating what to do. On the table by the door was her copy of *The Fellowship of the Ring.* She picked up the book, checked the book mark, flipped a few pages and then put the Tolkien novel back on the table.

She walked over to the living room bureau where sat Hugh II's various alcohols and attendant glasses. Molly picked up the decanter, pulled the crystal stopper, and walked over to her father's chair and table. She poured a little more scotch into the glass and then replaced the stopper. "More water?" she asked.

"No," he said without looking up. He turned a page, took a drag on his cigarette, and kept reading.

Molly replaced the decanter onto the bureau. Then she sat down on the small tufted footstool aside her father's feet. She grabbed her knees and rocked back and forth without any notice from her father. She leaned forward and placed her cheek on her knees so that she could glimpse her mother's picture that was also on the bureau. Then she placed her chin on her knees and stared at the floor. Then she gave a sigh, sat up, and looked up to the ceiling as if imploring divine assistance. Turning slightly on the footstool, Molly clasped her hands upon her knees.

"Daddy, I need to talk with you."

Hugh II kept reading.

After a half minute of silence, Molly said again, "Daddy, I need to talk with you."

Hugh II said, "Just a minute!" and kept reading. He finished the page, folded it as a bookmark, and closed the magazine which he dropped into his lap. He puffed his cigarette one last time and mashed it out in the ashtray. He sipped his drink and kept it in his hand as he turned and looked at Molly for the first time since she had walked into the living room.

Molly looked down at her clasped hands which she tapped once upon her knees. Then she looked into her father's eyes and said, "Daddy, I'm pregnant. I'm going to have a baby."

Hugh II said nothing. He kept looking at her with his glazed eyes as he brought his drink to his lips again. He lowered his glass and continued to stare at Molly.

Having long dealt with her father's inability to communicate with her, Molly did not wait for her father to comment. She continued, "Daddy, I am pregnant and I am going to have a baby—in about six and a half more months."

She hesitated only slightly, looked at her clasped hands again and then back to her father's eyes. She took a breath and said, "Daddy, my baby, my little daughter or my little son will also be my little niece or nephew. ...my little niece or nephew," she repeated. "My little baby will have two fathers—two daddies."

Molly said nothing more. She was squeezing her nails into her hands. She did not flinch from looking into her father's eyes. She was gritting her teeth in an attempt not to lose it completely. Her eyes began to well and a tear rolled down her right cheek. She would not break her stare to wipe it away.

Hugh II continued to look back at her with a countenance upon his face that gave no evidence that he had heard or comprehended what Molly had said to him. After each held their pose for fully a minute, Hugh's body stiffened. He put down his glass of scotch. He moved to the edge of his chair. His widened, bloodshot eyes were only inches from Molly's face. He snorted his alcohol laden breath upon her. He stood up and slapped Molly's face so hard that she did a backward somersault across the living room. Hugh II grabbed his shirt from the back of his chair. *"You slut!"* he shouted as he stormed out the front door and drove away.

Molly curled into a ball and wailed primordially.

Chapter 53

The Unkindest Cuts of All

It was the Tuesday following Mother's Day, 1962, my junior year in high school. As the school day ended, I walked behind the high school and junior high school toward Lincoln Street. As I went, I thought about the fact that I would have two baseball games to hear on the radio that night. The *Kansas City A's* were playing the *Indians* in Cleveland so that game would begin just past 6:00 p.m. in the CDT Zone. As that game wound down, the *Cardinals* would begin a game against the *Giants* in San Francisco. That would be a 9:00 p.m. start time in Kansas. I would fall asleep listening to Harry Caray's play-by-play. Outstanding!

Only two weeks of school remained till summer vacation. There was spring in the air and a spring in my step. I was rejoicing in the beauty of the day after a long winter. That preoccupation doubtless explains why I was half-way down the first block of Lincoln Street from the junior high school before I noticed them. They stopped me in my tracks and I nearly dropped my literature book. They were large and they were orange:

Xs!

As my eyes swept the trunks on my side of the street and then across to the other side, I saw that every American Elm Tree that was within the confines of the parking between the sidewalks and the street was marked with a scraggly orange **X**. Those **Xs** were the marks of impending death!

Two weeks prior, the *Journal* had reported that Kansas State University, the Montgomery County Agricultural Agent, and Coffeyville's own municipal staff had confirmed that bark beetles had infected the majority of the city's American Elms with the international blight of Dutch elm disease. Similar reports came from virtually every city, town, and hamlet across eastern Kansas. All arborilogical authorities agreed there was nothing to do but hew

301

every infected elm and unceremoniously burn it with kerosene in an attempt to halt what was now a national elm tree catastrophe.

When I read these reports, I realized destroying so many trees would have a significant impact upon neighborhood aesthetics all across Coffeyville and into the surrounding countryside. But I had not calculated the impact Dutch elm disease would have upon Lincoln Street. Standing there, surveying the collection of marked elms, I groaned audibly.

As I resumed my walk toward home, I began to look up and around at the canopy of elms—the only spring, summer, and fall image I had of my little neighborhood for the past half-dozen years. What would the street look like without these stately elms? I realized that what I was observing on Lincoln Street would be repeated on virtually every street in Coffeyville. *How can this be???*

The closer I came to the 700 block of Lincoln Street, the slower I walked. As I crossed Washita, I saw that the elm in front of the Rousters bore an **X** as did the two elms in front of our neighbor, the Boles. Then I saw that the elm in front of our house was marked. I went to the tree and ran my hand slowly across the bark as if I were gently touching the newly dead. These trees were not dead, but they were dying. As loving masters must sometime euthanize a beloved, faithful, but ailing pet, so it was that all of these beautiful elms were going to be *"put down"* and the ache that would come upon Coffeyville was akin to everyone in town losing the family dog.

The elm trees in front of the duplex, the Lundquists, and the Madigans were also sporting orange tattoos. I took my literature textbook inside the house and then returned to take the car and drive down the street. In the four blocks that comprised Lincoln Street, I counted thirty-seven **Xs**—every elm in the parking strips!

That Tuesday was the first day the city workers and hired hands had begun marking trees. Arbitrarily, the first batch to be tagged with orange were those trees east of Cherokee and north of Eighth Street. As I drove up to Fifth Street, I caught up with some of the workers systematically going about their tasks. A few residents were talking with the supervisors, a couple with great agitation.

Later that day, I read in the *Coffeyville Journal* that chainsaw crews were still a few weeks away from beginning their cut and burn efforts. The city government informed homeowners that they would have to make appointments to have elm trees on their own property inspected by city workers or certified private inspectors. Homeowners would have sixty days from the date of the inspection to remove any infected trees at their own expense. It was a windfall for people who owned chainsaws, hauling trailers, and a can of kerosene!

A gravel burn pit was established on the northeast corner of McGugin Field. The Coffeyville Fire Department oversaw the infernos which only took place during daylight hours and when the prevailing winds were from the southwest—toward Altamont and Parsons—so Coffeyville proper would not have to inhale the smoke of burning trees, some planted by the citizens' own hands.

As is the case with people, towns are not meant to be stripped naked in public.

Chapter 54

Joplin

Three days after Molly told her father of her pregnancy; Hugh Madigan II knocked once on her door and pushed it open. Molly was still in bed. She did not acknowledge her father other than by pulling the covers around her more tightly.

"Molly, I'm going to work. I'm coming home early to take you to be examined. Pack a change of clothes." He closed the door.

Molly had vomited twice during the morning. She stayed in her room, in robe and slippers, sipping some iced tea, while she reread *To Kill a Mockingbird*. A little after 1:00 p.m., she thought about fixing a sandwich but decided against it, opting rather for a piece of toast and more iced tea.

She went into the den and started to open the top of the piano to pull out a cigarette. But she was already a little lightheaded from the lack of food. She didn't want to get dizzy from the hit of the nicotine. So, she returned upstairs and showered. As she applied makeup, she tried to disguise the bruise on her cheek. There wasn't much she could do but wait for it to disappear on its own. "Yeah, as a matter of fact, I did walk into a door. I must need glasses."

She placed a change of clothes into a paper sack.

In light of her father's comment that he would be home "early," Molly thought that he would show up between 3:00 p.m. and 4:00 p.m. She cared not when he showed up. She was content to read. When he did show up, there would be a new risk of a blowup. The sooner they were to and from the exam the better, no matter how much Molly feared the exam process and the anticipated disapproving looks by doctor and nurse.

At 4:30 p.m. Hugh II walked into the house with car keys in hand. He shouted up the staircase. "Let's go, Molly." He returned to the car and had it started by the time Molly showed up with her sack which she placed on the backseat.

Hugh II turned left on Washita and left again on to West Eighth Street which is also U.S. 166. They drove the seven blocks to downtown, past the radio station and newspaper, past the Midland Theater, past the Oasis Café, the bus stop, across the railroad tracks, and past the grain elevators. On the east side of town, they crossed over U.S. 169 and picked up speed as they passed Walter Johnson Park and the Pig Stand Bar. On they went, through the little towns of Edna, Chetopa, and Baxter Springs.

Not a word had been said between father and daughter from the time they left Lincoln Street. As they came into Baxter Springs, Molly said, "I need to pee."

"Later!" her father said.

"Where are we going?" Molly inquired with a scowl.

"To have your news gossiped around Coffeyville would not be good for your future or my business. We're going farther down the road on 166. Discretion is something you'll one day have to understand and practice."

It was only a few more miles till they crossed into Missouri, turned northeast and came to the outskirts of Joplin. It had been ninety minutes since they left Lincoln Street. The sun had been down for the last half hour. It was just after 6:00 p.m. As they drove along what Molly knew from past visits to be Joplin's main drag, the retail stores were closed. The traffic was light. The only parked cars were outside restaurants or bars.

As they were about to leave downtown Joplin, Hugh II turned right and drove another two and one half blocks to an alleyway. He made a right turn into the alley and drove back toward downtown. As he reached the end of the alley, he turned left into a small parking area behind a large house that was apparently used for professional purposes. The headlights illuminated a sign that said, "Parking for Doctor's Office Only. Violators will be towed!"

"What are we doing back here?" Molly asked.

"What I said, Molly—the exam. It's after hours. The doctor doesn't want the locals to know they can call on him at night. This is a favor to me. It's also a favor to you which you won't understand until you're older and wiser, sadder and wiser. His name is Dr. Wolfe and his wife helps him. Now, grab your sack and let's go."

In the dark, they walked along a gravel walkway to a small porch. There was a doorbell which Hugh II rang. The porch light came on. A moment later, the woman Molly presumed was Mrs. Wolfe—though the woman never identified herself to the Madigans—opened the door. She was dressed in a white nurse's uniform with a sweater. She was wearing house slippers. Apparently, the house was the doctor's office and home.

"Please come in," the nurse said. She closed the door behind them and turned out the porch light. The room in which they were standing appeared to be a storage room for cleaning supplies, mops, brooms, and the like. There was the odor of janitorial disinfectant.

"Please follow me." They walked down the hallway which had two exam rooms on one side and three closed doors on the other. At the end of the corridor was the waiting room.

"The doctor will be down in just a minute. He's finishing his dinner. We've had a busy day with all the flu going around," she said. "Sir, please have a seat. Young lady, please follow me."

"Excuse me," Molly said, "but I really need to use a restroom."

"Of course," the nurse said. "It's the first door on the left." Hugh II sat down in the waiting room.

When Molly emerged from the restroom, the nurse led Molly to the closed door closest to the back entrance. Behind the door was another, larger exam room. Molly was clutching the sack with her clothes to her chest. She was slightly relieved that the nurse's attitude had been matter-of-fact and professionally perfunctory. She'd have to deal with this for another six and one-half months.

In the exam room, there were a small chart table, chair, a stool on wheels, a large medicine cabinet, exam light, a blood pressure cuff hanging on the wall, sink, and other assorted medical paraphernalia. Along one wall was a hospital bed. In the center of the room was the exam table. The nurse went directly to the exam table and positioned the stirrups. She drew down a fresh paper coverlet for the table. She pulled a hospital gown from the cabinet. Then she turned back to Molly.

"Please sit in the chair while I take your temperature and blood pressure," the nurse instructed. Molly sat. The nurse took Molly's medical history. Molly blushed and bristled when the nurse asked if she had any history of venereal disease. *"No!"* Molly replied emphatically. After the questioning, the nurse placed the chart on the table.

"Miss, please remove all of your clothing. You may change behind that screen. There is a small table there and two hangers. Please put on the gown so that it opens in the front.

The nurse opened one of the upper doors of the medicine cabinet. She withdrew a small paper pill cup which she handed to Molly. The pill cup contained two white tablets, slightly larger than aspirin. The nurse also retrieved a paper cup and filled it with water from the sink.

"Please take these tablets now. They'll relax you. That will make the doctor's time with you easier."

Still clutching her sack, Molly tossed the tablets onto her tongue, returned the cup to the nurse, and took the water.

"I presume you have had pelvic exams previously?" the nurse asked.

"Yes," Molly replied looking at the tile floor.

"Fine. After you change, please sit on the exam table. I'm going to step out for a few minutes. I'll come back to finish preparations before the doctor comes in." The nurse left, closing the door behind her.

Molly placed the cup onto the chart table. She looked around the room once, took a deep breath, and went behind the screen. With her bladder now empty, she realized she was very hungry.

A few minutes later, Molly was seated on the exam table trying to keep warm. Her feet were bare. The hospital gown was barely big enough to go around her and provided little warmth. She was tired, tired to the core, but she knew for the baby's sake she would have to get with the program and do whatever an incestuously impregnated teenage girl was supposed to do. Molly remembered that *Mockingbird's Scout* had an older and wise neighbor and confidante, *Miss Maudie Atkinson.* Molly wished *Miss Atkinson* would suddenly materialize in that cold exam room, even if it were merely to hold Molly's hand.

Molly leaned onto the upright back of the exam table and wished the nurse would get her butt back into the exam room. Gauging the nurse's age, Molly thought the doctor must really be an old fart. What a job he has, looking up women's vaginas and fondling their breasts!

The combination of no food, fatigue, and cold were causing Molly to feel like she could use a nap. She would have nothing else to do but sleep in the car on the way back home. With any luck, they should be back on Lincoln Street by 10:00 p.m.

The nurse returned. Molly's head bobbed up as she realized she had almost fallen asleep.

"Now, Miss, please lie back and place your feet in the stirrups." Self-consciously, Molly positioned her body as instructed. The nurse placed a sheet as a drape over her lap and knees. Molly was grateful for the extra layer, thin though it was.

Molly's legs and feet were hardly comfortable but her back, shoulders, and arms relaxed as she stared at the ceiling light.

The nurse came along side and placed the blood pressure cuff back on her arm, but did not inflate it. She pulled a stethoscope from her pocket, put it on, pulled back Molly's gown, and listened to her heart. The she moved the stethoscope down to her belly. She moved it from spot to spot, side to side.

"What are you listening to?" Molly asked.

"The baby's heart."

"Oh! May I listen," Molly asked, lifting her head slightly.

Then the room faded to black.

Chapter 55

For Peep's Sake

It was a blustery Friday afternoon in late February. The temperature was in the high thirties. Snow was expected sometime that night as a front moved through. The branches of the elm trees, bare as they would be in the winter, were waving in the air. I had on my suede jacket, white stocking cap, and gloves. With my gym bag tossed over my right shoulder, I had my books on my left hip. I caught up with Scott Brentano as we marched along Lincoln Street toward our respective homes"

"Hiya, Scott," I said.

"Hi, yourself," Scott replied. "Man, I should've worn gloves. My fingers are going to be ready to snap off before I get home. Woo-eee," he said as he tried to hunch his neck lower into his jacket collar.

"Hey, wanna go to the Midland tomorrow afternoon," I asked. "It's a John Wayne movie—*North to Alaska*."

"Yeah, I wanna," Scott said as he huffed along. "But I can't."

"Why not?" I wadded my gym bag under my left arm.

"I'm grounded," Scott declared.

"Grounded? Wow! I don't remember you being grounded ever before."

"That's right, Billy-boy, never ever before. But now I've been called to account for a young life of misadventure."

"What did you do," I asked?

"I got caught, Billy. But it won't happen again," Scott huffed.

"No, I mean what did you get caught at," I pressed.

"I got caught scoping out the divine knockers of Delite McCutchen," he said.

"Delite McCutchen? She's a junior, right?"

"Right-a-roni, Billy. But her breasts are not juniors," he said.

"Wait a minute," I said. "No way Delite McCutchen or any other girl you know is gonna show you her breasts. What really happened?"

"What really happened," Brentano began, "is that every night after supper Delite McCutchen takes a bath. Her room is opposite our house's guest room on the second floor. After supper, I'd tell my folks that I was going to my room to work on homework. I always keep the door to my room closed—I like my privacy. The guest bedroom door is also kept closed to cut down on heating. I routinely slip into the guest room to see if Delite has left her curtains open and her shade up. Half the time she does, so I've had a ringside seat to peep into her room."

"Wow!" I said. "But how did you get caught?"

"It's a sad story, Billy-boy! I got caught because Delite apparently learned I was peeping. She was like that *Lady Godiva* chick without the horse. She would come over to her open window naked as a jaybird and comb her wet hair, staring right across at our window where I was down on my knees peering under the shade."

"Come on, Scott," I demanded with exasperation. "What's the punch line here?"

"The punch line, Billy-boy, came last Thursday night. I was in position. The light was on in her room so I figured she was playing with her tubby-toys. I was patient, very patient—who wouldn't be patient if you could get a shot at a rack like Delite McCutchen's?"

"All of a sudden she backs into the frame of her window, combing her hair. She's got her back to me and I always see her from the waist up. This goes on for a minute and I'm anticipating she'll turn for the big reveal. Sure enough, she turns around and I knew something was not right."

"What? What wasn't right," I wanted to know.

"She had something over her titties. I focused and then saw that it was a card or a piece of construction paper hanging over her breasts."

"Why was that?" I asked.

"Because she'd written on the card. She'd taken one of them big black markers and written on the card. It said, *'Hi, Scott!'* I was so startled I jerked on the shade and it sprung out of my hand and flippity-flopped all the way to the top with a bang. I fell flat on the floor but Delite obviously knew she'd caught me because of the pull-down shade flying up."

"Then what happened," I asked with my eyes still wide at this close encounter of the breast kind!

The worst possible, Billy-boy. Guess who was just passing by in our hallway? None other than dear ol' Mom. She banged the door open and demanded, *"What's going on in here?"* But she couldn't see me from the door 'cause I was trying to crawl under the bed. Naturally, she walks into the room and sees my legs poking out from under the bed. "Scott, get out from under there this minute," she yells.

"She comes over to where I am and watches me crawl out. I stand up in front of the window to block her view, but she pushes me aside. She looks right across and Delite's curtains are still open. "Then she exclaims, 'Why there goes Delite McCutchen in her bathrobe!'"

"Really," I said, trying to keep a straight face.

"That's when I knew she'd figured it out. She turned on me and grabbed my left ear. She hadn't grabbed my ear since I was nine. She marched me downstairs and into the living room where Dad was drinking a beer and watching Bob Hope. My sister was lying on the floor, petting the dog. I had to confess in front of everyone. They grounded me."

"Oh, man, that's rough. But at least you got some great shots of *Delite's delights,"* I chuckled at my turn of phrase.

"Laugh on, chum, but my punishment included more than being grounded."

"Oh, my gosh!" I said. "What else did they do to you?"

"Friday night, we finished dinner. I hadn't said a word, trying to lie low. My mom and sister cleared the table and I figured we're going to have dessert. But then my mom and sister come back and sit down. They aren't carrying dessert. Instead, Mom plops a stack of *National Geographic Magazines* into the middle of the kitchen table.

"My dad says, 'Scott, because you have such an interest in female mammary glands, I went to the library today and checked out a few *National Geographics*. I thought your mother and I could look at the pictures with you and Sally and have a nice family discussion about the human body.'"

"I nearly wet my pants which I also haven't done since I was nine," Scott said.

"What a bummer, Scott," I said. "When will you become ungrounded?"

"I have no idea, Billy-boy, no idea! Probably the twelfth of never! But if I've learned anything from this fiasco, it's this: You always gotta keep a firm grip on a window shade!"

Chapter 56

D Day and Zinnias

My dad grew up on a farm. Doubtless influenced by that background, every few years he would mark out a small portion of our backyard to plant a petite garden of tomatoes, onions, radishes, and carrots. But most years, he limited his green thumb efforts to only two plants, tomatoes and zinnias.

Home grown tomatoes are delicious, especially if you can pluck them vine ripe, wash them off, slice them up, and serve them up. Dad's problem was keeping the tomatoes alive long enough to ripen on the vine. The sun was a killer. So were bugs. So were various kinds of blight. Nevertheless, he persevered and our summer meals were the better for it.

My dad also loved flowers. When it came to growing flowers, his one and only specialty was zinnias.

Named after a chap named *Zinn* who discovered the hearty weeds in the American and Mexican southwest, our yards always had one or two patches expressly for the multicolored zinnias. I thought they were pretty. They didn't give off much of a scent. They grew quickly and were able to withstand more heat than tomatoes so they survived more of the summer than other blooms. My mother would regularly clip two or three of the flowers to put in a small vase on her dresser.

That late spring, I had finished reading *The Longest Day*, the Cornelius Ryan book Captain Jack had exhorted me to read. The book detailed the planning and execution of the *D Day* invasion of France, June 6, 1944. When I read Ryan's epic account, America was less than twenty years removed from D Day. I found it fascinating, one of the first serious history books I read outside of a textbook.

The book gave me an understanding of what was involved in *Operation Overlord*, the invasion plan developed by the Allied Forces under the command of General Dwight D. Eisenhower. My uncle, who had night-sweats and nightmares left over from WWII, parachuted behind enemy lines in the pre-dawn darkness of D Day.

After reading *The Longest Day*, I realized that it was no wonder my Uncle Merle screamed in the night. Duty, honor, and country are severe taskmasters.

As I read all that had to take place on both sides of the English Channel for the invasion to be successful, it occurred to me that Mlle. Madeleine Madigan would have been an effectual member of the French resistance.

Therefore, I decided I would give Molly the copy of *The Longest Day* that Captain Jack had given to me. I knew he would approve. To have both Molly and I read the book would be an encouragement to the veteran. Of course, I had no idea whether Molly would want to read it.

Molly's eighteenth birthday was the next day, June 21, the longest day of the year. Since she had once given me a memorable birthday present, I thought I would give her the book plus a bouquet of zinnias. From my perspective the *"good time feeling"* Molly had once given me for my birthday exceeded the items I was offering to her. I knew my dad would not object to the flowers being clipped and shared. He and Mom regularly carried bouquets (as well as sacks of tomatoes) to friends.

Along with my usual hours, I was lucky to get some summer fill-in work for vacationing workers at the newspaper. I knew I'd be putting in a full day on the morrow at the *Journal* so I decided to carry Molly's gift to her the day before. She'd probably be doing things with her family on her birthday anyway.

I dug through closets to find some wrapping paper for the book. I found no ribbon. I found a small card that had no writing upon it. It took me twenty minutes to create:

Happy birthday, Molly!
May you have *the longest day* of happiness!
Your friend,
Billy

It was mid-afternoon. I walked across the street to the Madigan's, up to the front door, and knocked. I held the package and bouquet behind me. The main door was open so, as I peered through the screen door, I figured someone was at home. I did not want to deal with the twins. No one came. I knocked again. Then I saw Molly coming barefoot down the stairs in her usual garb of short shorts and *Van Heusen*.

She came to the screen. "Hi!" I said.

"Hi," she replied. I knew in an instant that she was not in a rollicking good mood. *"Dang, I hope this doesn't blow up in my face!"* I thought to myself.

"I've got a couple of things for you," I said.

"What? Why?" she barked back.

"Molly, tomorrow is your birthday. I brought a couple of gifts for you—if you want them, that is. Look, may I come in or you come out? I'm not going to be able to hand you anything with this screen door between us."

She smiled. "That's sweet, Billy. Come in."

We stopped just inside the door. I held out the zinnias. "Here!" I said. "I hope you'll like these zinnias. They're from our yard. I cut them myself."

She draped her arms around my neck and gave me a kiss on the cheek. "Thank you, Billy. They're beautiful. Come sit down."

We went into the den. She held the flowers in her lap as if she were a maiden soon to be called to dance around a *Maypole*. Before I sat down, I handed her the book. "There's this, too."

"What's this, Billy?"

"Open and see," I responded.

She read the card, though I couldn't tell if she liked it or even understood the bit about *"the longest day of happiness"* as she hadn't unwrapped the book yet. She took nearly as much time to unwrap the package as I did in wrapping it.

When she finally peeled the book out of the wrapping paper, I said, "It's a book Captain Jack gave me. I read it. It's about D Day in WWII, June 6, 1944. The author—a guy named Ryan—he's Irish like you—Ryan named his book *The Longest Day* because of something one of the Nazi generals said before the invasion. It was Rommel. He said that the first twenty-four hours of the invasion would be decisive. He said that for the Allies, as well as Germany, it would be *'the longest day.'*

"Of course, I know that June 6 is not the longest day on the calendar. That's usually June 21, as you very well know, and that's tomorrow. So, I thought it would be neat to give you *The Longest Day* for your longest day birthday. I hope that doesn't sound too dorky. Really, I hope you'll read the book, Molly. It's well done. And Captain Jack will be glad."

Molly held onto the zinnias with one hand and riffled through the used book with the other. "You and Captain Jack are the most important men in my life. If these pages have your mutual fingerprints on them, then I am honored to add mine. Thank you, Billy."

Molly smiled at me.

Silence.

Because Molly and I had developed an actual friendship, Molly regularly smiled at me—as she did to many others. But on that June 20, the day before her birthday, when Molly proffered a smile of gratitude, a mental flashbulb went off in my mind. To this day that beautiful smile is securely imprinted deep in my little gray cells!.

In that ultimate *"Kodak moment,"* I was not merely seeing a nearly eighteen-year-old girl. The set of the smile, the lips, the beautiful dark eyes—they were all from some gorgeous woman from the future named Madeleine. Lit by the sunlight through the windows, Molly's smile revealed a futuristic radiance. Of course, I knew nothing of the future. I was clueless of the pain and sadness that was churning behind Molly's smile.

Return to reality: While that singular smile took my breath away, I was not going to ruin the moment or the memory by lingering any longer. "Gotta go!" I said. 'Have a great birthday! Have a beer for me!" and I turned to leave.

"Bye, Billy," Molly said. "Thank you so much!"

But then I surprised the both of us.

Before I reached the door, I halted, turned around, and walked over to the sofa as Molly held the book and zinnias. I, Billy Howard, invisible man, dork, dweeb, and theretofore grossly lacking in social grace and confidence, bent over and kissed Molly Madigan *on the lips.* She was wide-eyed and started to smile again as I said, *"Feliz cumpleaños, Molly"* and walked out the door.

My Spanish teacher would be so proud! *Hubo otro regalo de cumpleaños que seguir dando!*

Chapter 57

Housecleaning

Molly had not slept. At 3:00 a.m., she eased out of bed, cinched her *Van Heusen*, pulled on her robe and put on her tennis shoes. She opened her bedroom door and stepped into the hallway. She could hear her father snoring. The twins' door was closed.

Slowly, she walked down the stairs, skipping the two steps that squeaked. On the first floor, she walked into the kitchen. Opening the cellar door, Molly flipped on the cellar light and went down the steps. As always, the cellar was musty and dank. She walked to a shelf unit that had assorted cans of paint, garden shears, a sprinkler head, and a tool box. From the top shelf, Molly pulled down a bag and carried it over to the workbench. She pulled the overhanging light string to give herself a better view. She heard something do a fast rustle on the other side of the cellar, doubtless a rat which she ignored.

She unzipped the bag and withdrew the rifle. It was a *Remington 121 Fieldmaster*, .22 caliber. Molly opened the action to confirm the rifle was not loaded. It was not. She brought the rifle to her shoulder and sighted down the barrel toward a package of *d-CON* rat bait. With her left hand, she grasped the sliding forearm of the rifle and racked it back and forth. With her right hand, she released the safety and pulled the trigger. Click. She did it again. And one more time. She lowered the rifle and ran her finger over all the parts to see if there was still a fine veneer of oil. There was.

Molly placed the rifle on its cover. She went back to the shelf unit and pulled down a partially used box of Remington ammunition. She loaded fifteen rounds into the tubular magazine. Having slung the weapon over her shoulder, she replaced the rifle cover and box of bullets to the top of the shelf unit. Then Molly pulled the rifle from her shoulder and clicked the safety into place. After pulling the bench light string, she climbed the cellar stairs, carrying the rifle in one hand. She flipped out the cellar light and gently closed the door.

She walked through the kitchen and into the den. She stopped at the piano and placed the rifle behind the upright, butt down and parallel to the wall, so there was little chance of it falling. No one else in the family came anywhere near the piano, let alone looked behind it.

Molly walked to the front door to peer into the street. There was nothing to see except for the elm trees silhouetted by the corner street light. Those shadows would be gone with the elm trees within the week.

Molly returned to her room. Without taking off her tennis shoes or robe, Molly lay down on her bed and slept soundly.

Molly woke up around 9:15 a.m. She was on her back. She kicked off her tennis shoes and stared at the ceiling. Her thoughts wandered: *"What to fix for supper? Do I have enough shampoo? Do the Beatles have bad teeth like all the other Brits?*

"Today is Thursday," she thought. *I was born on a Wednesday. How does it go…*

> *'Wednesday's child is full of woe.*
> *Thursday's child has far to go.'*

"That hit the nail on the head! Molly thought." She rolled onto her left side and went back to sleep, fitfully, for another hour. When she awoke again, she was drenched in sweat. She buried her head in her pillow and wept.

Molly showered. She had plenty of shampoo. Downstairs, she cleared the breakfast table, rinsed the plates, and stacked them in the sink. She ate a piece of toast. Then she dusted and vacuumed the downstairs.

When she was done with the chores, Molly walked to the front door and opened it to peer out onto Lincoln Street. She saw no one out and about in the 700 block. But she could hear the lumberjacks and their chainsaws. She walked out onto the porch, leaned over the rail and looked west.

The slaughter of the elm trees now reached from the junior high school to the middle of the 800 block of Lincoln Street. The cutters appeared to be in front of Captain Jack's house. She wondered if Captain Jack would watch the carnage or go to the river to fish and drink.

Molly stepped back into the house and closed the door to mask the sound. On the table was her copy of *Les Miserables.* Oh, how she loved *Cosette!* On top of the book was a twenty-dollar bill and a grocery receipt. On the back of the receipt, Hugh II had written, "Molly, buy yourself something." Molly thought, *"Apparently the bastard never heard of Hallmark."*

At 5:45 p.m., Molly, Hugh II, Cormac, and Hugh III sat down for dinner. The kitchen table sat six persons, one at each end, two on each side. As usual, Molly sat at the sink end of the table, aside the stove. The chairs next to Molly were empty. The three males sat at the other end. Molly had already prepared her plate, blessed herself and her food before calling the others. She ate nothing till they were seated. Slightly off center toward Molly, a chocolate cake sat on the table. It had chocolate icing on the top, none on the side. With part of her birthday money, Molly had bought the cake at *Safeway.* There was no birthday inscription, no candles. No one remarked about it. No one proposed singing *"Happy Birthday to You!"*

Out of the twenty dollars, Molly had $6.87 left over when she finished shopping downtown for her own birthday gift funded by her father. On her way home, she stopped at Holy Name Catholic Church for twenty minutes. In the sanctuary, she knelt behind a pew to pray. As she left, she lit four votive candles and dropped the remainder of her shopping money into the poor box.

For the special occasion of her birthday dinner, Molly had dressed in a white blouse, blue neckerchief, blue skirt, and her new shoes. Molly had prepared a sliced tomato salad, meatloaf, scalloped potatoes, and green beans. Hugh II said nothing throughout the meal. He held a folded-over copy of *Farming Today* close to his face, moving it away only slightly as he lifted and lowered his fork to his mouth. The twins talked about how Gus Kenoly broke his leg when he lost control of his bicycle riding down from Big Hill and flew into a ravine. *"Idiot!"* they both agreed.

Molly also said nothing throughout the meal. That, too, was not untypical in recent times. Molly noted that in her silence she had become like her late grandmother's *make-no-waves* presence at the dinner table. She bit her lip as she lamented again that the collapse of her family would not have occurred if her mother were still living.

Molly finished eating first. She stood and placed her dishes into the sink. She reached into the cupboard and pulled out a coffee cup. At the back of the counter was a jar of *Maxwell House Instant Coffee*. She ladled out a tablespoonful of the granules. On the stove, a small pot of water was at a slow boil. She lifted the pot and poured the water onto the coffee. She stirred it. Then she placed it at her father's place. By now, he, too, had finished eating and was smoking a *Pall Mall* cigarette, America's largest selling smoke, as he read. Molly took his dishes. The twins had cleaned their plates, had seconds, but left their milk glasses half-full.

While Hugh II adjourned to the living room for an evening of scotch and reading, Molly sipped iced tea as she washed the dishes. Via her battery-powered portable record player, she played the themes from *The Apartment* and *Exodus,* both by concert pianists Ferrante and Teicher. When she finished washing the dishes and racking them to dry, Molly opened the cupboard and pulled out four small plates. She took a butcher knife and carved the cake, placing the pieces on their sides. She put a fork on each plate.

She carried one serving to her father and placed it on the table next to his chair. Hugh II was not smoking but he was still reading. As she returned to the kitchen, Molly yelled up the stairs. "The cake is ready."

Molly sat down at the kitchen table and began to eat her cake. A few minutes later the twins came in, grabbed the cake plates, and headed back to their room where they were doubtless reading *Mad Magazine* or jerking off. They had not bothered to acknowledge Molly's birthday with word, card, or gift.

After Molly finished her cake, she took a final sip of iced tea and then poured the remainder into the sink. She washed and rinsed her cake plate and fork and placed them in the drying rack. Grabbing a kitchen towel her grandmother had embroidered, she dried her hands. She placed a cover over the leftover chocolate cake.

Molly went into the den, sat down at the piano and played *The Bumble Boogie* and briefly tried to improvise the newly released *Cast Your Fate to the Wind* by Vince Guaraldi. When she finished playing, she closed the keyboard cover, stood up, and walked to the entrance to the living room.

"Thank you for the twenty dollars, Daddy. I bought myself a pair of white flats at *Read's*. I'm wearing them." Hugh II said nothing. He did not look away from the tabloid *Kansas Agriculture Gazette* which was still right before his myopic eyes.

"How was the cake, Daddy?"

"A little dry," came a voice from behind the magazine.

Molly stood there for another moment. Then she rubbed her hands two or three times down the side of her thighs as if she were wiping her hands clean. She made the sign of the cross to bless herself.

Molly turned and walked to the back of the piano. She retrieved the rifle and clicked off the safety. Then she walked to the entrance of the living room and pumped a round into place. The ratcheting prompted Hugh II to peer over the top of his magazine.

Molly aimed and fired. The bullet pierced Hugh II's forehead. His head dropped to his chest, dead through and through. The *Kansas Agricultural Gazette* plopped to the floor. Molly immediately went to the footstool aside her father's chair and knelt one knee upon it. She again pumped a bullet into its chamber.

From their upstairs bedroom, the twins shouted, *"What the hell? What's going on?"* They bounded down the stairs. Molly again lifted the *Remington Fieldmaster* to take aim just as she had done when she and Lindy blasted tin cans to oblivion out at the Lundquist's farm.

Cormac was the first to enter the living room. He had scarcely begun to comprehend what had happened in the room when Molly shot him in the center of his chest. He fell backward into his brother. Hugh III tried to grab Mac but the life-ebbing body just slid down Hugh III's chest and legs to the floor.

Hugh III stood in place with Cormac's blood on his hands. He looked across at his father's corpse and Molly with the reracked rifle aimed at him. The first bullet hit Hugh III in his crotch. He gave a shout and doubled over, still standing. Holding his gushing groin with both hands, he lifted his face toward Molly. *"Fuck you, big sister!"* he shouted.

Molly shot him in the throat. He gurgled and flailed. His spinal cord had been severed. He fell upon his twin.

Molly placed the rifle at her father's feet. She stood up. She picked up her father's scotch glass, cake plate, and fork and carried them around the bodies. She avoided getting any blood on her new white flats. Molly walked into the kitchen, rinsed the dishes, and placed them into the sink.

She dried her hands. She picked up the *Jergen's* bottle she kept by the sink and put a dab of the lotion in her right palm. She stood by the sink for a moment, smoothing the moisturizer evenly upon both hands. Then she walked to the phone and dialed Carolyn Rousters.

"Hello."

"Hi, Carolyn."

"Hi, Molly! Any birthday cake left?"

"Carolyn, I need you to come over here now. I just killed my family."

Chapter 58

Trying Times

During her trial, Molly Madigan said not a word in her own defense. She was not concerned that she might incriminate herself further. She did not remain silent as an act of defiance against the legal system or the social system. She kept her mouth shut as an act of resignation.

When Molly hung up after telling Carolyn Rousters that she had just killed her family, she concluded,

> *"It's over. This family is over. I'm over. It's all done. History. The Madigans are no more. I am here, but I am not here. They can do whatever they want to do to me. It can't be any worse than what's already been done to me and what I have already done to others and myself. I will live till I die. Then I will char in hell. Sorry, Jesus and Blessed Virgin! I messed up big time!"*

When Carolyn blasted out of her house following Molly's phone call, I was just exiting my car having come back from getting gas and the tires checked. Carolyn screamed at me that Molly was in trouble and the two of us sprinted to the Madigan house.

Molly had come outside and sat down on the steps of her front porch as Carolyn and I came running up to her. She said nothing to either one of us. To the police, to the prosecutors, to the court, Molly said nothing. The sun finally set on that longest day in June 1962. It was not *"the longest day* of happiness!"* It was a day that turned into a moonless night, black and bleak on Lincoln Street.

The state of Kansas looked unkindly upon patricide and fratricide. But it also frowned upon incest, abortion, parental neglect and abuse.

As the investigation began, the public knew about the patricide and the fratricide. Incest, abortion, and parental neglect had yet to be revealed.

From the beginning of her legal ordeal, Molly received help from three unexpected sources.

As a matter of honor, duty, and affection for Molly, Captain Jack secured Kansas City attorney, Elliott Bideau to defend Molly. From the beginning, Captain Jack smelled a rat. Assuredly, this was murder most foul, but he knew Molly, he knew Hugh Madigan II, and he knew the obnoxious twins, Cormac and Hugh II. There had to be more to this story than first met the eye.

Another of Molly's staunch allies turned out to be Lindy Lundquist. By virtue of her age, Lindy was old enough to observe Molly's world with some objectivity. Because Lindy was still a young woman, Molly had no problem in relating to Lindy. Because Lindy was a nurse, Molly had some revelatory conversations regarding her family situation. After Lindy reported those conversations to Elliott Bideau, the police, investigators fanned out in various directions. The case was not going to be as open and shut as first anticipated.

Molly's third ally was Kansas Fourteenth District Judge Abraham Lincoln Sappenfield. The presiding judge at Molly's trial was seventy-two-years-of-age. A graduate of Washburn School of Law in Topeka, Sappenfield had served as a judge for thirty-one years at the time State of Kansas v. Madeleine F. Madigan came before him.

Judge Sappenfield's benefit to Molly's defense was the same benefit he showed to her prosecutors. Defense attorneys, prosecutors, and appeal courts counted Judge Sappenfield as a learned jurist who was fair, impartial, and assiduous in his oversight of any trial before him.

November 15, 1959: Herb, Bonnie, Kenyon, and Nancy Clutter had their Holcomb, Kansas, farmhouse invaded by Perry Smith and

Richard Hickock. Smith and Hickock blew the Clutter family's lives away with a shotgun. Less than five months later, Smith and Hickock were captured in Las Vegas, extradited to Kansas, tried, convicted, and sentenced to hang.

In June 1962, Truman Capote was still doing research for what would become *In Cold Blood* that documented the Holcomb bloodletting. For whatever reason, Molly's trial didn't garner the same degree of press coverage as converged on Holcomb. Nevertheless, Coffeyville's hotels and motels did a good business with visiting journalists.

The *Coffeyville Journal*, in its initial report of the deaths, headlined *"Daughter Kills Father, Brothers in Family Dispute."* First thought was that Molly had committed her dastardly deeds because she had been grounded for some infraction. That must have prompted her to kill her father. Her brothers were doubtless killed for teasing her about the punishment or so the early conjecture went.

In reality, the case was not forty-eight hours old when the picture of the Madigan clan began to change markedly. Lindy Lundquist had come forward and reported what Molly had told her. Three teenage friends of the twins were brought to police headquarters by their parents. Each youth reported that one or the other of the twins had bragged about forcing Molly to have sex with them. Of course, the friends didn't believe the trio until the twins were dead.

A Bartlesville, Oklahoma, man named Harry Inman, who worked for the same farm implement company as Hugh Madigan II, told authorities something that was theretofore unknown. To wit, a few months earlier, Hugh Madigan II had called him for a conversation on the *q.t.* Madigan said, "I've got an Army buddy whose high school son has knocked up his girlfriend. This kid's got a chance to get a football scholarship next year but having a baby won't help his cause. The girl's not interested in changing diapers either."

Inman continued, "Madigan wanted to know if I knew any back-alley doc who would solve the kid's 'problem.' I told him I knew of no such person and really didn't want to know an abortionist. That ended the conversation."

Of course, Molly remained publicly silent throughout all of this. She would talk to her attorney, Elliott Bideau who turned out to be much like Captain Jack. Lindy Lundquist spent time with Molly on a regular basis and was always in the courtroom, seated next to Captain Jack who took notes on the testimony.

Not surprisingly, my own feelings regarding Molly were greatly conflicted. The twins were assholes, but Mr. Madigan had been kind to me following Mac's bicycle accident.

I figured *"Thou shalt not kill!"* was self-explanatory. But Lindy was a straight arrow and she was standing with Molly—not defending her, but being a friend when most people in town and on Lincoln Street were rushing to disassociate themselves with the entire Madigan family, especially Molly.

My parents were enraged and indignant at what had happened down the street, though early on they—like everyone else—didn't know the full story. At first, they were frightened that somehow, someway, I might have been involved in light of how much time I had spent visiting with Molly. *"Thanks for the vote of confidence, Mom and Dad!"* was my judiciously silent reaction. My mother said she didn't want to hear Molly's name mentioned ever again in our house.

Fortunately, Captain Jack and Lindy would talk with me. Captain Jack was far more open and opinionated. Again, without ever suggesting Molly should be exonerated, Captain Jack kept asserting that the full story was not yet known. He didn't pretend to know the full story but he insisted his gut told him there was something *"rotten in Denmark."* The first time I heard that, he had to explain what *Hamlet's* phrase meant. It was during the time of the investigation and trial that I noticed Mrs. Patterson was now cleaning house and cooking for Captain Jack five days a week.

I concluded that it would be some while before I would come to a settled perspective about Molly, what she had done, and what may have been done to her. I was bothered by the fact that she had a dark undercurrent flowing through her life that I knew nothing about. Carolyn Rousters and Lindy knew more about that undercurrent than I did. I don't suppose I would have understood all that Molly was up against even if she had told me. I was uninformed in so many ways.

Still, what I did know was that Molly had been my friend. At a time when I did not have a large cadre of friends and virtually no close friends who were girls, Molly was very much a friend and very much a girl. I gave Lindy a few notes of encouragement for Molly.

Lindy said she would deliver them, but would not discuss any conversations she had with Molly unless Molly specifically says, *"Go tell this to Billy."* Molly never said any such thing.

Despite repeated requests for interviews, Molly never spoke to the press. At first, newspaper coverage was very harsh against Molly. But then some of the facts regarding incest, abortion, the character of the twins, and the alcoholism of Hugh II began to leak. Captain Jack was still playing bridge with Hubert Richards, the publisher of the *Journal*. The tone of the reportage began to change. No one suggested that Molly hadn't done a terrible thing. But now news stories included potentially mitigating factors.

Pretrial motions were filed. Prosecutor Nick Quaglione wanted Molly to submit to a medical exam to determine if she had ever been pregnant, experienced an abortion, or given birth. Molly had refused to volunteer for such an exam. Though he could have directed an exam be administered, Judge Sappenfield sided with the defense. Molly, who had never hinted she was innocent by reason of insanity, was ordered to be examined by a psychiatrist. The psychiatrist reported that Molly was uncooperative but illustrated no behavior which would prompt the physician to declare Molly insane. Molly told Lindy the state had wasted its money.

The defense argued that Molly should be tried as a juvenile, not an adult, even though the murders had taken place on Molly's eighteenth birthday. The defense argued that Molly's birth certificate showed she had been born at 10:36 p.m. The killings had taken place around 6:30 p.m. So, the defense reasoned, the defendant was not technically eighteen, the age of majority. Judge Sappenfield said *"Nice try, but no cigar."*

The Smith and Hickock trial spanned seven days. Molly's trial lasted four-and-a-half days, from opening presentations by the attorneys to the verdict being rendered. In 1962, Kansas statutes that defined first degree murder, second degree murder, justifiable homicide, excusable homicide, and manslaughter had been on the books since 1859 when Kansas was still a territory, two years before it became the thirty-fourth state of the union.

On the one hand, it was obvious that Molly had premeditated the shootings. On the other hand, there was much stress-inducing conduct by brothers and father.

Captain Jack said the trial had proceeded in an orderly manner. He and Lindy sat right behind the defense table. Molly always appeared in a skirt and white blouse with her hair hanging shoulder length. She always looked right at whoever was giving testimony but betrayed no emotion. She never looked at the jury. She never conferred with her attorney while in the courtroom.

Captain Jack said he was not offended by the prosecution. He was pleased at the efforts of Eliott Bideau. According to Captain Jack, Judge Sappenfield played things right down the middle.

In his instructions to the jury, Judge Sappenfield said, in light of the circumstances of the case, the jury could acquit or find the defendant guilty of first or second degree murder or manslaughter. The jury began deliberating at 3:30 p.m. on a Thursday. They halted deliberations for the day at 6:00 p.m.

That night, I walked some magazines down to Captain Jack's. Mrs. Patterson answered the door and invited me in. Lindy, Eliott Bideau, and Captain Jack were seated at the dining room table. Coffee cups and empty pie plates were before them. A fourth spot was obviously for the Negro housekeeper/cook. I was not surprised and certainly not offended.

"Have some pie, Billy. We've got plenty."

"No, thanks, Captain Jack." I would have preferred to stay. "My mom said I had to come right back and get going on my homework."

As I began to turn for the door, I looked back and asked, "Do you think there'll be a verdict tomorrow?"

"Don't know, Billy. Can't say," Captain Jack responded.

Elliott Bideau said, "Juries aren't very predictable. We'll just have to wait to see what the morrow brings."

"Tell Molly *'hello'* for me," I said as I went out the door.

That night after I went to bed, after I tried to lift up some sort of coherent prayer regarding the need for justice and mercy for all, I cried myself to sleep. I hadn't done that for years. I didn't do it again for many, many years. I was just so sad about what had happened to Molly, her family, and the rest of us on Lincoln Street.

Friday morning at 10:15 a.m., the court was informed that the jury had reached its verdicts. At 11:00 a.m., the prosecution, defense, judge, jury, press, and spectators were in their places. Judge Sappenfield told Molly to face the jury, which she did, and looked right at the foreman, Neale Cook, a retired fireman.

"Mr. Foreman, has the jury reached a verdict?" Judge Sappenfield asked.

"It has, your honor," the foreman replied.

"Please hand your verdict slip to the court clerk," the judge directed.

After Judge Sappenfield had reviewed the verdict silently to himself, he returned the verdict slip to the clerk who carried it back to Foreman Cook.

"Mr. Foreman, please disclose your verdicts."

> "In the matter of State of Kansas v.
> Madeleine F. Madigan, we, the jury, find her
> guilty of second degree murder in the deaths
> of Hugh K. Madigan II, Cormac R.
> Madigan, and Hugh K. Madigan III."

The Judge said, "Ladies and gentlemen of the jury, are these your verdicts, so say ye one, so say ye all?" The jurors spoke their collective agreement and then were polled individually. Four of the jurors were wiping away tears.

Molly showed no emotion. Lindy wept silently. Spectators began to talk among themselves until Judge Sappenfield gaveled everyone back to silence. With thanks, the judge dismissed the jury. The prosecution and defense were told by the judge that if they had any motions to file, they were to be in the court's hands within a week. Sentencing was scheduled for two weeks hence.

Molly shook Elliott Bideau's hand, hugged Lindy and Captain Jack and then was taken back to her cell.

I was in the crowd of perhaps twenty people who had gathered on the court house steps awaiting word of the verdict. I knew of no way Molly could be found *not guilty.* I was frightened big time that Molly would be hanged.

As the press and spectators began to file out of the courthouse, it quickly became apparent that Molly's life had been spared but that she was going to prison for a long time. There seemed to be nothing to be glad about.

When the day of sentencing came, I put on a suit and tie, and, with Captain Jack running interference for me, I got into the courtroom, seated between Captain Jack and Lindy. When Molly was brought in, she stared right at me for a moment, perhaps uncertain that it was I she was seeing. She had only seen me in a suit three or four times. But she broke her gaze without any sign of recognition or emotion and sat down beside Elliott Bideau.

"All rise!" the bailiff cried. Judge Sappenfield entered the courtroom and began going through some preliminaries. Then he said, "Miss Madigan, please rise."

Molly and Elliott Bideau stood.

The judge said, "Miss Madigan, have you anything to say before the court pronounces sentences?"

Elliott Bideau responded in behalf of his client, "No, your honor."

"Well, I admire her grit," the judge thought to himself. Then he spoke aloud, "Very well."

The judge began to read his sentencing comments:

> *"Miss Madigan, you have committed terrible crimes against your family and the people of the State of Kansas. We can only conjecture as to how your family came to this end. But such conjecture in no way mitigates the horrific reality of the killings that occurred by your hand."*

Judge Sappenfield continued for another couple of minutes, moralizing, philosophizing, and citing the merits of obedience to societal laws. Then came the bottom line:

> *"Madeleine F. Madigan, in light of the deaths by your hand of your father and brothers, I hereby*

sentence you to three terms of not less than twenty years nor longer than your natural life. These sentences are to be served in the Kansas Bureau of Prisons in a correctional facility deemed appropriate. These sentences will be served concurrently."

With that, the judged banged his gavel one last time. "All rise!" the bailiff demanded as the judge went to his chambers.

Lindy had warned me that Molly never spoke to any courtroom spectators, including Captain Jack or Lindy. Such was the case on this day, the last day I would ever see her in Coffeyville. Molly did turn to us and gave each one of us a hug and a kiss on the cheek. Not knowing what to say or how to say it, I stammered, *"I-I'm so sorry, Molly. I'll write you."* She was led away by a matron.

Elliott Bideau filed appeals. Molly was denied bail pending the outcome of those appeals. All appeals were denied. Molly was transferred from the Montgomery County jail to the Kansas Bureau of Prisons.

On the day of Molly's sentencing, I left the courthouse and drove west on Eighth Street to go home. I turned north on Beech Street and then west onto Lincoln Street. Again, I was slapped in the face by the denuded landscape. I immediately pulled over and stared down the four blocks of Lincoln Street. *Blasted Dutch elm disease!* Gone were the trees. Gone was the canopy. Gone was the shade. Gone was the protection. The cold winter sun glowered upon the lane. I squinted my eyes against the brightness. This shamefully deforested Lincoln Street was somebody's neighborhood but it sure as hell didn't look like my neighborhood! Welcome to *The Twilight Zone!*

I tasted ashes in my mouth.

"Damn! Damn! Damn! Damn! Damn!"

Part IV

1962 - 1988

Chapter 59

"I'll Write You!"

I told Molly I would write to her and I did. I wrote to Molly in a manner that I have never written anyone else. To explain what I mean, consider the words of Nineteenth Century British cleric and wit Sydney Smith who said:

> *"Correspondences are like small clothes*
> *before the invention of suspenders;*
> *it is impossible to keep them up."*

Under other circumstances, I would completely agree with The Reverend Mr. Smith. But, as it turned out, for some cosmic reason, most likely rooted in friendship and loyalty, I wrote to Molly at least once per month for the entire time she was in prison at Lansing.

The first letter I sent to Molly was postmarked on the fifteenth of the month. For the remainder of the time that I mailed epistles to Molly, I made certain that it was dispatched on or before the fifteenth of the month. The cost of a first class postage stamp was only five cents when I began writing Molly. My last letter to her in prison carried twenty-two cents worth of postage.

When Molly was first imprisoned, Sister Marie Claire of St. Theresa's, Captain Jack, Lindy Lundquist and several others sought to visit her. Molly refused to receive any visitors. Captain Jack reported that he knew of several people, including himself, who wrote to Molly on a regular basis. None received a reply.

Until the last five years of her confinement, I kept no record of my correspondence to Molly. From the beginning, I could have photocopied my letters, but I rarely did as I could think of no purpose to it at the time. For the first few years I alternated between hand-written letters, usually penned on notebook paper as I matriculated college, and typed letters on white, twenty-pound bond. Eventually, I purchased an *Apple II* computer with 48k of memory. I then stored any and all of my correspondence on five-and-one-quarter inch floppy disks.

As the years accumulated, I wondered what Molly did with the letters she received from me or anyone else. Did she automatically trash them upon receipt? Did she read them? Or was it too difficult for her to read them? Instead of being notes of information and encouragement, were they daggers to her heart as reminders of the life she could have had?

During my junior year of college at Kansas University, I made my first attempt to visit Molly. No dice. I tried to visit once a year for the first few years thereafter. Then it dwindled down to every two or three years. I was never told anything other than the inmate had refused the visit.

In my conjecture, which I realized could have been far from reality, I believed that Molly had amputated her past life. To state the obvious, *she had no future in her past.* Hopefully, she had come to peace with life in prison. Who knew how long she would be incarcerated?

In those days, in an attempt to maintain some linkage with my Kansas roots, I subscribed to the *Lawrence Journal-World* and the *Coffeyville Journal* as I traveled the globe as a broadcast journalist for *Voice of America.* The Lawrence paper regularly reported on state parole hearings. Molly's name never appeared as she refused to request a meeting with the parole board.

Besides acceptance of her prison reality, I prayed that Molly would develop some positive routines for her life—work, study for a college degree, reading the classics, playing the piano. I was relieved that I never received a letter back from the correctional facility stamped with *"Deceased."* I was convinced that I would go berserk if I were ever imprisoned as Molly was. A few times, I actually contacted the Kansas mental health prison in Larned to see if Molly had been transferred out of the mainline prison population. Fortunately, she was never registered there.

Life goes by. Life goes on. As the passing years increased the distance between Lincoln Street and me, the cadre of past friends who once meant so much to me began to dwindle to a precious few. Molly was always among the precious few.

Chapter 60

"You're from Where?"

I should have expected it, but I did not. Even among Kansans at KU, the mere mention of *"Coffeyville"* caused others to giggle, snort, or horselaugh. Many thought the name of the town was *"Cof-FEE-ville."* In fact, the town was named after Colonel James A. *COFFEY* who established a trading post in 1869 to service the Indian Territory two miles south in what became Oklahoma.

After graduation when my civilian endeavors were declared not sufficiently in the national interest and I was inducted into the United States Army, the mere mention of *"Coffeyville"* provided no end of amusement to drill sergeants and over-boozed officers. For the record, I would, from time to time, encounter someone who would say, "Oh, that's where the Dalton brothers met their Waterloo." I even met a non-com who surprised me by saying, "Coffeyville? *'The Big Train,'* Walter Johnson, was from Coffeyville, wasn't he?"

Alas, no one ever remembered that Wendell Wilkie, a former Coffeyville High School teacher prior to World War I, launched his unsuccessful 1940 Republican campaign for the presidency in Coffeyville. (In a battle of philanderers, Wilkie won only ten of the forty-eight states, losing the electoral vote 449-82 to FDR.)

"Coffeyville" received the same rude treatment in Vietnam, graduate school, California, Washington, D.C., and various European stops where the natives for some reason thought the moniker *"Coffeyville"* was a hoot.

Even my esteemed editors and publishers have wheezed with laughter when they have noticed from whence I have come. On the lecture circuit, I routinely mention my hometown, Coffeyville, at the beginning of my talk to soften up the audience as they ponder whether a *"hick from the sticks"* will have anything meaningful to say. I note that even Jesus had this problem as His disciple Nathanael, on first meeting the Lord, asked, *"Can anything good come out of Nazareth?"*

I am happy to report that I heard nary a giggle when *"Coffeyville"* was mentioned at the two Pulitzer Prize Award Ceremonies where my writing was honored.

Chapter 61

The Easter Twister

When I had reason to return to Kansas to visit my parents, speak at a Kansas university, or attend a writers' conference somewhere in the *Sunflower State,* I would fly into Wichita, Kansas City, or Tulsa. Every three or four years on one of my visits to Kansas that landed me in Wichita, I would take the time to go to the north-central part of the state's largest city to drive around *St. Theresa's School for Girls.* The school was located in the upscale Eastborough section of Wichita, near country clubs, parks, and not far south of Wichita State University.

I had never seen the place while Molly was a student there. The first time I saw the school was four or five years after Molly's imprisonment as I was leaving the state after visiting family. The fifteen acre campus included three two-story brick buildings, one of them housing the *"Welcome Center and Administrative Offices"* and the elementary day school. Another building provided separate wings with classrooms for junior high school and senior high school students. The third building provided separate wings for the secondary school students who were boarding. Each building also provided accommodations for the *Benedictine* sisters who administered and taught at the Catholic school.

Over the years, I noticed that the grounds were well kept as were the athletic fields. Catholic generosity, student fees, and various grants appeared to be keeping St. Theresa's in fine fettle. Of course, what I knew of the school was mainly based on increasingly dated hearsay from Molly Madigan.

Then there came the day that St. Theresa's School for Girls received unfortunate national attention. Fifteen years after Molly was sent to prison, St. Theresa's School for Girls was ravaged by a tornado. The twister cut a swath a half-mile wide through central Wichita. It had hop-scotched from the southwest, hitting Conway Springs, but crossed over Condray with its tail in the air. The capricious storm touched down two blocks southwest of St. Theresa's and ploughed through everything in its way for the next two miles. When its tail lifted from Wichita, the tornado dissipated, leaving heavy rain, destruction, and death in its wake.

The tornado was called the *"Easter twister"* because it hit Wichita at 4:18 p.m. on the Saturday of Easter weekend 1978. Because of the holiday weekend, students were away on Easter break. No lay faculty or administrative workers were on campus. Only the resident nuns were present when the twister hit. Nine Benedictine sisters were killed. The remaining resident nuns had injuries that ranged from critical to not-a-scratch.

Even before the nuns were buried, Catholic Diocese of Wichita Bishop John Mahaffy announced that classes would reconvene at the end of the Easter break. Debris was cleared from the school parking lot and athletic field. Portable classrooms were installed. It was hardly a pleasant spring semester, but students, faculty, diocese, and many Protestant churches pitched in to help St. Theresa's make it through the final eight weeks of the school year.

As the spring term ended, the principal, Sister Anna-Marie, who had survived the tornado with only a dislocated shoulder, declared that St. Theresa's would reopen in the fall and a building campaign was launched.

By then, my first literary gusher had come in, so I sent a check to St. Theresa's School for Girls in remembrance of Madeline Madigan. I received a cordial form letter from Sister Anna-Marie thanking me for my contribution. From that point forward, I received regular updates and solicitations for added support. Occasionally, I sent an additional check, always in memory of Madeline Madigan.

Two years after the tornado, the newly constructed St. Theresa's School for Girls was dedicated and opened for classes. From what I read, it was a gala and emotional event. A memorial to the dead nuns had been erected in the lobby of the school's main entrance. Despite the sad remembrance, the dedication ceremonies were festive. Pope John Paul II sent a congratulatory greeting.

While I was happy to learn of the rebuilt campus, I gave no thought to attending the ribbon cutting. I had only one connection to the school. I knew she would not be in attendance, being otherwise engaged. I wondered how Molly was passing her days and what kind of toll the incarceration was taking upon her spirit and soul.

Chapter 62

Return to Sender

In January 1983, my letter to Molly was returned inside a prison envelope. Stapled to my unopened letter to Molly was an imprinted card that said:

**Addressee is no longer incarcerated
by the State of Kansas Department of Corrections.
The DC does not provide forwarding addresses.
Thank you!**

After twenty years, maybe a month or so more, I deduced that Molly Madigan was finally *"free at last, free at last!"* Sentenced to twenty-years to life in prison, I prayed that Molly would figure a way to get out of lock-up at the earliest possible time, even if that meant her behavior had to be *"good."* That would be a first for her, I rudely mused.

I reluctantly respected her wish for no visits, though in fact I tried to visit her several times during the score of years of her imprisonment. I knew of none of her former Coffeyville friends ever being granted an audience by Molly. My letters to her at the beginning of her prison term had been gestures of affection. With the passage of time, my monthly letters became acts of personal discipline. I sought to avoid being perfunctory, to keep the missives current and chatty. At times, I worried that my narratives, intended to be an encouragement to her, might in reality generate depression on her part. How easy would it be for her to learn of my comings and goings when she could do no such thing?

I regularly included reports of when the month had not gone well for me, when publishers rejected my brilliant prose, when editors hacked the carefully constructed meter of my sentences. I hoped this would communicate to her that life on the outside was not always sweetness and light. Of course, I realized that such thinking was foolishness on my part. Spending twenty years in an eight-by-six foot cell would test every fiber of any person's being.

Oh my Lord:
Did Molly and I actually swing
under the green leaves of an elm tree on Lincoln Street?

Whatever the case, I was finally released from my commitment of monthly letters. Captain Jack would have been proud that I had followed through on a pledge that I made when I was only seventeen. There was much water under the bridge since then, some of it recorded in the two-hundred-forty-plus monthly letters. I would miss the monthly missive.

Subsequently, I regularly speculated about Molly's circumstances outside of prison, I also wondered whether the Molly I remembered for so many years had any basis in present-day fact. Had time and my musings turned the Molly I recalled into someone who never was?

"It isn't so astonishing,
the number of things that I can remember,
as the number of things I can remember
that aren't so."

Mark Twain

Chapter 63

The Incredible Shrinking Graduates

In 1983, twenty years after I was graduated from Field Kindley Memorial High School, I was invited to give the school's commencement address. The event took place on Ise Athletic Field behind the high school on Wednesday, May 25, two days before the Memorial Day weekend began.

The stands and field area around the platform were packed with graduates and their celebratory relatives. Even the bleachers on the visitor's side of the football field had some spectators. The far-side spectators had no admission ticket to the grandstand as a graduate's family member. Nevertheless, they wanted to enjoy the hoopla and hear *old-what's-his-name* make his speech and stare at the back of his head.

Graduating students marched to their seats accompanied by the requisite *"Pomp and Circumstance."* Superintendent of Schools Robey McGinnis welcomed the crowd and presided over the opening exercises. After the *Pledge of Allegiance* and *National Anthem*, Pastor Glenn Muncy of First Baptist Church offered the invocation.

When it was my time to speak, I noted that it was great to be back in Coffeyville.

> *"My primary reason for accepting the invitation to speak here tonight is to be able to shake the hands of those surviving faculty members who are still mumbling to themselves about the far-fetched reality that the loquacious Billy Howard of the class of '63 should be connected in any manner to the Pulitzer Prize-winning Billy Howard of 1983—except for the intervention of alien life forms."*

In an attempt to quell such disbelief, I presented Superintendent McGinnis with my framed *Pulitzer Prize Certificate* awarded to me for the novel *Obermeyer's Pear Garden.* The certificate featured printer Benjamin Franklin. I asked that the prize be rotated through Coffeyville schools for a one year period, hopefully to inspire students to write well and have confidence that if I could do well, they could, too.

Whereas the *Nobel Prize for Literature* includes a gold medal and over one million dollars in prize money, the Pulitzer Prize is a paper certificate and ten thousand dollars. In light of my publishing success, I presented the superintendent with a check for ten grand to be used by the high school to reward speaking and writing excellence, *no matter the economic need* of the student. I wanted to underwrite merit and actual accomplishment, not the always-with-us needy. The superintendent accepted the check with thanks.

Then I launched into the core of my presentation, seeking to recite every graduation cliché known to man or beast. Having attended many such affairs, I was convinced the main thing the gathered crowd would appreciate most about my remarks would be brevity. Thus, at the earliest reasonable time, I sat down.

I was recalled to my feet when the students began marching across the platform to receive their diplomas. I was privileged to shake the hands of one-hundred-ninety-three graduates. However, I was mindful that this number was nearly twenty-percent less than had been graduated in 1963. The number of annual graduates peaked in 1964. Like so many small towns across America, Coffeyville was shrinking and shrinking and shrinking. Sigh.

Chapter 64

Rubens

The day following the graduation ceremonies was Thursday. There was no urgency for me to return to Fort Worth, my home of three years after having abandoned the good life in California. I had booked my motel through Friday night. I would fly from Tulsa on Saturday afternoon.

My time in Coffeyville, with no further engagements planned, would provide me with some excellent laid back thinking time. Much of that rumination would be accomplished in my ritualistic cruising of Coffeyville streets as I had done as a teenager twenty years before. I drove around town recollecting people, places, and things, pondering the changes in the town.

Sadly, due to economic downturn and population decline, community deterioration was easy to see. Many folks would not even paint their houses as they believed they would not get any return on the investment. What a contrast to how the town looked— or how I thought the town looked—when I was riding my bicycle along Lincoln Street and throughout the town.

Be that as it may, I still wanted to walk along both sides of Lincoln Street, disheveled as it might be. I parked my rental car on the north side of the street, just one house from the east end of the four-block long Lincoln Street. Trees of some sort had been planted to replace the elms and the new timber was providing some shade along the street. But there was no elm canopy of shade. I looked past the new trees as I strolled.

It was mid-afternoon. The temperature was in the low eighties. With school out, there was little automobile traffic and no other pedestrians. In the first block, there was the house of my sixth grade teacher, not one of my favorites and vice versa. Mr. Burchinal, my drama coach, lived just off Lincoln on Grant Street between Lincoln and Eighth.

In the second block—my block—there were the Madigans' house with Lindy's across the street, the duplex, the Barbers' house was on the north side, and across the street from their house was my family's house, gone to seed. It was hard to look at it. The former Boles and the Rousters homes were also in marked decline.

As far as I knew, none of the Lincoln Street families to which I have referred in the previous chapters remained resident on these first two blocks of Lincoln Street. As I crossed Washita on the north side, I looked over at the Whitfield house with its nicely manicured lawn. In the middle of the block was Captain Jack's old house. It was in pretty good shape and the spirea bushes were nicely trimmed. A month before my stroll, I received a letter from Captain Jack who had moved to the Hawaiian island of Oahu to live in the shadow of Schofield Barracks with Mrs. Patterson. The couple never married but the Hawaiian polyglot environment was then friendlier to mixed race couples than the heartland of the U.S.A.

As I approached the secondary schools' campus, I observed that block four of Lincoln Street was in very poor shape.

I arrived at Cherokee and looked across it at Roosevelt Junior High School, home of the once and **always** *Rough Riders.* Moments later, I crossed to the south side of Lincoln Street and headed back to the car.

I was almost done with my half-hour ramble down memory lane. I was approaching Mrs. Whitfield's house and grounds. Several years before, Mrs. Whitfield had gone to her final reward. I knew nothing of the present owners, other than the fact that they seemed to be taking good care of the place. It was the best looking house and lawn on all of Lincoln Street. The two-story house was newly painted. I noticed that a sprinkler system had been installed. Such lawn care was way beyond my skill set, past or present. I was delighted to be a writer rather than a gardener.

When I was still half-a-house away from the Whitfield property, the front screen door swung open. Racing toward me was *a black schipperke!* I froze. How could it be? *Van Gogh* still alive? Or was the fiend a phantom back from the dead? *Can dead dogs become zombie mutts?* Whatever it was, it was running full-tilt at me? I fully expected the hound to lunge for my ankles or leap toward my vitals. I was staring at imminent assault!

But as soon as the schipperke reached me, it began to bound happily into the air. It did not bark. It did give some growls of apparent delight for which I was in no way prepared. The dog ran a circle around me and then flopped onto its back, giving the appearance of a canine desperate to have its belly scratched. *"This is a trap!"* I thought to myself. *"I am about to be mauled by a twelve-pound Flemish rat killer."*

Despite myself, I knelt aside the schipperke and began to stroke its tummy. It spoke little whines of contentment. Surely this could not be *Van Gogh*. Perhaps his demented son or grandson?

"Rubens!" a female voice exclaimed.

The dog leapt up and ran toward a black-haired girl who appeared to be of high school or college age. The dog jumped into the air and was caught by the young woman who displayed Eurasian features.

The lass, in summer dress and sandals, had a purse over her shoulder. She walked over to me and said, "Hello. I'm Dala." She extended her hand which I shook. As soon as our hands disengaged, she said, "You've already met *Rubens*. He's the best! But we're late for the vet. Routine check-up. Gotta go!" Dala turned and walked to the street and around a red Corolla.

Dala opened the driver's side door and Rubens took his seat on the passenger side. As Dala removed her purse from her shoulder to enter the car, she looked across the Corolla's roof to me and said, "Please go right on into the house. The screen door is open. Mom's waiting for you. Maybe *Rubens* and I will see you later."

With that, Dala eased into the car and drove away, east on Lincoln Street with *Rubens* smiling at me through the car's back window.

I was grinning. This was the most surreal encounter I had had in some while. Why should I follow the instructions of *Dala* and her jolly lap-dog *Rubens?* Why is *"Mom"* waiting for me inside the screen door? Indeed, who is *"Mom?"*

At that point, I had little doubt that a pack of ravenous schipperkes was awaiting my passage through the screen door. I would be reduced to skeletal remains within minutes. Nevertheless, it seemed like a pleasant enough day to be eaten alive.

I walked up the porch steps, opened the screen door, and entered a foyer, which had a staircase ahead, and a large room to the right. I ventured through the arched opening into the room, apparently the living room, empty, silent, immaculate, and stylish. I began to look around. As I was doing so, a woman with blonde hair walked in carrying a tray, two glasses, and what appeared to be a pitcher of lemonade.

"Hi, Billy. How was your walk?" she asked as she set the tray on a table.

"Harriet?"

As a teenager, Harriet Whitfield had spent several summers with her grandmother, the proud owner of *Van Gogh,* the schipperke from hell! Harriet was regularly involved with the Lincoln Street irregulars during those summer months. But it had been nearly a score of years since we had seen each other. That was during the summers of our first and second years of college. While I was rooting for the *Kansas Jayhawks*, Harriet was attending school in Columbia, home of KU's arch-rival, the *Missouri Tigers.*

Harriet and I greeted one another with a hug and then sat down with the lemonade to catch up with one another.

"I heard of your grandmother's passing. I didn't know your family continued to reside here," I said.

"Only for parts of the year," Harriet said. "When I went to Columbia, my parents moved to Bangkok year around. I would visit them during the summers. They would come back here for Christmas. We'd spend some time in Kansas City, Columbia, and here. But I believe this will be my last or next to last trip to spend time in this house."

"Why is that?" I asked.

"My parents are going to retire from Thailand. They'll continue to promote the mission, but they will use Kansas City as their base. They'll put this house up for sale. But, if you've taken a look around town, you know that there are plenty of homes for sale and not many of them are in as good as shape as this one. That ought to be a positive. But what it really means is that few local people will want to spend money for this property because of the maintenance. Also, they would be afraid of ever getting their money back. My parents understand that. Fortunately, this house has been paid off for a long time, so they will still receive some profit to help with their retirement."

"I'm sure you've seen our old house, or Molly's or the Rousters or even Lindy's," I said. "None of them are anywhere as well kept as your family's home."

A bell rang in the kitchen. "I was making cookies when I saw you walk by," Harriet said. "Oatmeal raisin, made to Grandmother Whitfield's recipe." Harriet left to retrieve the cookies. When she returned, the scent of the cookies was all that the *Keebler Elves* could ever want. Harriet topped off the lemonade glasses.

"I know your parents were missionaries in Thailand, but did they have work in addition to evangelism?"

"They were medical missionaries sent by the American Baptist Churches. That's the denomination of First Baptist of Coffeyville. My parents ran a home for Thai women who had been involved in human trafficking, prostitution, drugs and the like. My dad is a physician and my mother a nurse. My folks would visit brothels to check the health of the girls—some were as young as ten. Any of the girls who showed up at the mission house in an attempt to get off the streets were given lodging and taught how to sew or type or cook or some other skill so that they could support themselves without having to sell their bodies. My B.S. is in Biology and then I stuck around Columbia to get an M.A. in Public Health Administration."

"So you were also a missionary?"

"Well, not a commissioned missionary, other than Jesus saying, *'make disciples of all nations.'*" Harriet said. "But I was a part of the team. My parents made regular trips to Bangkok from Kansas City while I was growing up. I spent time in Thailand with them. When I went to university, my folks went full-time to Thailand.

"I was full time with the mission from 1969. Two years later, I married a physician named Pretchett Koppensott—isn't that a mouthful! He was a great man! His father had also been a physician. Pretchett had received a scholarship to the *University of Texas* and received his medical degree there as well. We had known of one another for years. We had seen one another a few times in Thailand and in the states. But we had never considered a relationship until we both returned to Bangkok full time. He was fluent in English and I had become fluent in Thai. Communication was never a problem."

"You've used the past tense regarding Pretchett," I said.

Harriet looked away for a moment. "Yes. Pretchett and another nurse from the mission daily made calls on brothels to check the women. Everyone knew they were from the mission. One day they were in a house with a red door from where several girls had fled and taken up residence with us. While Pretchett and Elizabeth—the nurse from Green Lake, Wisconsin—were treating the girls, the pimp walked into the room and shot Pretchett in the back of the head and Elizabeth in her forehead. The pimp was strung out on drugs. He then put the gun into his own mouth and pulled the trigger."

"Oh, Harriet, I am so sorry to hear this!" I said. "How long ago did this happen?"

"It's been just over ten years. Dala was only nine at the time."

"So, Dala, the beautiful young lady with *Rubens,* is your daughter?"

"What a blessing—what a marvel she is, Billy! She grieved so deeply when her daddy died. It was the same with me. But my parents, the mission staff, the women at the home, all gathered round, poured out prayer and kindness to us, so that we could make it through. I would not wish our experience on anyone, but Dala is a very strong, bright, courageous, and kind young woman. From the time she was twelve, she began working with me in dealing with the girls at the mission home. She is street smart way beyond her years.

"We came back to Kansas City when she began high school. She had some culture shock but now she is truly bi-cultural and can move in either society with aplomb. We go back to Thailand during the summers and again my parents come here for Christmas and New Year's. Two weeks from now, Dala and I will head for Bangkok. We'll come back in mid-August."

"I presume she is a college student now," I said.

"Yes. She'll begin her sophomore year this fall at the University of Missouri. She's pre-med. And she is a *Missouri Tiger*, through and through! Sorry, Billy. However, I always looked for you in the crowd when the *Tigers* took on the *Jayhawks*."

"I was there," I said. "But I blend well with a crowd."

"Not anymore you don't!" Harriet said. "We attended the graduation ceremonies last night. You were great! I tell my friends that my family is one of only a handful that have had their lawn badly mowed by a two-time Pulitzer Prize winner!"

"Badly mowed!" I protested. "Well, sadly you are right. No wonder *Van Gogh* wanted to tear me to pieces."

"Yes, *Van Gogh* was a terror, except to the family. He was very territorial. He died about the time that I went to college. Grandmother replaced him with *Van Eyck.* Grandmother painted as a hobby and she was very fond of the Flemish school of artists. *Van Eyck* survived grandmother by a year. It seemed only right that Dala and I should carry on the tradition with *Rubens.* He's a lover, not a fighter."

When Dala returned with Rubens from the veterinarian, I was invited to spend the remainder of the afternoon with them and then have a real-deal Thai dinner. How could I refuse? Also, I did not want to give *Rubens* any excuse to be annoyed with me. As it turned out, Rubens was, indeed, a love-bug, happy to be petted while perched on my lap.

With the happy assent of Harriet, Dala, and Rubens, I extended my stay in Coffeyville by a week. I was fortunate to spend quality time with the Koppensotts, having Thai cuisine at least once per day. Strolling on Lincoln Street had been serendipitous...*and especially good for the palate!*

Chapter 65

Molly's Playground

Despite my several moves across the United States, Europe and the Middle East, updates from St. Theresa's School for Girls continued to reach me. I rarely spent much time with the school's newsletters. Nevertheless, I never requested my name be taken off the mailing list. It had been several years since I had made any further contribution to the school.

For whatever reason, sometime in the early 1980's, I took time to read one of the newsletters. All the publications of St. Theresa's included some sort of fund appeal and a postage-paid return envelope was always included. In this particular issue, there was a story about how St. Theresa's soup kitchen had expanded in various ways to serve the homeless and downtrodden of Wichita. The article noted that the mission had increased involvement of students from St. Theresa's School for Girls.

The article continued that more and more mothers were seeking assistance at St. Theresa's food and shelter station on Wichita's downtown skid row. The mission was called "The Samaritan's Inn." Originally, it served men only. But with the passage of time, the mission sought to serve either gender. While scores of mothers with children were being housed each night, more beds were needed. The article also said that in the future the mission hoped it would have the funds to purchase and convert an adjacent warehouse into a playground for the children. That's when the idea of *"Molly's Playground"* sprang full blown into my mind. I love the right side of my brain!

I picked up the phone and called St. Theresa's. I asked to speak to Sister Mary Claire whom the newsletter had identified as the school's new principal. After a brief wait, Sister Mary Claire answered.

I identified myself as a friend of someone who had attended St. Theresa's many years ago. I said I had made a few contributions to the school and, as a result, had been receiving its newsletters and fund appeals. I said that I had read the article about the need for increased services for homeless women with children and that a playground was one of the long-term goals. I said I would be interested in underwriting the cost of purchasing the warehouse, razing it, and building a playground. Sister Mary Claire was delighted with my offer. She came across as one used to receiving *"miraculous calls."* I was encouraged by that.

We talked for fifteen minutes. She said she would get back to me within the week regarding costs for the projects.

When Sister Mary Claire called back a few days later, she stated that she had checked my name in the school's giving records. She expressed gratefulness for the contributions. She asked if Madeleine Madigan had been a close friend or family member.

I said, "friend," and nothing more.

"Are you Catholic, Mr. Howard?"

"No. Baptist," I said.

"Well, the Lord in His wisdom has accomplished many great things using Baptists. We are delighted that the Savior has prompted you to have a sensitive heart toward the ministries of St. Theresa's. I have the information you requested regarding the warehouse and the playground."

Sister Mary Claire shared the costs involved in securing permits, razing the warehouse, accomplishing the landscaping, and building a state-of-the-art playground.

"Let me be frank with you, Mr. Howard," she said. "Because of my long experience in dealing with the grace and generosity of God and His servants, I have provided you with *Cadillac* estimates. This project can be done for less. But I wanted to honor God and not shortchange your reward in Heaven by quoting you what would be top-of-the-line for this good work. I hope that does not offend you."

"Not at all, Sister," I replied. "God deserves only the best." (Praise God, another literary gusher had come in!)

I agreed to underwrite the *Cadillac* version of the project. But then I said, "I do have one request regarding this project, Sister Mary Claire."

"What would that be, Mr. Howard."

"I would like for the finished project to be called *"Molly's Playground."*

"In honor of your friend," Sister Mary Claire said. "That's very kind of you. I don't believe that would be a problem, Mr. Howard. I'm sure the Lord is pleased by your gracious gift."

I sent the check to underwrite the project with a little extra for on-going maintenance.

A year later, the warehouse was history and *"Molly's Playground"* was opened to the children of St. Theresa's city mission, The Samaritan's Inn. I did not attend as I had indicated to Sister Mary Claire that I wanted my contribution to be virtually anonymous. It was my connection with a phantom of the past that caused me to undergird the playground. Again, I thought it unlikely that the person who connected me with St. Theresa's was going to be present at the dedicatory event. I doubted that Molly was on the donor list, but in reality I knew nothing of her present circumstances.

The dedication festivities took place on the fifteenth of the month. Over time, I had learned to accept coincidence as merely that, coincidence.

Twenty-five years had now passed since that fateful June 21 on Lincoln Street. As I thought about it, I grew tired, very deeply tired. As William Wordsworth lamented, sometimes *"the world is too much with us."*

Chapter 66

Herman's Hermits
and
St. Theresa's Catholic School for Girls

For as long as I can remember as an adult, I awaken each day with a song going through my mind. I love a wide variety of music, so the melody that greets me as my feet first hit the floor ranges from classical to country.

I enjoy the tunes because I never give any forethought to this personal hit parade. Often I am surprised as I begin to hum a song that I haven't thought about in a very long time. Songs may repeat another day but not without a significant interval of other songs—except for the occasion of my trip to visit St. Theresa's School for Girls and its community outreach at The Samaritan's Inn rescue mission.

Wichita State University Humanities Department invited me to speak at a luncheon for the department's faculty with a question and answer period following. During the afternoon, I would enjoy a colloquy with five undergraduates and five graduate students on whatever literary themes or topics the students wanted to discuss. My official day at WSU would conclude with a cocktail reception, lecture open to the public, and a book-signing.

To get a good night's rest for a full day, I flew to Wichita the day before, arriving in the early afternoon. I checked into my hotel and spent a relaxing afternoon and evening reading in my room and having room service deliver supper. As an otherwise pleasant evening progressed, I began to think I should have gone to a movie because *Herman's Hermits* were beginning to wear on me.

The day before my flight to Wichita, I woke up with Herman's Hermits cover of *"I'm into Something Good"* streaming through my mind. The song, which peaked at number thirteen on American pop charts in late 1964, was one that may never have had any first-thing-in-the-morning play time in my mind. But, again, that was one of the things I appreciated about whatever or whomever was serving as my personal wake-up DJ.

Not unusually, the entirety of the song was not being rendered. In this case, it was merely the closing refrain:

"Something tells me I'm into something good!
"Something tells me I'm into something good!
To something good, O yeah, something good,
To something good, something good, something good!

That's what was playing in my head as I awoke the day before my trip to Wichita. That's what was playing in my head the day I flew to Wichita. It was still looping through my mind that night as I was reading *War and Remembrance* by Herman Wouk in my hotel room. (Maybe it was the *"Herman"* connection that forced the constant replay.)

The day of my lectures, the uninvited refrain was again present to greet me. Purposefully, humming some other song or playing the radio, would deliver me from the Hermits for a while. But that night, as soon as I began to drive away from the WSU lecture hall, there it was again. At that point, my reaction was, *"Whatever! Do your worst, Hermits! Ultimately, you shall be conquered!"* Besides the next day I was going over to St. Theresa's School for Girls. If necessary, I figured I could have an exorcism.

St. Theresa's School for girls was located to the east of downtown Wichita and south of Wichita State University, home of the *Wheatshockers*. In the 1980s, the area was called College Hill near Eastborough which was the city's *poshest* neighborhood, if *"posh"* and *"Wichita"* can be used in the same sentence. Through various Catholic benefactors, St. Theresa's was able to secure fifteen acres next to Prairie View Golf Course which was a part of the exclusive Prairie View Country Club. Until the aerospace industry abandoned Wichita, Prairie View Country Club touted a first class chef and multi-starred amenities that were surprising to find in the heartland of America.

With Herman and his British pals in the backseat of my rental car, I pulled into a "Visitor Parking" slot in front of St. Theresa's administration building. Inside, I presented myself at the reception desk to a woman whose nameplate said Elena Mendoza

"Hello. I'm Billy Howard. I have an appointment with Sister Mary Claire.

"Yes, Mr. Howard," the pert Elena responded. "She's been expecting you. Please have a seat and I'll tell her you are here."

With that, I sat and Elena departed to the inner offices. Moments later she returned, accompanied by a nun.

"I'm Sister Mary Claire, Mr. Howard. "It is so good to meet you in person finally! Welcome to St. Theresa's School for Girls!" she said. "Won't you come back to my office, please?"

Sister Mary Claire's office was well lit by sunlight but spare in furnishings. "Please be seated, Mr. Howard. After our several telephone conversations over recent years, it is wonderful to meet with you face-to-face. I am happy to say I have read three of your books. Truly, you are a gifted writer!

"Thank you," I said.

"Did the *Wheatshockers* take good care of you yesterday?"

"They did, I'm happy to say. Thank you for asking. I had some excellent conversations with students and faculty."

"May I offer you some coffee, tea, or a soft drink?" she asked.

"Thanks. Unadulterated tea would be great."

After asking Elena to bring us tea "without milk or sugar," Sister Mary Claire said to me with a wry smile. "We're not big into 'adulteration' around here."

While we waited for the tea, we exchanged pleasantries and banalities regarding weather and the joys or hassles of travel.

"Let me be bold, Mr. Howard, in asking if you might someday consider spending some time with our honor students to discuss literature and the realities of being a writer."

"I'd be delighted!" I said. "When I return to Texas, I will send you some dates of when I will pass through Wichita again. Perhaps one of those occasions would suit the students' schedule."

"That would be wonderful, Mr. Howard. When you send those dates to me, please tell me about your fee for speaking. St. Paul tells us the laborer is always *'worthy of his hire.'*"

"Well, I appreciate and agree with the apostle's teaching, but for St. Theresa's there would be no fee," I said. "I would enjoy the opportunity to interact with your students." '

"That's very kind of you, Mr. Howard. It is always wise to '*lay up treasure in heaven,*' as our Lord said."

As if on cue after taking her first sip of tea, Sister Mary Claire said, "I know you have a busy schedule here in Wichita, Mr. Howard. I am very grateful you have chosen to spend time with us today. So that I don't delay in saying what I consider most important, I want to thank you for your generosity in supporting the ministries of St. Theresa's and The Samaritan's Inn. Reasonably, we expect the Catholic community to support these works and they do. We count it an added blessing of God when a non-Catholic, especially one as removed from Wichita as you are, chooses to join in our efforts. Your contributions have been much appreciated. Today, at long last, you will have an opportunity to see the fruit of your kindness up close."

"You're welcome, Sister. My impression is that good things have been happening here for a long time. I'm glad to do my little bit. You and your staff seem to be doing a splendid job. I always enjoy reading your newsletters."

"In our telephone conversations, you have said your support of St. Theresa's has been in remembrance of Madeleine Madigan." The nun continued, "Did you know her well?"

"She and her family were neighbors on Lincoln Street in Coffeyville where we both grew up. She lived down the street. She was a friend. Sadly, I knew nothing of her family situation until the killings took place. I'm sure you know the story very well."

"Of course, Mr. Howard, and there is no reason to dwell on that unhappy circumstance. I knew her as a student when she was resident here. She was a challenging but nevertheless brilliant student. In those days, I was her music and piano instructor. She played beautifully!

"I still recall the occasion when she and a classmate climbed up a water pipe to the roof in the middle of the night to check out the view and sneak cigarettes. It wasn't funny then, but today it is amusing to recall as comic relief to the grim reality of so much of Madeleine's life. We are all very sorry for what happened with Madeleine and her family. But, as the proverb says, '*it is an ill wind that blows no good.'* From those unfortunate experiences, you have chosen to underwrite some good works here at St. Theresa's and also at The Samaritan's Inn.

"So, here is what I propose," Sister Mary Claire continued. "We'd like to give you a tour of the rebuilt school, including a visit with a few of our students of various ages and backgrounds. They will share some of their life and school experiences with you. Sister Maxine and Sister Lois will be with the students. They both teach English and Literature here. That gathering should only take about forty minutes. Then you may return to your hotel for a rest. Is it possible for you to join us at The Samaritan's Inn at 5:00 p.m.?"

"Of course," I said. "I'm looking forward to seeing your ministry there."

"We'll begin with a tour of our rescue mission facilities, followed by some excellent cuisine. Tonight, I understand that we're serving salad, meatloaf, corn on the cob, and green beans with apple or cherry pie for dessert."

"Trust me, Sister, I will clean my plate," I said.

"Then," Sister Mary Claire continued, "we'll show you *Molly's Playground.* I believe you will be very pleased with the beautiful setting and amazing playground equipment, so different from when we were kids. The children and the parents truly adore the place!"

"That's great to hear," I said, as I finished sipping my tea. "Truth is, Sister, I could use some playground time."

Sister Mary Claire walked me back to the reception area. Two uniformed students were talking to the receptionist. Sister Mary Claire interrupted. "Mr. Howard, let me introduce you to Tiffany Stamper and Kanika Ferguson." The girls gave a slight bow as they extended their hands. "I'm happy to meet you, ladies," I said.

"We thought that your tour of St. Theresa's would be best accomplished if guided by two of our charming students. Tiffany is a senior and Kanika is a junior. They both are resident students. Each has given her parents and the school reason to be proud of their time with us. Girls, please return Mr. Howard in one piece and at peace by 3:00 p.m."

"Yes, Sister!" the girls responded in unison.

As we walked down the hallway, the blonde, Tiffany, said, "Please call me 'Taffy.' Everyone here does. My mother was inspired by Audrey Hepburn in *Breakfast at Tiffany's* and that's how I got named. Around here, it's a little too over the top. Here, I'm just plain 'Taffy.'"

"'Taffy' it is!" I smiled.

Kanika was Afro-American. (Descriptors were changing.) Her skin was ebony. She had her hair in an early Michael Jackson puff-ball, a frizzy globe.

"I was born in Nigeria," Kanika said. "'*Kanika*' means '*black cloth*.' My parents were Mennonite missionaries to Nairobi. They are white. They adopted me when I was two years old. We came to the United States when I was nine. God in Heaven has smiled very large on me. I love St. Theresa's even though I am not Catholic!"

Taffy and Kanika did a splendid job showing me around the campus, the classrooms, the athletic fields, the theatre, the dorms, and the student union. The two girls were animated in their descriptions of life at St. Theresa's. In my mind, I readily recalled walking the halls of Field Kindley High School. In such musings, I was eternally young. In the reality of walking the halls of St. Theresa's with two girls who could be my daughters, I felt like the *Ancient of Days!*

Following the enjoyable tour and conversations with other students and nuns, Taffy and Kanika returned me to the reception area where I thanked them. They each gave me a farewell hug. Hugs are good!

Elena, the receptionist, presented me with a packet that she said included the latest information on the school and The Samaritan's Inn. "Sister Mary Claire thinks you might enjoy looking through the brochure on The Samaritan's Inn since that is where you will tour and dine this evening."

"Thank you, Elena," I said. "I recognize a homework assignment when I hear it. I promise I will review it all by the time I show up at the rescue mission."

My hotel was only a mile away. My brief drive was again accompanied by Herman and his reclusive friends. *"Let's all join in now: 'I'm into Something Good!'*

Annoyed, I thought, *"I get it, Herman—really I do! Now, it would be a big help to my sanity if you and the boys would just blurt it out and tell me what the 'something good' is! Herman, are you there? Can you hear me? Surely you must, for I keep hearing you!"*

Chapter 67

What's in a Name?

Back at the hotel, I pulled a bottle of water from the in-room fridge, sat down at the desk, and began leafing through the *Wichita Eagle-Beacon.* When I finished the paper, I peeled off my shirt and tie and cleaned up for the evening event. This time I put on a polo shirt. The open collar would be reasonably comfortable in the heat and humidity of Wichita, situated along the *Chisholm Trail.*

Once I was nattily dressed, I sat back down at the desk and picked up the packet Sister Mary Claire had prepared for me. Most of the material in the packet pertained to St. Theresa's School for Girls. It appeared to be the kind of information that was sent to prospective students and their families. There was an introductory letter signed by Sister Mary Claire, Principal, and Sister Karen Lyn Director of Admissions. The school catalogue was full of photos depicting the K-12 students having a spirited good time learning about the always fascinating *Pythagorean Theorem* and the purposefulness of the *Crusades.*

Though not Catholic and not wanting to be Catholic, I had nevertheless bought into the good works of St. Theresa's, originally as a remembrance of Molly Madigan. By the time I was invited to tour the campus, my support was in appreciation of the institution's ministries which I had come to value. I was a Protestant, a product of public schools, and had met very few priests or nuns along the way. My only boarding experience had been courtesy of the U.S. Army and I sincerely hoped that life at St. Theresa's was more hospitable than life in the Basic Training barracks of Ft. Polk, Louisiana, (May it sink into the sea!).

After grabbing another bottle of water, I turned to the glossy brochure regarding The Samaritan's Inn. It was a typical double-fold brochure which could easily be slipped into a jacket pocket or purse. The front cover showed the unimposing two-story facility.

Turning the page, I saw that downstairs were the reception area, kitchen, dining area, two meeting rooms, and two offices. The kitchen served between 50-400 persons—men, women, and children—each morning and night, seven days per week, all year around. Also on the ground floor were a sleeping room, showers, sinks, and toilets for men. The brochure said the rescue mission could accommodate 125 men per night.

Upstairs were comparable facilities for women with special accommodations for women with children. The brochure said The Samaritan's Inn hosted between sixty to eighty women and children each night, a number that had markedly increased in recent years. There were also two offices upstairs, including one that was labeled "Director."

The brochure noted that The Samaritan's Inn was supported by funding from Catholic Charities plus numerous Wichita individuals, families, churches, community organizations, and businesses. The rescue mission appeared to be a strategic help to the city and I was eager to take the tour, to say nothing of enjoying a meatloaf supper.

The back panel began with a headline that said,

"From the Director...

"Jesus told the parable of a wounded traveler who was avoided by other travelers passing by until an unlikely Samaritan sojourner treated and bound the injured man's wounds. The Samaritan then carried the ill-treated man to an inn where the Samaritan paid the cost to help the hurting man recover.

In our quest to be a good neighbor, The Samaritan's Inn is a way station for the hurting and homeless of Wichita. Please contact me if I may assist you in being a part of this important community service. Also, please remember The Samaritan's Inn as you pray and give. Together we can brighten and encourage the lives of many men, women, and children who need food, shelter, and healing!

Sincerely,
Maddy Finch
Director

I froze in place!

I stared at the signature block.

And stared.

After I don't know how long, I stood up, still holding the brochure, still staring at the Director's name: *"Maddy,"* short for *"Madeleine." "Finch"* as in *"Atticus," "Scout,"* and *"Jem."*

Molly Madigan had been reborn as *Maddy Finch* and was serving as Director of The Samaritan's Inn!

I resurfaced to real time about fifteen minutes later. I found myself gazing out my hotel room's window at not a thing, despite the wide, flat horizon of central Kansas as seen from the hotel's twelfth floor. My head had exploded with a billion recollections and questions. The detonation was too much to process all at once. I found myself smiling in a manner that my cheeks began to ache. *I would see Molly—Maddy—again!*

But then I sobered at the thought that I knew *nothing* of the Maddy Finch who was Director of the rescue mission. Even if she were still *"Molly,"* she would be *changed*, very changed. Twenty-five years change everyone, especially if you've been caged for twenty of those years.

My stomach sank. I didn't even know for certain that I would meet Maddy during the tour or at dinner. Perhaps she was off duty or purposefully chose to be away, lest she have to deal with an awkward encounter. Good grief, the last time Molly and I had a conversation was the day I presented her with *The Longest Day* and a bouquet of zinnias. That was the day before her infamous eighteenth birthday, a long day, indeed!

I went into the bathroom where I literally splashed cold water on my face. Whatever was going to happen was going to happen. *Que sera sera!*

I heard Herman say, *"'Que sera sera?'* That was bloody brilliant, Billy! How many Pulitzers did you say you've won?"

As I pulled out of the parking lot to drive to the mission, *Herman's Hermits* began to sing yet again, *"I'm into Something Good!"* This time I welcomed the tune. Some day in the future, I would chat with my subconscious or the *Higher Musical Power* about how this ditty accompanied this remarkable reunion with Maddy Finch, nee, Madeleine Fiona Madigan. At long last, Herman and colleagues went on break as I arrived at The Samaritan's Inn.

Chapter 68

Sob Story

As I turned off the ignition, I took several deep breaths in an attempt to calm myself. Upon exiting my car in The Samaritan's Inn parking lot, I was greeted by an approaching nun who said, "Good evening, Mr. Howard! Welcome to The Samaritan's Inn. I'm Sister Lenore."

"Good evening, Sister Lenore. It is good to be here. And how did you know that I'm Billy Howard?" I asked.

"That's no mystery, Mr. Howard. Most of our clients don't have cars and most of our workers showed up earlier. Those who are here for supper usually aren't dressed as nicely as you are. And to top it off," Sister Lenore said, "I've seen your picture on your book covers."

"Thank you for your attentiveness, Sister Lenore. What are your responsibilities at The Samaritan's Inn?" I asked.

"For the past two years, I have been the Assistant Director. Our Director is Ms. Maddy Finch. She wanted to be here to give you the tour and have dinner with you, but she had a doctor's appointment with some tests which always take some time. But she said that she will be here by the end of dinner and looks forward to greeting you personally."

"Yes, I look forward to that time. Is Ms. Finch well?"

"As far as I know, yes, praise the Father! She's a high energy person. But, as you may know, the march of time requires us all to show added diligence in the stewardship of body and soul. When I was in high school and college, I jogged regularly. I loved it! But since joining our order, my habit is not conducive to jogging. And my knees don't like the thought of jogging, either!" Sister Lenore said with a chuckle.

Let me cut to the chase as quickly as possible:

The tour of The Samaritan's Inn was great, upstairs, downstairs, and all around the house!

Sister Lenore, other nuns, Father Michael from Blessed Sacrament Catholic Church, and community volunteers all appeared to be happy campers, all glad to be doing something that meant something for the community.

Sister Lenore showed me Maddy's spartan office. There were three photographs in the room. The visage of Pope John Paul II hung on the wall. On a shelf behind Maddy's desk were two small framed photos. The first was of the late Christian apologist and author C.S. Lewis. The second was of the former aide to President Richard Nixon, Charles Colson, who was jailed for his role in the *Watergate Scandal*. While incarcerated, Colson *"got religion"* and upon his release founded *Prison Fellowship.*

When it came time for our meatloaf dinner, I sat at a table with Sister Lenore, Sister Mary Claire, a young mother with her two-year-old daughter, a grizzled man in his fifties, and one of the kitchen volunteers. Sister Mary Claire asked the group to describe their varied experiences with The Samaritan's Inn. Accepting the fact that the group was a stacked deck, they were nevertheless sincere in their appreciation of the rescue mission. My own research about The Samaritan's Inn had long before convinced me of the institution's merit, but it was nice to hear some first-hand reports.

While I was listening to all of this, I hoped the group was not put off by how quickly I gobbled the excellent food or the fact that I was regularly looking to the clock on the wall. Since reading the inn's brochure this afternoon, my only focus had been upon the reunion with *Maddy* or *Molly* or whomever she chose to be!

Following supper and the testimonies, everyone left except Sister Mary Claire.

"Now, Mr. Howard, it is with much gratefulness that I want to show you *"Molly's Playground."*

"Just lead the way, Sister Mary Claire," I said. I then took some more deep breaths and popped a mint into my mouth.

Opposite the reception area, we passed through a set of double doors to a large side yard. Outside the double doors were two sidewalks that went in different directions. The first was a regular cement sidewalk that went to the front of the building. The other sidewalk was comprised of bricks painted yellow and one did not have to be a rocket engineer to know to *"follow the Yellow Brick Road."*

Spaced alongside the winding walkway were bronze sculptures of children having fun, running, playing *"Ring around Rosie,"* looking at bugs, chasing a dog, and so on. The side yard was beautifully landscaped with flowers and bushes of various sorts.

The yellow brick road wound its way to and fro to a destination that was only about fifty yards from the inn but took perhaps eighty yards to traverse. Coming out from behind a hedgerow of bushes, we glimpsed the accoutrements through an arched arbor that had emblazoned upon it in multi-colored letters the name *"Molly's Playground."* How sweet it was!

The playground equipment was state of the art. Swings, merry-go-round, geodesic climbing bars, teeter-totters, slides and more were arrayed in gay profusion. The ground itself was some sort of synthetic matting so that a kid would really have to work hard to break a bone in his or her body. As Sister Mary Claire and I watched, a half-dozen kids were playing under the watchful eyes of four moms. The entire playground area, I noticed, was also under the watchful eyes of security cameras.

Ringing the playground equipment were two types of benches. They were far enough away to give the kids the impression that they were on their own, but close enough for quick parental intervention, if necessary. Four benches were the regular *"bus stop"* type that could seat two to four people. The benches alternated with two-person rest stations that were V-shaped. They were metal rocking chairs divided by a cement table. These were well-suited for conversations. It was at one of those V-shaped rest stations that Sister Mary Claire and I were seated.

"It's magnificent and beautiful, Sister Mary Claire! Your team did a marvelous job! I'm very glad to have had a role to play in this project," I said as I continued to survey the grounds in the early evening of that summer night.

"We are all pleased, Mr. Howard. The landscape architect and the contractor provided greatly discounted services. The sisters and clients were in daily prayer for the playground's development.

Again, God has been gracious to us. Our new Bishop Redfield regularly brings people to the property to show them what can be done with some God-given imagination and God-honoring giving."

"Sometime, if you can, I would appreciate a photograph of *Molly's Playground* on a sunny day with plenty of kids," I said. "That would go well in my office. Unfortunately, I neglected to bring my own camera."

"Of course, Mr. Howard," Sister Marie Claire said. "We'll send that to you soon. We'll make copies to place in the inn and back at the school as well. I trust you saw Kanika and Tiffany working in the kitchen tonight."

"Yes, I did," I said. "It is an amazing thing to see teenage girls laughing as they scour pots and pans. And, on a different subject, in light of all we have been through together over the years, please call me 'Billy.'"

"That's very kind of you, Mr. Howard. But, alas, we will always use the honorific. Call it a Benedictine thing," the nun chuckled. "But, Mr. Howard, there is no prohibition against you calling me Mary Claire unless you convert to Catholicism. Did you know there is a fashion magazine named *'Marie Claire?'* I've not seen it as I fear it is much too worldly!"

I laughed. "I shall respect the Benedictine conventions," I said. "I suspect it will be a cold day you-know-where before I would call you merely *'Mary Claire,'* I said with a smile.

We sat silent for a minute or so, enjoying the activity of *Molly's Playground.*

Sister Mary Claire broke the silence. "For the first time as a Benedictine nun, I am going to violate a confidence for which I shall seek forgiveness and do appropriate penance.

"You should know, Mr. Howard, that since Maddy—as she calls herself now—petitioned to join our work more than four years ago, she has been a hardworking, joyous, and very fruitful servant of our Lord.

"I did not tell her of your previous donations to St. Theresa's in her remembrance. But when you confirmed that you wanted to go forward with constructing *"Molly's Playground,"* I thought she should know. I called her to my office and asked her to be seated. When I told her the plan for the playground, what it would be named, and who was the donor, she collapsed in her chair, got down onto the carpet on all fours, placed her head to the ground and sobbed, and sobbed, and sobbed.

"I sprang from my desk to her aid. When she calmed down, I asked her why she was reacting this way. She said—and I'm paraphrasing—the only person who stood by her all the time in prison was you. Even though she would not permit you to visit, she cherished your letters. She told me that she had not heard from you since she was dismissed from Lansing. She said she did not want to contact you because she felt you had more than proved your friendship. She had chosen not to reach out to you because she was afraid you would be mad at her for never responding. She said she was absolutely overwhelmed by the news of *Molly's Playground.* She gave great praise to the Father and gave great thanks to the Father, to you, and even to me for facilitating this project which she knew would be a great blessing to our children and parents.

"Mr. Howard, Cain slew Abel, Moses killed an Egyptian, King David arranged for the murder of Uriah the Hittite, and the Apostle Paul watched over the cloaks of those who stoned to death St. Stephen. God has a history of forgiveness and Maddy Finch has embraced that *amazing grace,* about which I know Baptists love to sing.

"You were a friend and anchor-point for Maddy. I hope you will be able to renew your friendship. I will continue to pray for each of you, no matter what may happen.

"Now I will leave you, Mr. Howard. Your formerly silent pen pal will join you shortly. Please come again soon," Sister Mary Claire said. "You have many friends here."

Chapter 69

I Want to Hold Your Hand!

I sat watching the children.

She placed her right hand upon my left shoulder. Not turning, I reached up with my left hand, took her hand off my shoulder, and pulled it to my cheek. Then I stood and turned. There she was! Short hair, still the color of Maureen O'Hara's. She wore a light blue blouse, navy skirt, red jacket, and navy blue pumps. She looked well and professional. She was smiling with the same smile that used to precede calling me a *"dork."* There was still a spark in her eyes. Only the fact that her eyes appeared slightly sunken betrayed what she had doubtless endured in forty-three years of life.

We moved toward one another and hugged. Our hugs were hard-pressed; as if we realized that we had lost one another before and did not want to be ripped apart at this special moment. The hugs eased but lingered. I realized, for whatever it was worth, that she and I shared a unique bond.

We parted our embrace. We held hands. We continued to look at one another, observing, under the wrinkles of time, the teenagers we once were when we swung from an elm tree on Lincoln Street.

"Billy! Billy, you look great! Like *Dorian Gray*, you must have a portrait that ages, instead of you."

"Hyperbolic flattery will get you everywhere!" I replied. "You look marvelous, Molly—I mean Maddy. It is so wonderful to see you, especially here!"

"Billy, you may call me 'Molly,' 'Maddy,' or 'Hey, you!'" she said. "Please, let's sit!"

We sat. I held her hand on the cement table. We just stared at one another, grinning.

Then, Maddy waved her right arm at the expanse of the playground. "Look at this, Billy! Isn't it marvelous? You have been so generous! Children and parents love this special place. And, Billy, when I learned that you wanted this beautiful facility to be called, *"Molly's Playground,"* I just wept and wept. You have no idea how much that kindness means to me, Billy. *Thank you! Thank you! Thank you!"*

"Mol—Maddy—Hey, you—when I made the offer to Sister Mary Claire, I had no idea that I would one day be able to sit here with you. I am so glad you're able to enjoy the playground and watch others take pleasure in *Molly's Playground!* Who knows," I said facetiously, "maybe I'll franchise the idea."

"Go for it, Billy," Maddy said, "and may it be the blessing elsewhere that it is here!"

Maddy shifted in her chair, leaned back, and took a deep breath. "Billy," she began, "there are some things I must say to you right now. This may not be easy for me because I am overwhelmed by your presence and the words I have to say have waited many years to be said.

"Again, thank you, Billy! Thank you! Thank you! What a friend you have been to me! Twenty-five years ago, I made a decision—right or wrong—to sever myself from my emotions and from my past. Some of my friends from that time did, in fact, make repeated efforts to contact me. Today, I know how very kind those gestures were. Maybe I should have been open to them. I could have refused your letters, also. I am so glad that I did not turn you away!

"The first four or five years I was in prison, I was numb, a shell. Bram Stoker who wrote *Dracula* would have called me *'the undead.'* I read your letters but during those early years I could not fully engage your words."

"What changed?" I asked.

"Me, of course!" Maddy said. "I read and I read and I read. It was an attempt to deliver myself from my dark reality. But great books that had moved people's feelings in passionate ways came across to me as pointless rhetoric. Reading kept me occupied. I wanted to be—*I had to be*—distracted. Intellectually, I understood everything. Intellectually, I understood that *Sydney Carton's* death by guillotine was a noble sacrifice. But I did not weep when *Old Yeller* was put down or when *Beth* died in *Little Women* or when *Madame Bovary* drank poison. I was numb to it all."

"And then?" I nudged.

"By chance—*or by divine appointment*—I began reading books by C. S. Lewis," she said. "I had never heard of him. Did you know he died the same day as John F. Kennedy? Anyway, Lewis had a remarkable literary range. I read *The Chronicles of Narnia* first. There was no pattern to my reading. Anything would do as I had no emotional connection to any book written by anyone. Reading simply filled the hours and days. In retrospect I have realized that my intellectual perspective at that time was *'what possible significance can any of this have to do with the life I now live in a six-by-eight cell?'"*

"I've read some of Lewis' essays on faith, but that's all," I said. "What did you read by him that made a difference?"

"Two books after *Narnia,"* Maddy said. "The first was *Mere Christianity.* The book is a compilation of essays Lewis wrote for the BBC at the beginning of World War II, ostensibly to buck up the Brits with a dose of Christian orthodoxy in order to confront the terror of the war. Despite my Catholic education, I never received such a clear explanation of the Gospel as what Lewis provided.

"The second book was *A Grief Observed* that Lewis wrote regarding the death of his wife, Joy Gresham, a Jewess who converted to Christianity before she met Lewis. It is a short book. Lewis recounts the grief and bleak depression he suffered at Joy's death due to cancer. Honestly, it seemed that Lewis himself was going to lose his belief in Christ.

"And that's when it happened. Apparently, my soul could not abide having Lewis abandon his convictions after he had done such a remarkable job of articulating faith and the transcendent superiority of Christ. Suddenly, I began to feel—*feel*—afraid that Lewis would deny Christ and Christianity. I feared turning the next page of *A Grief Observed.* Thankfully, Lewis was able to draw on the Lord's strength to climb out of that valley of despair.

"Billy, that was when all the bottled up emotions about my rape, the killing of my baby—you didn't know that, did you—my indefensible killing of my father and brothers, my imprisonment, my ruined life—that's when it all exploded. I was in my cell and I screamed and I began to sob and scream and wail. The guards came to see what the matter was and when I kept howling they carted me off to the hospital ward, tied me down, and sedated me.

"It was twenty-four hours before I woke up. When I did wake up and recalled what had happened, I began to weep quietly. These days psychologists would say I had a *'major cathartic release'* wherein I *'got in touch with my feelings.'* Did I ever! I was washed far downriver before I was able to drag myself to shore.

"Well, dear Billy," Maddy continued, "my feelings at that point were badly wounded and I wondered if I would survive. After another day at the hospital ward, I was taken back to my cell. I reread *Mere Christianity.* When I finished reading it for the second time, I asked the prison chaplain if I could have a Bible. I was in my mid-twenties and for the first time in my life without the admonition of a priest or nun, I began to read scripture. God scraped me up and breathed life back into me.

"Don't misunderstand, Billy. I was justly punished for committing terrible acts. Allegedly, society believes I have paid my debt—which is a crock, by the way. But that doesn't bother me, because while in prison I realized that Jesus paid my debt to God the Father. No matter what I've done to others or what they have done to me, today, Billy, *I am blessed!* "Oh, Billy, you should have been taking notes. All this could win you a third Pulitzer Prize. I am so, so proud to know you and *I am so, so, so grateful* for the kindness you showed to me for so many years. I can never make it up to you!"

There was a pause in our conversation.

I was the one trying to compose myself. Realistically, I could only imagine the prison ordeal that Maddy had endured. Reconnecting after twenty-five years, I was awash in memories, questions, *happiness.* I wondered if there was such a thing as getting the bends from rising too quickly through a sea of emotions.

"Maddy, I'm so glad to hear this part of your story," I said. "Over the years, I've always wondered how you were faring. I was so afraid your spirit would be crushed or that you might be physically harmed. I realize that you may have been to hell and back, but you are clearly a survivor. And regarding *Molly's Playground*, you can thank me by continuing to do the good works you are doing! Sisters Mary Claire and Lenore sing your praises! Why did you choose to come back to St. Theresa's?"

"For the first five years at Lansing, I worked in the prison kitchen. I did drudge work: Washing the floors, doing dishes, wiping down tables, serving food, three times a day. The work was hot and mind-numbing but, during those years, my mind was already numb. In retrospect, I realized that in those five years I learned

380

pretty much everything a person needs to know to administer a cafeteria from front to back.

"But when I began to recover, I actually wanted to do something more. That's when I bumped into *Prison Fellowship*—you know the ministry the *Watergate* guy, Chuck Colson, started up after he had been locked up by the Feds for only seven months. That ministry helped me get my head straight and my heart straight. *Prison Fellowship* encouraged me to take college courses that were taught at Lansing. You'll be happy to know, Mr. Smarty-pants that I have a Bachelor's Degree in English Literature. I even taught classes in literature at Lansing. The students were great, but then they were all a captive audience. That's a little prison humor, Billy. It's okay to laugh."

I laughed. I smiled. These were wonderful moments. Maddy had survived—more than survived, she had rallied! Good for her!

"Billy, come with me!" Maddy said.

We stood and she took my hand. She led me behind the benches to a tree. "Do you know what this is, Billy?"

"My first guess is a *'tree.'* My second guess is an *'elm tree.'* But I've heard nothing about Dutch elm disease being wiped out over the past quarter-century."

The tree was about twelve-feet tall, anchored by a guy wire and stake on the southwest side to prevent it from bowing in the wind. I had noticed that there were six such newly planted trees surrounding *Molly's Playground.*

Molly plucked a leaf from the tree. "Dutch elm disease has not been eliminated, sadly," she said. "But what has happened is that research labs have developed disease resistant varieties of the American elm which used to line our Lincoln Street. In fact, I'm told that this property once had several groves of American elms. These six are the first that have been reintroduced here. The landscape architect says he is eighty-percent confident that these elms will survive. Do you know if they have replanted elm trees on Lincoln Street?"

"They haven't, Molly. Within two or three years following the trees being removed, new trees were planted. They aren't elms. I don't know what they are. They're pretty mature now, but the branches do not arc over the street. There is no canopy of shade like we had."

Maddy took my hand again and began walking toward the playground equipment.

"As I recall, Billy, when you were but a skinny lad, you were quite a swinger!" she said with a smirk.

"Beg pardon?" I replied.

"Swinger, Billy! *Swinger!* Don't you remember the hours we talked away swinging back and forth across the sidewalk?"

"Yep, I do," I said. "I used to serenade you with my *humanatone*—you know, the nose whistle."

"Serenaded me with a nose whistle? Did you really think I thought that screeching was a serenade? When you got heavy into dating, did you continue to court girls with a—what did you call it—a *humanatone?"*

"No," I said. "You were the only lucky one."

"'Lucky,' huh? Well, maybe today I am. But not back then, I'm afraid."

We walked around the equipment and ended up at the swings.

"Look here, Billy. There are four sets of swings with four seats each. The seats are positioned at different heights for different-sized kids. But this fourth set of swings has two seats that are positioned for adults with extra-strong chains for the extra weight. *Let's swing, Billy!"*

And we did! For the next two and one-half hours, we talked— old times, new times, bad times, good times. The playground lights came on to illuminate the equipment and walkway back to The Samaritan's Inn. I suppose we looked like a couple on a date. We weren't. But we did feel like a couple of kids who had time-travelled to a long-ago and long-gone Lincoln Street.

"Wow, Maddy!" I said as I finally looked at my watch. "I hope I haven't worn you out. I know you've had a long day and you've got to be up and at'em tomorrow. By the way, and I don't mean to be inappropriately intrusive, but Sister Lenore said you had a doctor's appointment and tests today. I trust you are well."

"I, too, trust that I am well—*'by His stripes we have been healed,'* she said. "It was my annual checkup. I was poked and probed. Pre-menopause is always a cheery time of life for women. I had the usual tests and I got my boobs mashed for a mammogram. I assure you, Billy, that your hands were far gentler than the mammogram vise."

"Good grief, Maddy! Now I'm beet red!" I said, laughing. "Well, for the record, I've never received a *Hallmark Card* that could equal your memorable birthday gift to me!"

"Thank you, Billy! For the record, no one else ever received such a 'memorable' birthday gift from me. Let's walk."

We began to stroll the winding walkway back to The Samaritan's Inn. I placed my arm over her shoulder and she put an arm around my waist.

"Can we meet again tomorrow, Billy? We could have lunch or I could fix dinner for us."

"I would so love that, Maddy!" I said. "But your happy reappearance in my life has come upon me unawares. First thing in the morning, I'm flying back to Fort Worth and then I must drive to Houston where I have a couple of days of lectures and book signings. But let me tell you something I've been thinking."

We stopped on the sidewalk. I turned to face Maddy. "The truth is, Maddy, I've missed you big time! From this afternoon till about an hour ago, my head was bursting with so many considerations about our reunion. Then, it finally occurred to me: *What's the rush?*

"The reconnection has been made, thanks be to God! My schedule over the next three months is packed as I'm flying around the U.S. and making a handful of stops in Europe, Japan, and then a couple of weeks in Thailand. But I can bring the whole family here to show them St. Theresa's and The Samaritan's Inn on our way back to Texas. Then you can come with us to Fort Worth and we'll teach you how to do the *'Cotton-Eyed Joe.'*

"It's obvious that you've well-trained Sister Lenore to cover for you and I know that Sister Mary Claire would endorse the idea of a break for you. So, after this astonishing reunion, let us all be patient for just three months. Then come to Texas. Then we can begin taking advantage of the time."

"Taking advantage of the time," Maddy said. "Sounds good, Billy."

To my surprise, Maddy choked up and turned away.

"Maddy, what's wrong," I asked. "Did I say something wrong?" I turned her back to me and held her close for a moment. She quickly backed away and wiped her eyes.

"Oh, Billy, I'm sorry! Our reunion has been awesome. For so many years, I thought all my friends from the past were gone forever—due to my stonewalling them. I am so, so grateful to you. Nothing would please me more than for us to rebuild our friendship. I hope that can happen. I know it can't be forced. And I don't know what God has in store for me or us or St. Theresa's. I'm still pretty fragile and tentative when it comes to thinking about the future. I made it through prison by taking only one day at a time."

"I understand, Maddy!" I said. "Truth be told, taking things one day at a time makes *"heap big sense,"* to paraphrase *Big Chief Thundercloud* on *The Howdy Doody Show.* Good grief, I really must be tired if I'm quoting a puppet show. Let's get some rest, Maddy."

I walked her to her car. We stood facing one another. I laughed.

"What?" Maddy asked.

"Maddy, when we arrived here at your car door, I suddenly felt like I was on a first date and had just arrived back at the girl's front door."

"Hah," Maddy snorted. Imagine it's a date, if you wish, Billy Howard, but you'll have some explaining to do when you return to your home and hearth."

Maddy opened her car door and tossed in her purse. Then she closed the car door and turned once again to me.

"Billy, I know that you and your wonderful wife are not Catholic but I need the two of you to grant me an *indulgence.* I promise I will explain this to that beautiful woman. I am absolutely certain she will have no hesitancy in granting me this indulgence."

"If you say so," I chuckled. I'll have to research the fine print on indulgences but it's always easier to ask for *forgiveness* than for *permission.* What do you need?"

Maddy looked to the stars and gave a deep sigh. Looking back at me, she said, "Perhaps what I really need, Billy, is not yours to grant. But what I will ask you for is this: *Kiss me, Billy!* Don't kiss me platonically. Don't kiss me as an act of charity. Don't kiss me as a lover. Kiss me as the dearest and deepest of friends for that is what you are to me. *Kiss me, Billy! It's been a long, long time!"*

I stood before Maddy motionless and silent. I looked into her beautiful brown eyes. A tear rolled down her left cheek. I took her hands in mine and drew them to my lips. I raised her hands and she placed her arms around my neck. I took her waist and drew her to me.

The kiss was long and luxurious. It was a kiss wrapped in a gentle and time-transcending embrace.

When we stepped back and had caught our breaths, Molly said, "She's a very lucky woman, Billy! I'm happy for both of you! You cannot conceive of how happy I am for your children!"

Maddy stepped back and I opened her car door. She sat down and lowered her window.

"This has been such a special night, Billy! God is very kind! Have safe travel and tell the lovely Mrs. Howard that I can't wait to be with the two of you and your kids!"

Maddy grabbed my hand and kissed it. Releasing my hand, she said, "'Good night, sweet prince...!'"

As she drove away, I finished the Shakespearean line: "...and flights of angels sing thee to thy rest" dear Maddy!

"Never thought you would be standing here so close to me—
There's so much I feel that I should say,
But words can wait until some other day!

Kiss me once, then kiss me twice, then kiss me once again.
It's been a long, long time!
Haven't felt like this, my dear, since I can't remember when.
It's been a long, long time!
You'll never know how many dreams I've dreamed about you
Or just how empty they all seemed without you.
So kiss me once, then kiss me twice, then kiss me once again.
It's been a long, long time!"

Sammy Cahn and Jule Styne
Songwriters

Chapter 70

Have You Hugged Your Hometown Lately?

Probably everyone on this globe could pen his or her own tale of *"coming of age"* in their respective hometowns. In the telling of this tale, this memoir is not intended to gloss over the warts, foibles, foolishness, and, on recurring occasions, flat-out evil that stains the history of Coffeyville.

Through the decades, some observers of Coffeyville would call it

"…an All-American City!"

"…a great place to raise your kids!"

"a good place to find well-paying employment."

But others would say the opposite, that Coffeyville is

"…an armpit of a town with terrible odors in the air."

*"…has not a dang thing for the kids to do
and the houses are falling down."*

"Everyone who can is moving away."

"Jobs? Well-paying jobs? You gotta be kidding me!"

Some of the dark truths about Coffeyville are that:

*Girls didn't have to leave town to have
back-alley abortions.*

Female teachers with comparable training to male teachers were not paid the same.

When segregation legally came to an end, the Big Hill Municipal Swimming Pool and Roosevelt Junior High School were among the venues that, at first, did not get the memo--

When Negroes showed up for the first time at the Big Hill pool and plunged into the water, all the whites climbed out. That little swimming pool on the east side of town should have been just fine for anyone of a colored persuasion.

When Negroes—how dated the word now seems—showed up at the brand new junior high school, an administrator was out front to turn away colored students, Negroes, African-Americans, blacks... Well, you get the picture.

Scandal surfaced during the infamous Maude Martin murder trial, featuring the friendly but klutzy local surgeon, Dr. S.A. Brainard and his hired henchman and hit-woman.

But I have chosen not to expand upon these *"damn spots!"* as *Lady Macbeth* would call them, for one particular reason: Call it fate, luck of the draw, or grace, but when I was growing up in Coffeyville, I was more influenced by the *good* of the place than I was by the bad or the ugly.

There will always be more than enough embittered folk cursing the darkness of their pathetic, malevolent, and vile hometowns. But that ain't what this tome has been about. In light of its formative and positive influence upon my life, I say *"Thank you, Coffeyville!"*

What would you say to your hometown?

On a regular basis, we hear stories of athletes who have become wealthy because of their prowess at some sport. Some of the *nouveau riche* acknowledge the support of their parents by purchasing a new car or even a house for dear old mom and pop. That is a gracious and much appreciated gesture by the child.

Happily, my parents were on the job in watching out for my development. I have sought to express my gratitude to them in intangible and tangible ways over the years. Their involvement in my life has been sufficiently documented in other biographical essays.

In my view, however, Coffeyville also served *in loco parentis—"in the position or place of a parent."* I wish people who had a good experience growing up in their hometowns would tip their hats in some meaningful way to remember and encourage those dear hearts and gentle people who lived and loved in their hometown.

Therefore, in appreciation:

In 1985, local residents and dance instructors Clem and Winnie Hedley approached the Coffeyville City Council to report that people interested in fostering the arts had raised sufficient funds to build a multi-purpose ballroom and community center at Pfister Park on Big Hill, provided the city would donate the land for the structure. The facility would be able to accommodate a seated audience of three-hundred-fifty, a banquet audience of two-hundred-seventy-five, and a dance audience of two-hundred-forty. There would be a stage for the community theatre, a kitchen, and ample storage space. Monies were included for paving the parking lot.

The Hedley's said this facility would be deeded to the city upon its completion. The only request the donors had was that the facility be named *"Carly and Toni's Ballroom and Community Center,"* as a memorial to the late FKHS students Carla Delgreco and Toni Weinstein.

The city council unanimously accepted the donation and name stipulation.

"Piglet noticed that even though he had a Very Small Heart,
it could hold a rather large amount of Gratitude."

Winnie-the-Pooh
A.A. Milne

"I would maintain that thanks are the highest form of thought;
and that gratitude is happiness doubled by wonder."

G. K. Chesterton
Author and Theologian

Chapter 71

Married with Children and Dogs

By now, dear reader, surely you have noticed that the yarns, tales, conversations, and stories of my memoir have *not* been presented in a sequential or chronological order. This is not because I can't remember which came first, the *ZoZomobile* or *Captain Jack photographing elm trees.* This spattered recollection exemplifies how I recall the special days of my youth in Coffeyville. My memories of those days are pied and kaleidoscopic, not linear. In my mind, those dappled memories unite as a colorful whole.

You will recall my stroll around Lincoln Street the day after I had spoken at the commencement ceremonies of Field Kindley Memorial High School. It was during that walk that I was serendipitously accosted by *Rubens*, the jolly schipperke whose masters were and are Harriet Whitfield Koppensott and her daughter Dala Koppensott.

As it turned out, Cupid still had arrows to launch on Lincoln Street. Harriet and I were married slightly more than one year after we were reunited through Rubens' good offices. Our union received joyous affirmation from Dala. Rubens expressed no opposition, though the dog did appear somewhat puzzled as to why I began sleeping with Harriet using the side of the bed upon which the schipperke had previously sawed logs.

A few months after our wedding, we brightened Rubens life and added to our household merriment when we adopted *Reggie,* an always-bright-white non-shedding *Bichon Frise* puffball of a dog who would match Rubens in size and good humor. To see this black-and-white duo cavort is a delightful pastime and pleasant accompaniment for my writing.

Three years into our marriage, Harriet and I adopted four-year-old fraternal twins from a Bangkok orphanage. Our daughter is named Dawn Chatmanee Howard. Our son is Frederick Anada Howard. Dawn and Frederick adore Dala who reciprocates the feeling. The dogs are over the moon!

It's delightful to be married! Thanks again, Coffeyville!

Chapter 72

Breathtaking!

The morning following my wonderful reunion with Molly, I flew back to Fort Worth where Harriet picked me up at DFW airport. We then drove five hours to Houston where I had book signings and lectures. I had plenty of time to share with Harriet—who also had been and would continue to be—Molly's friend.

Of course, I shared with Harriet *"the kiss"* with Molly. When I told her, Harriet went silent and turned her face to stare out the passenger-side window. Then she quickly twisted her body back toward me, leaned toward me, and in a deep-throated hiss, Harriet said, *"You did what, Billy Howard? You did what with Molly Madigan?"*

Blood drained! I turned pale.

Harriet's burning eyes suddenly restored their usual glint and she burst out laughing. She touched my leg and said, "O Billy, I'm not angry! I'm not jealous! I am so very proud of you and all you've done to stand by someone you had no contact with for a quarter-century! Would that everyone had friends like you! I know Molly must be overjoyed! She could use some *overjoyed-ness* in her life! Maybe I should send you on mission trips to seek out and kiss righteous but pent up women."

My heart restarted and color was restored to my face.

"I mean it, Billy! I am truly proud of you! I know in whose bed you will be sleeping tonight. I'm the only woman on this planet who knows what makes you *"tick"* and *"talk"* in bed. Maybe we'll order room service at the hotel and have our own little *Tex-Mex* fiesta. What do you say, cowboy?"

O Lord, I love Harriet!

As our drive to Houston continued, Harriet said she would call Molly/Maddy to extend her own greetings, repeat my invitation to visit us in Texas, and, should there be any need, offer *absolution* for *"the kiss."* (Question for Catholics: Is *"absolution"* even necessary for an *"indulgence?"*)

The next day when I returned from lecturing, Harriet told me that she had had a thirty minute phone conversation with Maddy, a conversation which Harriet permitted to delay her shopping trip to Houston's *Galleria!*

Back in Fort Worth, our family had one week to prepare for three months of travel. My parents volunteered to host Rubens and Reggie during our absence from the States. Dala was actually stoked about being able to ride herd on Frederick and Dawn as the kids traveled with us. I questioned whether such a long period of travel could actually be fun or good for two precocious seven-year-olds or even a post-graduate student. But Harriet assured me that it would all work out!
Whatever!

The first month of our travel was devoted to a seventeen city tour commemorating the tenth anniversary of the publication of *The Sixteenth Frame* which had garnered me my second Pulitzer. The anniversary also marked the launch of my latest book, *Webster's Gestures!* Reviews and sales of books past and present were going very well.

The second month was more of the same but in Europe. We visited London, Paris, Rome, Lucerne, Vienna, Munich, Budapest, Prague, and St. Petersburg. Whether in the USA or Europe, all three kids were more impressed by arcade games than the turnout at the book signings or my appearances on local television.

Some landmarks thrilled Dala but Frederick and Dawn thought London to be dreary, Paris to be full of over-dressed people, and that Rome would be really nice *"if all the buildings were not so old!"* Dala declared caviar in St. Petersburg to be *"barf balls."* They did like the *"Dying Lion of Lucerne,"* the *Charles Bridge* in Prague, and *schnitzel* in Salzburg.

I enjoyed *Stella Artois*, Swiss chocolate, and our family dinners. Also, I really loved the lederhosen I purchased in Munich despite Harriet bemoaning my alleged knobby knees.

We spent two weeks in Japan and too much money at the shops in the *Ginza!* Just as we thought all three kids were about to implode, we arrived in Bangkok and were greeted by Harriet's parents and friends from the mission. All of us were revived as we enjoyed the country and rejoiced at the continuing good works with the *"red door girls."*

Harriet, her parents, and Dala were happy to show me their old digs. At first, Dawn and Frederick or *Chatmanee* and *Anada* were confused as to how to handle their own biculturalism. Dala was able to serve as their cross-cultural guide and the three of them revelled in their common bond. The kids settled in to enjoy Grandma and Grandpa (*Yāy* and *Kuhn-pū*). From deep within, Harriet and I smiled!

We spent a week in Bangkok and environs. Then the clan headed for *Karon Beach* at *Phuket.* We were all beach bums! *(bums chāyhād)*

Finally, it was time to return to the USA.....*where our breath again would be taken away!*

Departing Bangkok, jet-lag was force-fed to us as we crossed the Pacific to arrive in San Francisco. We spent two nights in a San Francisco airport hotel to relax and collectively come to agreement as to the actual time of day. We did not venture beyond the hotel swimming pool.

Having the appearance of refreshed bodies and restored rationality, our family flew from SFO to Wichita where we were met by my parents who had driven to Wichita with Reggie and Rubens in tow. It was another happy reunion!

While traveling, we had taken full advantage of the remarkable communication device known as the *"postcard."* We had a full retinue of friends whom we wanted to remember from some faraway place with a strange-sounding name. Maddy Finch received the most postcards, though we also remembered to send cards to Sisters Mary Claire and Lenore.

As per our conversations before leaving the states on our ninety-two day romp around the world, we wrote Maddy of our approximate arrival date in Kansas. We restated our desire for her to visit us in Texas and that she would be welcome to travel with us in our carpool to Fort Worth. We said we would call when we were ensconced in Wichita.

We arrived in Wichita on a Monday morning. The remainder of the day was devoted to catching up with grandparents and dogs and mid-western cuisine. After dinner, with grandparents gone to their room, Dala, Dawn, and Frederick next door in their room, and Harriet and I cuddling with Reggie and Rubens, I called The Samaritan's Inn and punched in Molly's extension. The new *PhoneMate* transmitted Sister Lenore who requested callers to leave a message *"after the beep."*

> *"Hi, Sister Lenore! Hello, Maddy! This is Billy Howard. As promised, Harriet and I have arrived in Wichita. We are eager to see you and catch up on your summer. Our kids and my parents plus our two dogs are also here. Everyone, with the possible exception of the dogs, is looking forward to meeting you and taking a tour of The Samaritan's Inn and St. Theresa's. Unless this does not work for you, Harriet and I will stop by the Inn around 11:00 in the morning to do some scheduling with you. Ladies, if you are available, Harriet and I would be delighted to take you to lunch. When it's convenient, call us at the Hyatt. We're in room 1218. Love you all! Good night!"*

By 9:00 a.m. the next morning, my parents and the kids were off to the *Sedgwick County Zoo*. I was feeding Reggie crust from a piece of toast left over from breakfast in our room when the phone rang. Harriet answered.

"...Why, of course.....No problem at all.....Tell her we will see her then. Thanks for calling.....Bye!"

"What's up?" I asked, as I gave the jealous Rubens the final piece of crust.

"That was Elena Mendoza, the receptionist at St. Theresa's," Harriet said. "Elena said Sister Mary Claire wanted to know if we could stop by her office this morning before heading over to The Samaritan's Inn. I didn't think that would be a problem so I said we would come by. If that's not what you prefer to do, I will call Elena back."

"No. It's no problem all," I said. "I hope nothing's wrong."

"If I had to guess, Billy, I suspect Sister Mary Claire merely wants to welcome you again to the friendly Catholic environs in behalf of the faculty, staff, and administration—and in behalf of His Holiness, the Pope as well." Harriet chuckled. I groaned. She continued: "Three copies of *Webster's Gestures* are there on the end table for you to inscribe."

After checking Rubens and Reggie into the hotel's doggie daycare, Harriet and I arrived at St. Theresa's shortly before 11:00 a.m.

We were greeted by Elena Mendoza. I introduced her to Harriet.

Elena said, "I'll take you right back to Sister Mary Claire's office, but first let me ask what I may bring you to drink. Water? Coffee? Tea? Soft drink?"

Harriet asked for tea. I asked for black coffee.

"Mr. and Mrs. Howard, please follow me," Elena said. She led the way to Sister Mary Claire's closed office door. She tapped on the door twice and then swung the door open for us. Inside the office, Sister Mary Claire and Sister Lenore were standing and smiling at our arrival.

"Welcome, Mr. Howard. And you must be the wonderful Mrs. Howard about whom Maddy shared." The women smiled at one another. Sister Lenore was introduced and hands were shaken all around. We were bid to sit on the settee opposite the sisters.

Elena said, "Sister Mary Claire, would you and Sister Lenore like something to drink?"

"I think not, Elena. Thank you."

"Very well, Elena said.

Till Elena returned with our drinks, the four of us bantered about our around-the-world trip, particularly how the human trafficking mission was progressing in Bangkok. Elena brought our drinks. After a few sips, the smiles of the nuns disappeared.

Sister Mary Claire spoke: "Dear friends, it is a privilege and pleasure to welcome you in behalf of St. Theresa's and The Samaritan's Inn. By my first-hand observation, you have proved yourselves gracious and unexpected donors for our mission, our faculty, staff, and students. Most especially you have shown yourselves to be loyal friends to Maddy Finch who has been such a strategic and fruitful part of The Samaritan's Inn."

Sister Mary Claire glanced briefly at Sister Lenore and then continued, "Sadly, I must now share with you some grievous news about Maddy. Maddy is..." Sister Mary Claire's voice choked. Harriet grabbed my hand. The pit of my stomach began to tighten.

"I am sorry to tell you that Maddy is gravely ill. In truth, she is dying, and most likely has only a few days left in this realm."

Air if not chunks of life were sucked out of Harriet and myself. We looked at each other with expressions of shock and confusion.

"God help us all!" I exclaimed. "Only a week before our trip, we were here with Maddy and she appeared in excellent health. That was barely one hundred days ago. What has happened?" I implored.

Sister Lenore picked up the narrative. "Billy, you may recall that on the very evening you visited The Samaritan's Inn to see *Molly's Playground* for the first time, I greeted you in behalf of Miss Finch because she had a medical appointment. Her exam and tests that day were simply part of her annual checkup. But when the results came back, more tests were ordered and it was determined that Molly had contracted pancreatic cancer. Unfortunately, it became metastatic and the cancer is now throughout her body.

Despite great progress that has been made in dealing with various cancers, pancreatic cancer has not been repulsed by drugs, chemo or radiation therapy. Even the onslaught of intercessory prayer that has been launched in Maddy's behalf has not prompted the Savior to intervene. We must trust His wisdom in having numbered each of our days, including Molly's."

"Pancreatic cancer!" I said. "That's what killed Molly's mother and apparently at nearly the same age." I heaved a deep sigh. Harriet and Sister Lenore were both wiping away tears.

"Thank you, Sisters, for breaking this to us as gently as possible. Where is Molly? Is she lucid? May we see her?"

"Maddy is here," Sister Mary Claire said. "For the past three weeks she has been bedridden most of the time, though she has been able to spend short times in a chair. She is being tended to around the clock under the supervision of Sister Beatrice who is also a registered nurse and a hospice nurse as well.

"During the past few days, Maddy has been in and out of wakefulness. When she is awake, she has been conversant. I fear her periods of wakefulness are diminishing. This is such a terrible disease, but the Father calls us to honor Him in every circumstance. I'm happy to say Maddy has not wavered in her confidence in our blessed Savior. She knows her earthly travail will soon pass."

Sister Lenore said, "We will take you to see Maddy. Please prepare yourselves. Her body has been ravaged. She is weak and wan, but the essence of our dear friend is still with us."

"My friends, Sister Lenore and I will go check on Maddy. Why don't you stay here until we come for you? I realize you have been blindsided by this as we all were. Let us lean on the Lamb of God."

The nuns left the room. Thank God Harriet and I had each other to begin processing such hideous news. We prayed.

Perhaps fifteen minutes later, Sister Lenore tapped on the door. She led us up a flight of stairs to one of the standard rooms used by the sisters. It had been outfitted as a hospital room. As we entered, Sister Mary Claire said, "Maddy, you have two dear friends to see you."

Maddy was seated in a recliner that elevated her slipper-shod feet. She was in a gown and robe. A gray blanket was over her legs and lap. Her hair had marked streaks of gray and was a little matted. But it had been freshly combed. Maddy's pallor was beginning to waxen. There was not much brightness to her eyes.

Indeed, she was but a shadow of her former self. But her smile was full!

"Billy! Harriet! How wonderful to see you! O Harriet, my darling friend, you are even more beautiful than I remember! What a lucky, lucky man you are, Billy Howard!" Her voice was raspy but there was still some force behind it.

Harriet knelt beside the recliner to embrace Maddy. I followed, kneeling to take and kiss Maddy's hand, bruised from various intravenous treatments. A saline solution was dripping into Maddy's other arm via an IV pole on wheels.

Harriet said, "Maddy, we are so sorry to learn of your illness. It was bad enough to lose you once. The thought of losing you again is ripping at my soul. We love you!"

"Truth be told, Maddy," I said, "to see you in good health or poor health—just to be with you—is still a blessing to me. Indeed, we love you and we will be here with you."

I placed two folding chairs in a row facing Maddy beside the right side of her recliner. Harriet took Maddy's hand.

Maddy said, "I asked the Father that you might return from your travels in time for me to see your beautiful faces again. See what's on the wall."

We turned and looked to the wall aside Maddy's bed. In chronological order, Maddy or someone had taped all the postcards we had sent to Maddy while we were circling the globe.

"What magnificent and storied places you've been! What did the children think?" Maddy asked.

"They loved it," Harriet said. "Would that you could have been with us, dear heart."

"Thank you, Harriet, but what has been found traveling through me has been a rude visitor. But, dear friends, I know that soon and very soon this petulant blight will be plucked away from me. You know and I know that Jesus is our Lord and our friend. He is with me. He is with us. But I have little patience for this dying. Let it be done! At this moment, it is life I want to hear about. Tell me about your family!"

And so we did. Harriet is never without photos. Each child was detailed. Maddy beamed as if she were the kids' aunt or God-mother. Harriet even had pictures of Rubens and Reggie. Maddy giggled and laughed till she began to cough. The coughing did not ebb and it became hacking. Sister Beatrice who had been standing aside with Sisters Mary Claire and Lenore moved toward Maddy with a syringe, but Maddy waved her off.

Slowly the coughing ceased. But Maddy was sweating profusely. She closed her eyes as she sought to catch her breath. Harriet stood with a hand towel and patted away as much of the perspiration she could reach. I thought Maddy was falling asleep. But after a minute's silent respite, she opened her eyes.

Maddy said, "Oh, I'm sorry for my little spell. These wracking waves come upon me whether I am awake or asleep. Soon they will descend to the pit and never bother me again."

I spoke up. "Maddy, this is not how we expected to spend time with you. We understand what's happening here. Harriet and I are already praying against it. If this fiendish sickness cannot be turned away, please tell us what we may do to comfort you in any way. Please!"

Maddy was tiring. I didn't want to wear her out which struck me as an absurd thought in light of her emaciated, nearly exhausted body, lying before me. Maddy closed her eyes and took a couple of deep breaths. Then she looked to us again and reached out to take my hand as she held on to Harriet with her other hand.

"My comfort here is well provided for by these dear sisters. Even morphine has its place. But my mind is not clouded at the moment, thanks to Jesus who is helping me stay awake.

"Billy, Harriet, I have two favors to ask of you. Life is intended to be for the living, not the dying, so if what I ask impinges upon you or your family or other responsibilities, not to worry."

"Cut the BS, Molly!" Harriet said pointedly. "Like Billy said, you are our dear friend and we want to comfort and encourage you in any way we can. Just tell us."

"You still call me to account and make me laugh, Harriet, just as you did when we were in the swings on Lincoln Street. Thank you! Here is what I would like:

"I know that our meeting here in Wichita was intended to be a brief interlude before heading to Fort Worth to visit you in your home. I would so love to do that but it ain't gonna happen. So, think about the time you have planned to be in Wichita. If you can be with me for some of that time, I would so love your mere presence and anything we could talk about would be icing on the cake."

"Yes, Molly, we'll be with you!" Harriet said. "What else?"

"I would love to meet Dala. How amazing and special she must be. And I've never known anyone named 'Koppensott' before." Maddy laughed and coughed. Taking another deep breath, Maddy said, "I would also love to meet Frederick and Dawn but I don't want my wasting body to frighten them. Do what you think best.

"Those are my requests," Molly said. "Thank you for hearing them."

Sister Beatrice came back to Molly's side. She gave no signal to us but Harriet and I recognized it was time to leave.

Harriet stood and said, "Molly, we're going to leave now so you may get some rest. If the sisters permit, we will be back later with Dala. Now please rest, dear friend. We love you." Harriet leaned over and kissed Molly's sallow and sunken cheek.

Sister Mary Claire and Sister Beatrice came out of Maddy's room with us. Sister Beatrice said, "You poor dears, how sad it is that you've had to meet your friend like this. But, truly, your presence is a tonic for her."

"Thank you, Sister Beatrice. We are very grateful for your care and the love that surrounds Maddy at St. Theresa's," I said. "Is it okay if we come back later?"

"Yes, Mr. Howard," Sister Beatrice said. "Your visit will boost her spirit. Your visit may exhaust her a little sooner than otherwise. But she will sleep awhile and then awake. She will be happy to see you any times you can be here."

"Forgive my question, Sister Beatrice. How many days or weeks do you believe remain for her?" I asked.

"Mr. Howard, we are not now talking of days or weeks. We have reached a point of hours or days. Maddy still has a strong will to live. But her body has already begun to shut down. She has indicated she wants no extraordinary measures. She has refused being hospitalized just as her own mother wanted to die in her own home. St. Theresa's and The Samaritan's Inn are the closest things to home and family Maddy has had since her imprisonment. She has no surviving blood relatives."

"We understand, Sister Beatrice," Harriet said. "We are going back to our hotel and have a family huddle. All three of our children have heard volumes about Maddy. Dala will certainly want to be with us when we return."

"That's splendid," Sister Beatrice said. "If you choose to bring your twins, I know Maddy will be delighted. If you decide that is not the best for your young children, Maddy will absolutely understand. Whatever the sins and shortcomings earlier in her life, we of St. Theresa's and The Samaritan's Inn have known Maddy only as a caring and productive woman of strong character and much love. Our imminent loss will be Heaven's gain."

Harriet and I walked from St. Theresa's in silence. We drove in silence back to the hotel where we dined in its main restaurant. Some other time, we would have enjoyed the cuisine and ambiance. I ordered a bottle of Chardonnay. We stirred our respective salads, but ate little of them.

When the waiter came to ask if we would like something more, I said, "Yes, bring us two servings of whatever you have that is chocolate and two black coffees as well."

Harriet was surprised and puzzled.

After some reflective silence, I said, "My precious Harriet, we were T-boned today big time. But we can't implode into our own cocoons of sorrow, at least not yet. We must deal with the kids and we must comfort Molly."

Harriet was in full agreement, so we sucked up the cake and made tentative plans for the next twenty-four hours as best we could. While most of what we actually ate at lunch was not particularly nutritional, we packed away enough food to sustain us through the afternoon and into the evening. We returned to our hotel room to await the return of my folks and the kids from the zoo.

Though we shared word of Molly's illness and her approaching extremis as gently as we could, all our family members were thunderstruck by this unexpected turn. This was especially so in light of the joyous anticipation all had shared as we looked forward to introducing Molly to the rest of the family and then having her as our guest in Texas.

Even though the twins were still a month shy of their eighth birthdays, their exposure to some grim realities in Thailand caused them to be undismayed at the thought of seeing a shrunken lady. My parents declined to go, saying that five new faces would overwhelm Molly. Just three would be better. We all ate supper at a nearby McDonald's and then went our separate ways.

At 6:30 p.m. Harriet and I tapped on Molly's door. Sister Beatrice came out. We introduced her to the kids and then Dala took the twins to a sitting area a short distance away so we could confer with the nurse.

"Maddy has had a good rest this afternoon, but her respiration is more labored," Sister Beatrice said. "I don't believe our friend will endure past the next twenty-four to forty-eight hours. I cannot overstate what a blessing your family's presence has been to Maddy. Please come in."

Our family time with Molly was brief but very positive. She was in her bed which was elevated to a sitting position. She brightened immediately upon seeing us, especially our children.

Without waiting for a formal introduction, Dala walked directly to the bedside and said, "Hello, Maddy. I'm Dala. My parents have told me so much about you. What a special lady you are!"

Maddy took Dala's hand. *"O how beautiful you are, Dala!"* Maddy said. "I hear you're on your way to become a physician like your grandfather and father. Maybe you'll be the one to find a cure for some disease, maybe even mine. I am so pleased to meet you!"

The twins were in no way cowering. "Maddy, these are our twins, Frederick and Dawn," I said. I stepped toward the bedside. Without prompting, the twins stepped with me.

Unhesitatingly, Dawn placed her hand on Maddy's. "I'm sorry you're sick, Miss Finch. We prayed for you this afternoon."

Maddy wrapped her near skeletal hands over Dawn's. "That is so special to me, Dawn!" Maddy said. "I pray for your family, too. Sometimes we must humble ourselves and accept what the Lord allows to happen in our lives whether we like it or not."

"Are you hurting, Miss Finch?" Frederick asked. I knew Maddy would be amused by the boy's directness.

With a slight chuckle, Maddy said, "No, Frederick, I am not hurting. Sister Beatrice sees to it that my medicines block the pain. But I'm not quite as energetic as I used to be.

"Do the two of you know that when your parents and I were just a few years older than you are now, we used to play and talk about important matters on Lincoln Street in Coffeyville? You've been there, haven't you?" Maddy asked.

"Yes, we have, Miss Finch," Dawn said. "Daddy showed us where you two used to swing. But the tree you used is not there anymore."

"No, it's not there anymore. Lincoln Street once had the most beautiful elm trees. But they got sick, too, and were taken down. That's pretty much the way it is for every living thing. But I'm not sad about that. I know that very soon I will be in the most beautiful place anyone could imagine."

"You mean Heaven, don't you, Miss Finch?" It was Frederick again.

"Yes, of course, Frederick—*Heaven!*" Maddy said. "One day, I'll see all of your family there. But don't rush! There's too much for you to do on this *'Big Blue Marble.'* Do you watch that TV show?"

"We do!" Frederick said. "Did you ever see my dad play a game called *'Marbles?'* He said he used to walk around with a bag full of marbles looking for a game."

"No, Frederick, I never saw your father's bag of marbles!" Maddy said. "In fact, I'm pretty certain that by the time he met me, your daddy had already lost all his marbles!" [Rimshot!] Maddy laughed. Dala, Harriet, and I groaned. The twins seemed bewildered. They exchanged a glance that seemed to communicate that *"living or dying, adults are very strange creatures!"*

Chapter 73

The Night Watch

Our family's visit with Molly lasted no more than twenty minutes before she fell asleep. Sister Beatrice said she most likely would not reawaken for another two or three hours. Therefore, I took the family back to the hotel.

Sister Beatrice said it would be fine for Harriet or me to sit with Molly any time of the night or day. Harriet and I decided that I would take the night watch with Molly and that Harriet would relieve me sometime in the morning. As I drove back to St. Theresa's, a humdinger of a thunderstorm moved across Wichita. In more ways than one, *"it was a dark and stormy night."*

When I reached Molly's room, Sister Beatrice was just coming out with another nun.

"Welcome back, Mr. Howard!" Sister Beatrice said. "Let me introduce you to Sister Rita Marie. We have been tending to Maddy. She awoke fifteen minutes ago, but she had another good rest. She will be glad to see you. There is a call button on her bed table. Don't hesitate to use it if you believe Maddy needs help."

Sister Rita Marie said, "I will be checking on Maddy regularly through the night, Mr. Howard. When I come back, may I bring you a cup of coffee or glass of water?"

"Sister Rita Marie, I'll take coffee black Thank you both for your care of Maddy."

When I stepped into Molly's room, her smile again appeared.

"Billy, you're back. I'm so glad!" Molly said. "Come sit by me. Let's talk till I conk out again. I'll try to keep my naps as short as possible."

The recliner had been pushed to the side of Molly's bed. As I sat facing her, I took her hand. When we were teenagers, as I was not one of Molly's love interests, I rarely held her hand. Sometimes when we swung under the big elm on the Madigan's parking on Lincoln Street we would hold hands to keep the swings in sync.

Molly held my right hand between her two hands. With her bony fingers, she gently caressed my hand.

"It was so wonderful to meet your children, Billy! Dala is such a bright and beautiful woman. Frederick and Dawn gave me chills—or maybe it was the cancer? No matter!" Molly said with a laugh. "Really, Billy—*not yet eight-years-old*—they are so charming. The five of you have been blessed by God to be turned into one international family!"

"I fully agree with you, Molly. I never imagined any of this!" I said.

"That's a lie, Billy Howard! I remember you telling me many times how you were going to write books, sell lots of books, and pick up various prizes of one sort or another. You were learning to write but you were too dumb to take Harriet out on a date when she spent her summers on Lincoln Street."

"You're right about trying to date Harriet. I actually thought about asking her to a movie but I was afraid of her grandmother and the mad dog she owned!" I lamented.

"I love hearing your voice, Billy!" Molly said. "When I first met you, your voice was still changing. Every once in a while you would squeak when we were chatting on the porch steps on Lincoln Street. Maybe you should have worked for KGGF instead of the *Journal!*"

Molly closed her eyes for a minute. When her eyes reopened, she lifted her head and looked around the room. "Billy, lean closer," she said.

I leaned toward her. "What? I asked. "Do you need something?"

"Yes. Two things," Molly said as she rested her head again. "I need a secret favor from you."

"Forget it, Molly! I'm not going to track down a cigarette for you!" I said.

Molly laughed so hard she began to cough. When she calmed down, she said, "Billy Howard, you are a Super Dork! I gave up smokes when I went to prison, another little gesture of self-denial, I suppose. No, Billy, I don't need a cigarette. I need a favor for after I'm gone."

"That is not my preferred topic of conversation," I said. "However, you're setting the agenda. What may I do?"

"Thank you, Billy. Here's the deal," Molly said. "I've left instructions for my remains to be cremated. Sister Mary Claire and some of the other nuns aren't happy about this—it's a Catholic hang-up, I guess. But it's mox nix to me. I will be cremated and I would like to give my remains to you in an urn I've picked out."

"As you wish," I said. *What are we going to do with an urn, I wondered.*

"Wait, Billy. There's more to this favor I'm asking. When you get the urn, dump the cremains onto a sheet of newspaper and divide my ashes into four parts. They don't have to be all that exact—just four parts. Place the ashes into four little paper sacks. Are you following all this, Billy?"

"Yes," I said. "Go on."

Molly breathed deeply, closed her eyes, and coughed. She rested for a few moments. Then she continued her request.

"I didn't want to take the matter of my remains to the nuns, Billy. But here's what I'd like for you to do. Take three of the little sacks over to The Samaritan's Inn. Go to *Molly's Playground.* Scatter one sack of me—*hah! That sounds funny! '...one sack of me'*—to the bench where we first talked with each other. Scatter the second sack near the elm tree I showed you. Spread the contents of the third sack around the swings. Sell the urn for scrap—they charged me almost one hundred dollars—and send the proceeds to The Samaritan's Inn anonymously. Would you do that for me, Billy? I know that the real me will be nowhere near the playground at that time, but I would still appreciate this being done."

"I will do it, Molly. What happens to the fourth sack of you?"

Molly closed her eyes and began to weep and then weep heavily till she began to cough. She covered her face with her hands. She recomposed herself and wiped her face with a tissue. She blew her nose. Then she looked back to me.

"Billy, the rest of my immediate family is buried in Coffeyville, out at Fairview Cemetery, northwest of town. You know the place. Please find the plots and scatter the last of my remains upon my mother's grave, only my mother's grave.....*Will you do that for me, Billy?"*

"Of course, I will Molly. Absolutely!" I said.

"Dear Billy, I can't imagine anyone having fun dying. The bother of my demise has been eased by you and your family. I am so, so grateful......But now, I'd better sleep."

Very quickly, Molly fell asleep, snoring lightly. I sat beside my now and long-ago friend and prayed in her behalf.

The thunderstorm continued through the night.

Sister Rita Marie came to tend to Maddy two or three times per hour. When she came by, I would step into the hallway to restore some of my alertness by walking and drinking Sister Rita Marie's graciously delivered coffee.

Around 1:00 a.m. Molly awakened. She wanted to know how I got the ideas for the books I had written. Despite her fatigue and emaciated state, Molly was quick to remember various characters from my books and her comments were deft. I thought about all the wonderful conversations Harriet and I would never have with Molly. *Damnable disease!*

Around 5:00 a.m. Sister Rita Marie told me in the hallway that Maddy's awake periods were diminishing in length. We both noticed that her breathing was more difficult. "Her systems are shutting down," Sister Rita Marie said. "I don't know if she'll see another sunset. But then, who knows if any of us will see another sunset?"

I estimated that Wichita was getting a six-inch soaking. The lighting and thunder subsided but the rain continued.

Molly wanted to hear about some of our Coffeyville friends: Lindy, Carolyn, Harley, Scott, Henryjuner, Geraldine, Brodie, Vonda and Dusty. I told her what I knew and she was fascinated. As she heard the stories of the former Lincoln Street denizens, I wondered if hearing about their lives that were uninterrupted by twenty-years in prison was depressing to her. Then it occurred to me that she was probably past the point of depression and had moved on to the *Cape of Good Hope.*

Soon after 8:00 a.m. Sister Beatrice relieved Sister Rita Marie. Maddy awakened and took some liquid nourishment. Then Harriet arrived in her raincoat, carrying her umbrella. She greeted Sister Beatrice, kissed me, took off her coat and put down her umbrella. Drawing alongside Maddy, Harriet kissed her cheek. "Good morning, dear friend."

Molly was again cheered by Harriet's presence.

"Oh Harriet, you should have been here through the night!" Maddy said. "Billy and I snuck past Sister Rita Marie, passed through the lobby, and climbed the rainspout to the roof! We must have puffed a full pack of cigarettes as we watched the rain come down. Even the security officer didn't spot us. It was the trail of dripped water that led Sister Rita Marie here after we came back. But I'm sure Sister Beatrice will forgive me. *Right?*"

"I'll prayerfully consider your request, Maddy. Now enjoy your friends," Sister Beatrice said as she left the room.

Harriet sat down in the recliner next to the bed. I stood at the foot of the bed, expecting to head back to the hotel as soon as Molly fell asleep again."

"Harriet, do you and Billy like black-eyed peas?"

"Sure do, Maddy. We always have them on New Year's Day for good luck. Do you like black-eyed peas?"

"Yes, but not as much as my parents did. I don't know how they got hooked but we would have black-eyed peas throughout the year. We even had fresh ones, not just the store-bought cans of black-eyed peas. My parents had a friend who grew them on their farm near Dearing. She would deliver black-eyed peas to my parents. I don't know if my folks ever paid for them.

"Neither of you ever met my mother. She was the rock of our family. When she died, we went from rock to sinking sand.

"Anyway, she and I would often sit on the front porch steps and shuck black-eyed peas. Have you ever shucked peas?"

"Yep!" I said as Harriet nodded her agreement, both of us thinking of shucking with our grandmothers.

"My mother and I would talk about all sorts of things while we were shelling peas of one sort or another. One time she was telling me about the importance of reading and especially reading great books, the classics of literature. She said, 'Molly, the more great books you read, the more you will see a pattern. Usually, things start off well and then something happens that is not good and things begin to fall apart. Sometimes the characters get themselves into great trouble, usually because of someone's wrong thinking, bad decisions, or even a flat-out evil heart. Then, in many of these stories, the main character bounces off the bottom, fights back, struggles, and climbs out of the mess. He or she may not live happily ever after, but they will have learned and they will live better for it.

"My mother—her name was Fiona—you would have liked her—my mother told me on more than one occasion that great books illustrate real life. She said, 'In real life, no matter how things start off, most people will have to walk through some dark valleys and really rough times sooner or later. But it's how you wind up that counts,' Mama said. 'It's how you wind up, Molly. Whatever happens to you, keep pressing on! Don't focus on the crap and mistakes and foolishness and heartbreak. Look to the Lord, Molly! The Lord will make a way so that you can end well.' That's what my mama used to tell me when were just shucking black-eyed peas on Lincoln Street."

Maddy sobbed once but quickly recovered.

"You are so finishing well, Maddy!" Harriet said, as she patted away Maddy's tears.

"I hope so! I used to get so sad when I thought of the terrible events of my past. Finally—*finally*—I reached the point where I could focus on the moment and live confidently for the future. Then I was able to remember some of the great times we had on Lincoln Street. Do you think Sister Beatrice would let me install some swings in this room?"

"For you, anything!" I said.

"Again, thank you both for being here," Maddy said.

Molly closed her eyes and seemed to doze for a minute or so. Harriet and I said nothing. Then Molly opened her eyes and looked to each of us. Harriet took her hand. Molly smiled and seemingly basked in the fact that she was being attended to by friends who loved her.

Suddenly, Molly jerked her head toward the window and squeezed Harriet's hand. Harriet and I looked to the window where the dark clouds and rain were still to be seen.

Molly's gaze was fixed on the window. "What is it, Maddy? May I get you something," Harriet asked.

"No, no, I'm fine!" Maddy said. Her smile widened. "The sun is back out. I'm so glad! I don't think I've ever seen it so bri…."

Her grip on Harriet's hand relaxed. She closed her eyes one last time. Molly's jaw slackened and her mouth opened slightly. Its momentary sting delivered, Death rattled away in defeat.

The next day, our family returned to Texas.

Molly's memorial service took place ten days following her death. Harriet, Dala and I flew from DFW back to Wichita. The twins remained in Texas with my folks. I was invited to speak at the memorial which I did with difficulty. More than eight hundred people were on hand for the celebratory funeral mass that took place at *Blessed Sacrament Catholic Church.*

Following the Memorial Service, Harriet, Dala, and I said our goodbyes to the nuns, promising to remain in contact. Another tearful farewell.

From the church, we drove to the Herndon-Gump-Tilcock Mortuary just off Kellogg to pick up Molly's urn. It was brass and shaped like a vase with a lid. Miss Gump, daughter of one of the owners, said that Molly had requested no nameplate for the urn. I thanked her and took my leave. We returned to the hotel for a quiet night.

The next day in Wichita and Coffeyville, Molly's earthly remains were scattered as per her instructions.

> *"Forasmuch as it hath pleased Almighty God of His great mercy to take unto Himself the soul of our dear sister Maddy here departed, we therefore commit her body to the ground; earth to earth, ashes to ashes, dust to dust; in sure and certain hope of the resurrection to eternal life, through our Lord Jesus Christ; who shall change our vile body, that it may be like unto His glorious body, according to the mighty working, whereby He is able to subdue all things to Himself.*

Amen!

The Common Book of Prayer
1662

Chapter 74

You've Got Mail!

I returned to our house after running a few morning errands to find Harriet in the kitchen preparing food for lunch and supper. I grabbed a baby carrot and nibbled Harriet's ear.

"The postman brought you some packages," Harriet said. "One is from Sister Mary Claire. The other two have the return address of Miss Maddy Finch. I put them on the dining room table," Harriet said.

"That's interesting," I replied. "I've always wanted to know how much postage it takes from Heaven to Fort Worth. Take a break and we'll open them." I retrieved a pair of scissors from a kitchen drawer.

All the packages were wrapped in brown paper. Indeed, Maddy's name was listed on two of the packages, but the return address was that of The Samaritan's Inn. I snipped into the paper of the largest box, virtually a cube. Inside were two #10 business envelope boxes. Taped to the top box was a folded-over note. It said,

> *"Hi, Mr. Howard!*
>
> *This big box and the smallest package are for you from Maddy. I hope you will enjoy these remembrances from our dear friend. Best wishes to Mrs. Howard and your children.*
>
> *Christ's servant,*
> *Sister Lenore."*

I took the lid off the top box. Inside were envelopes—letters—all addressed, stamped, and opened. I pulled out the first in line. It had my return address and had been sent to Molly while she was in prison at Lansing.

Harriet and I quickly deduced that Molly had saved all of my letters. That was news to us! Two thirds of the way through the top box, yellow sheets of paper began appearing behind each envelope. I pulled out the first such insert. It was a letter in Molly's handwriting addressed to me. Harriet and I realized that the first yellow sheet letter to me marked the occasion of her *"major cathartic release"* and the end of her *numbness* in prison.

Before us, were twenty years of my letters and approximately fourteen-plus years of Molly's responses. *Wow!* Harriet and I could scarce take it in. In fact, we limited our reading of those missives to one or two per week to give ourselves time to process what she had written in reply to my letters. It was a treasure trove. As she so often did due to her gift of mercy, Harriet wiped away tears. We moved on to the second package, smaller than the first. As I peeled back the brown paper, I again could not believe what I was seeing. It was the copy of *The Longest Day* by Cornelius Ryan that I gave to Molly the day before the bloodshed of her eighteenth birthday. For Harriet, I reviewed the story of my giving the book that I had received from Captain Jack to Molly.

"Open it. See if she wrote you a note!" Harriet said.

Inside the front cover was the birthday note I had written Molly. The faded ballpoint ink said,

"Happy birthday, Molly!
May you have *the longest day* of happiness!
Your friend,
Billy"

I slumped into a dining room chair. Harriet took the book from me and read the note. She wiped away more tears. Then she flipped some pages and came to a stop mid-way into the D Day chronicle. "Look, Billy!" she said.

Harriet held the book out to me. Flat in the middle of the book were two pressed zinnias, one white, one red.

It is amazing how some mementos from the past quake our souls and release a tsunami of engulfing emotions.

Harriet called a time-out for lunch (roast beef, Havarti cheese, smooshed avocado, and chopped sweet pickles on rye with iced tea). After we cleared the kitchen table, Harriet asked, "Are you ready to open the third package?"

"Let's do it," I said as I dried my hands.

The third package was from Sister Mary Claire. It looked as if it might contain something framed. I gingerly tore away the outer paper and opened the packing box. In fact, it was something framed, also wrapped in brown paper. Another note was taped onto the brown paper. It said,

> "Mr. Howard,
>
> You wanted a bright, sunny picture of *Molly's Playground!* That will follow another day. This after-sundown image of *Molly's Playground* was captured by Sister Lenore who is an amateur photographer of remarkable skill. This is a gift from St. Theresa's and The Samaritan's Inn. All our staff hope it will bring you joy! Perhaps it will also prompt you to pray for our ministries as well. Please come see us often!
>
> Christ's servant,
> Sister Mary Claire

The 24"-by-36" black-and-white photograph was framed in silver aluminum. An inscription at the top of the frame said,

> *"To Billy Howard, with love and appreciation from his friends at St. Theresa's Catholic School for Girls, The Samaritan's Inn, and Molly's Playground! May you not grow weary of well doing!"*

An inscription at the bottom of the frame said,

"Billy and Maddy Swing, Smile, and Reminisce!
Molly's Playground"

Apparently, the photograph was taken from the rooftop of The Samaritan's Inn. Taken after dark with the surrounding lights in full effect, the picture showed the entirety of *Molly's Playground*—the elm trees, the benches, and the playground equipment. Side-by-side on the swings were Molly and me. We were caught on the upswing with our legs extended. We were holding hands. We were in sync, just as we had been on Lincoln Street. On that blessed night, *all was well with the world!*

The Swing

"How do you like to go up in a swing,
Up in the air so blue?
Oh, I do think it the pleasantest thing
Ever a child can do!

Up in the air and over the wall,
Till I can see so wide,
Rivers and cattle and all
Over the countryside!

A Child's Garden of Verses
Robert Louis Stevenson

Chapter 75

Of Rear-view Mirrors and Windshields

"The shortest distance
between a human being and the truth is
a story."

Anthony de Mello
Jesuit Priest

One late night in Washington, D.C., Dr. Scott Bretano exhorted me to write a book about our common hometown, Coffeyville, Kansas. I told Scott his suggestion was not a new thought to me. However, though only twenty-five years or so had passed since we strolled the hallowed halls of Field Kindley Memorial High School, the world had altered itself considerably. I wondered whether readers of the late 1980s would grasp the pedestrian life found throughout America's *fly-over country* in the early 1960s.

Factually, life in the Midwest in those days was slow paced. Most of us were, indeed, provincial, naïve, ignorant, clueless, and not very conversant with the challenging ways of the world. Nevertheless, I'm glad that is where I had the privilege of growing up.

By my observation, Coffeyville residents did pay attention to the vagaries of life. Change crawled along as compared to the pace of transformation in the big cities. Nevertheless, most of us were able to develop sufficient adaptive skills to carry us through life in a small town *or* a metropolis. One way or the other, we learned to deal with sophisticated ladies, suave gentlemen, and the rice paddies of Vietnam.

A life lesson I have learned is that you can best discern where you are when you have a clear remembrance of where you have been.

From time to time, I enjoy leafing through my old school yearbooks. Our kids find rummaging through photo albums and boxes of pictures with commentary of Harriet or me to be very amusing:

"You actually wore that?"—Frederick

"Dad, why did you stop being skinny?"—Dawn

"Wow, Mom! You were hot!"—Dala

For the past year of recollection, research, writing, and rewriting, I have swum in a sea of nostalgia. For the sake of this now concluding project, I've sought to do justice to the way we were. This experience has also reminded me that the past is a nice place to visit, but I wouldn't want to live there. As far as the adventures of *Lincoln Street* are concerned, that was *then* and this is *now*.

I mention this because through the years, I have met various folks who are caught up in the past to the detriment of fully experiencing the present or anticipating the future. A well-used analogy about all of this is the comparison between the sizes of automobile rear-view mirrors and windshields. A rear-view mirror is a necessary safety tool. It is important to check what is behind you. But it is more important to observe what is happening before you, whether near or far.

This analogy is not a putdown of history, but rather a reminder that *not one of us will find his or her future in the past!*

As of this writing, Coffeyville is but a shadow of its former self. But being *down* is not the same as being *out*. I hope you will visit Coffeyville. There are good touristy, commercial, and family reasons to do so. Dusty Lang still sells suits on Ninth Street. The Midland Theater still shows double features. Spit Corner still gets drenched. The *Journal* still publishes. The Dalton boys remain in their graves. Field Kindley Memorial High School and Roosevelt Junior High

School remain in fine fettle though enrollment is markedly diminished from my day.

While in Coffeyville, I hope you will drive down Lincoln Street. Many houses are going to seed and the elm trees are long gone. But having said that, the city has planted maple, oak, Sweet Gum, linden, and catalpa trees where the elms once were. These are good looking trees in their own right. They will never form a canopy over the street as the elms once did. But they are providing cooling shade. As the kids of today play under this sundry assortment of trees, they are making their own memories. Perhaps one of those boys or girls will one day offer an engaging sequel to this account of *Lincoln Street*.

Anyone who tells tales or writes history must do so eclectically. That is to say, episodes and events must be culled and chosen from a vast sum of story material. My teenage confidants Tom Shaney, Scott Brentano, and Lindy Lundquist could write with the same date parameters as I have and come up with very different renditions of what I have presented. Thus, I fully expect some of my other peers to declare, *"That's not the way I remember those days."* I understand. We all have varied perspectives of anything and everything. But such differences or discrepancies do provide a basis for polite though pointed conversation.

As an exercise, dredging through the experiences of that bygone era has been enlightening to me. What I have recorded in *Lincoln Street* are the diverse occurrences that had a formative impact upon me, shaping whom I have become as an adult. For your own enlightenment, you may want to try such an autobiographical endeavor yourself.

Lincoln Street is my personal and heartfelt acknowledgement of the town that taught me about God, love, hate, hurt, heartache, laughter, learning, discipline, foolishness, friendship, and so many other subjects. As Captain Jack imprinted upon me, it is fitting to express gratefulness to our fellow humans. It is also fitting to express our gratitude to town and country where the community experiences painted the backdrop of our lives.

More than a quarter-century removed from the events recorded in *Lincoln Street,* I have accrued enough objectivity to say that no failures in my life—and I have had many—can I attribute to some flaw common to Coffeyville. I can truthfully write that my successes in life—and I have had a few—accrued in no small part from the life that once I lived on Lincoln Street.

Thank you, God, for Coffeyville! Thank you, Coffeyville, for Lincoln Street!

Billy Howard
Fort Worth, Texas
December 4, 1988

Captain Jack's List of Quotations about Gratitude

1.

*"Enter into His gates with thanksgiving,
and into His courts with praise:
Be thankful unto Him, and bless His name."*

King David

2.

*"Gratitude makes sense of our past,
brings peace for today,
and creates a vision for tomorrow."*

Melody Beattie

3.

*"O dear God above,
whatever may be my lot,
let me not damn what I lack,
but give thanks for what I've got!"*

Don Burgess

4.

*"Gratitude helps you to grow and expand;
gratitude brings joy and laughter into your life
and into the lives of all those around you."*

Eileen Caddy

5.

*"The first responsibility of a leader is to define reality.
The last is to say 'thank you.'"*

Max de Pree

6.

Let us be grateful to people who make us happy;
they are the charming gardeners who make our souls blossom.

Marcel Proust

7.

"Come, ye thankful people, come,
Raise the song of harvest home!
All is safely gathered in,
Ere the winter storms begin;
God, our Maker, doth provide
For our wants to be supplied;
Come to God's own temple, come;
Raise the song of harvest home!"

Henry Alford

8.

"Saying 'thank you' to someone
is like truing the wheels of a bicycle:
Subsequently, everything runs smoother."

A paraphrase based on remarks by Laura Trice

9.

"Feeling gratitude and not expressing it
is like wrapping a present and not giving it."

William Ward

10.

"I can no other answer make but thanks,
and thanks, and ever thanks."

William Shakespeare

ACKNOWLEDGEMENTS

Lincoln Street has told the story of the way things were—sort of, kind of, perhaps it was like that—or should of, could of, would have been, and some of it did happen and most of it could have happened and even the things that didn't happen when put together with the things that probably did happened, actually do tell the story of the way it was in Coffeyville in the late 1950s and 1960s. Mostly.

Lincoln Street is a *novel*, a fictional memoir that for me was a retelling of certain days now as gone as the wayward wind. The overwhelming majority of characters are fictitious. I purposefully mixed and matched surnames and given names from one of my yearbooks for the sake of faux authenticity. I mentioned a few actual people as my own personal salute to them for the positive impact they had upon me.

For life on Lincoln Street to come alive, I needed the help of folks who could relate to those times and the *"salt-of-the-earth"* people of Coffeyville and environs:

Thank you, God, for the ability to tell tales that have some point and purpose! *May God be praised in all things!*

Thank you, Lyn, wife of nearly fifty years, for standing with me through so much since we met in First Grade at Coffeyville's Garfield Elementary School!

Thanks to our daughter Kirsten Burgess Wilson who challenged me to participate in the *National Novel Writing Month (NaNoWriMo)* which gave rise to the first 50,000 words of *Lincoln Street*.

Thanks to Steve Wilson, Josh and Amy Burgess for their ongoing encouragement to *finish the book!*

Thanks to Coffeyville tree expert Derek Dick for advising me on the types of trees that have grown on Lincoln Street after the elms were cut down.

Thanks to Barbara Ginzburg, MLS, Washburn School of Law, who counseled me regarding murder laws that existed in Kansas in the early 1960s.

My astute speedster cousin Floyd Horton served as my automotive and drag racing authority.

Retired law enforcement officer Mike Abbott was my firearms adviser.

Readers of three Coffeyville Facebook sites *("Next Stop 'Coffeyville,'" "Coffeyville Memories 'Celebrate Nostalgic Coffeyville,'"* and *"You Know You're from Coffeyville, Kansas When....")* provided many answers to research questions about life in Coffeyville back in the day. Thank you!

Intercessory prayer for this project was facilitated by Dr. Lucinda Baker and other dedicated prayer warriors at First Baptist Church of Downey, California. Also, the Coffeyville Facebook Prayer Center kindly petitioned God for the completion of this novel. Other prayers were offered by friends at Christ Chapel Bible Church in Fort Worth, Texas. Many thanks to all!

Nuanced comments, chapter ideas, and even some dialogue suggestions were contributed by Claudia Crim, Maxwell Maltz, Harold Rush, Gary Schaub, and Sally Strasburger.

Helping with final revisions were my capable beta readers: Juliette Adams, Kris Crane, Gregory Hasman, Tandranika Johnson, James Kitchens, Nancy Plotkin, Terri Barnhart Richardson, Pamela Scott, Conni Stamper, and Christa Yancy.

The magnificent cover design was produced by the artist

ebookcover_xper
at
fiverr.com.

Thanks for reading *Lincoln Street!*

-----

*"And let us not grow weary of doing good,
for in due season we will reap, if we do not give up."*

Galatians 6:9 (ESV)

Contact
Don Burgess

eMail:
lincoln.burgess@att.net

FaceBook:
LINCOLN STREET - A Novel by Don Burgess

Twitter:
@donburgess_d

Website:
www.lincoln-street.com
Use this site to order PRINTED copies of *Lincoln Street.*

eBook
To order digital copies of *Lincoln Street,*
go to
https://kindle.amazon.com/.

Please recommend *Lincoln Street* to a friend!
Why not call or text them now?
You and *Lincoln Street* are day-brighteners!

Please post your own review of *Lincoln Street*
at Amazon.com!
Your opinion counts!

Thanks!